The Ocean Cat's Paw
The Story of a Strange Cruise

by

George Manville Fenn

Double 9
BOOKS

The Ocean Cat's Paw
The Story of a Strange Cruise
by George Manville Fenn

ISBN: 978-93-64289-57-3

Published by

DOUBLE 9 BOOKS

2/13-B, Ansari Road
Daryaganj, New Delhi – 110002
info@double9books.com
www.double9books.com
Tel. 011-40042856

This book is under public domain

ABOUT THE AUTHOR

George Manville Fenn was a very productive author of novels, a writer, an editor, and an educator from England. He was born on January 3, 1831, in Pimlico, London. He mostly learned on his own; he taught himself Italian, French, and German. During the years 1851–1854, he went to Battersea Training College for Teachers and then became the head of a state school in Alford, Lincolnshire. In the early 1850s, Fenn started to write short stories and pieces for newspapers and magazines. The Old Forest Ranger, his first book, came out in 1856. Afterward, he wrote more than 100 books, many of them for teenagers and young adults. He was one of the most famous writers of his time, and his books were well-liked and read by many people. He also worked as a reporter and writer for Fenn. Among the newspapers and magazines, he worked for was The Boy's Own Paper, which he ran from 1866 to 1874. He worked hard to make children's books better and was a strong supporter of education and reading. The Englishman Fenn passed away on August 26, 1909, in Isleworth.

CONTENTS

Chapter One
Rodd the Pickle

"Here's another, uncle."

This was shouted cheerily, and the reply thereto was a low muttering, ending with a grunt.

It was a glorious day on Dartmoor, high up in the wildest part amongst the rugged tors, where a bright little river came flashing and sparkling along, and sending the bright beams of the sun in every direction from the disturbed water, as an eager-looking boy busily played the trout he had hooked, one which darted here and there in its wild rush for freedom, but all in vain, for after its little mad career it was safely brought to bank, and landed. There was no need to use the light net which hung diagonally and unnecessarily across its owner's back, for the glittering little speckled trout was only about the size of a small dace, though it fought and kicked as hardily as if it had weighed a pound, and indulged in a series of active leaps as it was slipped through the hole in the lid of a creel, to drop into companionship with half-a-score of its fellows, which welcomed the new prisoner with a number of leaps almost as wild as its own.

The utterer of the grunt, a stoutly-built man who might have been of any age, though he could not have been very young, judging from his bristly greyish whiskers, was also busily occupied, but in a calmer, more deliberate way.

He had no creel slung from his shoulder, but a coarse clean wallet that was rather bulgy, its appearance suggesting that it was carried because it contained something to eat, while its owner held in one hand, slung by a stoutish lanyard, a big, wide-mouthed glass bottle half full of water, and in the other hand a little yellow canvas net attached to a brass ring at the end of a stick, the sort of implement that little boys use when bound upon the chase and capture of the mighty "tittlebat." And as his younger companion shouted and landed his little mountain trout, the net was being carefully passed under water, drawn out and emptied upon the fine lawn-like grass, and what looked like a little scrap of opalescent jelly was popped into the wide-mouthed bottle.

"You got one too, uncle?" shouted the boy, who was higher up the stream.

"Yes; some very nice specimens down here. Are you getting plenty of sport, Rodd?"

"Yes, uncle," replied the boy, who was carefully examining his tiny artificial gnat before beginning to whip the stream again. "They are rising famously; but they are awfully small. I shall get a dish, though, for supper."

"Uncle," as he was called, grunted again, and went on searching amongst the water-weeds with his net, his tendency being with the stream, while the boy, who did not scruple about stepping into the shallows from time to time, went on whipping away upward towards where one of the tors rose in a chaotic mass of broken, lichen-covered, fragmentary granite, apparently hiding in the distance the source of the little bubbling and sparkling stream.

Sometimes, as the boy struck in unison with the rise, he missed his fish, at others he hooked and held it till it broke away, and then again he transferred another to his creel, as intent upon his sport as his uncle was upon his pursuit, but still adding and adding to the contents of the creel for quite an hour. Then, in an interval when the fish had ceased to rise, the boy began to look downward, finding to his surprise that he was quite alone and close up to the towering mass of time-worn granite, many of whose blocks sparkled in the summer sun with crystals of quartz, and specks of hornblende, and were rendered creamy by the abundant felspar which held the grains together in a mass.

"I wonder what's become of Uncle Paul," muttered the boy. "Have I lost him, or has he lost me? What stuff! One's only got to go down the stream, and he's sure to be there somewhere, dipping for his what-do-you-call-'ems—hydras and germs and buds, and the rest of them. But oh, what a jolly morning it is, and what a jolly place Dartmoor is now the sun shines! Not very jolly yesterday, though, when the wind was sweeping the rain across in clouds and you couldn't see the tops of the tors for the mist. Oh, but it is beautiful to-day. I do feel jolly!"

The boy let his light tapering rod fall into the hollow of his arm, swung round his creel to the front, and, raising the lid, peered down at his speckled prizes lying upon a bed of newly-picked bracken fronds.

"Why, there must be fifty," he cried. "There, I won't stop to count. I'll catch a few more, and guess at fifty. That'll be enough for a nice lot for tea and some more for to-morrow morning's breakfast. Uncle Paul does enjoy a dish of trout. Humph! So do I. I suppose it's this beautiful fresh air up among the tors, and the tramping. It was a good long way up here from the cottage. I suppose it's that makes me feel so jolly hungry. Oh, look at that now! Uncle would carry the wallet, and he's got all the sandwiches. Never mind; I'll catch a few more of the little beauties, and then toddle back to meet him."

But the boy did not begin to fish directly, but stood gazing round at the glorious prospect of hill and dale and miniature mountain, here grey and sparkling, there flushed as if with the golden sheen of blossoming furze, while the lower slopes were of the magnificent purple of the abundant heath.

"Beautiful!" cried the boy ecstatically. "I am glad that we came up here to stay. So is dear old uncle. He's revelling in the specimens he gets, and we shall have another jolly night with the microscope. He'll give me a lecture upon all the little Latin beggars he pops into his bottle, and another for being so stupid in not recollecting all their cranky names. Never mind; it is jolly. Pity it isn't later, for then there'd be plenty of blackberries and whorts. I dare say there'd be lots of the little tiny button mushrooms, too, in the lower parts among the soft grass. But what's the use of grumbling? Uncle says that I am never satisfied, and that I am always restless, and I suppose it's because I am a boy. Well, I can't help being a boy," he mused thoughtfully. "I might have been a girl. Well, girls are restless too. I say, what's that?"

He shaded his eyes again and gazed at a speck of something that looked bright scarlet in the distance, and then not very far away he made out another, and again another speck or blotch of bright red. "Now, I wonder what's growing there," muttered the boy. "I don't remember anything scarlet growing and blowing. Poppies? No, I don't think they are poppies. They are at the edges of the cornfields, and there are no cornfields up here."

He fixed his eyes more intently upon the scarlet specks, and then burst out laughing.

"Well, they are not poppies," he said aloud. "Poppies don't move, and those are moving, sure enough. There, one of them has gone behind that block of stone. Pooh, how stupid! Why, of course!"

He jerked himself round to look in another direction, so sharply that his creel swung out for a moment from the strap, and came back against his hip with a bang, as he stood with his back to the sun, gazing at a distant grey, gloomy-looking pile of stone building, and then nodded his head with satisfaction.

"Poppies, indeed! My grandmother! That's what they are. Soldiers from over yonder. Part of the guard from the great prison, I suppose. Oh, poor beggars! How miserable, when you come to think of it—shut up yonder in that great gloomy place, for I don't suppose they let them come out much without soldiers to watch them—and all for doing nothing. Doing nothing! Mustn't say that, though, before Uncle Paul, or he'll go into a rage and begin preaching about Bony and the war, and going on about the French. Hullo!"

The boy started, for there was a dull thud, apparently from the prison, miles away, followed by a loud echo which seemed to come from close at hand, making him turn again as if to look for the spot from which it came, and seeing it too, for the report of the gun had as it were struck against the face of the tor above him, and then glanced off to strike elsewhere.

"How queer echoes are!" he muttered. "Yes, and how queer I feel—all hollow. That's made me think about it. I suppose that means twelve or one o'clock dinner-time. Oh, how stupid to go right away from uncle like this! I wish he'd come. But I won't go till I have made my fifty trout."

Turning his attention now to the stream, he began whipping away again, and finding that the little trout were rising as well as ever, with the result that Rodney Harding once more forgot everything else in his pursuit and went on up-stream nearer and nearer to the great tor, till at last he found himself in a little hollow amongst the rocks where the river had widened into a pool, hollowed out as it were at the base of a great cliff.

"Why, this is the end of it," he said, pausing to look round and upward at the towering pile of rocks. "No, it isn't. It must be the beginning—the source, I suppose they call it. Yes, the stream begins here, comes right from under that cliff. Why, it's like a little cave out of which the water streams."

He stopped short and threw his fly once or twice without effect, and then, moved by curiosity, waded into the shallow rippling water, which rose a little way above his boots, but as it began to invade his trousers he rolled them up to his knees, before wading onward till he was stopped by the piled-up cliff face where the water came gliding out and rippled about his legs.

"Why, it ought to be quite cold," he muttered, "instead of which it is warm."

Then, standing up his rod so that the top rested among the stones, he stooped down, bending nearly double before he could pass in beneath a rough stony natural arch and slowly force his way along a narrow passage for a few feet, before stopping short where the water nearly reached his knees.

"Oh, I say! I am not going to break my back short off at the hips by squeezing in here," he grumbled. "Besides, it's all dark; and what's the good? Here, I know! This isn't the source. This tor is only a piled-up heap of stones, and I dare say if I go round I shall find the little river coming in on the other side, and this is where it comes out. Well, let it. Here, I want my lunch."

He made his way back into the sunshine where all was bright and clear again, and, taking his rod, stepped out to the edge of the pool, where the dry sand felt pleasant and comfortable to his feet, and there he went on fishing again with more or less success, till he passed out of the little amphitheatre to where the rocks fell away on either side, half hidden by the heath and furze.

"Must have got fifty by this time," muttered the boy. "Now just one more to make sure, and then I'll be off, and— Ugh! Who are you? How you made me jump!"

" No, no, don't hit ! "

Chapter Two
After French Prisoners

There was some reason in Rodney Harding's words, for as he turned from the little river he had come suddenly face to face with a thin gaunt-looking lad of about his own age, very shabbily dressed and almost ragged, who was gazing at him fiercely, and stood with one hand as if about to strike. Recovering himself on the instant, Rodney, obeying his first impulse, began to loosen the bottom joint of his rod ready to use it as a weapon—a defence against the expected attack—but in an instant the strange new-comer dropped his hand to his side, turned quickly away to look outward across the moor, and then cried wildly, his voice sounding strange of accent, and husky as if from exhaustion—

"No, no, don't hit! I am so weak and so helpless. Help me. Tell me, which way can I go? They are close after me, and I can run no farther. Help!"

The poor wild-looking creature ended by sinking upon his knees amongst the heath, and raising his hands with a piteous gesture, while his imploring looks were quite sufficient to move the young fisherman's heart.

"Why, who are you?" he cried. "You are not a beggar."

"No, no! I confess. Oh, *mon ami*—I beg your pardon—sir! I forgot. I confess everything. It was for liberty; we were escaping, but the guard—the soldiers! They have been hunting us down like dogs."

"A French prisoner?" cried the boy.

"Ah, *oui*—yes, monsieur. It is my misfortune. But the soldiers. We have been separated."

"Who's 'we'?" said Rodney sharply.

"My father and I. I don't know which way he has gone. They have taken him perhaps, and now it is no use; I may as well give up, for I can go no farther."

He sank sideways amongst the heath and fern.

Rodd looked at him in horror, for the poor fellow seemed as if he was about to faint with weakness and misery, while he kept giving utterance to hysterical gasps as he was plainly enough struggling hard to avoid bursting into a passion of weak girlish tears.

"Here, I say, don't do that!" cried Rodd, stooping and catching him by the arm to shake him violently. "You don't know that the soldiers have caught your father."

"No, but I feel sure that they must have done so," cried the poor fellow, rising a little and gazing wildly in the speaker's eyes, while Rodd's energy seemed to galvanise him into action.

"Well, suppose they have? They'd only take him back into the prison again, would they?"

"I—I don't know," faltered the lad. "I heard firing, and they may have shot him down and taken him."

"Yes—may, may, may!" cried Rodd angrily. "But I don't believe our soldiers would be such brutes. It's only Frenchmen that do such things as that."

"What!" cried the lad, struggling to his feet. "How dare you speak so of our brave fellows! I appealed to you for help, and you insult me. Do you think if you were in France and flying for your life with your father—"

"Haven't got one," said Rodd shortly. "Died before I was born."

"Do you think then that if you alone had appealed to me for help I would have treated a poor escaping prisoner like this?"

"Oh, come, I say, don't go on like that. Any one would think you were a great girl. How can I help you? I daren't. What would my uncle say if he knew I'd helped a French prisoner to escape from his guards? You shouldn't, you know. It isn't right nor fair. Just because you have got into trouble, that's no reason why you should drag another fellow down too. Look here, what are you running away for?"

"Why?" cried the lad bitterly. "Because I am a prisoner, and I wanted to see my poor father free."

"Well, look here," said Rodd huskily; "I am very sorry, you know, and I'd help you if I could, but it's against the law, and— I say! Quick! Don't speak aloud. I can hear some one coming. Yes, it's the soldiers, I think."

"Oh!" cried the French lad wildly, and he gazed about him with every nerve quivering, his whole aspect being that of some hunted beast with the dogs close upon his track.

"Don't get up," cried Rodd. "I tell you, I mustn't help you; it's against the law; but if I were in your fix I know what I should do. Not afraid of the water, are you?"

"What, swim for my life? Nonsense! In a stream like this!"

"No, no. Wade into that hole opposite yonder, and hide there till the soldiers are gone."

"But they'd be sure to look there."

"Not they! They'd be afraid of spoiling their breeches and gaiters and washing out the pipe-clay."

"Ready for you to betray me to them," whispered the lad bitterly. "No; I'll surrender like a man."

"Oh!" growled Rodd, between his teeth. "If you weren't such a poor, weak, helpless-looking chap I'd hit you on the nose. How dare you speak to me like that?"

He raised his hand as if to strike, but there was a ring in his words which had thrilled the fugitive, who to Rodd's astonishment caught the hand in his, and quick as thought pressed it to his lips, and then dashed into the water and splashed his way to the mouth of the hole. The next moment the disturbed stream was the only trace left, for the fugitive had disappeared.

The young fisher stood gazing blankly at the low dark mouth of the hole, listening with every nerve on the strain for some sound from the hiding-place to strike his ear; but there was none. From behind, though, there came a loud voice, shouting—

"Here, this way; up by the stream!"

In an instant Rodd was full of action. Turning his back to the hole across the pool, he began to whip the surface with such effect that at the third cast there was a quick rise and he was fast in by far the biggest trout he had caught that day, though small enough all the same; and with knit brows he was playing it carefully just as a redcoat, followed by three or four more, came up at the double to the exit end of the pool and halted to stare at him wonderingly.

"Hi, young fellow!" shouted the leader, whose stripes betokened the sergeant. "What are you doing here?"

Rodd, whose heart was thumping against his ribs from excitement, did not so much as raise his eyes from the surface of the pool, but with teeth set, lips pursed up, and brows heavily knit, kept on playing his fish, paying not the slightest heed to the speaker and his companions.

"Fishing, eh?" said the sergeant, who, in spite of his important errand, could not take his eyes from the darting trout. "I say, we are after an escaped prisoner, and he came somewhere up here. Which way has he gone?"

Rodd did not take his eyes from the frantic darting of the fish, but gave line in silence as it flashed through the water to the far side of the pool, while the soldiers grounded arms and looked on with the deepest interest.

"Prisoners escaped," said the sergeant loudly, as he, too, still gazed at the rushings of the trout—"Frenchman—came up this way—Yes, a big 'un, youngster—Mind! You'll lose him!—One was quite a lad, and—Well done! You have got him yet!—We saw him run up this way, and—Well done!— You have handled a fly-rod before—Did you see anything of him?"

"Eh? What?" said another voice sharply, and a fresh comer suddenly appeared upon the scene in the shape of Uncle Paul, who stared in astonishment at the group as he stepped into the little amphitheatre from behind the rocks.

His appearance acted like magic upon the soldiers, who brought their muskets to the carry, while the sergeant sprang to attention and saluted.

"After escaped prisoners, sir. Asking the young gentleman if he had got one of them up here."

"Pooh! Nonsense! Absurd!" cried the gentleman addressed, just as Rodd brought his fish to land and went down on one knee to grip it in his left hand. "Prisoners, no!" literally barked the fresh comer, setting down his bottle and net, and taking off his straw hat to wipe his streaming face with a big yellow and red bandanna handkerchief. "Here, Rodd, boy," he cried, with a chuckle, "empty your pockets and then open your creel and show the sergeant how many prisoners you have caught. Hot up here, my lad!" he continued, and the sergeant and men grinned. "Thirsty?"

"Yes, sir," said the sergeant, grinning; "pretty tidy. We have had a precious good run."

"Well, there's plenty of beautiful water. Shall I lend you my drinking-cup?"

"Thankye, sir," said the sergeant.

"Thankye, indeed!" said the bluff speaker, with a chuckle, and he thrust his hand into his pocket. "There you are; there's a shilling for you to get some cider. I dare say you know where better than I can tell you. No, we have seen no prisoners."

"Thank you, sir! You are a gentleman," said the sergeant. "Didn't want to interfere with the young gent's sport, but we had got our duty to do.

Left face, my lads! Forward!" And the next minute the military party were on the tramp, to pass through the entrance to the little amphitheatre and disappear, just as Uncle Paul was lowering himself gently down upon a huge boulder stone and dragging round the wallet which hung from his right shoulder.

"Phew!" he gasped. "Pretty job I have had to find you, Pickle! I took a short cut, as I thought, and it proved a long one. I have had a round. Aren't you hungry, boy?"

"Starving, uncle," replied the lad, as he dropped the fish into the creel, hooked his fly on to one of the rings, and tightened the line. "But let's come out here on to the heath. It will be more soft and comfortable to sit down."

"Bah!" barked Uncle Paul. "I am not going to stir again till I have had something to eat and a rest. There, lay your rod down. Bother the soldiers! There was another party of them out yonder, shouted at me to stop, and because I didn't, made as if they were going to fire. Yes, they had better! But I had to stop; and then they began questioning me about their escaped French prisoners, and wanted to know who I was and where I was going, and I thought that they were going to make me a prisoner and march me off yonder, only I showed them my card and asked them if I sounded like a French prisoner. They were civil then, and I gave them a shilling. That's two shillings I have fooled away out here on this moor, where I should have said it wasn't possible for a man to spend a farthing. Come on; help yourself," and he held out the wallet for his companion to take one of the big sandwiches it contained.

"I think we had better go on outside, uncle," said the boy. "There's more breeze out there, and the rocks don't reflect the heat."

"Do you?" said Uncle Paul, with his mouth full. "There's quite wind enough in here to keep me alive, and I am so hot I don't want to go out to be blown on and catch cold.—My word, the old lady didn't forget the mustard! Come, eat away, Pickle. Let's start fair, or you will soon be a sandwich behind. My word, what an appetite this air does give one!"

"Yes, uncle," said the boy, who, in spite of an effort to control himself, could not help darting an anxious glance from time to time at the opening between the rocks.

"Capital sandwiches, Pickle," continued the uncle, eating away with the most intense enjoyment. "One doesn't want any other pickle with these. What does the old proverb say—Hunger's sweet sauce. Hullo! what are you getting up for?"

"Oh, I am going on eating, uncle," replied the boy. "I was only going to walk to the end and see how far the soldiers had gone."

"Hang the soldiers, sir!" cried the elder irascibly. "I wish they'd keep in their barracks instead of coming hunting their prisoners all over this beautiful countryside. Sit down and go on eating."

The boy resumed his place, and began making half-moons in the edge of his sandwich and trying to munch hard; but somehow his appetite was gone, and before he was half through the second sandwich he watched his opportunity, slipped it into his pocket, and as his uncle turned round to look at him he leaned forward and helped himself to a third from the wallet.

"Ah, that's better! Eat away, boy. We have got a long walk back, and you will have plenty of appetite for a good high tea. Hang the prisoners as well as the soldiers. If I had known that this great cage full of Bony's French frogs was up here I don't believe I should have come—that is, unless I thought that Nap himself was a prisoner here too, when I might have been tempted to come and have a grin at the wild beast in his cage. Eh, what? What did you do that for?"

He looked curiously at his nephew, who, after a glance across the pool, had involuntarily stretched out one hand to grip his elder's arm.

"Do you hear me, sir?" he cried sharply. "Why did you pinch my arm like that?"

The boy, whose face had looked rather white the moment before, flushed scarlet, and stammered out something confused and strange.

"Why, hullo, boy!" cried his uncle sharply, and he leaned forward in turn and caught the lad by the wrist. "Why, what's the matter with you? Haven't been overdoing it in the sun, have you? Here, take my cup and have a glass of water."

"No, no, uncle; I am quite right. There's nothing the matter with me. It's—it's—it's—"

"It's what?" said Uncle Paul sharply, as he gazed full in the boy's eyes and held tightly by his wrist. "Well, it's what?"

"Perhaps I am a bit tired, uncle. I have been working very hard, and I turned faint and hungry a little while ago."

"Humph!" grunted Uncle Paul. "Then do as I tell you. Drink a cup of that clear cold water."

"That's better," he continued, a few minutes later. "Now eat another sandwich. No nonsense, sir! Do as I tell you!"

The boy sighed and helped himself to another of the double slices and their contents, and for the next few minutes no word was spoken, the pair sitting opposite to one another and munching or ruminating steadily away, the younger feeling as if every mouthful of which he partook would choke him.

"Hah!" said Uncle Paul, at last; "it is a drawback to this beautiful place. The colours of the heath are glorious, and the views from up here are grand. I got some good specimens too, ready for our microscopic work to-night; and that was a nice trout you caught. How many did you get, boy?"

"Only one, uncle," said the boy vacantly.

"What!"

"I didn't see the other, uncle."

Uncle Paul drew a deep breath and fixed the boy with his eyes, as he said quietly—

"I asked you how many trout you got, Pickle."

"Oh, about fifty, uncle. Creel's half full."

"Ah! Then we will have some for high tea to-night, and some for breakfast in the morning, and give our landlady the rest. Nice woman that; full of stories about the prisoners, and Bony and his wretched scum. Ugh! The very name of the rascal raises my bile, and— There, I think I had better take you home and give you a dose."

"Yes, let's go on back now, uncle," said the boy eagerly, "but indeed, indeed I don't want a dose."

"Humph! Then pray why did you grip hold of my arm again like that, and stare across yonder over my shoulder as if you could see a raven hiding in one of the holes?"

"Oh no, uncle," cried the boy, with a forced laugh. "I couldn't see anything."

"Ha, ha!" ejaculated Uncle Paul. "Now, look here, Pickle; you and I have always had a sort of tacit agreement that we'd play fair together, and that there should be a mutual confidence."

"Yes, uncle, of course," cried the boy, whose face was burning.

"Very well, then, you are breaking truce. You are not playing the game, sir."

"Uncle!"

"Pickle! Now then, sir, out with it. You have seen those French prisoners."

"Uncle!"

"Yes, sir. Why did you pinch my arm—twice? Now then, honour!"

"I—I— You were talking about Bonaparte."

"Well, what of that?"

"I was afraid he'd hear you, uncle."

"What!" cried the other, and his mouth opened wide. "Bony! Here?"

"No, uncle, of course not, but one of the young prisoners. He was escaping."

"And you—you have turned traitor to your King, and been hiding a prisoner of war from his guard! Why, you young scoundrel! You lied to that sergeant, and said you hadn't seen them."

"I didn't, uncle!" cried the boy hotly. "It was you."

"Eh? What?" roared the elder. "You dare to! Eh?—Ah—so I did! But then I didn't know."

"No, uncle, and if you had seen and heard the poor lad as I did, I am sure you wouldn't have betrayed him."

"Betray! It isn't betraying, sir, to give up a prisoner of war."

"I felt as if it would be, uncle, under such circumstances," said Rodd, who began noting that his uncle had lowered his voice, and that his angriest words had been uttered in a whisper.

"Look here, my boy," he said now quite softly, "I knew that there was something up, or you would have been wolfing more than your share of those sandwiches. I saw you keep squinting at that hole over yonder. So you have hid him away there?"

"No, uncle," said Rodd; "I did nothing, but just as the soldiers were coming up, and he'd been begging and praying me to save him, I just said that that would be a good place to hide."

"Humph!" grunted Uncle Paul. "It was very wrong, my boy—very wrong; but look here, Pickle, is the poor fellow badly wounded?"

"No, uncle; only exhausted. He looked just like that hunted deer we saw the other day."

"Hah!" said Uncle Paul, nodding his head. "Humph! Well, you know, my boy, it isn't the thing, and we should be getting into no end of trouble if it were known. It's against the law, you know, and if you had caught him and held him you would have got a big reward."

Rodd got up and laid his hands upon his elder's shoulders as he looked him fixedly in the eyes.

"I say, uncle," he said, "you have been questioning me. It's my turn now."

"Yes, Pickle; I'll play fair. It's your turn," said Uncle Paul. "What is it you want to say?"

"Only this, uncle. Would you have liked me to earn that reward?"

"Hah! I say, Pickle, my lad, would you like any more sandwiches?"

"No, uncle."

"Then isn't it about time we began to make for home?"

Uncle Paul rose and led the way down-stream, gazing straight before him, and though he must have seen, he took no notice of the fact that Rodd did not throw the strap of his creel of fish over his shoulder, but left it by the side of the stone, along with the wallet, through whose gaping mouth a second packet of big sandwiches could still be seen.

Chapter Three
Mrs Champernowne's Pan

Mr Robson, when he came up from Plymouth for a natural history expedition into Dartmoor, did not select a hotel for his quarters, for the simple reason that such a house of accommodation did not exist, but took what he could get—a couple of tiny bedrooms in the cottage of a widow whose husband had been a mining captain on the moor; and there after a long tramp they returned on the evening after the adventure, to find their landlady awaiting them at the pretty rose-covered porch, eager and expectant and ready to throw up her hands in dismay.

"Why, where are the fish?" she cried—"the trout?"

"Eh?" said Uncle Paul.

"The fish, sir—the fish. I've got a beautiful fire, and the lard ready in the pan. I want to go on cooking while you both have a good wash. You told me that you would be sure to bring home a lot of trout for your supper, and I haven't prepared anything else."

"Bless my heart! So I did," said Uncle Paul. "Here, Pickle, where are those trout?"

Rodd gave his uncle a comical look, and stood rubbing one ear.

"Ah, uncle," he cried, "where are those trout?"

Uncle Paul screwed up one eye, and he too in unconscious imitation began to rub one ear.

"Ah, well; ah, well," said the landlady, "I suppose you couldn't help it. I have had gentlemen staying here to fish before now, and it's been a basketful one day and a basket empty the next. Fish are what the Scotch call very kittle cattle. Never mind, my dear," she continued to Rodd. "Better luck next time. Fortunately I have got plenty of eggs, and there's the ham waiting for me to cut off some more rashers."

As she spoke the woman hurried into her kitchen, from which sharp crackling sounds announced that he was thrusting pieces of wood under the kettle, and as she busied herself she went on talking aloud so that they could hear—

"Did you hear the gun fire, sir, somewhere about one o'clock?"

"Yes," grunted Uncle Paul. "Dinner-time, and we ate your sandwiches, Mrs Champernowne. They were delicious."

"I am very glad, sir. But, oh dear no, that wasn't the dinner-bell. That meant that some of the prisoners had escaped. Poor fellows! I always feel sorry for them."

"Mrs Champernowne!" cried Uncle Paul, and Rodd, who was in his room with his face under water, raised it up, grinning, for he knew his uncle's peculiar ways by heart, and he went on listening to what was said.

"Oh, yes, sir," cried the landlady, with her voice half-drowned by a sudden flap and a sizzling noise which indicated, without the appetising odour which soon began to rise to Rodd's nostrils, that their landlady had vigorously slapped a thick rasher of pink-and-white ham into the hot frying-pan; "I know what you think, sir, and what you told me only last night about being a loyal subject of King George, and these being our natural enemies, whom we ought to hate."

Ciss! went the ham, and Rodd felt as if he should like to shout "Hear, hear!"

"But I can't help remembering what I hear at church about forgiving our enemies; and I am sure you would, sir, if you knew what I do about those poor fellows, torn away from their own people and shut up behind prison bars, and all for doing nothing."

Just then there was a little spluttering noise as if the pan were chuckling.

"For doing nothing!" shouted Uncle Paul, and a sound from his room suggested that he had set down the washhand jug with a bang. "The scoundrels who invaded our shores?"

Ciss! said the pan.

"That they didn't, sir!" cried the landlady. "They didn't even try; and even if they had there were all our brave fellows round the coasts who would soon have stopped them."

"Hear, hear!" cried Rodd, very softly, for he was speaking into his sweet-scented towel, whose scent was that of fresh air and wild thyme.

"Well, well, that's right," shouted Uncle Paul; "but they wanted to."

Whish-ish, went the pan, and there was a good deal more spluttering, and in his mind's eye Rodd saw the great rasher turned right over, to begin sizzling again.

"And I don't believe that, Dr Robson," cried the landlady sturdily. "Don't you know that the poor fellows over yonder never get good honest shillings given to them and are enlisted of their own free will like our lads at home, but they are dragged away and are obliged to fight; and it was all owing to the angry jealousy and covetousness of that dreadful man, Bony, who has been the cause of all the trouble."

"Hah!" roared Uncle Paul, in a voice that almost shook the diamond-paned casement. "Say no more, Mrs Champernowne. You are quite right, and I admire your sympathies. Madam, you are a lady!"

"Oh, really, Dr Robson—"

"I repeat it, madam, you are a lady, and I applaud everything you have said. But what about that gun?"

"Oh, dear me, yes, sir; I was just going to tell you, but you put it all out of my head. It was the alarm gun to tell everybody that prisoners had escaped, so that all the people on the moor could join the soldiers in scouring the place as they called it, and hunting the poor Frenchmen down for the sake of the reward. Yes, I'd reward them if I had my way! Hunting their poor fellow-creatures, who are only trying for their liberty!"

"H'm! Ha!" grunted Uncle Paul, and there was a huckabacky sound about his words.

There was another furious hissing from the pan, followed by a fresh slap, for a second great rasher had been thrust in *vice* number one nicely cooked and just placed in the hot dish that had been intended for trout.

"Did they catch them, Mrs Champernowne?" shouted Uncle Paul.

"I haven't heard, sir," was the reply; "but dear, dear, they are pretty well sure to, for there's not much chance for the poor fellows. Oh, it makes my heart bleed when I hear sometimes that one of them has been shot down by the soldiers."

Rodd went on tip-toe across the creaking floor to open his door a little farther, listening with strained ear, for his bright young imagination pictured the thin pale youth, wild-eyed and breathless, out of his hiding-place and running for liberty across the open moor, and hearing again the distant reports of the muskets.

"But that doesn't often happen, sir, for between you and me and the post, seeing that the prisoners are only soldiers, after all, I don't believe that though they have their orders, our men ever try to hit them; and very glad I am."

"Ah, ah, ah, Mrs Champernowne, that isn't loyal, you know, that isn't loyal to his Majesty the King and your country."

"I can't help that, Dr Robson, and I am not speaking, sir, as a subject, but as a woman and a mother who has a brave stout boy in our good King's Guards. Now suppose, sir, that you were a mother." Uncle Paul grunted audibly.

"And had a boy the same as I have, and Bony Napolyparty had taken him prisoner. How would you like him to be shot down?"

Rodd literally jumped in his alarm, for there was a tremendously wild cissing from the pan and a horrible suggestion therewith that Mrs Champernowne had been turning the rasher with so much energy that she had thrown the cooking slice on to the fire itself instead of into its native pan, while a sudden gush as of hot burning fat came up the little stairs.

But the pleasant sizzling sounds began again directly, and Rodd, who was ravenously hungry, consequent upon the bad part he had played over the sandwiches beneath the tor, sighed in relief as he realised that the widow's energetic treatment had only splashed a little of the fat over the side of the pan.

As Rodd listened for a continuation of the political discussion, in which it seemed to him that Uncle Paul had got the worst of it, for neither the widow nor he spoke for the next three or four minutes, and the pan had it all its own way, there was some creaking of the boards as the naturalist stumped about, and when he did speak it was evident that he thought it wise to change the subject. And it was the inner man who now spoke—

"Our tea-supper nearly ready, Mrs Champernowne?"

"Oh yes, sir. The second rasher's about done. How many eggs shall I cook?"

"Oh, one, or perhaps two, for me," shouted Uncle Paul.

"Oh, I say!" muttered Rodd.

"Better cook eight or ten for my nephew," cried the doctor dryly. "He'll eat like a young wolf."

"What a shame!" muttered Rodd. "I'll serve him out for this."

"Fried, of course, sir?" came from the kitchen.

"Murder, woman, no!" roared Uncle Paul. "Fry! That is wild west-country ignorance, madam! Are you not aware, madam, that the action of boiling fat upon albumen is to produce a coagulate leathery mass of tough indigestible matter inimical to the tender sensitive lining of the most important organ of the human frame, lying as it does without assimilation or absorption upon the epigastric region, and producing an irritation that may require medical treatment to allay?"

"Dear, dear, dear, dear me, no, sir! Really, you quite fluster me with all those long words. Who ever heard that fried ham and eggs were bad for anybody?"

"Then I tell you now, madam," shouted the doctor, "that—"

"Don't you take any notice, Mrs Champernowne," shouted Rodd. "It's only uncle's fun."

"Wuff!" went Uncle Paul, with a snap like that of an angry dog. "Wuff!"

"Fried, please, Mrs Champernowne; four for uncle and three for me."

"Umph!" grunted the doctor, and a few minutes later he and his nephew, hunger-sharpened and weary-legged, were seated facing one another in the widow's pleasant little parlour, hard at work, and risking all the direful symptoms upon which the elder had discoursed, and thoroughly enjoying hearty draughts of Mrs Champernowne's fragrant tea.

There was silence in the kitchen, following the final hissings and odours emitted by the hard-worked pan, but a great deal of business went on in the little parlour, the first words that were spoken being by Uncle Paul, who growled out—

"Here, I suppose you had better tell the old lady to put on another rasher of ham to fry."

"For you, uncle?" said Rodd archly.

"No, sir, for you. You traitorous young dog, leaving all those beautiful trout up on the moor to be devoured by the enemies of your country!"

"Well, they can't eat them raw, uncle."

"Why not, sir? They are only so many ravening savages, ready to breathe out battle and slaughter if they got free."

"That poor boy didn't seem much of a savage, uncle," said Rodd quietly; and after a sidelong glance to see whether he dared say it, the boy continued tentatively, "I wish the poor fellow had been here to have this ham."

"What!" roared his uncle fiercely. "Bah! You wouldn't have left him a mouthful. Wolf—raven!"

"Yes, I would, uncle. I'd have left him all."

"Umph!" grunted Uncle Paul, taking up a very thin, old, much-worn silver table-spoon and looking at it with the eye of a connoisseur. "H'm! Ha! Queen Anne."

"She's dead, uncle," said the boy.

"Well, I know that, don't I?" growled Uncle Paul, as he tilted the empty dish, and carefully scraped all the golden brown fat and gravy to one side, getting together sufficient to nearly fill the spoon, and then making as if to put it upon his own plate, but with a quick gesture dabbing it down upon Rodd's.

"Fair play, uncle!" shouted the boy.

"Bah!" grunted the doctor. "Cut me a thin slice of bread, all crumb, Pickle. Thunder and lightning! I have got the best share, after all;" and then, with his face puckered up into a pleasant smile, he inserted a fork into the newly-cut slice of home-made bread, and began passing it round and round the dish until it had imbibed the remains of the liquid ham and the golden new-laid eggs, when he deposited it upon his own plate with a triumphant smile which seemed to Rodd to make him look five-and-twenty years younger.

"Shall I fill another cup of tea for you, uncle?" cried Rodd; and by the way, they were breakfast cups.

"No, no, Pickle; I—I—er—well, say half."

At that moment the door was opened, and, looking hot and out of breath, their landlady entered.

"I hope you haven't been waiting for anything, gentlemen," she cried, giving the table a comprehensive glance. "I am so sorry. I will cook another rasher or two directly."

"Madam, no," said Uncle Paul didactically. "What does the great classic author say?"

"Really I don't know, sir," cried Mrs Champernowne, with a perplexed look wrinkling up her pleasant face. "But it won't take many minutes."

"Enough, madam, is as good as a feast. This has been a banquet, eh, Pickle? I never enjoyed anything half so much before in my life. The ham was tenderness itself, the eggs new-laid—the bread—the butter—the tea— eh, Pickle?"

"Delicious, uncle."

"The fat of the land, Mrs Champernowne," continued the doctor; "the riches of these smiling pastures. Now if your friend Napoleon Bonaparte had come with his locusts to devastate the land, his hordes such as we have seen safely imprisoned yonder—"

"Yes, sir," interrupted Mrs Champernowne eagerly; "that's what I came to tell you. I thought I might just run over to my neighbour's, whose master has come back from the hunt, and I thought that you would like to hear. Those two French prisoners have got right away."

"Hooray!" shouted Rodd, springing from the chair, and to Mrs Champernowne's astonishment catching her round the waist and waltzing her about the room. "Three cheers for the poor prisoners! Hurrah! Hurrah! Hurrah!"

And Uncle Paul pushed back his chair, puckered up his forehead, stared hard at his nephew, and grunted out—

"Humph!"

"Oh, my dear, don't! Pray don't!" panted Mrs Champernowne, whom Nature had made middle-aged, round and plump. "You are taking away all my breath. But my neighbour's master says that he thinks they have made for Salcombe, where they will perhaps get aboard one of the orange boats and be put back in their own country."

"Hah!" said Uncle Paul, leaning back in his chair to take hold of his bunch of seals and haul up by the broad watered silk ribbon the big double-cased gold watch that ticked away from where it reclined warm and comfortable at the bottom of his fob.

"Confound their politics,
Frustrate their knavish tricks!"

"That was a very fine tea, Mrs Champernowne. Now, Pickle, my boy, I think it would be very nice to go and sit for half-an-hour in the arbour under the roses, while I kill the green fly—the aphides, Mrs Champernowne—which increase and multiply at a rate which is absolutely marvellous. Pickle, my boy, I hope you will never grow up as weak and self-indulgent as your uncle. Fill me my long clay pipe."

Chapter Four
Oh, Summer Night!

Mrs Champernowne's arbour was a very homely affair, consisting of four fir poles to form as many corners, and a few more nailed and pegged together to form gables. Nature built all the rest with roses and honeysuckle and some vigorous ivy at the back, the roses spiring up, the honeysuckle creeping in and out among the long strands and holding them together, while the ivy ran rapidly up the back till it could grow no higher, and then began to droop down till it had formed itself into a thick curtain which kept out the wind.

There was a very rustic table in the middle, formed by nailing two pieces of plank on to a tree stump, and a couple of seats, one on each side, pierced with holes that had once upon a time been made by ship carpenters' augers, when the wood was built up over the ribs of some stout ship which long years after was bumped to pieces by the waves upon the rocks and then cast up upon the southern shore, to be bought up and carted all through the county.

Yes, it was a very rustic place, but it suited its surroundings, and Uncle Paul looked supremely happy as he sat there slowly smoking his pipe and gazing dreamily before him at the beautiful landscape stretching far, and the garden of the one cottage within reach only a short distance away from the plot of ground where by the help of the neighbour sufficient potatoes were grown for the widow's use. "What a silent, peaceful evening, Pickle," said Uncle Paul. "Look yonder in the east; the moon will be up soon, and then it will be night, and we have done no work. How do you feel, my boy?"

"Tired and stupid, uncle. My legs ache right down to the ankles."

"No wonder, hopping about amongst those granite boulders. My back's a bit stiff too. There, let's go into the parlour, light up, and then you shall fetch down the microscope."

"Oh, not yet, uncle!—I say, have another pipe."

"A vaunt, you young tempter! Trying to lead me astray into idleness! No, let's get in. We have been playing all day; now let's go and get a bit of work done before we lie down to sleep."

"But I say, uncle, do you think that Napoleon will ever start another war in France?"

"Who knows, boy? His goings-on have brought nearly everything to a standstill, and there has been war enough to last for a hundred years."

"Yes, uncle; but do you think that Napoleon and the war put a stop to your expedition that you were to make in a vessel of your own?"

"Of course I do, Pickle," said Uncle Paul, smoking very slowly now, with his eyes shut, so as to make the little incandescent mass at the bottom of his bowl last for a few minutes longer. "Government promised me and my friends to make a grant for the fitting out of a small vessel, and for the payment of a captain and crew, and it was voted that we should have it; but do what we might, my friends and I could never get the cash, and it has always been put off, put off, on account of the expenses of the war."

"But, uncle—" began Rodd.

"No, you don't, sir," said Uncle Paul, with a soft chuckle. "None of your artfulness! You are trying to lead me on to prattle about Bony, so as to avoid my lecture upon the fresh-water polypes I have taken to-day. Get out, you transparent young scrub! In with you, and fetch down the case, and light the two candles on the parlour table. Nice innocent way of doing it. Think I couldn't see through you, sir? Be off!"

A few minutes later Uncle Paul's pipe was cooling on the parlour chimney-piece, kept almost upright by the waxy end leaning against a glass tube which had been formed into a sort of ornamental rolling-pin to be suspended over the fire, and to be much treasured by its owner.

It was not a very aesthetic piece of art or ornamentation, being only composed of coloured flowers carefully cut out of a piece of chintz, before being gummed upon the inside of the glass tube. This was then filled up with salt, and the ornament was complete.

The candles were burning brightly after each application of the snuffers; the polished mahogany microscope case stood on a side-table, and the brass tube that had been taken out was ready to receive one of the many slips of glass, some of which had little cup-like hollows ground out of one side ready for receiving a tiny drop of water and one or other of the specimens, the result of the past day's search.

Uncle Paul was on one side of the table with his big glass bottle; Rodd sat on the other, with his chin resting in his hands, trying to listen to his uncle's discourse, and with his eyelids drooping down now and again.

"Bother the flies and moths!" said Uncle Paul testily. "Who's to work with them circling round and round the candles, trying to singe themselves to death? What's that white one, boy?"

"Ghost moth, uncle," replied Rodd sharply, his uncle's question seeming to rouse him up to attention.

"Good boy! Well named. Trying hard to make a ghost of itself too. Why, there's a great Daddy Longlegs now! Here, you'll have to shut the window."

"Oh, don't, uncle! It will make the room so hot."

"Umph! So it will. Very tiresome, though, when one's trying to work. Now then, let me see; let me see. I want to examine this hydra, but I must put on a lower power, and— Oh, dear, dear, dear! Gnats! Moths! Tipulae and— Really, really, Pickle, that lamp gives no light at all;" and Uncle Paul leaned forward, took a pin out of the edge of his waistcoat, and began to prick at and try to raise the wick of the reflecting microscope lamp.

Then there was a little catastrophe, for after a most vigorous application of the pin the wick seemed to resent it as if it were some kind of sea worm, and drew back out of reach into its little brass cell.

"There, now I've done it!" said Uncle Paul. "Did you ever see anything so tiresome in your life, Pickle?"

"Yahah!" sighed the boy slowly.

"Why, what are you doing? Yawning!" cried Uncle Paul. "You are about the sleepiest chap I ever knew. There, I am afraid I shall have to wait for to-morrow morning's sunshine. Clear away, or help me. Let's put everything on a side-table, and I'll tell Mrs Champernowne that she isn't to touch what she sees there."

"Yes, uncle," said the boy, with something like alacrity, as the table was cleared and the candles re-snuffed, the effect of opening and shutting the snuffers seeming to act upon Rodd and making him yawn widely, while quite involuntarily Uncle Paul did the same. "Now then," said Uncle Paul.

"Aren't we going to bed, uncle?" said Rodd eagerly. "Bed? Nonsense! Because we are in a country place where people like going to bed almost in the middle of the day and getting up in the middle of the night, do you think we need follow their example? Absurd! I want to talk to you about some of the wonderful things I captured to-day. The waters on the moor swarm with the most beautiful limpid specimens."

Rodd sighed softly, and put his hand before his mouth to stop a yawn.

"Oh, by the way," said Uncle Paul, "did you change your trousers when you went up to wash?"

"No, uncle; they didn't want it."

"Weren't they damp?"

"No, uncle; I only got my shoes wet, and they were pretty well dry when I got home. Besides, you had got my other trousers in the big portmanteau in your room."

"Well, you could have come and fetched them. Always be careful to change damp things.—Come in!"

There had been a soft tap at the door, and Mrs Champernowne appeared.

"I beg pardon, sir, but what would you like for breakfast in the morning?"

"Breakfast, Mrs Champernowne? Nothing."

"Oh, I say, uncle!" said Rodd sharply. "We seem to have eaten enough this evening to last us for twenty-four hours."

"Oh no, sir," said the landlady. "Excuse me, but our moorland air will make you think very differently to-morrow morning."

"Humph!" grunted Uncle Paul.

"You see, sir, I did think that you'd bring home enough trout this evening to do for your breakfast too, and I am afraid there's nothing but ham and eggs. Would you mind them?"

"I'll tell you to-morrow morning, madam," said Uncle Paul.

"Then if you wouldn't mind, sir—I don't want to hurry you and the young gentleman—but it's my time, and if you will excuse me I'll say good-night."

"Good-night, Mrs Champernowne; good-night, and pleasant rest to you," said Uncle Paul heartily, "and— Yes? You were going to say something?"

"If you wouldn't mind, sir, being sure that the candles are well out."

"Oh, of course; of course."

"And it's a very hot night, sir."

"Yes, madam; we have found that out."

"So if you'll be kind enough to shut and slip the bolt of the front door I'll leave it for you to do so when you go up to bed."

"Certainly, Mrs Champernowne, certainly. Once more, good-night."

Their landlady smiled benevolently on both, and the next minute they heard the little old staircase creaking beneath her tread, this being followed by the cracking of the boards in the little room over the kitchen, the visitors both listening till all was silent again.

Somehow as Rodd sat opposite to his uncle, his head seemed to be unusually heavy, and he rested more and more upon his two thumbs, which he had placed for support beneath his chin.

There was a faint pinging sound, the trumpeting of a gnat flitting about the room, and then the deep boom of a beetle somewhere outside the open window. There was a hot delicious odour, too, floating in over the flowers in the garden, a portion of whose scent the warm air seemed to be taking up to mingle with that which it had swept off the moor.

And then as Rodd listened and gazed across the table between the two candles, whose tops were growing tiny brown mushrooms as they silently asked to be snuffed, it seemed to the boy that his uncle's face looked dim and misty, and then that it swelled and swelled and began to float up like a faintly seen balloon, till it died right away. And all was still but the *um-um-um* of the great beetle or chafer which had passed in through the window, and began circling round just below the whitewashed ceiling, against which its wings brushed from time to time with a faint fizz, till all at once Rodd started up, for his uncle exclaimed—

"Why, Pickle, what are you about?"

"I—I—nothing, uncle," said the boy hastily. "Why, I believe, sir, you were going to sleep!"

"Oh, I am quite wide awake, uncle," cried the boy.

"Humph, yes—now. You see, my boy, these hydras are most extraordinary things, and to-morrow morning in the bright sunshine we will get the microscope to work, and I'll show you how they—"

Burr—burr—burr—hum—hum—hum—um—um.

Was that Uncle Paul talking in a low tone with his voice getting farther and farther away, or was it that big chafer spinning round and round the room? Now it nearly died out, and then it grew louder again and seemed to double into a duet, just as if the great stag beetle had whisked in at the casement and had joined in the nocturnal valse, the duet seeming to be intended to lull the naturalist and his nephew to sleep in the soft musky sweetness of that delightful summer's night.

How long it lasted, who could say, but all at once there was a sudden start, and Uncle Paul's hand came down with a thump upon the tablecloth after he had knocked over one of the candlesticks, making so much noise that, wide awake now, Rodd made a dash and stood the candlestick up again, before snatching the candle from where it lay singeing the lavender and red-check cotton table-cover and beginning to deposit a big spot of grease.

"Bless my heart, Pickle!" cried Uncle Paul. "I believe I was going to drop asleep."

"I am afraid I was asleep, uncle," replied the boy. "You were saying that hydras—that hydras—er—er—er—something about hydras."

"Yes, yes, yes, but never mind. Perhaps we had better go to bed, and I'll finish what I was saying in the morning. There, light the two flat candlesticks, and we will have a good long snooze. That's right; put out the others. No, no; use the extinguisher! Don't blow them out, or there will be such a smell."

Then—

"Shall I shut the window, uncle?"

"Oh, no, I don't think you need. The place is like an oven. Heigho— ha—hum! Yes, I am sleepy. Come along. Good-night, my boy. I am going to sleep with my chamber window wide open, and you'd better do the same."

"But I say, uncle, we shall hardly want our candles. Look at the moon. It is almost as light as day."

All the same they took the candles up with them, the stairs creaking again beneath their tread as if uttering a protest against them for their forgetfulness in not attending to their hostess's request to close and bolt the door; but they were too sleepy to do anything more than slip off their things on reaching their rooms, while almost directly after, the moon was shining in right across Rodd's snowy white bed, the pillow being in the darkness, which also formed a black bar across the foot, so that only the boy's hands and breast lay in the light.

One moment after laying his head down in that black velvety darkness Rodd Harding was wide awake and thinking that all outside the window was silver, a broad streak of which came straight over him to die away in the wall on his left; the next, he was far away in the land of dreams, wandering over the moor, his confused visions taking the form of escaping prisoners flying before soldiers in scarlet coats.

And then after a blank pause which seemed to have lasted only a few minutes, Rodd opened his eyes upon the bright silvery light once more, to find that it struck across from the window in the opposite direction, for he was wide awake, listening to a soft tap, tap, tap, evidently administered by a knuckle upon his door.

Chapter Five
The Milk in the Cocoa-Nut

"Yes, all right, Mrs Champernowne; get up directly. I say, what's o'clock?"

"Oh, I don't know, my dear," came in agitated tones, "but would you come to the door and speak to me a minute?"

There was a bump on the floor as Rodd sprang out of bed, and then—

"What is it?" whispered the boy, who was moved by his caller's evident distress. "Don't say uncle's ill!"

"No, no, my dear, but I am in great trouble. You—you didn't shut the front door."

"Oh!" ejaculated Rodd.

"And—and, my dear, there have been thieves and robbers in the night. They have stripped my little larder, and I don't know what they haven't taken besides. Do, pray, make haste and dress, and come down and help me! I am in such trouble, I don't know what I shall do."

"All right; I'll make haste and come down," cried Rodd, feeling guilty all over, and then trying to excuse himself by shuffling the blame on to the right shoulders. "It was uncle she asked," he muttered, as he ran round to the other side of the bed for the chair upon which he had hang his clothes when he undressed. "Why, hallo!"

He stood staring at the chair for a moment or two, and then ran round the foot of the bed, opened the door two or three inches, and called in a subdued tone so as not to awaken his uncle, though if he had been asked why, he could not have told, beyond saying that he felt then that it was the right thing to do—

"Mrs Champernowne! Mrs Champernowne!"

"Yes, my dear," came from the foot of the stairs. "Oh, you have been quick!"

"No, no, I haven't," cried Rodd pettishly. "Here, I say, have you taken away my trousers?"

"Gracious me, no, my dear! What should I want with your trousers?"

"Take them down to brush perhaps," muttered the boy to himself, as he ran back to the other side of the bed and raised the counterpane. "Haven't slipped off and gone under," he muttered, and then as a fresh thought struck him he clapped his hands to his forehead and stood staring before him. "The thieves!" he exclaimed. "They haven't been in here and taken all my clothes?"

He was silent for a few minutes, as he stared vacantly about the room.

"They have, though!" he cried. "Here, Mrs Champernowne!—Boots and all. Oh, I can't tell her. Here, I must get my other suit out of the portmanteau. I won't wake uncle, because it's so early. Why, it can be only just sunrise; and he'd sit up and laugh at me. Oh, bother!"

Rodd ran round to the door again, opened it about an inch, and listened.

"She's in the kitchen," he muttered to himself, and slipping out on to the little landing he raised the latch of his uncle's door, glided in, and made for the big portmanteau that lay unstrapped beneath the window.

Raising the one half quickly, he twisted the whole round so that the two halves might lie open upon the whitely-scrubbed boards as silently as he could; but one corner caught against the leg of the dressing-table, jarring it so violently that a hair-brush fell on to the floor with a bang, and Uncle Paul sprang up in bed.

"Hullo, you sir! What are you doing there?" he cried.

"Getting out my other suit, uncle," said the boy quickly.

"What for? Don't do that! We are going over the moor again to-day."

"But I must, uncle," cried Rodd.

"Mush!"

"Yes. Oh, I shall be obliged to tell you. It was all your fault, uncle; you didn't fasten the door as Mrs Champernowne told you, and there have been thieves in the night."

"Been grandmothers in the night!" cried Uncle Paul contemptuously.

"It's true, uncle, and they came up into my room while I was asleep and took away all my clothes—boots and all."

"You don't mean that, Pickle! Here, I say, where are mine?"

Rodd sprang to his feet from where he was kneeling by the portmanteau, and ran round to the side of the bed, just as his uncle turned and faced him.

"Every blessed thing gone, boy. Why, Rodney, my lad, we have fallen into a den of thieves—robbed, and we may thank our stars we haven't been murdered!"

"Why, it's horrid, uncle! Didn't you hear them, then?"

"Hear them, no! I heard nothing till you knocked something off on to the floor. Here, stop a moment, boy! My purse! It was in my trousers pocket."

"Then it's gone, uncle," cried Rodd.

"Ah! Horror! My gold watch and seals!"

"Well, they weren't in your trousers, uncle."

"No, boy; I remember winding it up and laying it on the chimney-piece."

"It isn't there, uncle."

"My gold presentation watch, that I wouldn't have lost for five hundred pounds! Call up that wretched woman."

"Uncle, I can't!"

"Do as I tell you, sir! She's in league with the thieves."

"But, uncle!"

"Oh yes, I forgot. There, don't stand staring there like a bull calf that has lost its mother. Turn that portmanteau upside down. Put on some things yourself, and throw me some more. You can dress quicker than I can, for you haven't got to shave. Look sharp, and then run for the village constable."

"Why, there isn't one, uncle," grumbled Rodd, as he began to scramble into his other clothes.

"No, of course there isn't, sir. A miserable one-eyed place with only two cottages in it, and I dare say that old woman's in the other, sharing the plunder? What a fool I was to come!"

"No, you weren't, uncle, and Mrs Champernowne isn't sharing the plunder, for she came and woke me up to say that the thieves had been and carried off everything there was down-stairs. I say, uncle, it was all your fault."

"Don't you dare to say that to me again, sir!" roared Uncle Paul. "It is insolent and disrespectful. Oh, hang the woman's door! Why didn't she bolt it herself? Why, I'd got twenty guineas in that purse, besides a lot of silver. There, there's somebody knocking at the door! Who's there?"

"Please, sir, it's me. They've taken the bread and the butter, and a piece of freshly-boiled ham that I meant for you to have cold."

"And pray who's *they*, madam?" shouted Uncle Paul, who was in difficulties with buttons.

"Well, sir, I was thinking it must be the smugglers. They've been here several times before, when they have been crossing the moor with cargo; but it couldn't be them, for they always leave a little box of tea or a bit of silk, to pay for what they take. It must have been thieves, sir—thieves."

"Yes, madam; and they have taken my purse and gold watch too, besides two suits of clothes. There, go on down. We'll join you soon. I want to think what's to be done."

The stairs creaked as Mrs Champernowne descended, and just then something caught Rodd's eye—something bright and shiny, against the leaves of a big old gazetteer lying upon the side-table.

Rodd uttered an ejaculation.

"Oh!" he exclaimed.

"Something more gone?" cried the Doctor.

"No, uncle; there's your watch. And here's your gold pencil-case too," continued the boy, as he raised the corner of the book. "Why, they have been turning the watch-ribbon into a marker, and somebody has been writing here on the fly-leaf."

"Thank goodness!" grunted Uncle Paul. "That's something saved out of the fire. Never mind the writing. But they have taken our clothes."

"It's in French, I think, uncle, but I can't quite make it out."

"French!" cried Uncle Paul fiercely. "Why, of course! How stupid! I might have known. We have been attacked in the night by a gang of old Napoleon's scum. That man's bound to be the curse of my life. Don't stand staring there, boy. Can't you see?"

"No, uncle," said the boy sturdily. "What nonsense! Napoleon couldn't have invaded England in the night to come and steal our clothes."

"Bah! Idiot! Can't you see it's some of those scoundrelly French prisoners who escaped yesterday? That vagabond of a boy perhaps that you pampered off and were feeding with our good English provisions. Now you see the consequences. The ungrateful rapparee— Oh no, but that's Irish, and he'd be French."

"Yes, uncle," said the boy thoughtfully, for his uncle's fulminations fell blankly upon his ears as he stood trying to puzzle out some of the pencilled words upon the fly-leaf of the book.

"Here's *pardon*, uncle, and something else I can't make out, and *changer*. Why, that means exchange! Yes, and lower down here's *sous* something, only it's written over 'John Champernowne' and 'his book'; but that's in ink. What does *oreiller* mean, uncle?"

"Bolster," said Uncle Paul. "No: pillow," and he turned involuntarily towards the bed, where, unperceived before, a scrap of something red peered from beneath the clean white pillow-case. "Under the pillow," said Uncle Paul, and stepping to the side of the bed he snatched up the soft down cushion deeply marked by the pressure of his head.

Catching up what lay beneath, he uttered a loud ejaculation and tapped it sharply against the bed-post.

"What have you got there, uncle?"

"Pickle, my boy, it's my twenty guineas that we thought they'd stolen. What in the name of forceps and lancets did they tie them up in this old silk rag for? It's a bit of a pocket-handkerchief."

"Why, uncle," cried Rodd, laughing, "it isn't going to be so bad, after all. Somebody's been having a game with us."

"Game, eh? Queer sort of a game, Pickle," cried Uncle Paul; and with very little effort he tore open the silk envelope and poured out a little heap of bright gold coins upon the bed. "Napoleons, by all that's wonderful!" he cried. "Exchange! I begin to see now, boy. He's taken my good gold money, whoever he is, and left this French trash. Here, give me that book. Mind— don't drop my watch."

"I have got it safe, uncle," replied the boy, handing the big book to his uncle.

"Humph!" grunted Uncle Paul. "Not quite such a scoundrel as he might have been, whoever it is that wrote it. Exchange, eh? But there's been no exchange about our clothes. Humph! All in French, of course. If he had been a gentleman, and he couldn't understand plain English, he would have written it in Latin. Bah! How I do hate that pernicketty French! Let's see— let's see. Oh yes, here it all is. Ask pardon for two poor prisoners trying to escape—um, um, um—years of misery. Generous Englishman—some day—*remerciments*. Ah, it's all scribbled horribly—in the dark, I suppose. Oh, he's signed it, though, Pickle. 'Des Saix, Comte.' Oh, there are two of them, then. The other's signed his name too—quite a different hand. 'Morny des Saix, Vicomte.' H'm! Well, I suppose they are gentlemen."

"Noblemen, uncle."

"Bah! Noblemen wouldn't do a thing like that!"

"What are those other words, uncle, under the last name?"

"Um—um—um! 'May God bless you for what you did to-day. Your friend till death.' Why, Pickle, you ought to have been able to read that yourself."

"I did, uncle, but I wanted to be sure that I was right. Why, that must have been the boy I helped to escape."

"Yes, and he dodged us home, and as good as robbed us."

"Oh, uncle! Shame!"

"How dare you, sir! What do you mean by it, Rodney? Do you forget who I am, sir?"

"No."

"And pray who am I then, sir?"

"Dear old Uncle Paul, who has got out of bed the wrong way this morning!"

"H'm—ha! Well, I suppose you are right, Pickle. I did feel in an awful temper; but I don't feel quite so bad now that I have found my watch."

"And pencil-case, uncle."

"Ah, yes, my boy. That was the gift of a very grateful old patient."

"And then there are all those gold napoleons, uncle."

"Bah! Trash! Base counters, good for nothing, like the ugly head that's upon them," cried Uncle Paul irascibly.

"But I say, uncle; it might have been worse."

"But the clothes, my boy! The scoundrels! They'll go masquerading about in our things, and escaping, I'll be bound. But stop a minute. What did he say about exchange?"

"Oh, that meant about the money."

"Hullo! There's that wicked old woman again!—Well, Mrs Champernowne, what is it now?"

"The wood-shed, sir."

"Well, I don't want the wood-shed. Light the fire yourself."

"You don't understand me, sir. I went round there to get some kindling, and there's quite a heap of old clothes there that these wicked people have left behind."

Uncle Paul chuckled, for he was beginning to beam again.

"I say, Pickle, that accounts for the milk in the cocoa-nut. They must have taken our things down into the old lady's wood-shed, and turned it into a dressing-room."

"Yes," cried Rodd; "and that young Viscount is quite welcome to mine."

"Most generous, I am sure, sir," cried Uncle Paul sarcastically, "but would you be kind enough to tell me who pays the bills for your clothes?"

"Why, you do, uncle, of course. But I say, uncle, I do hope they'll escape; don't you?"

"Wha–a–at!"

"You do, uncle, only you pretend that you don't."

"Pretend!"

"Yes. Poor fellows! How horrible! To have to stoop to such a scheme as that to get away! But after all, uncle, it's glorious and brave. What an escape! Oh, how I should like to meet that poor fellow again!"

"What, to give him up to the soldiers?" said Uncle Paul sarcastically.

"Give him up to the soldiers!" cried the boy indignantly. "Why, I'd sooner put on his old clothes, and tell them a lie!"

"What!" cried Uncle Paul.

"Well, I'd pretend to be him so as to cheat them, and make them take me instead."

Chapter Six
What does that Sergeant want?

"Humph!" grunted Uncle Paul, as they descended at last, to hear the fire crackling in the kitchen, and the bright old copper kettle singing its morning song.

It was a lovely morning, with the sweet scents of the garden and moor floating in at the little parlour window, and as Uncle Paul took what his irreverent nephew called a good long sniff, he slowly and ostentatiously, moved thereto by the sight of the clean white cloth and the breakfast things, hauled up his great gold watch and examined its face.

"Twenty-five minutes, thirty-seven seconds, past six, Pickle. Rather early for breakfast. Well, I suppose we must take things as they are; but I am very, very sorry that they took away my old coat; it was a great favourite. And those things of yours, sir, are much too good to go climbing about tors and wading in streams. I wish that Count had knocked at my door like a gentleman and asked me, as he should. He should have had this suit instead. I'd a deal rather he had it than my old shooting jacket."

"Ha, ha!"

"What are you laughing at, sir?"

"Uncle Paul eating his words."

"What, sir?"

"You mean, uncle, that if Count de Saix had come and knocked at the door and asked you to help him, you'd have called me up and sent me to the prison for the soldiers."

"Now look here, Rodney, that's impudence, sir, and— Ah! There's the microscope, and the slides and the glasses. Have they been disturbed?"

"No, uncle. Just as we left them. I almost wonder they didn't carry off all those hydras."

"*Hydrae*. Be careful about your Latin plurals. But look here, do you want me to box your ears?"

"No, uncle."

"Then don't give me any more of your impertinent allusions. Hum— hum—hum! Half-past six. Very early for breakfast. But I begin to feel a little *appetitlich*, as the Germans call it; don't you?"

"Oh no, uncle," said Rodd, very mildly. "You said last night that we had eaten enough to last twenty-four hours."

"Now, look here, Rodney, you had the impudence to tell me a short time ago that I'd got out of bed the wrong way. I am afraid it's you, sir, that have done that, and if you don't take care we shall be having a very serious quarrel.—There! Run, quick! That kettle's boiling over."

But Rodd was half-way to the kitchen, and had snatched the kettle off before his uncle had finished speaking, warned of what was happening as he had been by the first angry hiss.

"It's all right, uncle," he cried. "No harm done!"

"But what's become of that old woman? She ought to be here now, seeing about our breakfast."

"Here she comes, uncle," and through the window they could see their hostess hurrying back with a big basket from the direction of the neighbour's cottage, and the next minute they heard her setting her load upon her white kitchen-table.

"Oh, I didn't know you were down, gentlemen," she cried, as she hurried into the parlour. "I have been over to my neighbour's to see if she could help me now that I am in such a fix."

"Well, could she?" said Uncle Paul.

"Oh yes, sir. As luck had it, she was baking yesterday, and she had plenty of butter and eggs, besides a small ham which had just been smoked."

"Oh, come," said Uncle Paul, "we shall be able to keep you alive for a few days longer, Pickle; and I suppose you will soon be able to let us have breakfast, Mrs Champernowne?"

"Oh yes, sir, very quickly. I shall only want time to fry the ham."

Uncle Paul gave an involuntary sniff, as if the aroma of the fragrant brown had floated to his nostrils.

"But you can't tell, sir, how sorry I am that such a thing should have happened to gentlemen staying in my house;" and the poor woman looked appealingly to uncle and nephew, and back.

"Don't you say another word about it, madam," replied Uncle Paul. "You make us a nice clear cup of coffee to take away the taste of the night's adventures."

"I will indeed, sir, and I won't say another word, only thank you for taking it so patiently and, if I might make the observation, in such a lamb-like way."

Rodd turned round very quickly, walked to the window, and began to whistle softly.

"I went over this morning to my neighbour's, sir, as you may see by the basket."

"Yes, madam," said Uncle Paul, who was staring hard at his nephew's back and scratching one ear vigorously.

"I told her all about it, of course, sir, and her master was there having his breakfast before he went out peat-cutting, and if you'll believe me, sir, he did nothing but laugh, and said he knew it was the prisoners, sure enough, and he had the impudence to say that it was a great blessing that they came to my cottage instead of to his, and lucky for the prisoners too, for they'd got a better fit."

"Ah, yes, Mrs Champernowne," said Uncle Paul, pulling out his watch and frowning very hard in its face; "but do you think your neighbour's ham will be as good as yours?"

"Oh yes, sir—better, I expect, for it was a lovely little pig when it was fatted up and killed last Christmas; one of those little fat, short-legged, dunkey ones with turn-up snouts. My husband used to say they were the Chinese breed, and that was why the ham and bacon always went so well with China tea. You may depend upon that ham, sir, being beautiful."

"Very singular fact, Mrs Champernowne," said Uncle Paul blandly. "Then perhaps you wouldn't mind cutting the rashers a little thicker. I am rather ashamed of my nephew's appetite; but then you see he's only a hungry, growing boy."

Uncle Paul took out his watch again, and this time their landlady took the hint, and hurried into the kitchen, from which delicious odours soon began to escape, and in the midst of the examination upon the window-sill, where the bright sun lit up the lenses of the microscope, the magnified hydrae, with their buds and wondrous developments, were set aside, to be superseded by the morning meal.

"Ah, yes," said Uncle Paul, thoroughly mollified now by Mrs Champernowne's preparations, "there are worse disasters at sea, Pickle, and I'd worn that old coat off and on for a good many years."

"You couldn't have worn it off and on, uncle," said Rodd dryly.

"Look here, sir; if your mother, my dear sister, had had the slightest idea that you would have grown up into such an impertinent, two-edged-tongued young scrub, I don't believe she'd have died and left you in my charge. I suppose you meant that to be very witty, sir. Please understand that I was only speaking figuratively. Now we will just spend about an hour over those specimens, and then, as it is so beautiful and fine, we will be off on to the moor again. You will take your fishing-rod, of course?"

"Oh yes, uncle."

"Then turn up the bottoms of those trousers before we start."

"No, uncle; I shall put my leggings on over these," said Rodd coolly, "and I should advise you to do the same." Both Uncle Paul's ears seemed to twitch, and he scratched one as if it itched; but he said nothing, for just then Mrs Champernowne tapped at the door, to enter smiling, with a packet of letters.

"Postman, sir," she said, placing the letters upon the table. "You won't mind me speaking another word, sir?" she said.

"Oh no, Mrs Champernowne," said her visitor, rather gruffly. "What is it?"

"I think you told me, sir, that the prisoners did not take any of your valuables, your money, or anything of that sort?"

"No, Mrs Champernowne," cried Rodd eagerly. "They took uncle's money, but they left a lot of French napoleons instead."

Uncle Paul made a snatch at a very big blue letter, and darted a furious look at his nephew.

"I am very, *very, very* glad, sir," cried Mrs Champernowne, "and, poor things, they are to be pitied, after all."

She backed smilingly out of the room, and Uncle Paul held the big blue letter, which was doubly sealed with red wax, edgewise at his nephew, as if he were going to make a sword-cut at him.

"Now, look here, Rodney," he said; "it has been dawning upon me for a long time past that I have indulged and spoiled you, with the result that you are growing into a most impertinent young rascal. Have the goodness for the future, sir, to allow me to speak for myself. When I require your conversational assistance, I will ask you for it."

"Yes, uncle, and—"

"Well, sir, what?"

"Aren't you going to open that big letter, uncle? I want to know what's the news."

"What is it to you, sir?" cried Uncle Paul, who had been opening a very keen-looking, peculiarly-shaped, ivory-handled knife. "Have the goodness to let my business be my business. I have a very great mind to put this letter,"—and as he spoke he carefully cut round the seals—"and the other missives away in my writing-case until I am alone—" Here Uncle Paul unfolded a letter upon the top of which was stamped the Royal Arms, and smoothed it out upon the tablecloth—"and read it in peace, without being pestered by an impertinent boy. Bless my heart! Why, Pickle, my boy! Hark here! It's a letter from the Government. Jump up and shout, you young dog! Hang Bony and all his works! It's all right at last."

"Why, what is it?" cried the boy excitedly, as his uncle went on eagerly reading the bold round hand that formed the formal contents.

"Hark here! 'His Majesty's advisers see their way to recommend that the long-deferred grant for the sea-going natural history expedition to the West Coast of Africa to be carried out by Dr Robson at his earliest convenience be made, and that the grant to the full amount will be paid in to Dr Robson's bank as soon as formal application has been received.' There, sir, what do you think of that? At last! At last! Pickle, my boy, they say that everything comes at last to the man who waits, and here it is."

"Oh, Uncle Paul!" cried the boy, with sparkling eyes. "I am so glad—so glad!" And as he spoke he dashed at the reader, to catch him tightly by the two sides of the collar of his coat.

"Mind my clean cravat, Pickle."

"Bother your clean cravat, uncle!" shouted the boy. "Look here, sir; you always promised me that if ever that money came and you went on that expedition, you'd play fair."

"What do you mean, sir, by your playing fair?"

"You said, uncle," cried the boy, sawing the collar he held to and fro, "that I should be very useful to you, and could help you no end over the netting and dredging and bottling specimens, and that you'd take me with you."

"Ah," cried Uncle Paul, "that was when you were a nice, good, obedient boy, and hadn't learnt to say sharp impertinent things, and didn't go about setting free escaped prisoners and getting your uncle robbed."

"Gammon, uncle! I see through you, and—I say, what does that sergeant want?" For there was the tramp of heavy feet, and the non-commissioned officer who had been at the head of the squad of men they had met, marched past the cottage window.

Chapter Seven
He Says

"Eh? What?" exclaimed Uncle Paul excitedly.

"You don't mean that he is coming here?"

"He is, uncle," replied the boy nervously, and his colour began to go and come.

"Tut, tut, tut, tut!" ejaculated Uncle Paul. "This looks serious, my boy. Well, I don't know. Perhaps he's only heard of the visit that has been paid here."

"I beg pardon, sir; here is Mr Windell, one of the sergeants of the prison guard. Could he see you for a few minutes?"

"Well, I'm rather— Yes, yes, show him in, Mrs Champernowne. Rodney, my boy, you sit still and hold your tongue. I don't know what this man wants; but you leave it to me."

Rodd nodded his head, and fancied that he felt relieved, but he did not, for his heart was beating faster than usual, and he was suffering from a strange kind of emotion.

"Good-morning, gentlemen," said the sergeant, saluting stiffly as he was shown in.

"Good-morning," said Uncle Paul stiffly. "Do you wish to see me?"

"Yes, sir; only about a little matter upon the moor yesterday. After we left you I did not feel satisfied about those prisoners."

"Indeed?" said Uncle Paul coldly.

"No, sir. The governor yonder likes to have things thoroughly done, so about three hours afterwards I went over the ground again."

"Yes," said Uncle Paul, without taking his eyes from the sergeant's face.

"And there I found out something else."

Uncle Paul was silent, and Rodd's heart went on now in a steady *thump — thump — thump — thump*.

"Thought I'd come on, sir," said the sergeant, turning back to the door, going outside, and returning with Rodd's creel, which he slowly opened and took from within, neatly folded up, the canvas wallet. "Belong to you gentlemen, don't they?"

"Yes," said Uncle Paul slowly; "those are ours. Well?"

Rodd's heart now seemed to stand quite still till the sergeant replied to his uncle's query.

"That's all, sir; that's all," said the sergeant, and Rodd's heart went on again. "You had left them behind, and I thought I'd bring them on."

"Thank you," said Uncle Paul quietly. "Very good of you, and I am much obliged."

"Don't name it, sir. Going to have another fine day, and hope the young gentleman here will have plenty more sport. There's a lot of trout up there, only they are terrible small. Good-morning, gentlemen."

"Good-morning, sergeant," said Uncle Paul quietly, and Rodd's mouth opened a little and then shut, but no sound came. "Wait a moment, sergeant," continued Uncle Paul, thrusting his hand into his pocket and feeling about amongst some five-and-twenty or thirty coins, all of which felt too small, for he wanted a larger one; but feeling that, he took hold of three together, when something made him stop short with his hand half out of his pocket, and he thrust it back again. "Dear me," he said, quickly now, "I really have no change."

"Oh, there's no need for that, sir," said the sergeant.

"Yes, yes," said Uncle Paul. "Rodd, my boy, have you half-a-crown in your pocket?"

"I think so, uncle," said the boy quickly; and then his face looked blank. "No, uncle; I haven't anything at all," he cried in dismay.

"Oh, pray don't mind, sir," said the sergeant, moving to the door. "Good-morning, sir; good-morning. I don't want paying for a little thing like that."

"Stop, please," said Uncle Paul hurriedly. "Rodd, my boy, go and ask Mrs Champernowne if she'll be kind enough to lend me half-a-crown."

Rodd hurried out, feeling exceedingly hot, and with a peculiar moisture in the palms of his hands, returning directly afterwards with the required coin, though the unexpected demand had made their landlady open her eyes rather widely.

"There, that's right, sergeant," said Uncle Paul, "and I am sure my nephew is much obliged. He wouldn't have liked to lose that creel."

"Thank you, sir. Very glad I found it. Good-morning once more."

The man saluted both, giving Rodd a very peculiar look which seemed to go through him, and then turning upon his heels, he marched out of the room and shut the door, while Uncle Paul sank back in his chair, took out a clean red and yellow silk handkerchief, and wiped his forehead.

"Rodney, my boy," he said, "I felt as if we had been doing something underhanded, and nearly brought out three of those napoleons to pay that man."

"Oh, uncle," said the boy huskily; "it would have been like telling him that the poor fellows had been here."

"Yes, my boy, and that you had been helping them to escape."

"Oh!" ejaculated Rodd, and he darted to the window. "No," he gasped, with a sigh of relief. "He's gone."

"Well, we knew he'd gone, boy."

"Yes, uncle, but I was afraid that he'd stop talking to Mrs Champernowne, and she would tell him about their coming here. But he didn't stop, and he has gone right away."

"Hah!" ejaculated Uncle Paul. "Well, you see how near we have been to getting into trouble with the authorities; for of course they are very strict over such things as these. There, now I must write an important letter to send off in acknowledgment of that despatch; so you be off now for about half-an-hour, and go and play like a good boy."

"Yes, uncle," said Rodd, rather grumpily; and he went slowly out, with the intention of getting somewhere on to the high ground where he could watch the sergeant's red coat till he was out of sight. "I wish Uncle Paul wouldn't talk to me like that," he muttered, as he went out of the garden gate. "Go out and play like a good boy! It does make me feel so wild! He'll be saying good little boy next, and I am past sixteen; and he wasn't doing it to tease me either, for he was quite serious, what with the prisoners, and the sergeant coming like that. Bother him! He looked at me as he went away just as if he suspected that I'd left the sandwiches and the fish where that poor fellow could get them. Here, I mustn't let him see that I am following him. I'll go round by that other track and get up behind those stones. Then I can see the whole way to the prison. Oh, he didn't know anything, or else he'd have spoken out. But that's the worst of doing what you oughtn't to. You always feel as if everybody suspects you. Well, I didn't want to do any harm, and Uncle Paul didn't think it was very wrong, in spite of his grumbling about the French. If he had he wouldn't have called me Pickle. It would have been Rodney, and his voice would have sounded very severe, for he can be when he likes. Spoiled and indulged me! That he hasn't!"

The ascent was so steep by the track he had chosen that the boy was soon high above the cottages, hurrying along by a ridge of stones which led up to what looked like a young tor, so situated that it sheltered the two cottage gardens, and the enclosed field or two where the neighbour's cow was pastured, from the north and east wind, and also acted as a lew for Mrs Champernowne's bees, which could reach their straw hive homes comfortably without being blown out by the wanton breezes which travelled across the moors.

Rodd was pretty well out of breath when he reached the little tor, and so he drew in a fresh supply as he dropped upon his knees and crawled round the last stone to his proposed look-out, feeling certain he would be able to see the sergeant's bright scarlet coat with its white belts, as he marched straight away for the prison.

He did see him, but not so far off as he had anticipated, and the sight took his breath completely away again, for as he crept round he became conscious of a peculiar scent that was not wild thyme but tobacco, and before he realised what it was, he came plump face to face with their late visitor, who was seated upon the soft close turf with his back against a stone, basking in the sunshine, and evidently enjoying a rest.

"Here we are again, then, sir!" he cried, in his sharp military way. "I thought I'd just sit down here for a bit on the chance that you might come up and like to have a word or two to say to me."

He looked very hard at Rodd as he spoke, and the boy felt his face burn, while the next moment there was a sensation as if the cool wind were fanning his hot cheeks.

"Come out to speak to me, didn't you, sir?" said the sergeant.

Rodd was silent for a few moments, for his throat felt dry, while he passed his tongue over his lips to moisten them.

"No," he said, at last, with an effort. "I came up here to see if you had gone, and watch you back to the prison."

The sergeant laughed softly, and thrust one finger into the bowl of his pipe, before sending out a fresh cloud of smoke.

"Ah," he said, "I am not surprised. Well, here we are. Do you want to say anything to me?"

Rodd opened and shut his lips again, but no words came till he made an effort, and then said, with his utterance sounding very dry —

"You want to speak to me?"

"Right, sir. Yes, I do. You remember when I came upon you up yonder by that pool?"

Rodd nodded and frowned.

"Well, I suppose you noticed that there was a hole at the bottom of those rocks across there, where the little stream came out?"

"Yes," said Rodd, with his brow puckering up.

"Well, yesterday evening, as I said to your uncle, I went over the ground again to see if I could find any track of those escaped prisoners."

Rodd nodded shortly.

"Well, I took off my gaiters and shoes and stockings and waded across the pool, and nearly doubled myself up to get into that hole; and after I had gone a little way I found that there was quite a dry cave there with streaks of light coming down from above between the piled-up stones."

Rodd nodded again.

"Just in the highest part where the water did not reach, some one had lit a fire with bits of ling and dry peat. It was still warm — at least, the ashes were, and somebody had been busy cooking trout there, grilling them, thriddled on a stick of hazel; and very curious it was too, for somehow or other, the water, instead of running down, had been running up backwards like, and carried with it that there fishing-basket of yours, and the wallet, and laid them upon that nice dry sandy place close up to the fire along by which there were ever so many heads of those little fish, and their backbones. Rum, wasn't it? Do you think an otter could have done that?"

"No," said Rodd, after a few moments' pause; and he spoke sharply and angrily. "No, I don't think that."

"More don't I," said the sergeant dryly, and he half closed his eyes and sent a faint little curl of smoke into the air. "Now, young gentleman, what do you think would happen if I was to go yonder to the governor at the prison, and say that I believed you had helped the King's enemies to escape? You didn't, of course, eh?"

Rodd moistened his lips again, and his frank young face looked very much puckered and wrinkled as he pulled himself together and looked almost defiantly at his questioner, who exclaimed —

"Well, you heard what I said."

The boy nodded.

"Well, speak out. You didn't, of course?"

Rodd drew a deep breath, moistened his lips again, and then out the words came. "Yes," he said, "I did!"

"Hah!" said the sergeant, as he fixed the boy with his keen grey eyes and spoke to him as if he were one of his recruits. "Well, I like that. Spoken like a man. My old mother used to say, 'Speak the truth, Tom, and then you needn't be afraid of any man.' Look here, youngster, I am only a soldier, and you are a young gentleman, or else you wouldn't be visiting and making holiday here; but do you mind shaking hands?"

"Yes," said Rodd hotly, "I know: I suppose I have done wrong, and you have got your duty to do; so go and do it."

"Here," cried the sergeant, "grip, boy, grip! I like you for all this more and more. I had my duty to do, and I did it as far as I could; but I was too late. The prisoners had escaped, and we have heard this morning, the news being brought by a miserable-looking sneak of a fellow who had come to the governor to ask for the reward for not taking them, that they got down to Salcombe very late last night and boarded one of the orange boats in the little harbour, where I expect they had friends waiting for them, for the schooner sailed at once, and I dare say they are within sight of a French port before now. Yes, I had my duty to do, me and my lads, but the prisoners escaped, same as I would if I had been in a French prison, shut up for doing nothing, and because our two countries were at war. There, I am not going to blame you now it's all over, as you own to it like a man. They both came to you, I suppose, for a bit of help, and you gave it to them. But when I was on duty I should have nailed you if I had caught you in the act. There, that'll do. Thought I should like to tell you about it, and hold you like at the point of the bayonet, and see what you'd say. I know it's precious hard to tell the truth sometimes, and it must have been very hard here. But you did it like a man. But I say: you never thought that basket and wallet would tell tales when you left those poor beggars a mouthful to eat; and I hope if there's any more war to come and I'm took, and make a good try to slip away—I hope, I say, that I shall come upon some brave young French lad who will do as good a turn to me as you did to those poor fellows, who were making a run for freedom, and to get out of the reach of our bayonets and guns."

Rodd thrust his hand into his pocket, and flushed up now more than ever, for the sergeant caught him by the wrist.

"No, no, my lad," he cried; "none of that! I didn't come here to get money out of you. I was a boy once myself. Only a common one, but pretty straightforward and honest, or else I don't suppose I should have won these three gold chevrons which I have got here upon my arm. Well, I wouldn't have taken pay then for doing a dirty action, fond as I was of coppers with the King's head on; and I wouldn't do it now. So don't you make me set up my hackles by trying to offer me anything for this. Besides, I've got a whole half-crown your uncle gave me, and I am not even going to ask you whether he had a finger in this pie."

"No, he hadn't—he hadn't indeed," cried Rodd warmly. "On my honour, sergeant, I did it all."

"All right, my lad, I'll take your word; but just you take my advice. The law's law, and they're pretty sharp about here, so if you hear the gun fire and the soldiers are out after any poor fellows who have escaped, don't you get meddling with 'em again. Time I was off back." And without another word the sergeant sprang up and strode away, leaving Rodd watching him for a time and admiring the man's upright carriage and bold elastic step, till happening to cast his eyes in another direction, he found himself looking down upon Mrs Champernowne's cottage, and, with letter in hand and straw hat on head, Uncle Paul, looking in all directions as if in search of his missing boy.

Chapter Eight
The Salcombe Boats

"I am very, very sorry, sir," said Mrs Champernowne. "Of course I am only a poor widow, and I let my apartments to gentlemen who come down fishing or to take walks for their health over the moor. But your stay down here has been something more than that. It has been a real pleasure to me ever since you and the young gentleman have been here. And not only am I very sorry that you are going away, but it has quite upset me to hear that you are going sailing away over the stormy seas, searching for all kinds of strange things in foreign abroad."

"Oh, come, come, Mrs Champernowne," cried Uncle Paul, as he saw the poor woman lift up her apron and put one corner to her eye. "There oughtn't to be anything in a naturalist's expedition to upset you."

"Ah, you don't know, sir," said Mrs Champernowne, speaking to Uncle Paul, but shaking her head sadly at Rodd all the while. "I have had those who were near and dear to me go sailing away quite happy and joyful like, just the same as you and Mr Rodney might, and never come back again, for the sea is a very dangerous place."

"Oh, perhaps so, and of course there are exceptions," said Uncle Paul; "but as a rule people do come back safe."

"I don't know, sir," said the old lady, shaking her head sadly. "The sea is very unruly sometimes. Hadn't you better take my advice, sir, and stop here? The moor's very big, and surely if you and the young gentleman look well you'll be able to find plenty of things to fill your bottles, without going abroad."

"Can't be done, Mrs Champernowne," said Uncle Paul smiling. "Dartmoor isn't the West Coast of Africa, nor yet the Cape of Good Hope, so, much as we have enjoyed being here, we shall have to say good-bye, and live in hopes of coming to see you again some day, for I haven't half worked out the moor, nor yet a hundredth part."

"I am very, very, very sorry," said the old lady again, "but no doubt, sir, you know best. When do you think of going, sir?"

"To-morrow morning, Mrs Champernowne. We can't let the grass grow under our feet, can we, Rodd?"

"No, uncle," was the reply; and the next morning the portmanteau was packed, the fishing-rod and naturalist's nets tied up in a neat bundle, a light spring cart was drawn up at the door, and uncle and nephew were soon on their way to the cross roads to take their chance of finding room upon the Plymouth coach, which came within a few miles of the widow's cottage.

They were fortunate, as it happened, and that evening they were safely back at Uncle Paul's home, a pleasant little country house on the high grounds overlooking the glorious harbour dotted with vessels, which included several of the King's men-of-war, and within easy reach of the docks.

"Ah," cried Uncle Paul that evening, as he strolled out into his garden, in company with Rodd, who was carrying a telescope that looked like a small cannon; "that was a fine air up on the moor, my boy, but nothing like this. Take a good long deep breath. Can't you smell the salt and the seaweed? Doesn't it set you longing to be off?"

"Well—yes, uncle," replied the boy, smiling and screwing up his face till it was all wrinkled about the eyes; "but I begin to be a bit afraid."

"Afraid, sir? What of?"

"That I shan't turn out such a good sailor as I should like to be."

"Why, what do you mean? Now, look here, Rodd; don't you tell me that you want to back out of going upon this trip."

"Oh no, uncle," cried the boy eagerly. "I want to go, of course!"

"But what are you afraid of?"

"Well, you see, uncle, coasting about with you in a fisherman's lugger for a few days, and always keeping within sight of land, is one thing; going right away across the ocean is quite another."

"Well, sir, who said it wasn't?" cried Uncle Paul. "What then?"

"Suppose I turn ill, uncle?"

"Well, sir, suppose you do. Am I not doctor enough to put you right again?"

"Oh, I don't mean really ill, uncle. I mean sea-sick; and it would seem so stupid."

"Horribly; yes. You'd better be! Pooh! Rubbish! Nonsense! You talk like a great Molly. Now, no nonsense, Rodney. Speak out frankly and candidly.

You mean that now it has come to the point you think it too serious, and you want to shirk?"

"I don't, uncle; I don't, indeed, and I do wish you wouldn't call me Rodney!" cried the boy earnestly.

"I shall, sir, *as long as I live, if you play me false now.*"

"Oh, uncle, what a shame!" cried the boy passionately. "Play you false! Who wants to play you false? I only wanted to tell you frankly that I felt a bit afraid of not being quite equal to the sea. I want to go, and I mean to go, and you oughtn't to jump upon me like this, and call me Rodney."

The boy stood before the doctor, flushed and excited, as he continued—

"You talk to me, uncle, as if you thought that I was a regular coward and afraid of the sea."

"Then you shouldn't make me, sir. Who was it said afraid? Why, you have been out with me for days together, knocking about, in pretty good rough weather too."

"Yes, uncle, but that was all within sight of land."

"What's that got to do with it? It's often much rougher close in shore, especially on a rocky coast, than it is out on the main."

"I wish I hadn't spoken," cried Rodd passionately.

"So do I, sir."

"I couldn't help thinking I might turn very sick for days, and get laughed at by the crew and called a swab."

"Oh," said Uncle Paul, laughing, "you talked as if you were afraid of the sea, and all the time, you conceited young puppy, you mean that you are afraid of the men."

"Well, yes, uncle, I suppose that that really is it."

"Humph! Then why didn't you say so, and not talk as if you, the first of my crew that I reckoned upon, were going to mutiny and give it all up?"

"Give it up, uncle?" cried the boy. "Why, you know that I am longing to go."

"Ah, well, that sounds more like it, Pickle," said Uncle Paul, looking sideways at the boy through his half-closed eyes. "Then I suppose it is all a false alarm."

"Of course it is, uncle," cried Rodd.

"Well, we may as well make sure, you know, because once we are started it won't be long before we are out of sight of land, and there'll be no turning back."

"Well, I don't want to turn back, uncle."

"Then you shouldn't have talked as if you thought you might. Are you afraid now?"

"Not a bit, uncle. I am ready to start to-morrow morning."

"Ah, well, you won't, my boy, for there's everything to do first."

"Everything to do?"

"Of course. It's not like taking a few bottles and pill-boxes and a net or two to go up on the moor. Why, there's our ship to find first, and then to get her fitted with our nets and sounding-lines and dredges and all sorts of odds and ends, with reserves and provisions for all that we lose. Then there's to còllect a crew."

"Oh, there'll be plenty of fellows down by the Barbican or hanging about down there who will jump at going."

"Don't you be so precious sanguine, my fine fellow. This will be all so fresh that the men won't be so ready as you expect. The first thing a seaman will ask will be, 'Where are we bound? What port?'"

"Well, uncle; tell them."

"Tell them what I don't know myself unless I say Port Nowhere on the High Seas! It will be all a matter of chance, Pickle, where we go and what we do, and I may as well say it now, if any one gets asking you what we are going to do, your answer is included in just these few words—We are going to explore."

Rodd nodded in a short business-like way.

"All right, uncle; I'll remember," he cried promptly. "Then you are going to hire a ship and engage a crew?"

"Well," said Uncle Paul thoughtfully, "we are landsmen—I mean landsman and a boy—but we may as well begin to be nautical at once and call things by the sea-going terms. No, my boy, I am not going to engage a ship—too big."

"Why, you won't go all that way in a lugger, uncle?"

"Bah! Rubbish!" cried Uncle Paul shortly. "Here, give me hold of that glass."

He took the telescope, drew out the slide to a mark upon the tube which indicated the focus which suited his eye, and then as he began slowly sweeping the portions of the harbour which were within reach he went on talking.

"Isn't there anything between a lugger and a ship, sir? You know well enough if you talk to a sailor about a ship he'd suppose you meant a full-rigged three-masted vessel."

"Yes, of course, uncle. And a barque is a three-master with a mizzen fore-and-aft rigged."

"That's better, my lad. But what do you mean by fore-and-aft rigged?"

"Well, like a schooner, uncle."

"Good boy! Go up one, as you used to say at school. Well, what do you think of a large schooner for a good handy vessel that can be well managed by a moderate crew?"

"Oh, I should think it would be splendid, uncle; and she'd sail very fast."

"That depends on her build and the way she is sailed, my boy. But that's what I am thinking of having, Pickle."

"But with a good crew, uncle."

"Yes; I want the best schooner and the best crew that are to be had, my boy."

"But it will cost a lot of money, uncle."

"Yes, Pickle; but I am proud to say that the Government has not been mean in that respect, and if what they have granted me is not enough, I shall put as many hundreds as are required out of my own pocket to make up the deficiency, so that in all probability I shan't have a penny to leave you, Pickle, when I die."

"When you die!" cried the boy scornfully. "Who wants you to die? And who wants you to leave me any money? I say, Uncle Paul, who's talking nonsense now?"

"How dare you, sir!"

"Then you shouldn't say such things, uncle. Talking about dying! There will be plenty of time to talk about that in a hundred years."

"Well, that's a very generous allowance, Pickle, and if we get such a schooner as I want, with a clever crew, and you work hard with me, why, we ought to make a good many discoveries by that time. A hundred years hence," continued Uncle Paul thoughtfully, as he apparently brought his telescope to bear upon a sloop of war whose white sails began to be tinged with orange as the sun sank low; but all the time he was peering out through the corners of his eyes to note the effect of his words upon his nephew. "But let me see—a hundred years' time. Why, how much older will you be then, Pickle?"

"Why, just the same as you would, uncle; a hundred years older than I am now. Pooh! You are making fun of me. But I say, uncle, be serious. How are you going to manage to get your schooner?"

"Set to work, and lose no time, my boy. But I am rather puzzled at the present moment, and I am afraid—"

Uncle Paul lowered the glass as he spoke, and turned his eyes thoughtfully upon his nephew, who had uttered a low peculiar sound.

"Of being sea-sick, uncle?" Uncle Paul smiled.

"I suppose that's what you call retaliation, young gentleman. Well, no, sir, I'm not afraid of that—at least, not much. I remember the first time I crossed the Channel that I was very ill, and every time I have been at sea since I have always felt that it would be unwise to boast; but I think both you and I can make our voyage without being troubled in that way. But we won't boast, Pickle, for, as they say, we will not holloa till we are out of the wood. Let me see; isn't there an old proverb something about a man not boasting till he taketh off his armour?"

"I think so, uncle, but I cannot recollect the words."

"Well, I don't want any armour, my boy, but I do want a well-found schooner—a new one if I can get it; if not, one that will stand a thorough examination; and I don't know that such a boat's to be got just now it's wanted. There are plenty of ramshackle old things lying about here, but I want everything spick-and-span ready for the extra fitting out I shall give her. Copper-fastened, quick-sailing, roomy, and with good cabin accommodation so that we can have a big workshop for the men who help us, and a sort of study and museum for ourselves. Now, Pickle, where shall we have to go to find such a craft? Portsmouth—London? What about Southampton?"

"Southampton. Yes. Some fine yacht, uncle."

"No, boy. She'd be all mast and sails. Do well for a coaster, but I want an ocean-going craft, one that will bear some knocking about. A cargo boat whose hold one could partition off for stores. Now then?"

There was silence for about a minute, and then Uncle Paul spoke again.

"There, out with it, boy, at once. Don't waste time. Say you don't know."

"But I think I do know, uncle," cried the boy.

"Eh? What? Where? Tchah! Not you!"

"But what about one of those boats the French prisoners escaped in?" cried Rodd eagerly.

"Eh? What? One of those trim orange boats that go on the Mediterranean Trade, that they build at Salcombe?"

"Yes, uncle. Don't you remember that one we were looking at a few months ago, that came in here after the storm, to get a new jibboom?"

"Why, of course I do, Pickle!" cried Uncle Paul eagerly. "Think of that, now! Why, I might have been fumbling about with a hammer for months and not found what I wanted, and here are you, you impudent young rascal, proving that you are not quite so stupid as I thought, for you hit the right nail on the head at once."

Chapter Nine
Captain Chubb

The next day was spent in Plymouth, and letting the idea of a visit to Salcombe rest in abeyance for a time, Uncle Paul called on different shipping agents, made inquiries in the docks, looked over two or three small vessels that he was assured would be exactly the thing he wanted, and which could be handed over to him at once if decided on; and at last, utterly wearied out, he returned home with Rodd very much impressed by the feeling that it was much easier to say what he required, than to get his wants supplied.

He was a little better after they had had a good hearty tea meal, but there was a great deal of truth in Rodd's mental remark that Uncle Paul was as cross as two sticks. Rodd quite started, feeling as he did that he must have spoken aloud, and Uncle Paul have heard his words, for the doctor turned upon him sharply, stared him full in the face, and exclaimed —

"Now, look here, sir; didn't I explain to each of those agents exactly the sort of vessel I wanted before they gave me their orders to go and view the craft where they lay in dock or on the mud?"

"Yes, uncle, you told them exactly," replied Rodd.

"Do I look like an idiot, Rodd?"

"No, uncle. What a question!"

"Then how dare the scoundrels deal with me as if I didn't know what I was about! I said a schooner as plain as I could speak."

"You did, uncle."

"And one sent me to see that ramshackle old brig that looked as if it might have been a tender out of the Armada, and the two others sent me to see a barque that would want twice as big a crew as I should take, and the other to look over that abominable old billy-boy that you couldn't tell bow from stern, which so sure as she bumps upon a sandbank would melt away like butter. Thinking of nothing else but making a bit of commission, ready to sell one anything; but I am not going to be tricked like that. — Yes, what do you want? What is it?"

For the neat handmaid who attended on the doctor's wants had tapped at the door, and receiving no answer from her master, whose voice she could hear declaiming loudly, opened the door and walked in, with—

"Somebody wants to see you, sir, if you please."

"Then tell somebody I don't please," said the doctor shortly.

"Yes, sir," said the maid, going.

"No, stop! I don't want to be rude, even if people have put me out. What does Mrs Somebody want?"

"Please, sir, it isn't a Mrs, it's a Mister," said the girl.

"Go and see him, Rodd," said the doctor shortly. "I expect it's somebody wants subscriptions, and I haven't got any."

"Please, sir," interposed the maid, "the—er—gent—person—said he'd heard say that you wanted a captain."

Uncle Paul grunted, frowned, and then in a surly tone exclaimed—

"Well, there, show him in."

The next minute the maid re-opened the door, showing in a heavy, sun-tanned, middle-aged man, who thrust the cap he carried into the yawning pocket of a dark blue pea-jacket, stared hard at the doctor, glanced at Rodd, and then turning sharply on his heels he stood with his back to the latter, stiff, squared, and sturdy, looking as the boy thought like a hop-sack set on end, and stared at the maid where she stopped, literally fixing her with his eyes for a few moments, before, quite startled at the fierceness of his gaze, she darted out, closing the door loudly.

"Business. Private!" literally growled the visitor.

"Well, what is it?" said the doctor shortly.

"'Eard you wanted a skipper, and come up."

"Well," said Uncle Paul, looking very hard at his unprepossessing visitor, while Rodd felt as if he wanted to laugh, but held the desire in check, "I may want one by and by, and a crew too; but I must have a ship first."

"What sort?"

"Well, you are pretty blunt," said the doctor.

"Yes," said the visitor, with a nod; and he waited, but turned his eyes from the doctor and looked very hard at the nearest chair.

"Ah, yes," said the doctor. "Sit down, Captain—Captain—"

The doctor waited for an answer, but the only answer made was by a movement, his visitor taking two steps towards the chair, and plumping down so heavily that the brass casters creaked.

The doctor glanced at his nephew, and then at the stranger, who seemed to be frowning at him with all his might.

"Er—what did you say your name was, captain?"

"Didn't say," said the visitor huskily. "Wanter know?"

"Well—yes," said the doctor. "I don't see how we are to transact business without."

"Chubb, Jonathan."

"Well, Captain Chubb?"

"Plymouth."

"Oh, I see; Captain Chubb, of Plymouth," continued the doctor.

"Right. Go on."

"Well, I gave you to understand that I wanted a ship before I engaged a captain."

"Skipper; not R.N."

"I see; but I wished to be polite," said the doctor.

"Skipper," grunted the man.

"Where have you sailed?" asked the doctor.

"Everywhere."

"Ah! Then you have had plenty of experience."

The visitor nodded, and the doctor was going to speak again, but the visitor interposed with a sidewise nod in the direction of Rodd, and said—

"Your boy?"

"Well, yes, in a way," replied the doctor.

The captain grunted.

"Boys always are," he said, and Rodd turned upon him angrily.

"I said in *a* way, not in *the* way," muttered the doctor.

"'Most the same," growled the captain. "A boy, the boy, means boy. What sort of a ship? First, where do you want to go?"

"I don't quite know myself," replied the doctor, "so we will say as you did, everywhere."

"Right," said the captain. "What for?"

"Why do you ask?" replied the doctor, rather tartly.

"Had four offers. Wouldn't take them."

"Why?" asked the doctor.

"Smuggling contraband."

"Oh, I see," said the doctor quickly. "Well, it's nothing of that sort."

"When do you sail?"

"As soon as I can get a ship."

"Plenty lying about waiting for cargo. Take your choice."

"That seems to be easier said than done, captain, for I am hard to please."

"So'm I," said the visitor, staring hard at Rodd, beginning with the crown of his head and then looking him slowly down where he sat till he reached the carpet by Rodd's right foot, and then making his eyes cross over, he began at the toe of the boy's left foot and slowly looked him up to where he had started at the top of the boy's forehead, where a tickling sensation had commenced, consequent upon the starting out of a faint dew of perspiration.

"I'm glad to hear it," said the doctor, "for I want a well-found craft, new or nearly so, built of the best materials."

"Good; ought to be. What sort?"

"Well, I should like a large schooner, fast and with plenty of room below."

"Cargo?" grunted the captain.

"No. Provisions, etcetera," said the doctor, who was beginning to feel annoyed.

"Ho!" came in a grunt, and then after a keen look at Rodd's uncle, he uttered the one word, "Weepens?"

"Weepens?" said the doctor.

"Yes. Long Tom and small-arms."

"Oh, arms. Yes, I should certainly have one of those big swivel guns amidships, and a couple of smaller ones, as well as muskets, cutlasses and boarding pikes."

So far the captain's features seemed as if they had been carved out of solid mahogany, but now they began to relax; his lips parted, and he showed a small even set of beautifully white teeth, while his eyes looked brighter to Rodd and seemed to twinkle; but he remained silent.

"Well," said the doctor, "what are you laughing at?"

He checked the word which had nearly escaped his lips, because he thought it would be rude, and he did not say grinning.

"Cat," said the man solemnly, and to Rodd's great discomposure he turned to him and winked.

"Cat?" said the doctor sharply.

"Ay, ay! Out of the bag."

"I don't understand you," said the doctor warmly.

"Won't do for me, master. Not in my way."

"Well," said the doctor, "I am afraid I must say you are not in my way."

"Poor beggars!"

"Well, really, my good man," began the doctor, "I am a bit of a student, and take a good deal of interest in natural history. Cats may be poor beggars, but that is no business of mine."

"Yes, if you are going to sail. Think of your crew."

"I am thinking of my crew, and I want to engage one," said the doctor.

"Men hate black cats. Unlucky."

"I have heard of that superstition before, Captain Chubb," said the doctor, "but that seems to be quite outside our business now. As a captain— or skipper—I should have thought you would have been above such childish notions."

"Am," said the man. "T'other won't do for me. I've seen it all. Won't get a skipper from this port."

" Look here, youngster—Guinea Coast, eh ?"

"Why?" said the doctor indignantly. "I am ready to give an experienced captain good payment."

"Want commission."

"Oh, nonsense! I couldn't pay on commission."

"Nowt to me. That's what a skipper would want. Ought to be ashamed of yourself."

"Well, of all—" began the doctor; but the skipper did not let him finish.

"Too bad," he said, growling; "and to take a boy like that!"

"My good fellow," said the doctor, "if I choose to take my nephew with me upon a natural history expedition—"

"Natural history expedition! Catching blackbirds! Oh, I say!"

He shook his head slowly at the doctor, whose face grew so red with wrath as he turned towards Rodd, and looked so comical, that the boy could not contain himself, but bent his face down into his hands and burst into a roar of laughter.

"You are a nice 'un," grunted the captain, shaking his head now at Rodd. "You'll grow into a beauty!"

It was the boy's turn to look angry now, and he glanced from the captain to his uncle and back.

"Look here, youngster," cried the captain; "Guinea Coast, eh?"

"Possibly," said the doctor.

"Bight of Benin?"

"Maybe," said the doctor, the short speech seeming contagious.

"Ketch the fever?"

"Probably," said the doctor.

"Both on yer."

"Well, sir, I shall risk that," continued the doctor.

"Both on yer off your heads, seeing niggers. Rattling their chains."

"Are you mad, man?" cried the doctor. "Yes."

"I thought so."

"Makes me. Call yourself a Christian! Give it up, and do something honest."

"Well, of all—" cried the doctor again.

"Good five guineas better than five hundred got by buying and selling your fellow-creatures," continued the captain, who was growing quite fluent. "Go to Bristol with you! Won't do for me."

"Mr—I mean, Captain Chubb," began the doctor, "allow me to tell you that you have done nothing but insult me ever since you have been here."

"Honesty," grunted the captain.

"Honesty is no excuse for rudeness, sir. Now have the goodness to go."

"Going," said the captain, rising. "But you are a bad man. To take that boy with you too! Shame!"

"Will you have the goodness to tell me what you mean, sir?"

"No good to bully, sir. I know. Off on the slave trade."

"What!" cried the doctor.

"But look out. King's cruiser will nab you. Sarve you right."

He moved stiffly, and took two steps towards the door, but stopped and turned sharply upon Rodd, clapped his big hairy hand on the boy's shoulder, and gripped it fast. "He's a bad 'un, boy. Don't go." Rodd glanced at his uncle, who was staring with bewilderment, while he, who during the last few minutes had seen clearly what their visitor meant, burst into another roar of laughter and gripped the skipper by the jacket, as he turned to the doctor.

"No, no," he stuttered. "No, no; don't go, captain! Uncle Paul, can't you see? He thinks you are going to the West Coast to buy slaves!"

"Well!" cried Uncle Paul, his voice sounding like ten ejaculations squeezed into one—"Well!"

Chapter Ten
At Cross Purposes

Captain Chubb stood looking back at Uncle Paul, then at Rodd, then back at Uncle Paul.

After that he gave a slow, puzzled scratch at his shaggy head as if hard at work trying to make out a mystery, before turning once more to Rodd.

"I say, youngster," he cried, "you don't mean that, do you?—Warn't I right?"

"Right? No!" cried Rodd, laughing more heartily than ever. "The idea of Uncle Paul going out with a slaver!"

"Did you mean that, Captain Chubb?" said Uncle Paul, beginning indignantly, and then softening down as he caught sight of his nephew's mirthful face.

"Allus says what I mean," grunted the captain. "Then I was all wrong?"

"Wrong, yes," said Uncle Paul. "We were all at cross purposes."

"Ho!" ejaculated the captain, and he took off his cap that he had put on with a fierce cock, turned it over two or three times in his hands, and then looking into it read over the maker's name to himself, as if fully expecting that that would help him out of his difficulty.

"Say, squire," he said; "I didn't mean to be so rude."

"No, no, of course not," cried Uncle Paul. "There, there; sit down again. It was all a mistake. Perhaps we shall understand one another better now."

"Well, I don't know," grunted the skipper. "Better go perhaps."

"No, no, man; I'm not offended. You thought I was a blackguardly ruffian who wanted to trap you into commanding a slaving craft for me, so that I could engage in that horrible trade of baying and selling my fellow-creatures; and you spoke out like a man. Here, shake hands, Captain Chubb. I honour you for your outspoken manly honesty."

"Mean it?" grunted the skipper, hesitating.

"Mean it, yes," said Uncle Paul, "and I hope this will be the beginning of our becoming great friends."

"Humph!" grunted the captain, and extending his heavy hand he gave Uncle Paul a shake with no nonsense about it, for though Rodd's uncle did not wince, he told the boy afterwards that it was the most solid shake he had ever had in his life.

Rodd fully endorsed it, as he knew directly after exactly what the skipper's salute meant, for Captain Chubb, after releasing the uncle's hand, extended what Rodd afterwards said was a paw, to the lad himself.

"Well, now then, Captain Chubb."

"Very sorry, sir, I'm sure. Thought I saw broken water and a shoal. Hadn't I better go?"

"No, no, captain," cried Uncle Paul. "I am beginning to think you are just the man I want."

"Ho!" said the skipper. "Mebbe. Let's see."

"Well," continued Uncle Paul, "I want a vessel, a schooner. Do you know of a likely one that could be purchased and made ready at once for a trip down the West Coast?"

Captain Chubb looked hard at the speaker, then at Rodd, with the effect of making the boy feel as if he must laugh, for there was something so thoroughly comical in the stolid face, that nothing but the dread of hurting the visitor's feelings kept him from bursting into a roar, especially as, after fixing him with his eyes, the skipper seemed to be taking careful observations, looking up at the ceiling as if in search of clouds, at the carpet for sunken rocks, and then, so to speak, sweeping the offing by slowly gazing at the four walls in turn.

"Schooner," he said at last gruffly.

"Yes," said Uncle Paul; "a smart, fast-sailing schooner."

"Well-found," grunted the skipper.

"Of course, and with a good crew."

"*And* a good crew," growled the skipper.

"Yes. Can you show me where I can get such an one?"

"No. Look-out."

He picked up and put on his cap again, took it off, and looked in the lining, and then gave his right leg a smart slap.

"Dunno as I don't," he roared. "What do you say to a horange boat?"

"Orange boat?" cried Rodd. "Why, uncle's been thinking of one of those!"

"Well, why not?" said the captain; "a Saltcomber?"

"Yes," cried Rodd.

"Well-built, fast, plenty of room below for cargo or what not, plenty of provisions and water, but no guns."

"That's just the sort of vessel I want," cried Uncle Paul. "Do you think one's to be had over there?"

"Sure on it. See one last week as they was just getting up her standing rigging."

"What, a new one?" cried Rodd.

"Ay. Fresh launched, and being made ready for sea."

"Capital!" cried Uncle Pad. "Who does she belong to?"

"Ship-builder as yet."

"And what would be her price?"

"Dunno. All depends," grunted the captain. "Most likely as much as the builder could get; but if a man went with the money in his pocket, or say in the bank, ready to pay down on the nail, he could get a smart craft that would do him justice at a fair working price. What do you say to coming over and having a look at her?"

"Yes. How are we to get there? By coach?"

"Tchah!" ejaculated the skipper. "Who's going in a coach when he can be run over in one of our luggers? You say the word, and I have got a friend with a little fore-and-after as only wants him and a hand and mebbe me to give a pull at a sheet. He'd run you over in no time."

"By all means, then, let's go," said Uncle Paul, to Rodd's great satisfaction.

"Well, yes," growled the skipper. "But who's a-going with you?"

"My nephew," said Uncle Paul.

"Ah, yes; and I suppose he's a good judge of such a craft, and could vally her from keel to truck. Don't seem a bad sort of boy, but he won't do. Nay, squire, you want somebody as you can trust. A'n't you got an old friend, ship-owner or ship's husband—man who's got his head screwed on the right way, one you knows as honest and won't take a hundred pounds from t'other side to sell the ship for them?"

"Well, no; I'm afraid I don't know such a man," said Uncle Paul.

"Have to find one," grunted the skipper. "Won't do to buy a ship with your eyes shut. Got yourself to think of as well as your money. You don't want to engage a skipper and a crew of good men and true, and drownd them all at sea."

"Well, no," said Uncle Paul dryly; "our ambitions don't lie in that direction, do they, Rodd?"

"No, uncle, but no man would be such a wretch as to sell you a ship that wasn't safe."

"Not unless he got the chanst," said the skipper, frowning. "I know some on them, and what they have done, and I don't want to command a craft like that. Been at sea too long."

"Well, then," said Uncle Paul, "you must have had great experience, and could judge whether a schooner's good or not."

"Dessay I could," said the skipper, "but I aren't perfect."

"But you ought to be a good judge," said Uncle Paul.

"Mebbe, but I wouldn't go by my own opinion if it was my trade instead of yourn."

"But look here," cried Uncle Paul, "I should like you to see the vessel and act for me."

"Tchah! Not likely, squire. What do you know about me?"

"Well, not much, certainly," said Uncle Paul, "and I should want a character with you as to your being a good seaman."

"Of course; and if you didn't like me, and I warn't up to my work, why, you could get rid of me. But that's a very different thing to buying a ship."

"Yes," said Uncle Paul, "but what about the ship-builder? Is he an honest man?"

"Oh yes, I think so."

"Couldn't he give good references?"

"Well, yes. Old established; built a lot of craft. Dessay he'd find a few to say a word for him."

"And I suppose I could have the opinion of some well-known ship valuer?"

"Yes," grunted the skipper, "but he's only in trade. You want to know what some old sailor says."

"Such as you," cried Rodd.

The skipper looked at the boy and smiled.

"Well, mebbe," he said, "but I don't want the job."

"Well, we'll talk about that another time," said Uncle Paul. "What I want is for you to help me by going over with us to have a look at the schooner."

"Ah!" said the skipper.

"And you may as well give me a reference or two to somebody who knows your abilities—somebody well-known in Plymouth, a ship-owner, somebody for whom you have sailed. Will you do this?"

"Ay," said the skipper.

"Well, whose name will you give me? To whom shall I apply?"

"Anybody. Everybody in Plymouth."

"That's rather wide," said Uncle Paul.

"Wider the better," said the skipper. "You ask the lot what they thinks of Captain Chubb."

As he spoke the skipper rose and put on his cap, but took it off again quickly.

"Time to-morrow will you be ready to start?" he said.

"At your time," said Uncle Paul promptly.

"Say nine?" asked the captain.

"Certainly; nine o'clock to-morrow morning," replied Uncle Paul.

"Good. I will be off the landing-place at the Barbican with a boat. Night, sir. Night, youngster. Natural history expedition, eh? And I thought you was going blackbirding! Haw, haw, haw!"

This last was intended for a derisive laugh at himself, but it sounded like three grunts, each louder than the last.

The next minute the skipper was outside, and his steps were heard growing distant upon the gravel path.

"Well, what do you think of our captain, eh, Rodd?"

"I think he's a rum 'un, uncle; but he isn't our captain yet."

"No, my boy, but if I have my way he will be, and if I hear that he's a skilful navigator, for I want no further recommendation. The way in which he, an old experienced hand, one who would be able to see at a glance how thoroughly I should be at his mercy if he were a trickster whose aim was to make as much money out of the transaction as he could, proved that he was as honest as the day and ready to lay himself open to every examination, that alone without his display of honest indignation when he suspected me of being about to engage in that abominable traffic—there, I want no more. As these sea-going people say, Pickle, Captain Chubb is going to hoist his flag on board my schooner, for as far as I can judge at present he seems to be the man in whom we shall be able to trust."

Chapter Eleven
Through the Storm

"It's enough to make a man say he'll throw up the whole affair," cried Uncle Paul, running his fingers in amongst his grizzly hair and giving it a savage tug.

"Uncle! Why, what's the matter now?"

"Yes, you may well say what's the matter now! Everything's the matter. The worry's almost maddening."

"What, is there anything fresh, uncle?"

"There, don't you take any notice, boy. I get regularly out of heart. There's always something wrong. It's as if we were never to be off. All these weary, weary months gone slowly dragging on."

"Why, uncle, they seem to me to go like lightning," cried Rodd.

"Oh, yes, of course. You are a boy, with plenty of time before you. I am getting an old man, and with little time to spare to do all the work I want to. I seem to get not a bit farther."

"Why, you do, uncle. It's astonishing what a lot we have done. Let's see; it's just fifteen months since you bought the schooner."

"Fifteen, boy? You mean fifty."

"Fifteen, uncle; and she was nothing like finished then."

"No, and as soon as the men knew that she was sold, I believe they made up their minds to spin the job out as long as they could."

"Oh, but, uncle, they did it all very beautifully; and see what a lot of alterations you had made."

"Had made, indeed! Wasn't I led on into having them done by that old scoundrel Chubb?"

"No, uncle. He always consulted with you first, and advised this and that so as to make the vessel better."

"Humph!" grunted Uncle Paul.

"Then see what a lot you had done, fitting up the work-room, and the bottles and tanks, and getting in the dredging apparatus. It does seem a long time to you, but see what a lot there was to do. You know you were never satisfied."

"I was, sir! Don't you get accusing me of such things, Rodney. You grow more impertinent every day. Now put a regular check upon yourself, sir. If you are like this as a boy I don't know what you are going to be when you grow to be a man."

"Well, uncle, I won't say another word about it."

"Ah! No sulking, sir! I command you to go on speaking at once."

"Very well, uncle; but you did say that you would have everything of the best, and that nothing should be left undone, to hinder the expedition from being successful."

"Did I say so, Rodd?"

"Why, yes, uncle, over and over again."

"Well, well, I did mean it. But I am getting quite out of heart. Every day it seems as if there is something fresh to throw us back. Now it's stores; now it's something else wants painting; now one of the crew wants a holiday, just at a time too when things are so nearly ready that I might want to start at any moment."

"Well, I shall be glad when we do get off now, uncle," said the boy thoughtfully.

"Then you had better give up thinking about it, boy. It looks to me like another six months before we can be ready."

"Oh no, uncle! Captain Chubb said to me yesterday that if I wanted to get anything else to take with me I must get it at once."

"Then don't you believe him, Rodd. He's a dilatory old impostor. I don't believe he means for me to go at all. By the way, did you have the men up and give them that big medicine chest?"

"Yes, uncle; the day before yesterday."

"Oh, and were those little casks of spirits got into the store-room?"

"Yes, uncle. I saw the men get them on board myself."

"That's right. But look here, Pickle; were you with them all the time?"

"Yes, uncle. You told me to be, before you went up to London."

"That's right, Rodd. But—er—did you—did you hear the men make any remark about them?"

"No, uncle; but I saw them smell the bung-holes and look at one another and laugh."

"Humph!" said the doctor, smiling. "By the way, I think I'll go on board now and have a look round. There are several things I want to see to, those casks and kegs among the rest."

"They were all put just as you gave orders, uncle."

"Yes; but I want to test the spirits all the same. Here, we may as well go on board at once."

"Very well," cried the boy eagerly. "Is there any little thing we can take with us?"

"No, my boy. As far as I am concerned, I think I can say everything is ready."

It was not long before the doctor and his nephew were down at the landing-place and being rowed across the harbour to where a beautifully trim full-sized schooner lay moored to one of the great buoys; and on coming alongside they were hailed by Captain Chubb, whose face seemed to shine with animation as he helped his chief on board.

"Morning, sir!" he cried. "I was just wishing that you would come on board."

"Bah!" exclaimed Uncle Paul. "What wants doing now?"

"Nothing. Not as I know of."

"Oh, are you sure?" said Uncle Paul sarcastically, "Sartin, unless you have got some more bottles or cranky tackle to be stowed away, sir."

"Oh, indeed," said Uncle Paul shortly. "You don't mean to say you have done at last?"

"Me, sir? Why, I was ready six months ago, only you had always got some new scheme you wanted fitted in."

"Ah, well, never mind about that now," cried Uncle Paul. "Then we may set sail any day?"

"'Cept Friday, sir. The men wouldn't like that. To-night if you like."

"Ah, well, we won't go to-night," said the doctor.

"Only give your orders, sir," said the captain shortly. "Like to take a look round now? Fresh provisions are all on board."

"Oh no," said Uncle Paul, "I know it all by heart."

"Looks a beauty now, don't she, sir?"

"Oh yes, she looks very well. Here, Rodd, come down with me into the work-room."

The doctor strode off aft at once, the captain following slowly with the boy; and as their chief descended the cabin stairs Captain Chubb cocked his eye at his young companion.

"Bit rusty this morning," he whispered.

"Yes; uncle's getting out of patience," whispered back Rodd.

"No wonder," said the captain. "Well, 'tarn't my fault. I never see such a doctor's shop and museum as he's made of the craft."

"Now, Rodney!" came from below sharply.

"Coming, uncle!" cried the boy, snatching at the brass rail, which, like every bit of metal about the beautiful vessel, shone as brightly as if it were part of a yacht.

The doctor was standing at the foot of the stairs with his hand upon a door, which he had just unlocked, and he led the way into a well-lit portion of the vessel which had originally been intended for the stowage of cargo, but which was now fitted up with an endless number of arrangements such as had been deemed necessary for the carrying out of the expedition.

One portion was like a chemical laboratory. Upon dresser-like tables fitted against the bulkhead were rows of railed-in bottles and jars, and beneath them new bright microscopes and other apparatus such as would gladden the heart of a naturalist. But the doctor gave merely a cursory glance at these various objects, with whose arrangement he had long been familiar, and made his way to where, set up on end upon a stout bench, were about a dozen specially made spirit casks, each fitted with its tap and a little receptacle hung beneath to catch any drops that might leak away.

"Here, I want to test these," said the doctor; "and, by the way, ask Captain Chubb to step down."

There was no need, for almost at the same moment the captain's heavy step was heard upon the metal-covered cabin stairs.

"Anything I can do, sir?" he asked, in his gruff way.

"Yes, look here, captain," said the doctor, and he took a bright glass measure from where it hung by its foot in a little rack, safe from falling by the rolling of the vessel; "I was just going to test these spirits, and I thought I should like you to be here."

"Hah!" said the captain. "I've thought a deal about all them little barrels put so handy there, ready on tap, and it's the only thing I don't like, Dr Robson."

"Why?" said Uncle Paul shortly.

"Why, it's just like this, sir. I have picked you out as sober a crew as ever went on a voyage, but sailors are sailors, sir, and I don't think it's right to be throwing temptation in their way."

"But this, my workshop, where I bottle my specimens, will always be kept under lock and key."

"Nay!" snorted the captain.

"But I tell you it will," cried Uncle Paul. "Nobody will have any business here but my nephew and me."

"That's what you mean," said the captain, "but how about times when you are busy, or forget and leave it open? Can't warrant always to keep it shut."

"Well," said Uncle Paul, with a curious smile, "I have thought of that," and going to one of the little casks he turned the tap and let about a couple of tablespoonfuls of liquid that looked like filtered water flow into the little glass measure, covering the bottom to about an inch in depth. "There," said the doctor, holding up the glass to the light; "just taste that, captain."

"Nay. I don't mind a drop of good rum at the proper season, but I don't care about spirits like that."

"I only want you to taste it," said the doctor. "It's too strong to drink."

"I know," said the captain. "Burns like fire."

"Just taste, but don't swallow it."

"Nay—Well, I'll do that. But it looks like physic."

The speaker just dipped his fore-finger into the liquid, and touched his lips, to cry angrily—

"Why, it's pison!"

"No," said the doctor; "proof alcohol for preserving my specimens. If by accident any of the men taste that they won't want any more, will they?"

"Don't know," said the captain. "Maybe they'd water it down."

"Fill that measure with water, Rodd," said the doctor.

The boy took the glass to a big stone filter covered with basketwork, and filled the measure to the brim.

"Now try it, captain," said the doctor.

This time with a scowl of dislike, the captain raised the glass to his lips, but set it down again quickly and hurried to a little leaden sink in one corner of the laboratory.

"Worse than ever, doctor."

"Well, do you think the men will water that down?"

"Not they! One taste will be quite enough."

"You don't think I need label those casks 'Temptation,' do you?"

"Nay, sir. If you want to be honest to the lads, I should put 'Pison' upon them in big letters."

"I would," said the doctor dryly, "but, as you say, sailors are sailors, and I don't think they'd believe it if I did."

"What have you put in it, sir?"

"Ah! that's my secret, Captain Chubb."

"Well, I hope none of the lads will touch it; but it's sperrits, you know. Won't answer for it that if one of them was helping you to bottle up some of them things as we shall fish up when we gets into the Tropics, he wouldn't be trying a sip."

"I shouldn't be surprised either," said the doctor, "but if he did he wouldn't do it again."

The skipper looked at him sharply.

"Don't mean that, do you, sir?" he cried.

"Indeed, but I do," replied the doctor.

"Going too far," growled the skipper. "Look here, doctor; I've fell into all your ways like a man, and have helped to drill the chaps into handling your tackle, which is outside an able seaman's dooties; but I don't like this 'ere a bit."

"I can't help that," said the doctor, bristling up. "I shall of course tell them that they must not touch this stuff, of which no doubt I shall use a great deal, and it will be in direct opposition to my orders if they give way to the temptation."

"Right enough," said the skipper, "but seamen's weak—like babies in some things—and a good skipper has to be like a father to them, to keep them out of mischief. Don't know no better, doctor. You do, and it's too strong, sir; it's too strong."

"Then let them leave it alone," said the doctor hotly.

"That's right, sir, but maybe they won't. Don't mean to say that I am stupid over them, but when I get a good crew I like to take care of them. Here, I'm getting out of breath. Can't make long speeches. Cut it short."

"Then say no more about it," said the doctor.

"Nay, it won't do. Taking out a good crew of smart lads. Want to bring them all back, not leave none of them sewed up in their hammocks and sunk in the sea with a shot at their heels. Look here, sir; how many of them there kegs have you doctored?"

"All of them. Why, my good fellow, you don't think I have put poison in, do you?"

"Said you had."

"Pooh! Nonsense! My boy Rodd and I tried experiments to see how nasty we could make the spirits without being dangerous. There's nothing there that would hurt a man; only you mustn't tell them so."

"Oh–h–h! That's another pair of shoes, as the Frenchies say;" and the skipper went up on deck.

"Thick-head!" growled the doctor. "Did he fancy I was going to kill a man for meddling? Bah!"

"He did, uncle. He doesn't know you yet."

"Well, I suppose not, my boy, but I am beginning to think that we are getting to know the crew pretty well by heart. Well, all we want now is a favourable wind, then we will hoist our sailing flag; and then—off."

"For how long, uncle?"

"Ah, that's more than I can say, Rodd, my boy. We'll see what luck we have, and how the stores last out. We'll get started, and leave the rest."

Two days later the start had been made, with everything as ready as the combined efforts of the doctor's and Captain Chubb's experience could contrive, and with his face all smiles Dr Robson stood beside Rodd, watching the receding shore as they, to use the skipper's words, bowled down Channel.

"Good luck to us, Pickle, my boy!" cried the doctor. "It's been a long weary time of preparation, but it has been worth it. We have got a splendid captain—a man in whom I can thoroughly trust, and a crew of as smart, handy, useful fellows as I could have wished for."

"Yes, uncle; and haven't they taken to all the arrangements about the tackle!"

"Yes, Pickle. They have all proved themselves not only eager and active, but as much interested as so many boys. Splendid fellows; and old Chubb knows how to handle them too. Fetch my glass up, Pickle. Let's have a look at the old country as long as we can."

Rodd darted off to the cabin hatch, but he staggered once or twice, for the schooner as she rose and fell kept on careening a little over to leeward, and in passing one of the sailors—a fine bluff-looking young fellow—the man smiled.

"Here, what are you grinning at, Joe Cross?" cried Rodd, who, after many months of intercourse with the crew, was fully acquainted with all, and knew a good many of their peculiarities.

"Oh, not at you, Mr Harding, sir. It was a little bit of a snigger at your boots."

"What!" cried Rodd.

"Just a little guffaw, sir. You see, the deck's as white as a holystone will make it, and your boots is black, and black and white never did agree. It's beginning to get a bit fresh, sir, and if I was you I'd striddle a bit, so as to take a bit better hold of the deck with your footsies. I shouldn't like to see you come down hard."

"Oh, I shan't come down," said Rodd confidently; but as he was speaking the schooner gave a sudden pitch which sent the boy into the sailor's arms.

"Avast there!" cried the man. "Steady, sir!—Steady it is! There, let me stand you up again on your pins. You mustn't do that, or you'll have the lads thinking you're a himmidge, or a statty, a-tumbling off your shelf."

"Thank you. I am all right now," said Rodd. "My boots are quite new, and the soles are slippery."

"I see, sir, but it wasn't all that. You see, our Sally's been tied up by the nose for so many months in harbour yonder, that now she's running free she can't hold herself in. Ketch hold of the rail, sir. That's your sort! There she goes again, larking like a young kitten."

"I didn't know she'd dance about like this on a fine day," said Rodd rather breathlessly.

"Bless your heart, sir, this arn't nothing to what she can do. See how she's skipping along now. Aren't it lovely?"

"Well, yes, I suppose so," said Rodd; "but if it's like this in fine weather, what's it going to be in a storm?"

"Why, ever so much livelier, sir. She'll dance over the waves like a cork. She's a beauty, that's what she is. Mustn't mind her being a bit saucy. There's nothing that floats like a Salcombe schooner, and I never heard of one as sank yet."

"Yes, uncle; back directly!" cried the boy; and he made his way onward to the cabin stairs without mishap, and re-appeared directly afterwards with the doctor's big telescope under his arm, to make his way as well as he could to where Uncle Paul was standing forward at the side with his left arm round one of the stays.

"Walk straight, boy—walk straight!" cried the doctor, laughing. "What made you zigzag about like that?"

"Didn't want to come down on the deck and break the glass, uncle," said Rodd rather sulkily. "The schooner oughtn't to dance about like this, ought she?"

"Oh, yes. It's no more than the lugger used to do when we have been out fishing."

"Oh, yes, uncle; and she's so much bigger too. Besides, we were sitting down then, and here one has to stand."

"You can sit down if you like," said Uncle Paul.

"What, and have the sailors laugh at me? That I won't! I want to get used to it as soon as I can."

"Then go and get used to it," said Uncle Paul. "You can't do better. I should like to do the same, but a man can't hop about at fifty, or more, like a boy at fifteen."

"Why, uncle, I am nearly eighteen."

"Then go and behave like it, boy. Look at the sailors. They keep their feet well enough, without seeming as if they are going to rush overboard."

"Oh, I shall soon get used to it, uncle," cried Rodd.

But instead of improving that day his progress about the deck was decidedly retrograde, for as the time went on and the Channel opened out, the wind from the north-west grew fresher and fresher, and the captain from time to time kept the men busy taking in a reef here and a reef there.

Topgallant sails came down; flying jib was hauled in; and towards evening, as she span along as fast or faster than ever, not above half the amount of canvas was spread that she had skimmed under earlier in the day.

Every now and then too there was a loud smack against the bows, and a shower of spray made the deck glisten for a few minutes; but it rapidly dried up again, and as the schooner careened over and dashed along, Rodd stood aft, looking back through the foam to see how the waves came curling along after them, as if in full chase of the beautiful little vessel and seeking to leap aboard.

The sun had gone down in a bronzy red bank of clouds, and after being below to the cabin tea Rodd had eagerly hurried on deck again, to find that the sea around was beginning to look wild and strange.

Whether he made for Josiah Cross, or Joe, as he was generally called, came up to him, Rodd did not know, but as he stood with one arm over the rail he soon found himself in conversation.

"Are we going to have a storm?" he said.

"Well, I dunno, sir, about storm. More wind coming."

"How do you know?"

"How do I know, sir?" cried the man. "Why, if you come to that, I don't know. Seem to feel it like. I don't say as it will. Wind's nor'-west now, and has been all day, but I shouldn't wonder if it chopped right round, and then—"

"There'll be a storm," said Rodd eagerly.

"Well, I don't say that, sir; but like enough there will be more wind than we want to use, and we might have to put back."

"What, now that we have started at last?" cried Rodd.

The man nodded.

"Oh, that would be vexatious," cried Rodd, "to find ourselves back in Plymouth again!"

"There, you wouldn't do that, my lad," said the man. "If we did have to put back, I should say the skipper would run for Penzance. But there, the wind hasn't chopped round yet, and it's just as likely to fall as it gets dark and we will get our orders to hoist more sail."

But the sailor's first ideas proved to be right, and not only did the wind veer round, but it increased in force and became so contrary and shifty that during the night it began to blow a perfect hurricane, and gave Captain Chubb a good opportunity of proving that he was no fine-weather sailor.

It proved to be a bright night, being nearly full moon, with great flocculent silvery and black clouds scudding at a tremendous rate across the planet, while one minute the schooner's rigging was shadowed in black upon the white, wet deck, at another all was gloom, with the wind shrieking through the rigging, and the *Maid of Salcombe* proving the truth of the sailor's words, as she was literally dancing about; like a cork.

"Hadn't you better come below, Rodd?" said the doctor.

"No, uncle; don't ask me. I couldn't sleep, and I want to look at the storm. It's so grand."

"Grand? Well, yes," said the doctor; "but we could have dispensed with its grandeur, and it seems very unlucky that after all these weeks of glorious weather it should have turned like this. Ah, here's Captain Chubb. Well, captain," he continued, "where are we making for? Mount's Bay?"

"No. Give it up. Nasty rocky bit about there, so I laid her head for Plymouth; but we shan't get in there to-night."

"Where then?" asked the doctor. "Wouldn't it be better to run for the open sea?"

"No," said the skipper shortly. "This wind's come to stay, and we must get into port for a bit. We don't want to get into the Bay of Biscay O with weather like this. It's going to be a regular sou'-wester."

"What port shall we make for, then?" asked the doctor, while Rodd caught all he could of the conversation, as the wind kept coming in gusts and seemed to snatch the words and carry them overboard in an instant. "Havre," grunted the captain laconically. There was silence for some time, for it became too hard work to talk, but in one of the intervals between two gusts, a few words were spoken, the doctor asking the skipper if he was satisfied with the behaviour of the schooner.

"Oh yes," He grunted; "she's right enough."

"You are not disappointed, then?"

"No. Bit too lively. Wants some more cargo or ballast to give her steadiness; but she'll be all right." All the same this was an experience very different from anything that Rodd had had before, and it was not without a severe buffeting that in the early dawn of the morning Captain Chubb had succeeded in laying the little vessel's head off Havre, so that, taking advantage of a temporary sinking of the wind, he was able to run her safely into the French port, and this at a time when it was a friendly harbour, the British arms having triumphed everywhere, the French king being once more upon the throne, and he who had been spoken of for so long as the Ogre of Elba now lying duly watched and guarded far away to the south, within the rockbound coast of Saint Helena.

Chapter Twelve
Private Ears

The schooner was run safely into port, but just before she cleared the harbour mouth, down came a tremendous squall of wind as if from round the corner of some impossible solid cloud behind which an ambush of the storm had been lying in wait for the brave little vessel.

Down it came all at once, just when least expected, and in a few seconds as it struck the little vessel, rushing, in spite of the small amount of canvas spread, rapidly for the shelter, every one on deck snatched at the nearest object to which he could cling. The schooner bravely resisted for a while, careening over and then rising again, and then down she went with her masts almost flat upon the foam, and then lying over more and more as Rodd clung hard with one hand and involuntarily stretched out the other to his uncle as if to say good-bye. For he felt certain as the water came surging over the leeward rail that the next minute their voyage would be ended, and the *Maid of Salcombe* be going down.

It was one horror of breathlessness in the shrieking wind, while the storm-driven spray cut and lashed and flogged at the crew.

"It's all over," gasped the boy, in his excitement, though somehow even then there was no feeling of fear.

Another minute as she still dashed on, plunging through the waves, the vessel began to right again, the masts rising more and more towards the perpendicular, and the water that seemed to have been scooped up in the hollows of the well-reefed sails came streaming back in showers upon the deck.

Another minute and Rodd began to get his breath again, panting hard and feeling as if some great hand had been grasping him by the throat and had at last released its hold, while as the schooner now skimmed on, every furlong taking her more into shelter, the squall had passed over them and went sweeping along far away over the town ahead, and the boy felt a strong grip upon his arm.

Rodd turned sharply, to face Cross the sailor, who held on to him with his left while he used his right hand to clear his eyes from the spray.

"All right," he said, with his lips close to the boy's ear, so as to make himself heard, while Rodd winced, for as the man leaned towards him he poured something less than a pint of salt water from off his tightly-tied-on oilskin sou'-wester right into his eyes.

Rodd nodded without attempting to speak, and the sailor laughed.

There was something so genial and content in the man's looks, that it sent a thrill of satisfaction through the boy's breast, telling as it did that they were out of danger, while, as they rapidly glided on, the shrieking of the wind through the rigging grew less and less and the motion of the schooner more and more steady as the harbour was gained.

"Say, my lad," said Cross, "I thought we was going to make our first dive after specimens, and the *Saucy Sally* seemed to be holding her breath as she stuck her nose down into it and then jibbed and threw herself over sideways as if she knowed there wasn't depth enough of water for the job."

"Hah!" gasped Rodd hoarsely, for he had been taking in spray as well as wind, and he had now nearly recovered the power of breathing easily and well. "Why, Joe, I thought we were sinking."

"Nay, my lad; not us! The *Sally* was too well battened down, and couldn't have sunk; but I was getting a bit anxious when it looked as if we was going to miss the harbour mouth and go floating in ashore lying down as if we had all gone to sleep."

"Yes, it was horrible," said Rodd, with a sigh of relief. "But what would have happened if we had missed the mouth and gone ashore?"

"Why, what does happen, my lad, when a ship does that? Bumps, and a sale arterwards of new-wrecked timber on the beach. But here we are all right, and instead of being ashamed of ourselves we can look the mounseers full in the face and tell 'em that if they can manage a better bit of seamanship than the skipper, they had better go and show us how."

Joe Cross said no more, for Captain Chubb was roaring orders through a speaking trumpet, the last bit of canvas was lowered down, and before long the schooner was safely moored in the outer harbour as far away as she could safely get from the vessels that had taken refuge before them, some of them grinding together and damaging their paint and wood, in spite of their busy crews hard at work with fenders and striving to get into safer quarters, notwithstanding the efforts of the heavy gusts which came bearing down from time to time.

The nearest vessel was a handsome-looking brig which they had passed as they glided in, noting that she was moored head to wind to a heavy buoy. As they passed her to run nearer into shelter Rodd had noticed the name upon her stern, the *Jeanne d'Arc*, which suggested immediately the patriotic Maid of Orleans.

He had forgotten it the next moment, the name being merged with the thought that while the schooner had had so narrow an escape of ending her voyage, the brig had been lying snugly moored to the buoy. But now as they glided on it became evident that the brig had broken adrift, for all at once, as she lay rolling and jerking at her mooring cable, the distance between her bows and the huge ringed cask seemed to have grown greater, and from where Rodd stood he could see the glistening tarpaulins of her crew as they hurried forward in a cluster, and Captain Chubb bellowed an order from where he stood astern, to his men.

"Aren't coming aboard of us, are they?" thought Rodd, as, heard above the wind during a comparative lull, Captain Chubb was roaring out fresh orders to his crew; for he had fully grasped the danger, and the men were ready to slip their cable moorings and glide farther in under bare poles.

But fortunately this fresh disaster did not come to pass, for as the brig bore down upon them there was a rush and splash from her bows, an anchor went down, checking her progress a little, then a little more, as she still came on nearer as if to come crash into the schooner's bows, and Captain Chubb raised his speaking trumpet to his lips to bid his men let go, prior to ordering them to stand by ready to lower their own anchor in turn when at a safe distance, when the brig's progress received a sudden check, her anchor held, and she was brought up short not many yards away.

"Smart," said Captain Chubb, "for a mounseer;" and he looked at Rodd as he spoke, before tucking his speaking trumpet under his arm and then giving himself a shake like a huge yellow Newfoundland dog to get rid of the superabundant moisture. "Well, squire," he continued, as he came close up, "what should you do next?"

Rodd looked at him as if puzzled by the question. Then putting his hands to his mouth he shouted back—

"I should get farther into the harbour, in case that brig broke away again."

"Of course you would," said the captain, with a grim smile. "Now, don't you pretend again that you aren't a sailor, because that was spoken like a good first mate. But we will wait for a lull before we let go, for I don't want to lose no tackle. But the gale aren't over yet."

"But we are safe, captain?" said the boy.

"Yes," grunted the captain. "Better off than them yonder," and he pointed to a good-sized vessel which had been running for the harbour, but in vain, for she had been carried on too far and was swept away, to take the shore a mile distant.

The lull foretold by Captain Chubb enabled him to slip from his moorings and get the schooner into a sheltered position which he deemed sufficiently snug and far enough away from the brig, whose captain did not manifest any intention of coming farther in.

As they were parting company Rodd was standing right forward close to Cross, who stood spelling out the name of the brig they were leaving behind.

"*Jenny de Arc*" he grunted to Rodd. "That's a rum name for a smart brig like that. Wonder what she is. I never see'd Jenny spelt like that afore. That's the French way of doing it, I suppose."

Rodd took upon himself to explain whose name the brig bore, and the sailor gave vent to a musical growl.

"Shouldn't have knowed it," he said; "but as I was a-saying, I wonder what she is. Looks to me like what they calls a private ear."

"Why, that's a man-of-war, isn't it, Joe?"

"Well, a kind of a sort of one, you know, sir. One of them as goes off in war times to hark in private for any bit of news about well-laden merchantmen, and then goes off to capture them."

"But what makes you think that, Joe?" asked Rodd. "Why, look at her rig, sir. See what a heap of sail she could carry. I don't hold with a brig for fast-sailing, but look at the length of them two masts, and see how she's pierced for guns. She has shut up shop snug enough on account of the storm, but I'll wager she could run out some bulldogs—I mean, French poodles—as could bark if she liked. Then there's a big long gun amidships."

"I didn't see it," said Rodd. "Maybe not, my lad, but I did."

"Well, but a merchantman might carry guns to defend herself, Joe."

"Ay, she might, sir; but she wouldn't, unless she was going on a job like ours and wanted to scare off savages; and that aren't likely, for I should say we are the only vessel afloat as is going on such a fishing expedition as ours. And then look at her crew."

"What about her crew?" said Rodd. "It seemed to be a very good one so far as I could see."

"A deal too good, sir. Who ever saw a merchantman with such a crew as that? Didn't you see how smart they were in obeying orders and getting down that anchor?"

"Why, no smarter than our crew," said Rodd rather indignantly.

"Smarter than our crew, Mr Rodd, sir! I should think not!" cried the sailor. "Why, they are French! Still it was very tidy for them. I should like to know, though, what they are. I do believe I'm right, and that she is a private ear. Not been watching us, has she? Seems rather queer."

"Why should she be watching us?"

"Why should a private ear be watching any smart schooner, except to make a prize of her?"

"Oh, but that's in time of war," cried Rodd. "Ay, sir, but your private ears aren't very particular about that. This is near enough to war time still, and if I was our skipper I should keep a good sharp eye on that craft. But he knows pretty well what he's about. His head is screwed on the right way. But I say, Mr Rodd, how should you like a bit of the real thing, same as we used to have when I was in a King's ship?"

"What, a naval action?"

"Oh, you may call it that, sir, if you like. I mean a bit of real French and English, and see which is best man."

"Oh, nonsense! That's all over now, Joe."

"I don't know so much about that, sir."

"But we are in a friendly port, Joe, and no French ship would dare attack one of ours."

"No, sir, I know they daren't do it," said the man stubbornly; "but if they could catch us asleep they might have a try. But there, don't you be uncomfortable. There's too much of the weasel about our skipper, and he'll be too wide awake to let any Frenchman catch him asleep."

"Ah, you are thinking a lot of nonsense, Joe," said Rodd. "The war is all at an end, and Napoleon Bonaparte shut up in prison at Saint Helena. There'll be no more fighting now."

"Well, sir, I suppose you are right," said the man, with something like a sigh; "but you see, like some of my mates, I have seen a bit of sarvice in a King's ship, and we have got our guns on board, and we have just now been lying alongside—I should say bow and stern—of a Frenchman so as we could slew round and rake her; and it sets a man thinking. But there, I suppose you are right, and there will be no fighting for us this voyage."

"Of course there won't be. We are friends now with France."

"Yes, sir, and the French pretends to be friends with us; but all the same if I was the skipper I should double my night watch and be well on the look-out for squalls. — Ay, ay, sir!"

Joe Cross answered a hail from the skipper, and was directly after busy at work helping his mates to make all snug aloft, for the wind had sunk now into a pleasant soft gale which seemed to suggest fine weather; but Captain Chubb shook his head and frowned very severely as he looked out to windward.

"Nay, my lad," he said, "we have made our start and got as far as here, but it don't seem to me like getting away just yet, for there's a lot of weather hanging about somewhere, and as we are in no hurry and are snug in port, I am not going to run the risk of losing any of my tackle while the wind is shifting about like this. If I was you I should go in for a general dry up, and maybe you and your uncle, if the rain holds off, would like to go and have a look round the town."

The skipper moved away, and Rodd went to the side to have another look at the French brig, and then, not satisfied, he went below to fetch the small spy-glass, finding his uncle busy re-arranging some of his apparatus in the laboratory, and as he did not seem to be required, the boy took the small telescope from where it hung and made his way back again on deck, where he focussed the glass and began to scan the brig, scrutinising her rig and everything that he could command, from trucks to deck, making out the long gun covered by a great tarpaulin, and then bringing the glass to bear upon such of the crew as came within his scope.

And as he watched the well-built, smartly-rigged vessel with such knowledge as he had acquired during his life at the great English port, he made out, though fairly distant now, that there seemed to be something in Joe Cross's remarks, so that when he closed his glass to go down below, he began to dwell on the possibility of the smart brig being indeed a privateer, and this set him thinking of how horrible it would be if she did turn inimical and make an attempt at what would have been quite an act of piracy if she had followed the *Maid of Salcombe* out to sea and seized her as a prize.

"Why, it would break uncle's heart, after all his preparations for the expedition," mused the boy; "and besides it would be so treacherous. But Captain Chubb would not give up, I am sure. I never thought of it before, but he must have thought a good deal more about an accident such as this happening when he was taking such pains to drill and train the men. What did he say — that as we were going along a coast where the people were very savage and spent most of their time in war and fighting, we ought to be prepared for danger, in case we were attacked. Was he thinking of the French as well as the savages when he said this? Perhaps so. If one of his men thought so, why shouldn't he? Well, I will ask him first time I get him alone. Hullo! What are they doing there? Somebody going ashore from the brig."

Rodd could see with the naked eye the lowering down of a ship's boat over the brig's side, and that made him quickly focus his glass again, and while he was busy scanning the boat as it kissed the water and the oars fell over the side, Joe Cross came up behind him and made him start.

"Well, sir," he said, "what do you make of her now?"

"Nothing, Joe," said the boy, "only that it seems a very nice brig."

"Very, sir, and well-manned. Look at that."

"What?" asked the boy.

"That there boat they've lowered down, and how she's manned. She's no merchantman. Look at the way they are rowing. Why, they're like men-of-war's men, every one. I don't like the looks of she, and if the old skipper don't get overhauling her with them there eyes of his I'm a Dutchman; and that's what I ain't."

"Ah, you make mountains of molehills, Joe," said Rodd.

"Maybe, sir; maybe. But I suppose it's all a matter of eddication and training to keep watch. There, you see, it's always have your eyes open, night or day. For a man as goes to sea on board a man-of-war, meaning a King's ship, has to see enemies wherever they are and wherever they aren't, for even if there bean't none, a chap has to feel that there might be, and if he's let anything slip without seeing on it, why, woe betide him! There y'are, sir! Look at that there boat. You have hung about Plymouth town and seen things enough there to know as that there aren't a merchant brig."

"Well, she doesn't look like a merchant's shore boat, certainly," said Rodd, with his eyes still glued to the end of the telescope.

"Right, sir," cried Joe Cross. "Well, then, sir, as she aren't a merchant brig's boat, and the brig herself aren't a man-of-war, perhaps you will tell me what she is? You can't, sir?"

"No, Joe."

"No more can I, sir; but if we keeps our eyes open I dare say we shall see."

Chapter Thirteen
In the French Port

In spite of the knocking about by the storm, the schooner was none the worse, and in the course of the day as the weather rapidly settled down and the western gale seemed to have blown itself out, while the sailors had been busy swabbing the rapidly drying planks, and, the wind having fallen, shaking out the saturated sails to dry, Uncle Paul strolled with his nephew up and down the deck, waiting till the skipper seemed to be less busy before going up to him.

"Well," said Uncle Paul; "are we damaged at all?"

"Not a bit," was the gruff reply. "It's done her good—stretched her ropes and got the canvas well in shape."

"But how do you feel about the schooner?"

"As if she was just what we wanted, sir. Given me a lot of confidence in her."

"Then as the weather is settling down you will sail again to-night?"

"No; I want to get a little more ballast aboard, and this is all a little bit of show. We shall have more weather before long. I shan't sail yet."

The work being pretty well done—that is, as far as work ever is done in a small vessel—Rodd noticed that some of the men had been smartening themselves up, and after hanging about a bit watching the captain till he went below, Rodd saw them gather in a knot together by the forecastle hatch, talking among themselves, till one of the party, a heavy, dull-looking fellow, very round and smooth-faced and plump, with quite a colour in his cheeks, came aft to where Rodd and his uncle were standing watching the busy scene about the wharves of the inner harbour, and discussing as to whether they should go ashore for a few hours to look round the town.

"I am thinking, Pickle, that after such a bad night as we had, we might just as well stay aboard and rest, and besides, as far as I can see everything's muddy and wretched, and I fancy we should be better aboard."

"Oh, I don't know, uncle. We needn't be long, and it will be a change. But here's the Bun coming up to speak to you."

"The what!" cried Uncle Paul.

"That man—Rumsey."

"But why do you call him the Bun?"

"Oh, it's the men's name for him," said Rodd, laughing. "They nicknamed him because he was such a round-faced fellow."

"Beg pardon, sir," said the man, making a tug at his forelock.

"Yes, my man; you want to speak to me?"

"Yes, sir; the lads asked me to say, sir, that as it's been a very rough night—"

"Very, my man—very," said Uncle Paul, staring.

"They'd take it kindly, sir, if you'd give about half of us leave to go ashore for a few hours."

"Oh, well, my man, I have no objection whatever," said Uncle Paul. "As far as I am concerned, by all means yes."

"Thankye, sir; much obliged, sir," said the man eagerly, and pulling his forelock again he hurried forward to join the group which had sent him as their spokesman to ask for leave.

Rodd turned to speak to his uncle, and caught Joe Cross's eye instead, wondering at the man's comical look at him as he closed an eye and jerked one thumb over his shoulder in the direction of the group forward as they began whispering together, and then, thrust forward towards the side by his companions, the Bun began to signal towards the Frenchmen hanging about the nearest landing-place, where several boats were made fast to the side of the dock.

Just at that moment the skipper came up from below, saw what was going on at a glance, strode towards the group, which began to dissolve at once, the Bun being the only man whose attention was taken up by a boatman who was answering his signal. Just while the signaller was making his most energetic gestures he leaped round in the most startled way, for the skipper had closed up and given him a very smart slap on the shoulder.

"Now, Rumsey, what's this?" he cried.

"Boat, sir. Going ashore, sir."

"Who is?" said the skipper, frowning.

"Us six, sir."

"Us six! Why, you're only one."

"Yes, sir. These 'ere others too, sir."

"What others?" cried the captain, and Rumsey, looking anxiously around, found for the first time that he was alone.

"The lads as was here just now, sir—six on us."

"Oh, indeed!" said the skipper sarcastically, and raising his cap he gave his rough hair a rub. "Let me see; when did I give you leave to go ashore?"

"No, sir; not you, sir. Dr Robson, sir."

"Oh, I see," said the skipper.

This was all said loud enough for Rodd and Uncle Paul to hear, and Rodd began to grin as he looked at his uncle, whose face assumed a perplexed aspect, one which increased to uneasiness as the captain came up to them at once.

"Just a word, sir," he said. "Did you order these men to go ashore?"

"Oh no," cried Uncle Paul. "One of them came up to me, asking if I had any objections to their going ashore, and I said, not the least. I supposed, of course, that they had got leave from you."

"Of course, sir. Bless 'em for a set of artful babies! They aren't learned discipline yet. You, Rumsey, go and tell your messmates that if they try that game again with me they'll stand a fine chance of not going ashore for the rest of the voyage."

"Yes, sir, I'll tell them, sir," cried the man hurriedly; and he shuffled off as hard as he could to find those who had left him in the lurch.

"Here, you, Joe Cross," continued the captain, "you signal to that Frenchy boatman that he is not wanted."

"Ay, ay, sir!" cried Cross, hurrying to the side, where he began gesticulating angrily, in spite of which the boatman persisted in coming alongside and in voluble French declaring that he was ordered to come and would not go back until he was paid.

Meanwhile a little explanation was going on between the skipper and Uncle Paul.

"Don't want to be bumptious, sir," said the former, "but there's only room on board a craft for one captain. Those fellows jump at any chance to get ashore, and when they are there, there's no knowing when you'll get them on board again, besides which, they wouldn't be careful, and French and English don't get on very well together after all that's gone by. Here,

Cross, tell that jabbering Frenchman if he isn't off, he'll have to go back with a hole through the bottom of his boat. No, stop. Go and find Mr Craig. Tell him to set those six men something to do."

"Ay, ay, sir!" cried the sailor, hurrying off.

"There, it was all my fault, captain," said Uncle Paul, smiling. "I won't offend again. Here, Rodd, my boy, give that poor fellow a shilling for his trouble."

Rodd hurried to the side, hailed the man, and held out the coin, telling him in very bad French what it was for; but the fellow shook his head, held up four fingers, and began shouting "*Quatre!*" so loudly that the skipper heard.

"Cat, indeed!" he shouted. "Just what I should like to give him. Here, come away, Mr Rodd; he shan't have anything now."

But Rodd did not obey at once.

"One or nothing," he cried to the man, in French.

"*Quatre! Quatre!*" shouted the man.

Rodd shook his head and was turning away, but the boatman swarmed up the side, and reaching over the rail, shouted "*Quatre!*" again, till the skipper made so fierce a rush at him that he lowered his feet quickly down into his boat, catching the shilling that Rodd pitched to him, and then hurriedly pushing off for the landing-place.

"Oh, it's all right, Dr Robson," said the skipper, "only you must leave all this shore-going to me. I know my lads; you don't."

Just then Craig, the mate, came up on deck, looking very sour at having been awakened from a comfortable sleep, and did not scruple about setting the delinquents to work upon some very unnecessary task, to the great delight of their messmates, who, headed by Joe Cross, gave them pretty freely to understand what their opinion was of the scheme to get a run ashore.

It was towards evening that, after a hasty meal, partaken of in peace in the still waters of the harbour, tempted by a few gleams of sunshine, and for Rodd's gratification, Uncle Paul and Rodd were rowed ashore in the same boat as the skipper, who had business with the English Consul about his papers, the understanding being that the boat was to go back and meet them at nine o'clock.

"That's as long as we shall want to stay, Rodd," said Uncle Paul.

"Yes, sir," said the skipper; "and if I were you I'd turn in early for a good night's rest, for I'm thinking we shall have dirty weather again to-morrow, and there's no knowing how long it will last."

"But it looks so bright to-night," cried Rodd.

"Just here, sir," cried the skipper, "and it may be fine enough to tempt me off in the morning; but I don't feel at all sartain, and to-morrow night we may be having another knocking about."

They separated at the landing-place, and for the next two hours Rodd was making himself acquainted with the principal streets of the old seaport, time going very rapidly and the night coming on.

It was growing pretty dark, and after making two mistakes as to their direction, Rodd declared that he knew the way, and his uncle yielding to his opinion, the boy led on, till, turning a corner sharply, they almost came in contact with a couple of French officers walking in the opposite direction, the one a tall, stern, elderly-looking man, talking in a low excited tone to his young companion, whose attention was so much taken up as he deferentially listened to his elder, that he started back to avoid striking against Rodd, who also gave way.

It was now almost dark, and the next moment the French officers had passed on, as Uncle Paul exclaimed—

"Yes, I believe you are right, Pickle. You are. Those are ships' lights hoisted up to the stays. Well, don't you see?"

"Yes, uncle, but—"

The boy said no more, and Uncle Paul laid his hand upon his shoulder.

"What's the matter?" he cried. "Why don't you speak? Those are the lights in the harbour."

"Yes—yes. Yes, uncle, I see," said the boy hastily; "but—er—but—er—"

"Why, what's the matter with you? Don't feel done up?"

"No, uncle," replied Rodd hurriedly. "I was only puzzled; it seemed so strange."

"You mean you seem so strange," said the doctor, laughing.

"Yes, uncle, I feel so."

"Well, come along, and let's make haste aboard. I don't want to keep the captain waiting. We have lost so much time by missing our way. It's past nine, I'm sure."

"Yes, uncle," said the boy, speaking more like himself; "it must be. But I felt so startled in coming suddenly upon those two officers."

"Why, there was nothing to startle you, my boy."

"No, uncle, I suppose not; but somehow I felt that I had been close to that one who nearly ran up against me before, and when he said '*Pardon*' —"

"I didn't hear him say '*Pardon*,'" said Uncle Paul.

"But he did, uncle, just in a low tone so that I could hardly hear him, and then I felt sure we had met before."

"Nonsense!" cried Uncle Paul. "Look here, my boy, how much sleep did you have last night?"

"Sleep, uncle!" cried the boy, in a voice full of surprise.

"Why, none at all. Who could sleep through that storm?"

"I'll answer for myself," said the doctor; "I could not. Well, you were completely tired out, and are half dreaming now. Come along; let's find the boat and get on board for a light supper and a good night's rest."

"Yes, uncle," said Rodd quietly; "but take care; we are on the wharf. I can make out the shipping plainly now;" and as he spoke a familiar hail came out of the darkness, while as they answered the captain strode towards them.

"Thought you were lost, gentlemen. Been waiting half-an-hour. Take care; the boat's down here;" and striding along the top of the harbour wall the skipper led the way to the descending steps, where the boat was waiting, and they were rowed aboard.

An hour later Rodd was plunged in the deepest of deep sleeps, but dreaming all the same of the storm and of getting into difficulties with some one who was constantly running against him and whispering softly, "Pardon!"

Chapter Fourteen
The Suspicious Craft

"Oh, I say, Uncle Paul, isn't it horrible?" cried Rodd the next morning.

Breakfast was just over, and Captain Chubb had gone on deck, while the wind was howling furiously as if in a rage to find its playthings, some two or three hundred vessels of different tonnage, safely moored in the shelter of the harbour, and out of its power to toss here and there and pitch so many helpless ruins to be beaten to pieces upon the shore.

Down it kept coming right in amongst them, making them check at their mooring cables and chains, but in vain, for their crews had been too busy, and the only satisfaction that the tempest could obtain, was to hearken to the miserable dreary groans that were here and there emitted as some of the least fortunate and worst secured ground against each other.

"Isn't it horrible, uncle?" shouted Rodd, for the rain just then was mingled with good-sized hailstones, and was rattling down upon the deck and skylight in a way that half-drowned the lad's voice.

"Miserable weather, Pickle; but never mind. We must settle down to a good morning's work in the laboratory."

"Oh no, not yet, uncle; we don't seem to have started. It will only be a makeshift."

"But we might put things a little more straight, boy."

"Oh no, uncle; they are too straight now, and I want to go on deck."

"Bah! It isn't fit. Wait till the weather holds up."

"Oh, I shall dress up accordingly, uncle. But I say, where does all the rain come from? It must be falling in millions of tons everywhere."

"Ah, you might as well ask me where the wind comes from. Study up some book on meteorology."

"Oh yes, I will, uncle; but not yet."

"Very well; be off."

Rodd hurried out of the cabin, and five minutes later came back rattling and crackling, to present himself before his uncle, who thrust up his spectacles upon his forehead and stared.

"There," cried Rodd; "don't think I shall get wet. I wish I'd had it the other night. It's splendid, uncle, and so stiff that if I like to stoop down a little and spread my arms, I can almost rest in it. I say, don't I look like a dried haddock?"

"Humph! Well, yes, you do look about the same colour," grumbled the doctor, for the boy was buttoned up in a glistening oilskin coat of a buff yellow tint; the turned-up collar just revealed the tips of his ears, and he was crowned by a sou'-wester securely tied beneath his chin.

"I say, this will do, won't it?"

"Yes, you look a beauty!" grunted the doctor; "but there, be off; I want to write a letter or two."

Rodd went crackling up the cabin stairs, clump, clump, clump, for he was wearing a heavy pair of fisherman's boots that had been made waterproof by many applications of oil—a pair specially prepared for fishing purposes and future wading amongst the wonders of coral reef and strand.

The deck was almost deserted, the only two personages of the schooner's crew being the captain and Joe Cross, both costumed so as to match exactly with the boy, who now joined them, to begin streaming with water to the same extent as they.

They both looked at him in turn, Cross grinning and just showing a glint of his white teeth where the collar of his oilskin joined, while his companion scowled, or seemed to, and emitted a low grumbling sound that might have meant welcome or the finding of fault, which of the two Rodd did not grasp, for the skipper turned his back and rolled slowly away as if he were bobbing like a vessel through the flood which covered the deck and was streaming away from the scuppers.

As the skipper went right forward and stood by the bowsprit, looking straight ahead through the haze formed by the streaming rain, Rodd was thrown back upon Joe Cross, with whom, almost from the day when the man had joined, he had begun to grow intimate; and as he went close up to him, the sailor gave his head a toss to distribute some of the rain that was splashing down upon his sou'-wester, and grinning visibly now, he cried—

"Why, Mr Rodd, sir, you've forgot your umbrella."

"Get out!" cried Rodd good-humouredly. "But I say, Joe, how long is this rain going to last?"

"Looks as if it means to go on for months, sir, but may leave off to-night. I say, though, that's a splendid fit, sir. You do look fine! Are you comfortable in there?"

Rodd did not answer, for he was trying to pierce the streaming haze and make out whether the brig was visible.

For a few moments he could not make it out, but there it was, looking faint and strange, about a hundred yards away.

"That's the brig, isn't it, yonder?" he said at last.

"Yes, sir, that's she, and they seem to have got her fast now; but she wouldn't hurt us if she broke from her moorings, for the wind's veered a point or two, and it would take her clear away."

Rodd remained silent as he stood thinking, he did not know why, unless it was that the vessel with the tall, dimly-seen tapering spars bore a French name, and somehow—again he could not tell why, only that it seemed to him very ridiculous—the shadowy vessel associated itself with the two French officers he had encountered in the darkness of the previous night, when he heard one of them after brushing against him murmur the word "Pardon!" And he found himself thinking that if the vessel had been swept up against the schooner when her anchor was dragging, it would have been no use for her crew to cry "Pardon!" as that would not have cured the damage.

"Well, sir, what do you make of her?" cried the sailor, putting an end to the lad's musings.

"Can't see much," said Rodd, "for the rain, but she seems beautifully rigged."

"Yes, sir, and she can sail well too—for a brig—but I should set her down as being too heavily sparred, and likely to be top-heavy. If she was going along full sail, and was caught in such a squall as we had yesterday, and laid flat like the schooner, I don't believe she'd lift again. Anyhow, I shouldn't like to be aboard."

"No, it wouldn't be pleasant," said Rodd; "but I say, I can't see anything of that long gun you talked about."

"No wonder, sir. You want that there long water-glass, as you called it—that there one you showed me as you was unpacking it. Don't you remember? Like a big pipe with panes of glass in it as you said you could stick down into the sea and make out what was on the bottom. You want that now."

The man passed his hand along the brow edge of his sou'-wester to sweep away the drops, and then took a long look at the deck of the brig.

"No, sir; can't make it out now; but I see it plainly enough this morning, covered with a lashed down tarpaulin as if to hide it, and I knew at once. I can almost tell a big gun by the smell—I mean feel it like, if it's there."

"But do you still think she's a privateer?"

"Well, I don't say she is, sir, for that's a thing you can't tell for sartain unless you see a ship's papers; but she is something of that kind, I should say, and— Ay, ay, sir!—There's the skipper hailed me, sir. I say, Mr Rodd, sir, do mind you don't get wet!"

This was as the man rolled away sailor fashion, and emitting a crackling whishing sound as he made for the vessel's bows, where he received some order from his captain which sent him to the covered-in hatchway of the forecastle, where he slowly disappeared into a kind of haze, half water, half smoke, for several of the water-bound crew had given up the chewing of their tobacco to indulge in pipes.

But Rodd was in a talkative humour, and made his way to the skipper, saluting him with—

"I say, Captain Chubb, how do you manage to do it?"

"Do what, my lad?"

"Why, say for certain what the weather's going to be."

There was a low chuckling sound such as might have been emitted by a good-humoured porpoise which had just ended one of its underwater curves, and thrust its head above the surface to take a good deep breath before it turned itself over and dived down again.

"Second natur', youngster, and that's use. Takes a long time to learn, and when you have larnt your lesson perfect as you think, you find that you don't know it a bit."

"But you did know it," said Rodd. "You said that the storm would come on again, when it was beautiful and fine yesterday evening; and here it is."

"Well, yes, my lad, if you goes on for years trying to hit something you must get a lucky shot sometimes."

"Oh yes, but there's something more than that," said Rodd. "When I have been amongst the fishermen in Plymouth, and over in Saltash, I have wondered to find how exact they were about the weather, and how whenever they wouldn't take us out fishing they were always right. They seemed to know that bad weather was coming on."

"Oh, of course," said the skipper. "Why, my lad, if you got your living by going out in your boat, don't you think the first thing you would try to learn would be to make it your living?"

"Why, of course," cried Rodd.

"Ah, you don't mean the same as I do. I mean, make it your living and not your dying."

"Oh, I see."

"You wouldn't want," continued the skipper, "to go out at times that might mean having them as you left at home standing on the shore looking out to sea for a boat as would never come back."

"No," said the boy, with something like a sigh. "I know what you mean. Ah, it has been very horrible sometimes, and all those little churchyards at the different villages about the coast with that regular 'Drowned at sea' over and over and over again."

"Right, my lad. Things go wrong sometimes; but that's what makes sailors and fishermen get to learn what the moon says and the sun and the clouds, and the bit of haze that gathers sometimes off the coast means. Why, if you'd looked out yesterday afternoon when the wind went down and the glint of sunshine come out, there was a nasty dirty look in the sky. You wait a bit and keep your eyes open, and. put that and that together, and as you grow up you'll find that it isn't so hard as you'd think to say what the weather is going to be to-morrow. You'll often be wrong, same as I am."

"Ah! then I shall begin at once," cried Rodd eagerly, as he looked sharply round. "Well, it can't go on pelting down like this with hail coming now and then in showers. Showers come and go."

"Right!" said the skipper, clapping him on the shoulder.

"Oh!" cried Rodd sharply.

"Hullo! Why, you don't mean to say that hurt?"

"Hurt! No," cried Rodd, shaking his head violently. "You shot a lot of cold water right up into my ear."

"Oh, that will soon dry up. Well, what do you say the weather's going to be?"

"The storm soon over, and a fine day to-morrow."

"Done?" asked the skipper.

"Oh yes; but mind, that's only a try."

"Then it's my turn now, youngster, so here goes. I say we shall have worse weather to-morrow than we have got to-day."

"Oh, it can't be!" cried Rodd.

"Well," cried the skipper, chuckling, "we shall see who's right."

"Oh, but I don't want for us to have to stop here in this French port."

"More don't I, my lad, so we think the same there. You going to stop on deck?"

"Yes, till dinner-time," cried Rodd, and just then the haze of rain out seaward opened a little, revealing the brig with its tall spars and web of rigging.

This somehow set the boy thinking about the escape from accident when they came into port, and then of the encounter ashore, and he began talking.

"It's no use to go down below. It's so stuffy, and I want to chat. I say, captain, what do you think of that brig?"

"Very smartly built craft indeed, my lad—one as I should like to sail if I could do as I liked."

"Do as you liked?" asked Rodd.

"Yes; alter her rig—make a schooner of her. But as she is she's as pretty a vessel as I ever see—for a brig. Frenchmen don't often turn out a boat like that."

"What should you think she is?" asked Rodd. "A merchantman?"

"No, my lad; I should say she was something of a dispatch boat, though she aren't a man-of-war. I don't quite make her out. She's got a very smart crew, and I saw two of her officers go aboard in some sort of uniform, though it was too dark to quite make it out."

"But if she's a man-of-war she would carry guns, wouldn't she?" asked Rodd.

"Well, I don't think she's a man-of-war, my lad," replied the skipper; "but she do carry guns, and one of them's a big swivel I just saw amidships. But men-of-war, merchantmen, and coasters, we're all alike in a storm, and glad to get into shelter."

"Yes, it is a fine-looking brig. Is she likely to be a privateer?"

"Eh? What do you know about privateers?"

"Oh, not much," said Rodd. "But going about at Plymouth and talking to the sailors, of course I used to hear something about them."

"Well, yes, of course," said the skipper thoughtfully, as he too swept the drops from the front of his sou'-wester, and tried to pierce the falling rain. "She might be a French privateer out of work, as you may say, for their game's at an end now that the war's over. Yes, a very smart craft."

"But do you think she's here for any particular purpose?"

"Yes, my lad; a very particular purpose."

"Ah!" cried the boy rather excitedly. "What?"

"To take care of herself and keep in harbour till the weather turns right. Why? What were you thinking?"

"I was wondering why she came in so close after us, and then anchored where she is."

"Oh, I can tell you that," said the skipper, chuckling. "It was because she couldn't help herself."

"Then you don't think she was watching us?"

"No-o! What should she want to watch us for?"

"Why, to take us as a prize, seeing what a beautiful little schooner it is."

"Bah! She'd better not try," said the skipper grimly. "Why, what stuff have you got in your head, boy? We are not at war with France."

"No-o," said Rodd thoughtfully; "but her captain might have taken a fancy to the *Maid of Salcombe*, and I've read that privateers are not very particular when they get a chance. And the war's only just over."

"No. But then, you see, my lad, even if you were right, that brig wouldn't have a chance."

"Why, suppose she waited till we had sailed, and followed till she thought it was a good opportunity, and then her captain led his men aboard and took her?"

"Oh, I see," said the skipper dryly. "Well, my lad, as I say, she wouldn't have a chance. First, because she couldn't catch us, for give me sea room I could sail right round her."

"Ah, but suppose it was a calm, and she sent her boats full of men on board to take us?"

"Well, what then?"

"What then? Why, wouldn't that be very awkward?" asked Rodd.

"Very, for them," said the skipper grimly. "What would my boys be about?"

"Why, they'd be taken prisoners."

"I should just like to see her try," said the skipper. "If the boats' crews of that brig were to get a lodgment aboard my craft, how long do you think it would take our lads to clear them off?"

"Oh, I am sure our crew would be very brave, but I should say that brig's got twice as many men as we have."

"What of that?" said the skipper contemptuously.

"Well, then," said Rodd argumentatively, "she's got her guns, and might sink us."

"And we've got our guns, and might sink her," growled the skipper. "Look here, my lad; why did I give my lads gun drill and cutlass and pike drill, while you and the doctor were taking in your tackle and bags of tricks?"

"Why, to defend the schooner against any savages who might attack us when we are off the West Coast or among the islands."

"Right, my lad. Well, as Pat would say, by the same token couldn't they just as well fight a pack of Frenchies as a tribe of niggers? Bah! You're all wrong. It's quite like enough that yon brig may have been fitted out for a privateer, though I rather think she wouldn't be fast enough. But that game's all over, and we are all going to be at peace now we have put Bony away like a wild beast in a cage and he can't do anybody any hurt. There, you needn't fidget yourself about that. All the same, I don't quite understand why a craft that isn't a man-of-war, but carries a long gun amidships and has officers in uniform aboard, should be taking refuge in this port. I dunno. She looks too smart and clean, but it might mean that she's going to the West Coast, blackbirding."

"Ha, ha, ha!" laughed Rodd. "Why, that's what you thought about us, Captain Chubb."

"So I did; so I did, my lad," said the skipper good-humouredly. "You see, I am like other men—think I am very wise, but I do stupid things sometimes. Well, I'll be safe this time, and say I don't know what she is, and I don't much care. But I am pretty sure that she aren't after us, and I dare say, if the truth's known, she don't think we are after her. There, squint out yonder to windward. That don't look like fine weather, does it?"

"No; worse than ever!" cried Rodd.

"That's so, my lad, and you may take this for certain; we shan't sail to-day, and you won't see another vessel put out to sea. Take my word for it."

"That I will, Captain Chubb!" cried the boy earnestly, and the skipper nodded his head so quickly that the water flew off in a shower.

But, as some wag once said, the wisest way is to wait till after something has happened before you begin to prophesy about it.

Captain Chubb had probably never heard about the wisdom of this proceeding in foretelling events, for it so happened that in spite of the storm increasing in violence for many hours, his words proved to be entirely wrong.

Chapter Fifteen
An Exciting Time

About mid-day there was a sudden lull. The wind blew nearly as hard as ever, but the clouds were broken up, allowing a few gleams of sunshine to pass through, and soon after the sky seemed to be completely swept; the streaming wharves and streets began to show patches of dry paving, and nearly every vessel near was hung with the men's oilskins, Rodd being one of the first to shed his awkward garments and come out looking more like himself.

There was such a transformation scene, and all looked so bright in the sunshine, that the boy took the first opportunity to ask the skipper what he thought of it now.

"Just the same as I did before, my lad," he replied bluntly. "Here, it's only mid-day, and mid-day aren't to-night, and to-night aren't to-morrow morning. Just you wait."

"Oh, I'll wait," said Rodd, "but I think we ought to start off as soon as we can, and get right away to sea."

"Do you?" said the captain gruffly. "Well, I don't."

After dinner Uncle Paul had a few words with the skipper, and then shook his head at his nephew, who was watching them inquiringly.

"No, my lad," he said, "it won't do; the captain says there's more bad weather coming; but we'll go and have a look round the town if you like."

Rodd did like as a matter of course, and with the sun now shining brightly as if there were no prospect of more rain for a month, they were rowed ashore, Rodd noticing as they went that the crew of the brig seemed to be very busy, a couple of boats going to and fro fetching stores of some kind from the nearest wharf, but what he could not make out.

Then came a good ramble through the busy place, where everybody seemed to be taking advantage of the cessation of the storm, and Rodd noted everything to as great an extent as a hurried visit would allow.

There was plenty to see, the forts, one each side of the harbour, and a couple more on the higher ground, displaying their grinning embrasures and guns commanding the harbour and the town, while soldiery in their rather shabby-looking uniforms could be seen here and there, and sentries turned the visitors back upon each occasion when they went near.

"Rather an ugly place to tackle, Rodd, from the sea, but I suppose our fellows wouldn't scruple about making an attack if there were any need. But here, I think we had better get back on board."

"Oh, not yet, uncle. I haven't half seen enough."

"But I am getting sick of this tiresome wind," said Uncle Paul. "One can't keep on one's hat, and it is just as if these gusts were genuine French, and kept on making a rush at us from round the corners of the streets as if they wanted to blow us into the harbour."

"Yes, it is rather tiresome," replied Rodd. "But I should have liked to have had a look inside one of those batteries."

"Pooh! What do you want to see them for?"

"Why, just because they are French, uncle."

"Nonsense! You have seen all ours on the heights of Plymouth, and they are a deal better-looking than these. We have a good way to walk, so let's go down at once. There, look yonder."

"What at, uncle?"

"What at? Why, at the clouds gathering there in the wind's eye. You see Captain Chubb's right, and we shall have the rain pouring down again before long."

Rodd laughed as if he did not believe it, but making no farther opposition, they began to descend towards the harbour; but before they were half-way there the wind had increased to a furious pitch, the sea became a sheet of foam, and with wonderful rapidity the clouds had gathered overhead, till a black curtain was sweeping right over, and a few heavy drops of rain began to fall. Then down came a drenching shower, and they were glad to run for refuge to the nearest shelter, which presented itself in the shape of a great barrack-like building that seemed to be built about a square, and at whose arched entrance a couple of sentries with shouldered muskets were pacing up and down.

As Uncle Paul and Rodd approached at a trot, with the intention of getting under the archway, both sentries stopped short, and one of them held his weapon across breast high, scowling fiercely, and barred their way.

"Here, it's all right," cried Rodd. "We only want to shelter out of the rain for a few minutes;" and he pressed forward. "Come on, uncle. Never mind him!"

"*Halte là!*" cried the sentry.

But Uncle Paul's hand went to his pocket, and drawing out half-a-crown he pointed quickly at the falling rain and the archway under which they now stood, taking out his handkerchief the while, and beginning to brush off the drops which bedewed his coat.

The man glanced at the coin, then at his brother sentry, and both looked inward at the square behind them. The exchange of glances was very quick, and then the first sentry opened one hand, but kept it very close to his side, again looking inward to see that he was not observed, before grumbling out—

"*Eh bien! Restez!*" And then as if perfectly unconscious of the bribe he had received, he resumed his slow pace up and down under the shelter of the great archway.

It was all a matter of minutes, but long enough for the wind and rain to have gathered force, and while the former raved and shrieked, down came the latter in a sheet, or rather in a succession of sheets which made the roadways seem as if full of dancing chess pawns, and the gullies turn at once into so many furious little torrents tearing down the slopes towards the harbour.

"Nice, isn't it, uncle?" said Rodd merrily.

"Nice!" grumbled Uncle Paul. "I don't know what I was thinking about to give way to you in such treacherous weather. Why, it's worse than ever. How are we going to get back to the schooner?"

"Oh, it will soon be over, uncle, and if it isn't we must get to know where the nearest place is from that sentry, and make a rush for it to get some tea, and wait there till the shower is over."

"Shower!" said Uncle Paul. "It looks to me like a night of storm coming on, and as if we shan't get back to the schooner to-night."

"Well, it doesn't matter, uncle," cried the boy coolly. "There's sure to be a good hotel, and Captain Chubb will know why we haven't come back. As soon as there's a bit of a lull we will make a run for it, and we shall be able to get a lesson in French."

"Bah!" said Uncle Paul impatiently. "How the wind comes whistling through this archway! We shall be getting wet even here."

The two men on guard were evidently of the same opinion, for they turned to their sentry boxes and began to put on their overcoats, after standing their muskets inside.

But before this was half done, each snatched up his piece again and faced the entrance, for all at once there was the clattering of hoofs in the cobbled paved street, and a cavalry officer, followed at a short distance by a couple of men, dashed up to the front and turned in under the archway, drenched with rain, the officer saying something sharply to one of the sentries.

The man replied by pointing to a doorway at the back of the great entrance, while the officer swung himself from his horse, threw the rein to one of his men, and then lifting his sabre-tache by the strap he gave it a swing or two to throw off the water from its dripping sides, and then opened the great pocket to peer inside as if to see that its contents were safe.

The next moment, as if satisfied, he let it fall to the full length of its slings, gave a stamp or two to shake off the water that dripped from him, and then raised his hands to give a twist to the points of his wet moustache. He scowled fiercely at Rodd the while, and then marched towards the doorway with the steel scabbard of his sabre clinking and clanking over the stones.

"Pretty good opinion of himself, Pickle," said Uncle Paul quietly.

"Yes, uncle; but what a pair of trousers—no, I mean long boots—no, I don't; I mean trousers.—Which are they, uncle?" added the boy, who was rather tickled by the size and the way in which they were finished off at the bottoms with leather as if they were jack-boots.

"Wait till he comes out, Pickle, and ask him," said the doctor dryly.

"No, thank you, uncle; my French is so bad," said the boy, with his eyes sparkling. "But, my word, they must have been galloping hard to escape the rain! Look at those poor horses. They are breathed."

Rodd had hardly spoken when they became fully aware that they had taken refuge in the entrance to the town barracks, for the notes of a bugle rang out, echoing round the inner square of the building, and seeming to be thrown back in a half-smothered way from wall to wall, while the wind and rain raged down more fiercely than ever.

"Something must be the matter," said Rodd, with his lips close to his uncle's ear.

"Seems like it, boy. That officer must have brought a dispatch."

The object of the bugle was shown directly, for in spite of the rain the interior of the barracks began to assume the aspect of some huge wasps' nest that had suddenly been disturbed.

Soldiers came hurrying out into the rain, hurriedly putting on their overcoats; the great arched gateway filled up at once with men seeking its shelter, and the sentry who had received his half-crown came to roughly order the English intruders to go elsewhere; but it was only outside militarism, for he said in a low hurried tone in French—

"Run outside to the end of the barracks. Grand café."

"Come along, uncle. Never mind the rain," cried Rodd, catching at his uncle's wrist, as he fully grasped the sentry's meaning; and stepping outside the archway they ran together, or rather, were half carried by the shrieking wind, for some thirty or forty yards, almost into the doorway of a large lit-up building, for already it seemed to be almost night.

"Never mind the rain, indeed!" grumbled Uncle Paul. "Why, I'm nearly soaked. Oh, come, we have got into civilised regions, at all events;" for a couple of waiters, seeing their plight, literally pounced upon them and hurried them through the building into a great kitchen where a huge fire was burning and the smell of cookery saluted their nostrils.

The attentions of the waiters of what was evidently one of the principal hotels of the town were very welcome, and a glance teaching them that their visitors were people of some standing, they made use of their napkins to remove as much of the superabundant moisture as was possible, and then furnished themselves with a fresh relay to operate upon their backs.

"Queer, isn't it, uncle? I am quite dry in front. My word, how the rain did come down!"

"Messieurs will dine here?" said one of the waiters smilingly.

"*Oh, oui, pour certain*" replied Uncle Paul. "If you don't mind, Pickle."

"Mind, uncle? Oh, yes, of course. I am horribly hungry."

"You always are, my boy. Well, we must make the best of a bad business," continued the doctor, as, nodding to the waiter, he moved a little closer to the fire and turned his back, an example followed by Rodd.

"It makes a dreadful time, monsieur," said the smiling waiter. "Will he choose, or trust his servant to prepare a dinner upon the field of which the English milor' will be proud?"

"You speak capital English," said the doctor, rather sarcastically.

"I have been many times in public in London."

"Ah, that's right. Then give us a snug little dinner while we dry ourselves. But what's the meaning of all that upset at the barracks next door?"

"It is not quite that I know, sir," said the man eagerly; "but two officers came in upon the instant to put their cloaks where they should not water themselves so much, and I hear them say, a dispatch come quickly for monsieur the Governor to seize upon a ship. Oh, faith of a man! Hark at that!"

For there was a sudden crash and an echoing roar, while some of the utensils in the great kitchen clattered together, and a piece of earthenware fell from a shelf upon the stone floor, to be shivered to atoms.

"*Tonnerre, eh?*" said the doctor.

"*Non, non, monsieur*" cried the man, relapsing into his native tongue for a moment. "It is what you English gentlemen call a great gun from the fort; and look, look! The poor *cuisinière* much alarm, as you call it."

For just then, as if catching the contagion from the shrieking of the storm, one of the cook-maids threw herself back into a chair and began to scream.

It was a busy scene for a few minutes while the frightened hysterical woman was hurried out, while with the storm seeming to increase in violence, and amid the trampling of armed men outside, who were hurrying from the barracks, the two English visitors gradually picked up scraps of information which explained the excitement that in spite of the storm was going on outside.

"Messieurs would like to see," said the friendly waiter. "They will come up-stairs to the long *salle* whose windows give upon the harbour."

"But what's the matter?" cried Rodd. "Is there a wreck?"

"A wreck, sare?" said the waiter, shaking his head. "No, I know not wreck."

"Has a ship come ashore and is breaking up?"

"Ha, ha! No, no, no, no, no, no, no! You would say *naufrage. Non, non, non*! It is a sheep in the harbour; a foreign spy. They say it has come to set fire to the town."

"Then they have chosen a very bad night for it," said Uncle Paul, laughing.

"Monsieur is right. Nosing would burn. But the enemies of la France, my great country, not stop to think of zat."

"Oh, but that must be a rumour, Rodd," said Uncle Paul uneasily. "Why, surely they are not going to fancy that our English schooner is a spy and an enemy!"

The waiter's ears were sharp, and he cried at once—

"English! Oh non, monsieur. You are from the little two-mast. It is not you. It is some enemy of the King whose sheep is in the harbour, and great dispatches have come to the Governor that she is to be seized. Ah, there again, monsieur! Anozzer gun from the fort."

It was plain enough to hear, for the windows of the big badly-lit room into which the man had conducted them clattered in their frames, while the dull, heavy report was preceded by a vivid flash as of lightning.

"Ha, ha! You see. The sheep will not get away, for at the forts they are alert and will sink her if she try."

"Oh, but no vessel could try to put out in a storm like this, Rodd," said Uncle Paul.

"No, sare," continued the waiter excitedly; "the boats will go out with the soldiers and take the sheep."

"She is a man-of-war, I suppose?"

"Yes, sare. Not very big, but an enemy; but if she fight they will shoot from all the forts and sink her."

"But how do you know all this?" said Rodd.

"Many soldiers, horsemen, came galloping up to bring dispatches to the Governor. There, sare; you will look from the window," continued the man, using a clean serviette that he took from under his arm to rub the steamy window-panes, for the cold blast of the storm had caused the warm air inside to blur the glass with a thick deposit of vapour. "There, sare," continued the man; "zat is ze sheep."

"Oh, it's too thick to see for the rain."

"Yes, sare; but you see out zare in ze arbour ze two lights."

"Nonsense man!" cried Uncle Paul, half angrily. "That is the English schooner—ours."

"Oh, non, non, non, monsieur! Away to ze *gauche*—ze left hand. Ze sheep with two high, tall mast, that we all see here when she come in ze storm yesterday. We all here with ze officer of ze regiment see you come in through ze storm, and ze enemy sheep, a stranger, come after, and ze officer say she will run you down and sink you in ze harbour!"

"Oh, that one!" cried Rodd excitedly.

"Ah, I see, monsieur knows. You see her lights swing in the wind— two;" and the man held up a couple of fingers.

"Yes, I see where you mean," cried Rodd; "but she has only one light."

"Ah, ha! Monsieur is right. Zare is only one. Ze vind storm has blow out ze uzzer. Look, now zare is no light at all. Ze sheep put im out."

The violence of the rain was now abating, but the wind beat against and shook the window-panes and shrieked as it rushed by. It was evening, and a few minutes before it had been dark as night, but with the cessation of the rain the heavy forms and light rigging of the many vessels gradually became more and more visible, while fresh lights began to come into view, but in every case not moving and swinging about like those in the rigging of the safely moored ships, but gliding about from various directions as if they were in the sterns of boats that had put off from the harbour side.

"Messieurs see?" said the waiter excitedly. "Two boats come now from the fort on ze uzzer side. Look, look! Ze lights shine on ze soldiers' bayonet. They go to take ze sheep."

As the man was speaking the brig that had previously taken up so much of Rodd's attention stood out more clearly. Her riding lights were indeed gone, but there was a peculiar misty look forward, and it was now Rodd's turn to speak excitedly about what he saw.

"Why, uncle," he cried, "she's moving! They've slipped their cable and hoisted the jib!"

"Nonsense, boy! Not in a storm like this."

"I don't care, uncle; she has. Look; you can see her gliding along."

"Impossible!"

"It isn't, uncle. Look, you can see them plainly now; two boats full of men, and they are rowing hard, but getting no nearer to the brig. Here, I want to see; let's get right down to the harbour."

"What, to get wet again?" cried Uncle Paul.

"It doesn't rain now a drop. There's nothing but wind; and look, look; the people are running down now in crowds, and there goes a company of soldiers at the double. Oh, there's going to be something very exciting, uncle, and we must see."

"But the dinner, boy, the dinner! What is this to us?"

"Dinner, uncle!" cried the lad indignantly. "Who's going to stop for dinner when there are boats out yonder full of men going to board and take a ship?"

"Humph! Well," grunted Uncle Paul, "I suppose it would be rather exciting, and we shall be able to see; but I don't know, though. There'll be firing, and who knows which way the bullets will fly?"

"Oh, they; won't hit us, uncle. Come on."

Uncle Paul was rapidly growing as excited as his nephew, while the waiter, if it were possible, was as full of eagerness as both together, and forgetting all his duties and the dinner that he had ordered to be prepared, he cried—

"Ze rain is ovare; you come vith me. I take you out ze back way and down ze little rue which take us to the quay."

That was enough for Rodd, and the next minute they were following the waiter down the big staircase through the great kitchen once more, which was now quite deserted, and out into a walled yard to a back gateway, beyond which, mingling with the roaring of the wind, they could hear the trampling of many feet.

"Zis way; zis way!" the bare-headed waiter kept crying, as he put his serviette to quite a new use, battling with the wind as he folded it diagonally and then turned it into a cover for his head by tying the corners under his chin.

"Here, I say," cried Rodd, as the man kept on at a trot; "I want to get to the harbour."

"Oui, oui; zis way!" panted their guide, who nearly put the visitors out of patience by turning off two or three times at right angles and apparently taking them quite away from where they wished to go. "Zis way! Zis way!" he kept on crying, till at last the trio were alone, others who had been hurrying onward having taken different directions.

Bang went another gun from the fort, a report which seemed to be sent back instantly from the harbour walls, apparently close at hand.

"Yes, zis way; zis way!" shouted the man. "I show you before zey sink ze sheep."

And now he suddenly turned into a narrow alley formed by two towering warehouses so close together that there was not room for two people to walk comfortably abreast; but "Zis way, zis way," shouted the guide, "and you shall be zere upon ze field—*sur le champ, sur le champ*. Ah ha!" he cried directly after, as he suddenly issued from out of the darkness of the alley into the comparative light of a narrow wharf encumbered with casks, just beyond which was the dripping stone edge of the great harbour, and below them boats, barges, and lighters swinging from the great rusty iron rings and mooring posts of the quay.

"Vat you say to dat?" cried the waiter, turning round to face his companions, beginning loudly and ending in a choking whisper, for he had met a gust of wind face to face which stopped him for the moment from taking his breath and forced him to turn his back and make a snatch at the corner of one of the warehouses. "Faith of a good man!" he panted. "The vind blow me inside out! Aha! What did I say?"

"Capital!" panted Rodd, almost as breathlessly as the waiter, at whom upon any other occasion he would have burst out into a roar of laughter, so grotesque was his appearance with the white napkin tied under his chin. "Oh, this is a splendid place!"

"Here, you look out, Pickle," cried Uncle Paul. "Lay hold of something, or we shall be blown right off."

"All right, uncle. Why, if one of those gusts sent us into the harbour we should be drowned."

"Come a little farther this way, then, and if the wind is too much for us, why we shall only go down into this barge."

At that moment, as they looked across and downward towards the mouth of the harbour, there were the flashes of bright light to illumine the gloom of the evening, and the reports of a ragged volley of musketry coming from one of the two boats which they could now make out being rowed hard after the brig, as it glided rapidly along in the direction where the watchers now stood.

Then for a short space it passed out of sight behind a group of four vessels which were safely moored. Then it was out again, and as the lookers-on excitedly watched, they made out dimly that the vessel answered her helm readily and was gliding round in a tack for the other side of the harbour, while the two boats in pursuit altered their direction, the men rowing with all their might, as if to cut the brig off during her next tack.

There was another ragged volley, this time from the second boat; but if they were firing to bring down the steersman, it was in vain, for the brig sailed swiftly on, gaining a little way, as she made for the mouth of the harbour.

This was far distant yet, and her chances of reaching it even in the shelter of the harbour, with such a gale blowing, were almost nil.

"She'll do it, though, uncle," shouted Rodd, with his lips close to Uncle Paul's ear.

"Yes, my boy, I expect she will," was the reply; "but they've got some daring people on board, and I shouldn't like to be the man at the wheel."

"Ah, why don't they shoot? Why don't they shoot?" cried the waiter. "She is an enemy, and—"

The rest of his speech was unheard, for another flash cut the darkness, followed by the thud of a big gun, the shot coming as it were instantly upon the waiter's question; but it had no effect upon the brig, which came nearer and nearer to the pier-like wharves of the harbour, glided round again with the two stay-sails rilling upon the other tack, and then went off once more.

"She'll get away, uncle," cried Rodd excitedly, "and I don't know what they are, but one can't help admiring such a brave deed."

There was another report, this time from quite another direction.

"That must be from the fort up behind the town, Rodd," cried Uncle Paul. "It's too thick to see any splash, but they must be in earnest now, and will not be firing blank charges. It looks as if they mean to sink her if she doesn't stop."

"They've got to hit her first, uncle," cried Rodd excitedly. "Oh, I can't help it, uncle," he continued, with his lips close to his uncle's ear so that the waiter should not catch his words, "but I do hope they won't."

"Well, my boy, I can't help feeling the same, though she's neither enemy nor friend of ours, and we don't know what it all means; for I don't suppose," he said, with a half-laugh, "that she has got Napoleon Bonaparte on board."

Uncle Paul had not taken his nephew's precaution, and as a heavy gust was just dying out, the excited waiter caught a part of his speech.

"Ha, ha!" he cried. "You sink so? You say le Petit Caporal is on board?"

"No, no," cried Uncle Paul; "I didn't say so."

"No, sare; you think so, and zat is it. He has escape himself from ze place where you English shot him up safe, and he come in zat sheep to burn down ze town. But ah–h–h, again they will sink him. Faith of a man, no!" he cried angrily, for there was a shot from another battery, this time nearer the harbour mouth. "They cannot shoot straight."

For onward glided the brig, making tack after tack, and zigzagging her way through the narrow entrance of the harbour, at times partly sheltered by the great pier to windward, then as she glided farther out careening over in spite of the small amount of reefed sail she carried, but all the while so well under control that she kept on gaining and leaving the two boats farther and farther behind.

"Oh, if it were only lighter!" cried Rodd, stamping his foot with vexation. "Why, she'll soon be out of sight."

"Before she gets much farther," said Uncle Paul gravely, "she'll be getting within the light cast by one or other of the harbour lights, and that will be one of her critical times."

"Why critical, uncle?" cried the boy earnestly. "Because the men in the fort will have a better chance of hitting her, I should say."

"Oh, I hope they won't," said Rodd beneath his breath. "Why, it would be horrible, uncle," he half whispered, with his lips close to his uncle's face. "She must have a brave captain to dare all this."

"A very brave captain," said Uncle Paul earnestly. "But you think she'll get away, uncle?"

"No, Rodney," said the doctor, laying his hand with a firm grip upon his nephew's shoulder. "She may pass through the harbour mouth without being hit by the gunners, for it would require a clever marksman to hit so swiftly moving an object, rising and falling as the brig does now that she is getting into the disturbed water near the mouth."

"But suppose she passes through untouched, uncle? What then?"

"What then, boy? She will be out of the shelter given by the end of the jetty. It's too dim now to see, but once or twice I had just a glimpse of the waves washing over the harbour light, and there must be a terrific sea out there. Why, you can hear it plainly even here."

"No, uncle; that's the wind."

"And waves, my boy. Why, trying to sail out there in the teeth of such a gale as this, it will be almost impossible for her to escape. It seems to me to be an act of madness to attempt such an escapade, and cleverly as the brig is handled I think it is doubtful whether she will ever clear the mouth. But if she does she will catch the full force of the storm and —"

"And what, uncle?"

"Be carried away yonder to the east somewhere and cast ashore."

"Oh–h!" sighed Rodd; and it was almost a groan.

Chapter Sixteen
Escape

Three more shots were fired at intervals, as the brig kept making short tack after tack, and with each report the flash appeared to be brighter, indicative of the increasing darkness, while now a pale lambent light seemed to be dawning at times and making the shape of the brig stand out more clearly at intervals, but only to fade away again quickly, while there were moments when the vessel quite disappeared.

"Why is that, uncle?" asked Rodd quickly, as he looked vainly now in search of the flying craft. "Ah, there she is again! I began to think she had gone down. Why is she seen so dimly sometimes?"

"Hidden by the flying spray, I think," said Uncle Paul.

"Oh yes, of course," cried the boy. "Ah, there she is, quite clear now, and still going on nearer and nearer to the harbour mouth. No—now it's getting darker than ever.—There, now she's coming into sight again quite clearly."

"Yes, she's getting out where the harbour lights are full upon her," said Uncle Paul.

As he spoke there were two more reports, almost simultaneous, and Rodd felt a peculiar sense of pain attacking him, for at one moment when the two guns flashed, the brig could be plainly seen; the next, as the boy strained his eyes, all was black darkness, and he caught at his uncle's arm with his hands trembling and an intense longing upon him to speak; but no words would come.

It seemed like some minutes before a word was uttered, and then it was the doctor who spoke.

"I haven't caught sight of the boats lately," he said. "It is evident that they have given up the chase."

"Oh, uncle, uncle," cried Rodd, "I was not thinking about them, but of those poor fellows in the brig. One of those last shots must have hit, and they have gone down."

"Oh no," cried Uncle Paul; "I saw her once again. Just now.—Yes, there she is, tossing wildly in the waves. She must be beyond the mouth of the harbour, and—"

"Yes, I see her! I see her!" cried Rodd wildly. "No, she's gone again; but she was pitching and tossing horribly."

"Yes," said Uncle Paul. "It's going to be hard work for them now, for the waves out there must be tremendous. Well, my boy, it was a daring attempt, and whoever they are let's hope they may escape, but—"

Uncle Paul was silent, and once more the boy uttered a low groan.

Then no one spoke, but all stood straining their eyes to try and catch sight again of the vessel, which had seemed to be pitching wildly in the darkness; but they looked in vain, for all now seemed to be rapidly growing black.

The boy tried to speak, but no words would come, and even the waiter was silent, as he stood trying to catch sight of the vessel once more; but the darkness now was rapidly increasing, and though from time to time they could make out the faint outline of the lights, all seemed to become more dense and obscure, and the boy started violently as their guide suddenly exclaimed—

"It is no use now, sare. I sink she must have gone down."

Silence; but as Uncle Paul pressed his nephew's arm Rodd followed him slowly without a word, while the waiter shook his head and suggested that they should return to the *café*.

The boy gave one glance before stirring, and then uttered a sigh.

"Come, my boy," said his uncle; "perhaps there is no occasion to despair. It is quite evident that the captain of the brig knows what he is about, and may escape."

Rodd followed his uncle without a word, the waiter going on before them to show the devious ways along by the harbour and the old town.

As they drew near the yard Rodd felt a sense of hesitation. "I think I would rather get back on board the schooner, uncle," he said.

"Oh, but we couldn't do that, my boy," cried Uncle Paul. "I gave an order for dinner to be prepared."

"Yes, uncle, but I don't feel as if I could eat anything now."

"Why?"

"It seemed so horrible watching that vessel trying to escape under fire."

"It was evidently not hit, my boy."

"But it was going right out into the face of this storm, and even you thought she'd be driven ashore."

"Yes; perhaps I have been thinking the worst; but the brig's captain is evidently a clever sailor and knows what he's about. It is rather jumping at conclusions to consider that he will let his vessel be wrecked. Yes, it was nervous work watching a vessel like that; but there, we must hope for the best, and possibly there is no reason to despond. Whoever the brig belonged to had good reason for getting away, and they have succeeded in that. There, come along; let's have our dinner, and think no more about it. But hallo! What's the matter here?"

Uncle Paul's remark was caused by a loud angry voice scolding in French at the waiter who had just led them to the yard door, and it was evident that the man was in difficulties for absenting himself from his duties after giving the order that the visitors' dinner should be prepared.

"But I have been in attendance upon the gentlemen," he protested, with not much truth in his utterance. "I had to take them down to the side of the harbour to see the firing at the spy. Is everything ready? Because the gentlemen are anxious for their dinner."

Uncle Paul nudged his nephew, glad of the opportunity to change the bearing of the boy's thoughts, and shortly after the good meal prepared in the snug, warm room diverted Rodd's mind from the roaring of the storm, which was still beating round the great hotel; and they had just finished and were talking about going outside to see what the weather was like, when a very familiar gruff voice saluted their ears, as the waiter showed Captain Chubb into the room.

"Oh, here you are," he grunted. "Come ashore to look after you. 'Fraid you were lost."

"We are very glad to see you," said Uncle Paul. "Sit down. We thought it was not safe to try and get aboard."

"Well, it aren't very," said the skipper; "but we come in the boat to make sure you weren't both drowned, and if you'll risk it I think I can get you round by keeping under the lee of two or three vessels."

"What do you say, Rodd?" asked Uncle Paul. "Shall we risk it?"

"Oh, I don't think that there'll be much risk, uncle, if Captain Chubb considers it safe. I don't mind going with him."

The skipper gave the boy a nod and looked pleased; then nodding at Uncle Paul he said quietly —

"As we were ashore I told the men to get a few stores down to the boat, and that I'd meet them here. I dare say Joe Cross will be an hour, and by that time it will have lulled a bit, or else be a deal worse, and we'll see."

It took very little persuasion to make the skipper partake of some of the hotel fare, and naturally enough the conversation turned upon the incident that had lately taken place.

"Yes," said Captain Chubb, "the skipper of that craft has got some stuff in him, and he knew how to navigate his boat. I could have done it if I'd been obliged, but I should have wanted a deal of shoving before I hoisted sail. Storm was bad enough, and no room to tack; but what I shouldn't have liked was being fired at by two boats' crews and three or four forts. I know what being fired at is, young squire," continued the captain, giving Rodd a very peculiar look out of one eye, after closing the other, "and you may take my word for it it aren't nice."

"What, have you been out in a man-of-war?" asked Rodd eagerly.

"Nay, my lad, but several of our fellows have, and if you ask them, they can tell you what it's like too."

"Then you never were fired at?" said Rodd questioningly.

"Who says I warn't? I tell you I was, though it wasn't by forts. It was a Revenue cutter got trying to hit me."

"What, smuggling?" cried Rodd.

"Nay! Smuggling, indeed! It was her skipper—Lieutenant somebody or another—I forget his name—say Smith. He made a blunder, same as I did in taking you and the doctor here for slavers."

"Oh!" cried Rodd, laughing.

"Ah, it warn't anything to laugh at, my lad, with round shot coming a-splashing right across your bows. Certainly it was in a fog, and my craft didn't get hit, but more than once the balls came pretty near, and I remember thinking whether if the cutter did sink us we should all be able to swim ashore, and I come to the conclusion that we couldn't in our boots, for it was about nine miles."

"I should think not," replied Rodd dryly. "But, Captain Chubb—about that brig; do you think they'd get right away to sea?"

"I shouldn't think they'd try to, my lad."

"They seemed to be trying to."

"Not they. Her skipper, as soon as he got outside the harbour, would try to creep under the lee of the high ground somewhere out west. Whether he'd do it or not is quite another thing. Let's hope he did, for I don't care about hearing that good men and true have been drowned in a storm, even if they are French. I am not like your uncle here."

"Come, I say, Captain Chubb," cried the doctor indignantly, "how dare you say that! Surely a thinking man can have a feeling of antipathy against Napoleon Bonaparte and all his works without being accused of liking to see brave Frenchmen drowned."

"Beg pardon, sir. I suppose you are right," granted the skipper; "but I should like to hear that that there smart brig got safe away."

"Well, I hope so too," said Uncle Paul shortly, and with a look in his countenance that made Rodd think about some words a friend had once said about a red rag to a bull. "But I suppose you don't believe that vessel had some emissaries of Napoleon on board, come to set fire to the port of Havre?"

"Nay," said the skipper, drawing out the negative very deliberately. "Don't see any likelihood of their doing such a thing. What for? Suppose they did get it alight, that wouldn't bring Bony back. Nay, his game's about up now, and there will be quiet again over here for a bit, though I wouldn't venture to say for how long. Keeping quiet isn't in a Frenchman's nature."

"But there was evidently something very special about the vessel, or else the French Government wouldn't have sent orders for her to be seized."

"French Government did?"

"Yes, I believe so," replied Uncle Paul. "We saw the officer and his men come riding in with the dispatch."

"Nay. Order for the Revenue to put men on board."

"Oh no," replied Uncle Paul. "From what we saw and what we heard, it was something much more important than that. Why, hang it, captain, they wouldn't have turned out the garrison and manned all the forts to stop the progress of a smuggler, would they?"

"We wouldn't at Plymouth, sir; but there's no knowing what Frenchmen will do. But there, I give in. It must have been something stronger than that, and I am beginning to think that squire here's right, and that yon vessel, the—the—the—"

"*Jeanne d'Arc*" cried Rodd.

"Right," snorted the skipper. "She was something of a privateer, on mischief bent, and I shouldn't be a bit surprised if we was to hear something more about her. I don't know, though; if the storm blows itself out before morning we shan't lie long here in harbour, but make away south as fast as I can make the schooner bowl along."

"Then you think the weather will hold up soon?" said Rodd.

"Nay, I am not going to think, squire; I'll wait until I can be sure. Anyhow, I won't fill my pipe till we get aboard."

"Then you mean to try soon?" cried Rodd eagerly.

"Why not?" replied the skipper gruffly. "Look yonder; what do you say to that?"

"That" was the presence of Joe Cross, who was being ushered into the dining-saloon by the waiter, to announce that the wind had sunk a bit and only came in squalls, between two of which he thought he could easily run the boat alongside of the schooner.

And he did—while the next morning broke almost absolutely calm.

Chapter Seventeen
A Question of Fear

It was as if all the bad weather had been left behind, for after a little snatch or two, as Joe Cross called them, the cruise down south had been glorious.

The bluff, good-humoured sailor explained to Rodd what he meant by a snatch, something after this fashion.

"You see, sir, after we started from Havre the weather seemed to be a bit sorry for itself for being so dirty, and you know how we bowled along down south till the wind got into a tantrum again—got out of bed the wrong way, as you may say, and then everything was wrong. We were getting into the Bay, you see, where it comes quite natural to lay all that day. In the Bay of Biscay O! Then Nature got all out of sorts again. It seemed as if she was waxy to let us have it so comfortable, and made a snatch to drag us back again. But the old man was one too many for her, and kept on for them two bad days, when we sailed out of her reach and everything was fine."

"Yes, Joe, it was fine. All that coast of Spain and Portugal was lovely."

"Yes, sir, and you got grumbling 'cause your uncle wouldn't give orders for us to let go the anchor for you to go fishing."

"Well, see how grand it was, and how calm the sea used to get of an evening before we put in to Gibraltar."

"And then you weren't half satisfied, sir. You'll excuse me, Mr Rodd, sir, but you do make me laugh;" and to the boy's great annoyance the man half turned from him, leaned over the taffrail, laughed till his sides shook, and then pulling himself up suddenly wiped his eyes. "I am very sorry, sir," he said.

"Doesn't seem like it," cried Rodd warmly, as he made as if to go away.

It was one evening when the calm sea as it heaved seemed in places to glint forth all the glorious colours of a beautiful pearl shell, and the east wind was of a different complexion to that familiar to an English lad, for it was soft, balmy and sweet, suggestive of its having been blowing gently for miles and miles over beds of flowers.

"Oh, don't go away in a tiff, Mr Rodd, sir. It was only me, and you know what I am. I didn't mean no offence."

"Well, it was offensive," said Rodd. "How would you like to be laughed at?"

"Me, sir?" cried the man merrily. "Me who has been knocking about the sea nearly all my life, first in a west-country fishing-boat, and then in a King's ship, and been in action! Like being laughed at! Why, bless your heart, sir, it suits me down to the deck. I like it. Deal better than having the old man dropping on to me about something being wrong aloft."

"Well, I don't see that there was anything to laugh at," cried Rodd, softening down a little, for somehow the liking he had felt for the sturdy-looking sailor ever since he had come on board had gone on increasing, and Rodd affected Joe's society more than that of any one in the ship. At least he said so to Uncle Paul, who shook his head and with a grim smile joined issue.

"No, Pickle," he cried, "I won't have that. You seem to make better friends with the cook than with anybody."

"Oh, uncle," replied the boy, "you always do tease me about my appetite."

"Never mind, Pickle," said Uncle Paul good-humouredly. "Go on eating, and grow."

But to return to the conversation by the taffrail.

"No, sir," said Joe Cross, "of course you don't, sir. It'd be contrairy to nature if you did. We chaps can't see ourselves. There's the old Bun. He's been offended over and over again because people told him he was so fat. He can't see it, sir."

"Oh, he must," cried Rodd, laughing.

"There aren't no must in it, sir. He can't. He might find it out perhaps if he tried to get into a pair of boy's trousers—yours, for instance; but then that aren't likely, because you won't give him the chance, and what's more, he wouldn't want to. You try him some day about being too fat, and you see if he don't stare at you."

"He will, Joe, when I'm so rude to him. But come now, you are shuffling. Why is it that you laugh at me?"

"Well, sir, because I like you, for one thing, and another is because you are such an unreasonable chap."

"I? Unreasonable?" cried Rodd hotly. "That I'm sure I'm not!"

"Why, sir, wasn't you put out because your uncle and the old man wouldn't sail right into the Mediterranean Sea?"

"Well, there was nothing unreasonable in that. I am sure it would have been very interesting."

"Not it, sir. I've been there over and over again, and it always seemed to me just like any other sea, only a bit rougher sometimes, and it aren't got hardly any tide. You wait till we get a little further on, and you'll find plenty to make you open you eyes wider than ever you opened them before. I don't know a finer place for seeing wonders of the deep than along where we are going, as you say we are to, right along the West Coast of Afriky. Why, you might begin fishing and dredging directly after we had put in at Mogador, where the fish are wonderful, and you can't drop in a line without hauling something out."

"That's good," cried Rodd eagerly; "but I am afraid uncle won't let us have much time for ordinary fishing. He will be more on the look-out for curiosities."

"Ah, well, there's plenty of them too, sir—all sorts, and the farther you gets into warmer water the more there are."

"What sort?" asked Rodd.

"All sorts, and the nearer you are to land the more you get. Then I suppose some time we shall come upon that there Sargassey Sea."

"Where's that?" asked Rodd.

"Right away down south, sir. Let's see, if I remember right we falls in with that soon after you pass the islands."

"What islands?"

"Let's see; I ought to know, sir. The fust that comes near Europe is the Azores; then farther south there's that there island where all the sick people goes, Madeiry; then there's the Canaries, where the birds come from; only they aren't all yaller like people keeps in their cages. Most I seed there was green, and put me in mind of them little chaps as we have at home with the yaller heads—you know, sir; them as cries, 'A little bit of bread and no cheese.' And you see them up country, a-twittering among the hedges."

"Yes, I know," said Rodd sharply; "but what about the Sargassey Sea?"

"Ah! I'm thinking it was after that we come to that sea, only I aren't quite sure, sir. But if I recollect right, they say it shifts about according to what sort of weather we have."

"Well, so does every sea," cried Rodd, "when the waves are running high."

"Ah, but they don't run high here, sir. You see, the Sargassey Sea aren't like other seas, and I suppose it's only part of the Atlantic after all. It's all smooth like because as far as you can see it's all like one great bed of floating seaweed, so thick that you can hardly sail through it at times, and if you go out into it in a boat it's as much as you can do to dip your oars."

"Have you been out amongst it then?" asked Rodd.

"Yes, sir, more'n once. It was when I was in the *Prince George* off the West Coast of Africa, and we had got a surgeon on board there, and him and our second lieutenant had both got it badly."

"What, West African fever?" cried Rodd.

"No, no, sir; same as your uncle's got—looking after strange things as lives in the sea. I was one of the crew of the second cutter then, and in the beautiful calm weather we used to take the doctor and the second luff out in this Sargassey Sea, which used to look sometimes as if we were floating about in green fields."

"Oh, you mean the Sargasso Sea!" cried Rodd. "Nay, I don't, sir; I means the Sargassey Sea."

"Well, that's the same thing, only you spell it differently," cried Rodd.

"Oh no, sir; that I don't. That's a thing as I never pretended to do. I can take my spell at the pump or at any other job; but what you call spelling was never in my way."

"But you mean the same thing," cried Rodd. "It isn't Sar-gass-ey; it's Sar-gass-o."

"Ho! Sar-gass-ho, is it, sir?"

"Yes, of course."

"All right, sir; I'm willing. But my one was all alive with little things, little fish and slugs and snails of all kinds of rum sorts; and our second luff used to make us haul in great lengths of the seaweed as was floating about, and then help him to pick 'em out into bottles till they were quite full, and looking just as if they was pickles same as you see in the grocers' shops in Plymouth town."

"Well, the same as you saw uncle and me do that day during the calm?"

"Yes, sir, just like that, only yours as you did were small shop and ours was like big warehouse, though I don't think our doctor did much good with them, because so many of them used to go bad, and our cook and his mate used to have to throw no end away and wash the bottles."

"Ah, ours won't go bad," said Rodd confidently. "My uncle will preserve them differently to that."

"Oh, yes, I suppose so, sir. You see, we've all come out this time ready for the job; our officers on the *Prince George* only did their bit just for a day or two's holiday like, and our job was to look after the mounseers' cruisers, not to catch tittlebats and winkles, and it wasn't so very long after that we was at it hammer and tongs with a big French frigate, making work for the doctor of a precious different kind, and for our ship's carpenters too. Different sort of nat'ral history that was, sir, I can tell you, for we lost nineteen of our men and had a lot wounded; but we took the frigate, and carried her safe into Portsmouth Harbour."

"Ah!" cried Rodd softly, as his eyes flashed at the thoughts of the deeds of naval daring carried out by our men-of-war. "I wish I'd been there!"

"You do, sir?" said Joe. "Mean it?"

"Mean it? Of course! There, don't look at me like that. I wasn't thinking of being a man, but a reefer—one of those middies that we used to see at Plymouth."

"Ah, it's all very fine, sir," said Joe, shaking his head, "and it sounds very nice about firing broadsides and then getting orders to board when the two big men-of-war get the grappling-irons on board and you have to follow your officers, scrambling with your cutlass in your hand out of the chains from your ship into the enemy's; and all the time there's the roaring of the guns and the popping away of the marines up in the tops, and the men cheering as your officers lead them on. It's a very different thing, sir, to what you think, and so I can tell you."

"Why, Joe," cried Rodd, almost maliciously, "you talk as if you felt afraid!"

"Afraid, sir?" said the man, quietly and thoughtfully. "No, sir. No, sir; I never felt afraid, and I never knowed one of my messmates as said he was."

"Oh no, of course they wouldn't say so," cried Rodd, laughing.

"No, sir, that's right. But I aren't bragging, sir. I've been in several engagements like that, and my messmates always seemed to feel just as I did. You see, they'd got it to do, sir, and we always felt that it was only mounseers that we'd got to beat and captur' their ship; and then as soon as we had begun, whether we was crews of guns, stripped and firing away, or answering the orders to board, why, then we never had time to feel afraid."

"What, not when you saw your messmates shot down beside you?" cried Rodd.

"My word, no, sir!" cried Joe, laughing. "We none of us felt afraid then; it only made us feel wild and want to sarve the other side out. No, sir," continued the bluff fallow, in a quiet matter-of-fact way, and his voice utterly free of vaunt, "whether it's a sea-fight or things are going wrong in a storm, we sailor fellows are always too busy to feel afraid. You see, I think, sir, it has something to do with the drill and discipline, as they calls it, training the lads all to work together. You see, it makes them feel so strong."

"I can't say I do see," said Rodd.

"No, sir, because you haven't been drilled; but it's like this 'ere. One man's one man, and a hundred men's a hundred men—no, stop; that aren't quite what I mean. It aren't in my way, Mr Rodd, sir; I never was a beggar to argue. The fat Bun can easily beat me at that. This 'ere's what I mean. One man's one man, and a hundred men's a hundred one men. That's if they aren't drilled and trained like sailors or soldiers; but if they are trained, you see each one man feels as if he has got a hundred men with him all working together, and con-se-quently, sir, every chap aboard feels as if he's as strong as a hundred men. Now don't you see, sir?"

"Well, yes," said Rodd quietly; "I think I begin to see what you mean."

"Why, of course you do, sir. Say it's heaving a boat aboard, and it takes twenty men to do it. Why, if they go and try one at a time, where are you? But if you all go and take hold together, and your officer says to you, 'Now, my lads, with a will, all together! Heave ho!' why then, up she comes. Well now, I do call that rum! Look at that, sir. If here aren't the old man, just as if he had heard what we was talking about, passing the word for gun drill, or else a bit of knicketty knock with the cutlasses and pikes!"

Chapter Eighteen
A Strange Visitor

Upon hearing Joe Cross's announcement Rodd eagerly turned, to find his uncle just coming on deck to take his evening walk after a busy day with his specimens that he had dragged and trawled from the calm sea.

The captain had just given orders to the mate to summon all hands on deck, and one of the first proceedings was to call the men to attention, the next to send them to the small-arms chest, from which each returned with cutlass buckled on and carrying a boarding pike, which were placed in a rack round the mainmast.

Rodd took his position just opposite as the men fell into line; Uncle Paul seated himself as far off as he could get, in a deck-chair, where he sat and frowned; and then Captain Chubb diligently put his men through all the evolutions of cutlass drill over and over again, till he was satisfied, when he bade them fall out for a few minutes to rid themselves of their cutlasses.

In the interval Rodd went up to where his uncle was seated.

"I say, uncle," he said, "how the men have improved!" Uncle Paul grunted, and just then Captain Chubb strolled up.

"Well, sir," he said, "we shall soon have a crew now as smart as a man-of-war's."

"So I see," grumbled Uncle Paul; "and when you have got them perfect what are you going to do with them?"

"Ah, that remains to be seen, sir. There's nothing like being prepared."

"Better let the men rest after all they have done to-day. What with their deck cleaning and the work they have done for me, they don't want setting to play at soldiers."

"Playing at soldiers, eh, sir? I call it playing at sailors. No use to lock the stable-door after the steed's stolen. My lads may never be called upon to fight, but if by bad luck we are, I should like them to be able to use their fighting tools like men."

"Oh, it isn't likely," said Uncle Paul, "in a peaceful voyage like ours."

"Most unlikely things are those that happen first," growled the captain.

"But you worry the men with too much work, and I want them to be fresh and ready for me to-morrow morning. I don't want the poor fellows to be discontented."

"Discontented, sir!" cried the skipper hotly. "I should like to see them look discontented! But not they! They like it. Puts them in mind of their old fighting days. Now you shall see them go through their drill with the boarding pikes, and see how smart I have made them. I say they like it, sir; and I know."

"Then I suppose," said Uncle Paul, "you will set them to work lumbering about that great gun, pretending to load and fire it. Why, who in the world do you expect we are going to encounter out here on the high seas? We are not at war with the French."

"Captain Chubb thinks we may meet with the privateer," said Rodd merrily.

"Don't you make rude remarks, Rodney!" cried Uncle Paul angrily. "Well, there, captain, I suppose you will have your own way, but it seems to me great waste of time."

"Oh no, sir," said the skipper good-humouredly. "I suppose you mean to run in and up some of those rivers we shall pass by and by?"

"Most certainly," cried the doctor.

"Well, and what then, sir? You are going right out of civilisation there, and among black tribes and warlike people who are ready for anything, from attacking another tribe and bringing the prisoners down the river to sell for slaves, up to taking a fancy to any smart craft they can master, and then stripping her and burning her to the water's edge."

"And what becomes of the crews?" cried Rodd sharply.

"Well, Mr Rodd, that's rather a hard question to answer. If ever you go to Liverpool or Bristol and you get asking questions amongst the merchants there, you will find they have got some queer tales to tell. Sorry you don't like my plans, Dr Robson, but even if we never get into trouble we shall be none the worse for being prepared."

"Oh, I am not going to complain, Captain Chubb. Drill away as much as you like. You say the men like it, and it satisfies you. Then my boy Rodd, here, nothing will please him better than letting him have a canister of gunpowder to play with and pop off that gun. So I am in a minority, and I will give in. There, you'd better take Rodd and drill him too."

"I'll take you at your word, sir," said Captain Chubb, laughing, and making Rodd start with eagerness. "Fall in, my lads. Pikes."

The drilling went on till it was beginning to grow dusk, and then pikes were laid aside and orders given for the gun crew to take their places, Rodd closing up quickly in anticipation of something coming off.

"Rather warm weather, Mr Rodd, sir," whispered Joe Cross, as, aided by another of the crew, he proceeded to cast loose the lashings and strip the tarpaulin off the long gun. "If it warn't for the showers this 'ere pocket pistol might very well do without her greatcoat. I say, sir, didn't I hear your uncle tell the old man that you were to have a canister of powder just to fire her off once or twice?"

"Yes, Joe, but I think it was only to tease me."

"You ask the skipper to let you have one. It's all very well to go on ramming and sponging and making believe to load, but it is like having your grog served out in an empty glass. And if the old man grunts and shakes his head and grumbles about waste of ammunition, you just ask him if he'd mind you bringing one of your canisters of powder as you and your uncle's got for your double guns. He might let you then, if your old man don't mind. We could divide it into about four goes as wouldn't make much noise, and there'd be some sense in it. There would be something to ram down; and the lads would like it."

"But the captain wouldn't let you fire away any cannon balls, Joe."

"Well, no, sir, I suppose not, unless we got the cook up with a pudding-bag to hold it over the muzzle and catch them again."

"Wouldn't a straw hat be better, Joe?" said Rodd dryly.

"Well, now you talk of it, sir," replied the man, grinning, "I never thought of that. Perhaps it would if one of us held it lightly in his hand and eased off a good deal when we fired. If you didn't do that of course the ball might go right through."

"Well, I'll ask the captain, Joe."

"Yes, sir; do, sir. As I said afore, it would please the lads, and do good too, for it would clean the gun's teeth, sweep away all the scales and rust."

"Scales and rust!" cried Rodd. "Why, it isn't an iron gun; it's brass."

"Why, so it is, Master Rodd, sir. Why, only fancy me not thinking of that! But here he comes. Try it on, sir."

"Shall I, Joe?"

"Yes, do, sir; as I said, it would please the lads. They're just like a lot of school-boys when they gets a chance of a change."

"And Joe Cross doesn't care a bit," said Rodd.

The man gave the speaker a comical look as he replied—

"Well, sir, you see, I was a boy once, and I was born with a lot of human natur' in me, and I never got rid of it, and I am afraid I never shall. There, go on, sir," whispered Joe. "Pitch it into him at once."

Rodd moved towards the skipper as he came up, and as the latter looked at him inquiringly he began—

"You heard what my uncle said, captain?"

"What about, my lad?"

"Letting me have some powder to play with."

"Ay, ay! But you don't want that?"

"Oh, I don't know. I wish you would have a canister and let the men load the gun properly."

"Eh?"

"It would be like practice."

"Well, that's true. But it would be only waste of powder; and I'm not going to waste any of the cannon balls."

"No, I don't want you to do that."

"Besides, I don't want to use either of the powder-bags, and they're made for a regular charge."

"Beg pardon, sir," cried Cross. "Might make small charges up with a snuff of powder wrapped up in paper; and then I could prick and prime."

"Um–m–m!" the captain growled, and frowned, while the gun crew stood with parted lips, looking as eager as so many boys on the Fifth of November. Then the captain grunted.

"There, Mr Rodd," he said, "it will be a bit of practice for the lads, and it won't please you, of course. You don't want to see the gun really fired?"

"Oh, I have seen salutes fired, at Plymouth."

"Ah, so you have, of course, my lad. But those are bangs, and this would be a bit of a whiff."

"That doesn't matter," said Rodd. "It will be real, and not pretending to fire."

"Very well," said the captain, smiling grimly. "Maybe you'd like to fire?"

"Yes, I should," cried Rodd. "No; let Joe Cross and the other men do that. I'll stand aside."

There was a little more discussion, quite in opposition to ordinary drill, while the skipper went below and then returned with a pound gunpowder canister painted red.

"I say, look here, Chubb," cried the doctor. "Shall I have to move?"

"Oh no, sir; we shan't shoot you," replied the skipper grimly. "You'll be safe enough, unless the long gun bursts. But she's too new and strong for that. Here you are, Cross. Make that into four charges."

The speaker was in the act of passing the canister to the man, when the look-out man from forward suddenly shouted—

"Sail ho!"

"Where away?" cried the captain. "About five points off the starboard bow, sir. Leastwise, sir, it aren't a sail. It's a big boat, bottom upwards and just awash."

"Stop a minute," cried Rodd. "I'll fetch our glass."

"Bring mine too, my lad," cried the captain, and Rodd raised his hand in token of his having heard the order, as he dashed to the cabin hatch, to return directly after and find that his uncle was forward along with the skipper scanning the object about a quarter of a mile away.

"Catch hold, uncle," cried Rodd, and he held out the telescope with one hand, and the captain's big mahogany tubed spy-glass, decorated with coloured flags, with the other.

"No, focus it and use it yourself, boy. I'll have a look afterwards."

Rodd raised the glass at once to his eye, but by this time the skipper had caught the object, and began to growl remarks.

"Capsized long-boat," he muttered. "No, it's a fish—sick whale, I think. But I don't know. It's moving pretty well through the water. What do you make of it, my lad?"

"It's very big and long," cried Rodd excitedly, "and it may be part of a whale's back just showing above the water. I don't know, though. I never saw a whale swimming before. Here, I know! I think it's five or six porpoises swimming one after the other and close together."

"Nay!" growled the captain. "It's something—"

"It's gone!" shouted Rodd. "Oh, uncle, I wish you'd seen it. It seemed to sink down out of sight all at once."

"'Cause it didn't like to be looked at, sir," whispered Joe Cross. "But look out, sir," he cried eagerly. "There it is again, a little farther off."

"Have a look, doctor," said the skipper, passing the glass to Uncle Paul.

"Is it a whale?" asked the doctor.

"Nay, that's no whale, sir," replied the captain. "A whale don't go under water like that when she sounds. Down goes her head, and she throws her flukes up in the air."

"Then what is it?" cried Uncle Paul, with the glass now glued to his eye. "It's something very big. Yes, I can see plainly now—blackish-grey, and shiny as if slimy. It seems to undulate, for one minute the back seems to be only a few feet long, then three or four parts are above the surface at once, as if the creature were twenty or thirty feet long."

"Yes, sir; I can see that with the naked eye.—Nay, nay, sir; you keep the glass. It's more in your way than mine. Seems to me as if we have hit a curiosity for you, only it's rather too big to tackle."

"I think it's a great snake," cried Rodd excitedly. "I mean, a very large eel, swimming on the top, and he keeps throwing his head about as if he were feeding in the middle of a shoal of fish."

"Yes, it is something like that, Rodd," said the doctor; "but no conger eel could be as large as that, and really I don't know."

"Sea-sarpint, sir," whispered Joe Cross to Rodd, and looking longingly at the glass the while.

"Nonsense!" cried Rodd. "Here, you have a look, Joe," and he passed the glass to the sailor. "Now then," he said, "what do you make of it?"

"I say sea-sarpint, sir." The captain growled more deeply than ever.

"Sea-sarpint!" he said, in a tone of disgust. "There, hold your tongue, my lad. You're a naturalist, doctor; you haven't got no sea-sarpints in your books, have you?"

"No," replied the doctor, handing the glass to one of the men, as he caught his longing eye. "But this must be a very curious fish, and it is evidently feeding. I wish it were coming this way, so that we could have a better view."

Joe Cross lowered the boy's glass and looked questioningly at Rodd, giving at the same time a wag of his head in the direction of the nearest man.

"Yes, let him have a look," said Rodd hoarsely, and as the glass was passed the boy caught the sailor by the sleeve, and whispered, making Joe start and gaze at him inquiringly, before stooping down and giving his thigh a slap with his right hand.

"Ay, ay, sir!" he whispered. "Ask the skipper."

"Ask the *captain* what?" said the skipper sharply.

"I have been thinking, Captain Chubb," panted Rodd. "Have the long gun loaded with a ball, and let the men try and hit that thing. 'Tisn't above a quarter of a mile away."

"Eh? Have a shot at it, my lad?" said the captain, staring, and then shading his eyes to watch the object that was gliding along, making the water ripple strangely, while all around it was in violent ebullition, betokening that a large shoal of fish was feeding there. "Well, I don't know. What do you say, doctor?" continued the speaker. "I don't say that the lads could hit it, but they might."

"Certainly," said the doctor eagerly. "Try."

There was no occasion to give orders for a ball to be fetched up. Joe Cross and Rodd had darted off together, plunged down the hatchway, and were back again in an incredibly short space of time, the sailor carrying the ball, while Rodd had snatched up three or four big sheets of paper from off one of the laboratory lockers, and then as rapidly as possible a good charge of powder was emptied into one of the sheets, the gun's crew fell into place and rammed the charge home in the most business-like manner, the ball followed, Joe Cross thrust the pricker down into the touch-hole and primed, while another of the men ran with a piece of slow match to the cook's galley, where the water was being boiled for tea.

Everything was done skilfully and with speed, while all on deck were in a state of profound excitement and dread lest the great creature should disappear from sight and rob the spectators of their looked-for sport.

"Oh, do be quick!" cried Rodd.

"Yah–h–h!" came in a groan, for as the words left the boy's lips there was a violent ebullition where the great serpent or whatever it was had been playing, the beautiful ripple of the shoal of fish died out, and in the fast-fading light of the evening the sea all around lay gleaming and grey, as it gently heaved, with no other movement now.

"Oh, what a pity we were so long," said Rodd dismally. "I believe we should have hit it. I am disappointed!"

"Well, so am I, if you come to that, Rodd, my boy," said the doctor, "though I don't think the men could have made a successful shot. You see, it requires a great deal of practice to hit an object like that with a big gun."

"Whatever it was," growled the captain, "it was feeding on that shoal of fish, and when it made that dash it scared the lot away. There it is again! You, Joe Cross, take a good long careful sight. Don't hurry. Slow and sure. My word, you ought to hit that, my lad! It's a big 'un and no mistake. Silence there! Every man in his place. Slew the muzzle round a little more. Ready, Cross?"

"No, sir; want to lower a little;" and as he spoke the sailor thrust in one of the wedges a trifle. "That's about got it, sir."

"Looks as if he'd come to stay, doctor," said the captain excitedly, as he bent down to glance along over the gun's two sights, for the shoal of fish had risen once more, turning the beautiful smooth sea into a diaper-like pattern, while the strange object seemed as far as they could make out to be making a snatching dart here and another there, seeming to be like some whale-like creature with a long neck.

"Now she's steady, sir," whispered Joe Cross huskily, after taking the captain's place for another sight. "It's as near as I can get, sir. If you'll give me the word."

As he spoke the sailor drew back slightly, the captain cried "Fire!" and with a heavy, sharp crack a puff of white smoke darted from the muzzle and began to expand forward like a grey balloon, obscuring everything from the sight of the lookers-on for about a minute, before it rose clear, and then the darkening sea was all grey once more.

Chapter Nineteen
Chubb re Sea-Serpents

"Hah! Very disappointing—very," said the doctor.

"Yes, it's gone, I suppose, sir. One couldn't see where the shot hit for smoke, but I expect it turned up the water and scared the thing away. Well, it's best as it is. A great thing like that might have grown very dangerous if it had been hit."

"Oh, we don't know that," cried the doctor. "Well, I suppose we can do nothing more," he continued, as, following his nephew's example, he strained his eyes over the darkening plain.

"No," said the captain. "Cover up that gun, my lads, and break off. You, Cross, take charge of the gun, and well sponge her out. You others, pikes; fall in. Now then, right face. March!"

"I'm disappointed," said the doctor, as the men were marched off. "I should have liked to have had a closer examination of that creature. Well, captain, what next?"

"Tea," said the skipper bluntly.

The tropics were very near, and the night began to come on rapidly, so that the tea meal was partaken of by the light of the swinging lamp. But before it was over the moon rose above the sea very bright and silvery, and getting rapidly near the full, while later on as it rose higher it was nearly as light as day.

Rodd was anxious to get on deck again, to see if by any possibility the weird-looking object that they had seen that evening might rise to the surface; but anxious as he was to join the sailors and question them as to whether they had seen anything more, the conversation between his uncle and the skipper kept him below, where he listened to their different expressed opinions.

At last, though, he went on deck, and found all the men grouped together forward, and whispering to themselves about the visitor they had seen.

One man said it was a sign, and another grunted, while a third turned to Joe Cross to ask his opinion.

It was the stout heavy member of the crew who went by the name of the Bun, and seeming the most impressed of the whole crew he asked Joe Cross as above.

"Yes," said Cross slowly, "you are quite right, Ikey Gregg. It's a sign."

"What's a sign?" asked Rodd, coming up.

"The—the—Bun—Ikey Gregg says it is a sign, sir, that we see that big squirming wormy thing, and I says he's quite right, sir. It is a sign."

"Why, what can it be a sign of, Joe?"

"Sea's calm, sir, and that brings all the shoals of young fish up to the top to feed, and that there thing that feeds on them come up to the top to get a regular tuck out."

"Oh, that won't do," said Gregg the fat. "Things like that only come up to the top at particular times, and you mark my words, it means a storm."

As the man finished, he turned his eyes to right and left, scanning the beautiful silvery water before him, and then uttering a loud yell, he dashed by his companions, made for the forecastle hatch, and without troubling himself about the steps, leaped right down.

"What's the matter with Ikey?" said one of the men. "Showing us how he can jump?"

"Nonsense!" said Rodd. "It was as if he had been scared by something. He looked quite wild."

The boy walked close up to the rail and looked over, to see that the whole of the water right away from the bows was apparently ablaze with fire; but for a time he could make out nothing else, in spite of its crystal clearness and the way in which in addition it was laced and latticed as it were by the rays of the moon.

Seeing nothing for the moment likely to have alarmed the sailor, he was about to turn off, but only to start the next minute, and stand clinging with both hands to the rail, for some fifteen or twenty yards away the erst calm, heaving sea began to be violently agitated, running as it were with the swiftness of a mill-stream; and then something dull and glistening and shining like a halo appeared just beneath the surface, rising till it was quite clear of the water, and passing the schooner in one broad pale streak.

He was too much astonished to be startled, and for a few moments the only idea that he could form was that a good-sized vessel had careened over on to its side and was swiftly gliding along almost level with the water.

Then all at once something of the same moonlit glistening tint, but long and sinuous, slowly rose up eight or ten feet above the sea; then higher and higher till it was double that altitude, and in his excitement and agitation he realised that it was ended or begun by a snake-like head something after the fashion of that of a huge conger, the eyes being many inches across and dull and heavy after the fashion seen in a deep-sea fish.

One moment he thought it eel-like, the next that it was some serpent, while to his utter astonishment what he took to be its neck rose higher in a graceful swan-like shape, beautiful in curve as it was horrible in its gleaming, pallid, slimy aspect. One of the great eyes seemed turned to him with a peculiar glare, while as he fixed his own upon it as if unable to resist the attraction, he made out that from behind the curve the elongated body of the creature rose just above the surface, carrying out the semblance on a great scale to some swan-like half-fishy creature, and then with a quick rush as if the water were being hurled from it by enormously powerful fin-like paddles, the strange fish, reptile, or whatever it was, had passed on into the hazy moonlit night and was gone.

"Hullo here! Anything the matter, Rodd?" cried the familiar voice of Dr Robson, as he came quickly forward, followed by the skipper. "Where is it?"

"Where is it, uncle?" faltered the boy.

"Yes; that man Cross came running down to us in the cabin to say that they had seen the sea-serpent again."

Rodd slowly raised one hand from the rail to which he had been holding, and pointed outward over the sea.

"Well," said Uncle Paul, "what are you pointing out? Plenty of moonlight, and glorious phosphorescence, but where's the sea-serpent? Where did it show again? Why, what's the matter, boy?" he continued, catching his nephew by the arm and taking his hand. "Don't stand staring like that. Your hand's all wet, and like ice! Have you been frightened?"

"I—don't know, uncle, I suppose so," said the boy slowly and dreamily. "I never saw anything like it before, and—and—it came so close to the schooner. I think I thought it was going to make a snatch at me and take me under water. But don't ask me now, please. I don't feel quite right. I suppose I am cowardly; but it made Gregg run away."

"Then why didn't you," said the doctor jocularly, "if it was so horrible as that?"

"I couldn't, uncle," cried the boy passionately. "I turned cold all over and couldn't stir."

"Well, come down below for a bit," continued the doctor. "Why, Chubb, the boy's had a regular scare."

"Ah! and no wonder," said the skipper gruffly. "It scared the men too. They saw it."

"What, the same thing that you fired at?"

"Ah, that I don't know. That was a great long eely thing; but Joe Cross here says this was more like a great turtle, with flippers and a long neck, and a head like a snake."

No more was said till they were in the cabin, where soon after he had found himself in safety, shut in and with the swinging lamp burning above his head, Rodd heaved a deep sigh and then uttered a forced laugh.

"I couldn't help it, uncle," he said, "and I didn't think I could have been such a coward; but I am all right now. The other men did see it too, didn't they?"

"Yes, my lad; they saw it too," replied the skipper; "and next time we goes ashore, if we are stupid enough to talk about it every one will laugh and say we are making up tales for the marines. I've known skipper after skipper who has seen something of the kind in the warm seas and has told yarns about them. But men don't often do so now, no matter what they see, for one don't like to be laughed at. Well, sir, I suppose you believe there's more queer things in the sea than most people know of?"

"Well, yes," said Uncle Paul, "I am beginning to believe more and more that we who follow out natural history have a great deal to learn."

"Take my word for it, sir, you have. But I dare say you will be disposed to laugh at me and think that I am making up a bit of gammon, when I ask you if you remember what a frigate looks like when she has got all her ports open and her lanterns lit."

"I don't see why I should," said Uncle Paul quietly. "But of course I have seen a man-of-war like that by night; and a very beautiful object she is."

"Very, sir. But what should you say if I was to ask you if you had seen a fish looking like a little frigate with her ports all open and her lights shining in a couple of rows along her sides—lights that don't burn, sir, but shine brightly as if they did?"

"Well, I am not a man to laugh at anything new in science, Chubb," said the doctor quietly, "but between ourselves, your description is a bit too flowery."

"Not a bit, sir."

"I have seen," continued the doctor, "phosphorescent fish and insects, and even now, swimming round us, the sea is full of light-giving creatures, but nothing approaching your frigates with the ports open, or anything near them."

"Well, sir, I could take you right away to the eastward into the Indian seas—and I am not romancing, mind, but talking honest truth—I could take you and squire here, where you could drag up fishermen sort of fish, big-mouthed fellows ready to swallow what they catches, fish that guide themselves down in the dark deeps of the sea amongst the seaweed at the bottom, and there they hang out from the tops of their heads long barbels that look like worms, and fish with them for other fishes, to catch them to eat."

"Oh yes, that's right enough, captain," replied the doctor. "You know, Rodd, that great frog fish, the Father Lasher, as the fishermen call him. Why, captain, we have got them at home off the Devon coast."

"I know," said the skipper. "I have seen them; but those are not what I mean. He didn't give me time to finish, squire," continued the skipper, facing round to Rodd. "My ones out yonder in the Eastern seas always live down below where it's deep and dark, and where the fishes couldn't see their baits. So what do you think they do?"

"Swim up to where it's lighter," said Rodd. "Not they, sir. They grows a little bait as might be a little bit of meat at the end of their barbel-like fishing-lines, and wave it about in the water for the fish they want to catch to see."

"You said it was all black darkness deep down there," cried Rodd.

"So it is, my lad, and so that the fish may see it those little baits of theirs all glow with light, and shine out in the dark black water. Now, doctor, what do you think of that for a bit of nature?"

"Extraordinary!" cried the doctor. "But who told you that?"

"Nobody, sir. I have seen them with my own eyes."

"Yes, but what about the men-of-war with their ports lit up?"

"Of course I didn't mean men-of-war, sir. I thought I made you understand I meant fish. Fish about two foot long, with a row of lights down each side like lamps to see their way in the darkness. There, gentlemen, that's no story to tell to the marines, but a fact that I have seen with my own eyes; and if there's things like that deep down in the seas, I don't see anything wonderful in there being what some people calls sea-sarpints that might be as big as a great sparmacetti whale; and if you put some of them beside a cable a hundred foot long there isn't much rope to spare. I knew of a ninety-footer once, though they don't often get so long as that."

Chapter Twenty
A Warm Blush

Uncle Paul sat very quietly thinking for some time, while the other occupants of the cabin were waiting for him to deliver himself of what seemed to be gathering in his brain. "You see, Captain Chubb," he said at last, "human nature has always been prone to exaggerate. If a boy like my nephew here hooks a fish and loses it, he goes home and tells everybody that it was about five times as big as it really was."

"Oh, uncle!" cried Rodd indignantly. "I am sure I never did!"

"Well, well, perhaps not," said Uncle Paul shortly. "Don't say 'perhaps not,' uncle. That isn't fair. You know I always try to tell the truth."

"Well, well; yes, yes, yes, yes," said Uncle Paul testily. "I am not accusing you, Rodney. I am only alluding to what people who tell stories do."

"Why, of course, uncle, they say what isn't true if they tell stories."

"Will you oblige me, Rodney, by letting me continue what I was about to say?"

"I beg pardon, uncle."

"Yes, Captain Chubb," continued Uncle Paul, "there is that natural disposition born with us, one which requires a great deal of education to eliminate; that disposition to exaggerate in talking about things we have seen and others have not."

"Yes, sir, I know," grunted the skipper. "People will stretch."

"Exactly," said Uncle Paul—"magnify wonders that they have seen."

"Quite right, sir. I did just now about that sparm whale. I don't believe after all that they get to a hundred foot."

"Still," said the doctor, "we know what a spermaceti whale is; but this supposed creature which has been reported of over and over again under the name of the sea-serpent still lives only in the land of doubt—"

"Oh, uncle!" cried Rodd.

"Well, sir, I didn't see much doubt about that thing."

"H'm! no," replied the doctor thoughtfully; "but still you must grant that we did not have a fair examination, and that neither of us, even if we were clever with our pencils, could sketch an exact representation of the natural phenomenon."

"Nat'ral, sir?" said the skipper gruffly. "Well, to my mind it is a very unnatural sort of thing."

"I think I could sketch it, uncle, if I were clever with my pencil, which I am not, for I can seem to see it quite plainly now, as it raised its neck out of the water when it swam by."

"You think you could, my boy; but a great deal of it must have been under water, and your representation would be open to doubt."

"Humph! What was it like, youngster?" said the skipper gruffly.

"Just the same shape as a swan," said Rodd, with something like a shudder, "only enormously, big; but instead of having wings and feet it was just as if it had four great paddles."

"That's right," grunted the skipper; "just like what I see about ten years ago in the Indian seas. I didn't see enough of this one to be able to tell."

"Well," said the doctor gravely, "I for a long time have been of opinion that the reports that reach us from time to time about the sea-serpent must have some truth in them, though they have doubtless been greatly exaggerated."

"Don't hear of many reports now, sir," said Captain Chubb. "We seagoing people have been laughed at too much."

"Yes, I know," said the doctor, "and I have thought over these matters a great deal, and fully believe that we have a great many things to discover, both at sea and on land, quite as wonderful as the so-called sea-serpent. There's plenty of room, and I see no reason to doubt that there are great fish—"

"This warn't a fish," growled the skipper.

"Reptiles, then," grunted Uncle Paul, "which as a rule dwell far down in the depths of ocean, and which only occasionally seek, or are forced up to, the surface."

"Forced up, uncle? What could force up a great thing like that?"

"You ask that, Rodd? Why, what forces a fish up sometimes, to float upside down on the surface?"

"Oh yes, I know," replied Rodd; "something wrong with its swimming bladder."

"Exactly; and I should say such a creature as you saw would in its natural state be always living deep down in the ocean."

"'Cept when he comes up to feed," growled Captain Chubb. "This 'ere one was hard at work in that shoal of fish."

"I don't see that that interferes with my argument, Captain Chubb," said the doctor; "but what I was going on to say was this. There was a time in the history of this earth, when just such creatures as my nephew here described used to be plentiful."

"How long ago?" asked the skipper.

"Ah, that's more than any one of us can say; but I have seen their remains turned to stone, laid bare in a stone quarry—that is to say, their skeletons, which show pretty well what must have been their shape; and if they existed once there is no reason why some of their descendants, though very rarely seen, may not still survive, though I am half afraid that my nephew here must have some half-forgotten lingering memories of one of these creatures that he has seen in some geological work, and upon seeing that fish or reptile let his imagination run riot and finished it off by memory."

Rodd shook his head.

"I saw it plainly enough, uncle."

And the skipper gave his head a sapient nod, while the doctor shook his.

"What were you going to say, Captain Chubb?"

"Only this 'ere, sir. I have 'eard more argufying and quarrelling about sea-sarpints than about almost anything else. I say sarpints, but I mean these things, and I say this. It will never be settled properly till one of 'em is caught—which aren't likely—or one of them is cast ashore so as everybody can see fair and square. I believe in 'em, and I've good reason to."

"So do I, uncle," cried Rodd.

"Well," said Uncle Paul, "I have for a long time had my doubts, and now I am no longer a sceptic."

He looked very hard at the skipper as he spoke, and feeling that he was called upon to answer, the sturdy captain shook his head and brought his big hand down heavily upon the cabin table.

"That you are not, sir," he said; "your head's too full of science and knowledge and larning to be what you say. I don't quite exactly know what it means, but I'll answer for it you are not that; and now if you don't mind

I should like for us to go up on deck again and have a good look round. It's 'most as light as day, and if a thing like that is playing around we are just as likely as not to sight it again. What do you say, sir, to taking your glass and being on the look-out?"

"By all means," said the doctor. "Get the glass, Rodd. Hullo! What's the matter with you?"

"Oh, nothing, uncle," said the boy, hastily rising.

"Why, you took hold of the table as if you felt dizzy."

"No, no, uncle. I am all right."

"Not afraid, are you?"

"I—I was for a moment, uncle."

"Good lad and true! Naught to be ashamed on, and spoke out like a man," grunted the skipper.

"But I tell you I am all right now," cried Rodd angrily, and he darted a fierce look at the speaker.

"Of course you are, youngster; but you felt a bit skeart again, and 'nough to make you."

"Yes," said Rodd sharply, "I did feel startled for a moment, but it's all gone now. Come on, uncle; I have got the glass;" and the boy made a dash for the cabin stairs.

"I say," whispered the skipper, "that's better than brag, doctor."

"Yes," said Uncle Paul, drawing a deep breath; "a great deal."

They both then hastened up the stairs, to find Rodd half-way along the deck, hurrying with the glass under his arm to join the men, who were all gathered together at the bows, save their solitary messmate at the wheel.

"Well, my lads, did you make it out again?" shouted the skipper.

"No, sir," replied Joe Cross, who took upon himself the part of spokesman. "Aren't seen a sign of it. We have been casting it up among us that it got more than it liked in the shape of that bullet, and after going down, it turned waxy-like and come up again to have something to say to us, but turned worse and went down."

"Humph!" grunted the skipper. "Then you think we hit it?"

"Yes, sir; and some of the lads have been saying that if they was you they'd load the big gun well with a lot of grape-shot, and if the beggar come up again be on the look-out and let him have it."

"Some on us, Joe Cross; not all."

"Nay, but you meant it, Ikey Gregg," said Joe.

"Not me, messmate. I says it's dangerous to be safe to get meddling with things like that."

"Ay, ay!" came from two or three of the other men, but only in a half-hearted way.

But it was encouragement enough for slow, quiet, fat Isaac Gregg to continue—

"You see, gentlemen, it's like this. That there long-necked sarpint thing has only got to make a rush and chuck itself out of the water aboard us here, and break the schooner's back, and where should us be then?"

"I don't know," said the skipper shortly. "But what do you say, doctor?"

"Well, for my part, speaking for the advancement of natural history, Captain Chubb, I should like to see that creature lying dead upon the surface, and left floating long enough for you and your men to take measurements, while my nephew and I did the best we could with pen and pencil to describe what might very well be called one of the wonders of the world."

"And what do you say, squire?" asked the skipper, speaking eagerly.

"I say you'd better load the gun again, Captain Chubb," replied Rodd, speaking very hurriedly. "We might hit it if it came up, and then we could try and do what my uncle says."

"Right," growled the skipper. "Man the gun again, and you, Cross, come below with me and fetch a canister of grape-shot and a full business charge to load the piece. You lads who are not wanted for the gun, each of you take a musket and an axe. It aren't likely that we shall come to close quarters, but if we do—well, you know what."

Every man on board joined in a hearty cheer, and in a very short time the preparations were made, even the cook playing his part of keeping the galley fire ready, while directly afterwards he edged up to where Joe Cross was in conversation with Rodd.

"Thought I would come the old-fashioned dodge as well, sir," he said.

"Old-fashioned? What do you mean?"

"For firing the gun, sir. I've left the poker in between the bars to get red-hot. Put that to your touch-hole. Beats slow match hollow; don't it, Joe?"

"Ay, that it do, mate, if you have got the fire, and the poker's hot; but you have to come back to the slow match if neither one nor t'other's ready. Well, Mr Rodd, sir, it don't look as if any of us is going to have the watch below to-night."

"No, Joe, it doesn't. Do you think the monster will come up again?"

"Can't say, sir, I'm sure, and to speak honest, there are times when I hope it will and there are times when I hope it won't. Sea-sarpints aren't much in my line. I have had a turn in a whaler, and though a right whale is a nasty kind of a bird to tackle when she is in her flurry, you know what you are about. There's the harpoon in her, and you have got her at the end of your line, and you're waiting for her with your lances ready to put her out of her misery. But even if you have got a few shot in her, a sea-sarpint's different sort of cattle altogether, and I didn't like the looks of this 'ere one at all. She came up quite vicious-like to look after us. You see her eye, Mr Rodd, sir? I did, sir, for a moment. There was a sort of leery look about it, and it seemed to me as if she had just picked you out and meant to have you. All the lads here know I'm one as never brags, but if there's a bit of fighting on I am always ready to stick to my mates, just as I would now."

"Ay, ay, Joe! That's a true word," came in chorus.

"Thank you, messmates," said Joe modestly. "Well, then, I'll speak out. Between you and me and the post, my lads, I hope this 'ere annymile won't come up to give us a shot."

There was a low murmur at this which sounded very much like assent.

"It's narvous sort of work, you see. If the schooner had been fitted out as a sea-sarpinter with the right and proper sort of tackle, why, that's another thing. But then you see, she aren't been. We haven't got the proper sort of tools, and we aren't been drilled to use them even if we had."

"That's a true word, messmate," came in chorus.

"And that's why I says I hope she won't look us up to-night; but if she is following us up and keeping one of them great sarcer eyes upon our keel somewhere far away down below, I hope she'll leave it till morning. After sunrise we shall be able to see better, and have had time to get rid of a nasty unked sort of feeling which rather bothers me just now, though I don't know how it is with you. There, Mr Rodd, sir, you faced the thing splendid. I see you, sir. You didn't turn round and run away like Ikey Gregg. You stood fast there with your hands resting on the rail, staring the thing straight in the face. How you managed to do it I don't know. But do it you did, and I admired you, sir."

It was moonlight, and the change in Rodd's face passed unobserved, but it was scarlet, and felt so hot that the boy involuntarily raised his hand to his cheek, while a feeling of annoyance pervaded him as he looked at Joe Cross suspiciously, in the belief that the man must be bantering him; but as far as the boy could make out, Joe Cross's frank countenance was quite innocent of guile and he was speaking exactly as he felt.

But Rodd was not at rest, and in the calm still watch that followed, with every one on the look-out and ready to imagine that each phosphorescent flash in the sea meant the moving upwards of the uncanny enemy, Rodd waited till all was still and restful and they seemed likely to be undisturbed, to make his way to Joe Cross's side and get him alone.

Chapter Twenty One
Query—A Coward?

Joe had stationed himself on the larboard bow with his elbows resting upon the bulwark and his chin in his hands, gazing straight away to sea, his eyes fixed a little to the left of the dazzling path of light that extended from the moon to the schooner.

So intent was he upon something he fancied he saw, that he did not hear Rodd's approach, and started violently upon being touched.

"All right, sir; not asleep," he cried. "Oh, it's you, Mr Rodd! I fancied that it was the skipper, who thought he had caught me napping. Just you look yonder, sir. You are coming fresh to it. I have been staring till the little flashes of light make my eyes swim. Now then, just you look about half a cable's length left of that line of light, and see if you can't see something breaking water there."

Rodd gazed intently in the direction indicated for some little time without speaking.

"See anything, sir?" said Joe at last. "No."

"That'll do then, sir. It was my fancy. Well, we are having a quiet night of it, sir. No more signs of that old sea bogy, and like enough we shan't get a squint at it again."

"I don't suppose we shall now, Joe."

"Sleepy, sir?"

"Not a bit, Joe. Here, I want to speak to you about that thing."

"I am listening, sir. Talk away. Rather queer, warn't it, to come upon a thing like that just when you didn't expect it?"

"Yes, Joe; and you said something about my not being frightened."

"Yes, sir. You quite capped me."

"Stop a minute, Joe. I want to say something to you."

"All right, sir," cried the sailor, looking wonderingly at the lad, who was speaking to him in a husky impressive tone.

But Rodd remained speechless, and it was the sailor who broke the silence.

"I'm a-listening, sir. Heave ahead."

"Yes," cried Rodd desperately. "Look here, Joe; were you making fun of me?"

"Fun of you? No, sir. It was only my way, just to make things a bit more cheery, for every one on deck seems to be in the doldrums, all on account of that great squirmy thing."

"No, no, I don't mean that," cried Rodd. "I mean, making fun of me when you told the men I wasn't frightened."

"Fun on you? No, sir. Why, it was as I said. You quite capped me, to see you standing facing that thing without shrinking a bit. I should have expected to see you frightened to death."

"Then it was because you didn't look well, Joe," said Rodd, in a low hoarse voice, as he made a brave effort to set himself right with the man. "I was frightened—so horribly frightened that I couldn't stir."

"Well, and no wonder, sir. Enough to make you. Why, it would have frightened a brass monkey, let alone a man. Look at Ikey Gregg. I believe if you'd ha' 'eard him you would have found he was calling 'Mother!' Poor old chap. There aren't no way of proving it, as one don't know how heavy he was afore, but I believe he melted away a bit. Why, we was all like it, sir. It was a regular startler and no mistake."

"Do you mean honestly that all the men were very much frightened?"

"Why, of course, sir. I told you I was as bad as bad could be, and my hair stood right up on end—leastwise, it felt as if it did; and I can tell you this: I didn't feel like that when we were going into action, and that's saying a good deal, when a fellow didn't know whether the first sixty-four pounder that was fired wouldn't send its shot right into his chest. And so you felt regular skeart, did you, sir?"

"Yes, Joe; and it made me ashamed to hear you talking about me to the men as you did."

"Oh, well, I don't know as it matters, sir. I said just what I thought, and I rather like to hear what you say, because it seems to brighten me up a bit."

"Why? How?"

"Oh, because it makes me feel that I wasn't quite such a cur as I thought I was. There, it's all right, sir, and I suppose it's quite nat'ral for any one to feel afraid when there's something really worth feeling afraid on. I dare say we should both be just as bad again if that thing was to shove its head out of the water again close by here."

"Then you don't think I was such a coward, Joe?"

"You! You a coward! Tchah! Let me hear any fellow say you are, and I'll hit him in the eye. But there, it's just as if that thing knowed we were all ready and waiting for it, and so it won't show. I'm beginning to wish that the skipper would send everybody but the watch for their spell below; but I don't suppose he will, and so we must make the best of it. But if I was you, sir, and didn't belong to the crew, I should just slip off below and turn into my bunk till breakfast-time in the morning. What do you say?"

"No," said Rodd shortly; and he stopped on deck and watched with the men till the sun was well on high.

Then the suggestion of breakfast seemed so full of promise that after partaking thereof he went back on deck, to stand scanning the beautiful sunlit plain with the glass; but no further glimpse was seen of the strange monster that day, nor yet during the next six weeks, during which time they glided into port for fresh provisions twice, the second time in that of the sunny Canary Islands. There a week was spent in inspecting the beauties and the wonders of the old volcanic caverns, before they were well at sea again with the sun daily growing hotter and sea and sky more beautiful.

Days upon days were spent in exploring the attractions of the Sargasso Sea, till the doctor cried "Hold! Enough!" For the bottles in the laboratory were being filled up too fast, and there was too much to do yet in the farther south, towards which they sailed slowly and steadily on, till one day a holiday was announced, for the men had been hard at work rowing here and rowing there, hauling in drag and dredge, sounding and hoisting, harpooning fish, and busying themselves with the spoil they dragged on board, while Captain Chubb stumped up and down with his hands very deep in his pockets, scowling at his sullied deck, and wearing clouds upon his sun-tanned brow, till Dr Robson bade the men throw all the rest overboard, this order, for which the skipper had been impatiently waiting, being immediately supplemented by another, brief and prompt.

"Buckets! Swabs!"

And then as the slime of mollusc, fish and seaweed was washed away, and the deck of the schooner rapidly grew white again, the skipper smiled and entered into a pleasant chat with the tired naturalist and his nephew.

The men's holiday was spent after the fashion of such holidays, over the buffoonery enjoyed by the crew, especially in olden days, in crossing the line; and then it was onward again amidst glorious sunrises and sunsets, amidst calms and fervent seas that seemed to blaze back the heat of the sun.

It was all new to Rodd, and all glorious. He was never tired of seeing the flying-fish skim out of the water to seek safety, scattered by the pursuit of some bonito or dolphin, watching them till they dipped down into the smooth surface, as if to gather new strength, and then skim out again.

The dolphins and bonito were caught, the boy growing skilful in darting down the harpoon-like "grains," the modern form of Neptune fish-spear.

There were times too when the boy expressed his wonder that in spite of all the time they had been sailing south, it had been such a rare thing to meet or overtake another vessel.

"A pretty good proof," the doctor would say, "of the vastness of the ocean."

"And of how there is plenty of room, uncle, for any number of wonderful creatures such as we have never seen yet. But are you always going sailing on like this?"

"Why, aren't you satisfied?" said Uncle Paul.

"Satisfied, uncle? Oh yes, with what we are doing. But I haven't had nearly enough. I should like to go oil sailing like this for—"

"Ever?" said the doctor dryly.

"Oh no, uncle; I mean for long enough yet. But I say, isn't the world beautiful?"

"More beautiful, boy, than words can express," replied the doctor gravely. "But no. Now we are getting into the Southern Tropics I am thinking of going more to the east and into the great bay, so as to get within range of the African shores. Perhaps we shall make for the mouths of one or two of the rivers, and get within soundings where we can do more dredging. I anticipate some strange discoveries in those portions of the ocean; but at present we will keep on skimming the surface and finding what we can."

And so during the next two or three days they went sailing on, and found something that they had least expected, to Rodd Harding's great wonder and delight.

Chapter Twenty Two
The King's Ship

It was the afternoon of a blazing hot day, when the pitch was oozing out in drops in every exposed place, and Rodd had found it exceedingly unpleasant to touch any piece of the brass rail, bolt, the bell, or either of the guns, for the schooner was gliding on southward with every scrap of her white sails spread, and the wind that wafted her onward sent a feeling of lassitude through all on board.

Some days before, Captain Chubb had set his men to work to rig up a small awning aft, and the doctor having declared that it was too hot for work, he and Rodd had spent most of their time beneath this shelter, till the latter had struck against it, declaring it was all nonsense, for the sun came hotter through the canvas than it did where there was no shade at all, or else it seemed to, for there was no breeze in the shelter, and though what wind there was seemed as if it had come past the mouth of a furnace, still it was wind, and the lad declared that it was far preferable to stewing under the awning.

It was a lazy time, and the men, who had dressed as lightly as they could contrive, went very slowly about their several tasks, and at last when Rodd strolled towards the man at the wheel, he had to listen to a petition.

It was fat Isaac Gregg who was taking his trick, as he called it, and he began at Rodd at once.

"I've got something to ask you, sir," he said.

"Oh, bother!" cried Rodd, taking off his straw hat to turn it into a fan. "It's too hot to listen. Don't ask me anything, because if you do, I shall be too stupid to tell you."

"Oh, it aren't hard, sir," said the man innocently, as he let a couple of spokes pass through his hands and then ran them back again. "It's only as the lads asked me—"

"Well, well, go on," said Rodd, for the man stopped. "Phew! It's just as if the tops of the waves where they curl over were white hot."

"Yes, sir, it is a bit warm," said the man; "but I've felt it warmer."

"Couldn't," said Rodd abruptly.

"Oh yes, sir; much hotter than this."

"What! You've felt it hotter than this?"

"Oh yes, sir."

"Then why didn't you melt away? I should have thought you would run like a candle all into a lump."

"Ah, that's your fun, sir. Some of the lads has been telling you that I am fat. That's a joke they have got up among them, just because I'm a little thicker than some of the others. But as I was a-saying, sir, they ast me to ast you—"

"Now it's coming then," sighed Rodd. "Phew! Wish all my hair had been cut off. It gets so wet, and sticks to my forehead."

"Yes, sir, it's best short," said the man. "Just you look at mine. You should have it done like this."

As he spoke the sailor took off his hat and exhibited a head which had been trimmed down till all the scalp resembled a dingy brush, for it was cut with the most perfect regularity, for the hair to stand up in bristly fashion for about a quarter of an inch from the skin.

"Why, who cut that?" cried Rodd, with something approaching to energy, this being the first thing that had taken his attention that day.

"Joe Cross, sir. He's a first-rate hand with a comb and a pair of scissors. You let him do your head, sir and you won't know yourself afterwards."

"Oh yes, I should," said the boy sleepily, gazing down at the quivering compass and its many points.

"I mean you would feel so comfortable, sir."

"Oh, well, then, I will. Anything," cried Rodd—"anything not to be so hot!"

"That's right, sir. Ast me to ast you, sir."

"Well, you've been asking for the last half-hour. What is it?" cried Rodd peevishly.

"To ast the doctor, sir—"

"For some physic to make them cool?" snapped out Rodd. "Tell them to go and ask him themselves, and he'll say what I do—that they are not to eat so much nor drink so much, and not to work in the sun. There, that's all uncle would say."

"Yes, sir, but that aren't it," cried Gregg, making one of the spokes of the wheel swing from hand to hand.

"Then what do they want?"

"Why, sir, it seems rum, but Joe Cross and the other lads know better what's good for them than I do. You see, sir, they want to get to work again at your fishing and hauling, or rowing about, for they says they can keep much cooler when they are moving about and got to think what they are doing than when there's no work on hand and nothing to think about at all."

"Oh, very well," said Rodd grumpily, "I'll go and ask him, for I am about sick of this. I think there must be some volcanoes here, or something of that kind, for I never felt it so hot before."

"You aren't used to it, sir; but I thought you would, sir, and the lads said they thought you would too. Thank you, sir."

Rodd yawned, turned slowly on his heels, and strolled away to where Uncle Paul was sitting back in an Indian cane chair, resting the carefully-focussed spy-glass upon a half-opened book standing upon its front edges propped upon four more in the middle of a little table.

"Ah, Pickle, my lad! You had better stop in the shade. I don't want you to be getting any head trouble in this torrid sun."

"Oh, I am all right, uncle; but the men want to begin fishing or doing something again, keeping cool."

"Too hot till towards evening, my boy," replied the doctor. "But look here; you were saying only the other day how strange it was that we saw so few vessels. Well, here's one at all events—a three-master."

"Oh, whereabouts, uncle?" cried the boy eagerly.

"Away to the west yonder, hull down. There, take the glass."

As Rodd was arranging it to his own satisfaction the doctor went on quietly—

"Out here I am not going to give an opinion, but if we were in the garden at home in the look-out I should say that was a man-of-war coming into Plymouth port."

"Yes, that she is, uncle," cried Rodd, who had forgotten the heat in this new excitement.

"A man-of-war—that she is!" said Uncle Paul quietly. "That sounds ridiculous, Pickle. But one has to give way to custom."

"Yes," said Rodd—"a frigate. I can tell by her white sails."

"Not big enough for a frigate, my boy. A sloop of war, I should think. Now, what can she be doing down here?"

"I know, uncle," cried the boy excitedly—"looking after the slave ships."

"Ah, very likely," cried Uncle Paul. "I shouldn't be surprised. We are pretty near to that neighbourhood; and if she is it's quite likely that she'll overhaul us. Ah, here's Captain Chubb coming up. Look here, skipper!"

The captain, who looked very hot, and whose face proclaimed very plainly that he had been having an after-dinner nap, came slowly up, stooped within the awning, and in silence took hold of the spy-glass, whose glistening black sides were quite hot, and which Rodd thrust into his hands.

He wanted no telling what for, but raised and adjusted the glass to his own sight, took a quick shot at the distant object upon the horizon, and then lowered it directly. "British man-of-war," he grunted. "That's bad."

"Why?" cried Rodd sharply.

The skipper turned upon him, looked at him fiercely, and then almost barked out—

"You don't know, youngster?"

"No. What do you mean?"

"Means that I've got as smart a picked crew as a man need wish to have."

"To be sure," said Rodd; "of course you have. I do know that."

"Well," said the skipper gruffly, "I don't want to lose them; that's all."

Rodd and his uncle exchanged glances, while the skipper went and stood at the side and began scanning the sky, to come back shaking his head.

"No more wind, and not likely to be."

"Well, we don't want any more, do we?" said Uncle Pad.

"Ay; if a good breeze would spring up I'd show them a clean pair of heels."

"Oh, I see," cried Rodd excitedly. "You think that they would press some of our men and take them aboard. Oh, Captain Chubb, you mustn't let them do that!"

"I don't mean to, my lad, if I can help it. I hadn't reckoned on seeing one of them down here."

"Uncle thinks they're after the slavers."

"Nay, my lad, I don't think that. More likely after one of the palm-oil craft to see if they can pick up a few men out of them."

"Oh, that's a false alarm, captain," said Uncle Paul. "My papers and the work we're upon with a grant from Government would clear us."

"Ought to, sir," said the skipper gruffly, "but I wouldn't trust them. If a King's ship wants men, good smart sailors such as ours, men who have served, her captain wouldn't be above shutting his eyes and making a mistake. Anyhow I'm going to crack on as hard as I can till she brings us up with a gun, and then I suppose I shall have to heave to or risk the consequences."

"Hadn't you better risk the consequences, Captain Chubb?" said Rodd, in a half-whisper.

"Here you, Rodney, mind what you are saying, sir! It's the duty of every Englishman to respect the law, and I feel perfectly certain, Captain Chubb, that there is nothing to fear in that direction, so go quietly on as you are, unless you are obliged to heave to. Seeing how little wind there is, and how distant that sloop, I think it's very probable that she'll not overhaul us before it grows dark."

"Oh, uncle," cried Rodd, "she'll have plenty of time. The sun won't go down for an hour or so."

"Well, how long will it be before it's dark afterwards?" cried Uncle Paul. "You forget that we are in the tropics, and how short a time it is between sunset and darkness."

"Yes, sir; you are quite right there," said the skipper, "and that's what I'm hoping for. If we can only get the bit of time over 'twixt this and the dark, I shan't care, for she won't see us in the morning."

By this time one of the sailors forward had noticed the skipper using the glass, seen what took his attention, and communicated it to his messmates, with the result that all who had been below gathered forward and stood anxiously watching the beautiful vessel, whose sails glistened in the sunshine as if their warp was of silver and their woof of gold.

Rodd noticed at once what a change had taken place amongst the men. All listlessness had gone, and they were watching the King's ship, for such Captain Chubb had declared her to be at once, and were talking in excited whispers together, their manner showing that whatever the captain's opinion might be, theirs was, as sailors, that they would not trust a King's ship that was in want of men.

After a time Rodd was attracted towards them, and he strolled up, Joe Cross turning to him at once, to begin questioning him in a low tone.

"What does the skipper say, sir?"

"He said it was a sloop of war, Joe."

"Oh yes, sir, we know that," said the man irritably; "but we've been 'specting him here ever so long. So's our bo'sun. There, look; he's got his pipe in his hand. Didn't he say nothing about no orders?"

"No, Joe."

"Didn't he say nothing about hysting another stunsail or two?"

"No, Joe."

"Oh–h–h!" came in a groan from the men; and Rodd felt for them, for of late they had become more and more attached to their position, and seemed as happy as a pack of school-boys on board the beautiful little schooner.

"But he has been saying something, lads," continued Rodd, in a low tone.

"Ay, ay, of course," cried Joe. "Our old man don't want to lose us, and he knows best what he ought to do. Go on, Mr Rodd, sir; tell us what he means."

"I think he means to keep on quietly, in the hope of the schooner not being signalled to heave to."

"Go on, sir, please, quick!" panted one of the men. "You don't know what it means to us."

"Before it becomes dark," continued Rodd.

"Ay, ay, my lad! That's right, sir. Why, of course," cried Joe exultingly. "Trust our old man, boys;" and whistling loudly a few bars of the Sailor's Hornpipe, he snatched off his straw hat, dashed it down upon the deck, and began to cut and shuffle and heave and turn, going through all the steps as if it were cool as an early spring, while his messmates formed in a ring about him, half stooped with bended knees, joined in the whistle, and beat time upon their knees and clapped hands, till the figure was gone through, and Joe Cross brought his terpsichorean bit of frantic mania to an end, by bringing his right foot down upon the deck with a tremendous stamp which was followed by a hearty cheer.

"That's your sort, Mr Rodd, sir! It's all right," cried Joe, panting, and wiping his streaming face. "If anybody had told me that I could do that ten minutes ago, when I felt as if I had hardly stuff enough in me to lift a leg, I should have told him he was going off his head. Didn't think you could put sperrits into us like that, sir, with just a word, now did you?"

"I am very glad, Joe," said Rodd.

"Glad, sir? So's we—every man Jack on us. You see, it means a lot. When you have got a comfortable mess, and a skipper as makes you haul together in a brotherly sort of fashion, it aren't nice for a King's ship to come down and take its pick of the men. We as is able seamen don't want to shirk, and if we are obliged to go in time of war, why, we are ready to go and do our duty like men; but it do nip a bit at first, sir, 'specially at a time like this."

"Ay, ay, Joe!" came in chorus.

"You see, sir, mostlings life on board a ship is so much hard work, and you has a lot of weather of some sort or another to fight agen; but with the 'ception of that bit of rough time getting into the French port, this 'ere's been a regular holiday, and— Oh my! There she goes, lads!" groaned the poor fellow, for the hull of the sloop had been gradually rising more and more into sight, rapidly at last from the refraction as she had glided into a hotter stratum of air while nearing the schooner, and all at once a white puff of smoke had darted out of her bows, to be followed by a dull heavy thud, when the men turned as with one accord to gaze at their captain, as if hoping against hope that he would still hold on instead of giving an order to fat Gregg, the steersman, to throw the schooner up in the wind.

Chapter Twenty Three
Suspicious Visitors

There was a dead silence among the men as the soft white ball of smoke rose slowly and steadily, expanding the while and changing its shape till it became utterly diffused. The occupants of the schooner's deck were statuesque in their rigidity, the crew to a man gazing hard at the captain as they strained their hearing to catch his next command; the captain fixed his eyes from one side upon Uncle Paul, while Rodd stood upon the other with his lips apart, gazing questioningly in his uncle's half-closed lids, as the doctor leaned back in his deck-chair with a thoughtful frown upon his brow.

Then he started slightly, for the captain spoke.

"Well, sir," he said, "what's it to be?"

"What's it to be, Captain Chubb? I do not quite understand you."

"It's plain enough, sir. If I throw the schooner up in the wind we shall have a man-of-war's boat aboard us and some young officer in command in less than half-an-hour. First thing will be he'll ask for our papers, and then fall in the lads, run his eye along them, take his pick, and order the poor fellows down into the boat; and that means sending us back to port to fill up the best way we can, and perhaps not do it. On the other hand, I can make believe a bit and still keep forging on a little till the darkness comes, and then—"

The captain stopped.

"Yes," said the doctor; "and then—"

"Well, sir, it would go very hard if that sloop of war wasn't out of sight at daybreak to-morrow morning, and even if she wasn't I don't think she'd overtake us again."

"I feel sure you are wrong, Captain Chubb," said the doctor. "I repeat; my papers and the grant I have had from his Majesty's Government will, I feel sure, be sufficient to protect my schooner and crew from any action in the way of pressing from one of his Majesty's ships. You will have the goodness to obey the signal, and wait and see what follows."

"You mean to risk it, then, sir?"

"I mean to do my duty as a subject of his Majesty the King," said Uncle Paul gravely.

"Very well, sir. I am captain of this schooner, but I am your servant, and it is my duty to obey your orders," said the captain, in his gruffest tones; and he walked heavily to the man at the wheel.

The time had been short, but too long for the patience of the man-of-war, for before the skipper had opened his mouth to give his order to the steersman, another puff of white smoke darted from the sloop's bows, there was a heavy thud, and a cannon ball came skipping over the heaving sea like a flat stone thrown by a clever boy across the waters of a pond—dick, duck and drake fashion—while a thrill ran through all on board as they watched the shot pass right in front of the schooner's bows and give its final splash as it disappeared far away.

Then the captain spoke, the stem of the schooner gradually bore round, with the sails beginning to shiver as she faced more and more to the wind, and finally flapping to and fro; but almost at once as the spokes turned rapidly through Isaac Gregg's hands, a deep low murmur ran through the crew, while a pang-like spasm seemed to shoot upward to cause a choky sensation in Rodd Harding's throat.

"Silence there, my lads," said the skipper sternly, and Rodd noticed the gloomy look upon his countenance as he turned his back to the doctor and walked to the side to stand gazing at the distant ship.

Many minutes had not elapsed before Rodd, who had turned his back to the men so as not to see their faces, and to hide his own, saw through the telescope he was busily using, something moving at the side of the sloop—a something which glided down her side and which was soon afterwards succeeded by a faint glitter as of the movement of rays.

Then there was a splash, followed by the regular dipping of oars which seemed to throw up so much golden spray on either side, and the boy could plainly make out the sloop's boat being rowed out clear of the man-of-war, and gradually increasing its distance.

Rodd watched them for some time, and what was but a speck to his naked eye plainly showed in the field of the glass the regular movements of the men, and now and then a flash suggestive of the rowers wearing something brightly polished.

There were more flashes too caused by the sun's nearly horizontal rays, and these came from right astern, where the golden orange sunshine seemed to be intensified, looking wonderfully red; but ere long the watcher had grasped the fact that he was looking at the bright scarlet coats of so many marines, and then he was able to note the figures of two of the boat's occupants seated together.

"The officers in command," he said to himself.

It was a long row from vessel to vessel, and the sun had begun to dip, and sank quite out of sight as the sloop's cutter came alongside, the men tossed up their oars, and a smart-looking officer of about thirty sprang up the side, followed by a lad of Rodd's own age, who took his attention from the first.

The officer was received at the side by the doctor and captain, Rodd standing slightly behind looking hard at the midshipman, who stared harder, frowning and putting on an air of the most consequential kind, while, presumably involuntarily, his left hand played with the ivory and gilt hilt of a curved dirk, suggestive of a strong desire to draw it out of its sheath and flourish it before the schooner's crew.

The officer nodded importantly at the doctor, and then turned frowningly upon the skipper with the angry question—

"What's the reason you didn't heave to?"

"Didn't give me time," growled the captain surlily.

"No insolence, sir! You ought to have obeyed the first gun. You are an Englishman, and by the look of you have been long enough at sea to know the rules when you encounter a man-of-war. Now then, what ship's this?"

"*Maid of Salcombe*, Plymouth."

"Owner?"

"I am," said the doctor quietly.

"Oh! What are you trading in?"

"I am not trading," said the doctor quietly. "This schooner is upon a scientific expedition, under the auspices of the English Government."

"Oh," said the officer suspiciously; and he looked from the doctor to the skipper, and from thence ran his eye over the crew gathered forward, while the midshipman altered the pitch of his hat, turned towards Rodd, whom for the last few moments he had been ignoring, and looked him up and down in a supercilious manner which made the blood mount to the boy's forehead, and set him staring down at the middy's bright shoes, from whence he slowly raised his eyes as far as the belt which supported the dirk, and from there higher up to his hat, where he fixed his eyes upon the officer's cockade and kept them obstinately there, till the lad's nostrils began to expand, he grew as red in the face as Rodd, and his menacing eyes seemed to say, You insolent young civilian, how dare you!

"Rather a strong crew, skipper," said the lieutenant sharply.

"Yes, sir; picked men," replied Captain Chubb.

"And there's a look about them of the able seaman, R.N."

"Perhaps so, sir," replied the skipper, who gazed bluntly back at the intruder.

"Well-found schooner, skipper, and carries a press of sail."

"Yes, sir. Very smart craft," replied the skipper.

"Long gun amidships and a couple of small brass guns forward," continued the lieutenant, who seemed to miss nothing. "Very roomy hold below, I should say."

"Yes, sir. Built for a Mediterranean orange boat."

"And no cargo, I think you said."

"No, sir; only scientific traps, as Dr Robson here calls them."

"Yes," said the doctor, interposing.

"I am not talking to you, sir," said the lieutenant haughtily. "Your turn will come."

Rodd's uncle bowed, and turned away, frowning.

"Stop, sir!" cried the officer sharply.

"What insolence, uncle!" said Rodd aloud; and he turned away from the midshipman, to cross to his uncle's side.

"What's that?" shouted the lieutenant, and the middy clapped his hand to the hilt of his dirk.

"I said what insolence, sir. My uncle is a gentleman."

"And it seems that his nephew is not. Be silent, boy, and recollect in whose presence you stand. I am a King's officer. — Now, Mr — what is your name? Robson? Have the goodness to tell me how it is that, with a light, fast-sailing schooner, well-armed, and with a crew evidently fighting men, you are found here in the neighbourhood of one of the notorious slave-supplying rivers? You may just as well speak the truth, for in all probability your schooner will be a prize to his Majesty's sloop of war *Diadem*."

"I beg your pardon," said the doctor quietly. "Suspicious appearances can always be found by those who seek for them. If you will have the goodness to step below with the captain you can examine the papers and the scientific fittings of portions of the hold which were prepared under my instructions when I started upon the voyage. I don't think, sir, you will find any accommodation has been made for the reception of a black living cargo of those poor unfortunate objects of humanity in whom a certain vile nefarious traffic is carried on. Captain Chubb, pray take this gentleman below and show him everything he desires."

"Oh," said the lieutenant sharply, "if this is so, Mr Rodson—"

"Dr Robson, at your service," said the owner of the name, glancing sharply at his nephew, with a faint smile upon his lips, for at the utterance by the lieutenant of the syllable *Rod* the boy had started violently.

As the doctor spoke he took out his pocket-book, drew forth a card, and held it between two fingers in doctor's fashion towards the officer.

"Humph! MD, Plymouth. Oh, well, Dr Robson, I hope to find that I have been labouring under a mistake;" and he raised his hand to his cocked hat. "But I have my duty to do."

"Don't apologise, sir," said the doctor, who had changed as in a moment from the sturdy naturalist into the urbane medical man. "I quite see your necessity for guarding against imposture. Pray proceed."

The lieutenant nodded sharply, and leaving his guard of a couple of marines at the gangway, and the boat's crew ready to spring up the side at the slightest alarm, he followed the skipper to the cabin hatch, the doctor hesitating as if in doubt for a moment or two, and then following deliberately down the cabin stairs.

Chapter Twenty Four
The King's Middy

Rodd, full of excitement, was burning to follow too and see what he looked upon as the officer's discomfiture; but there was that middy, who seemed to be left in command of the marines, and he felt a peculiar sensation which completely mastered him, filling him as it did with a desire to have what he afterwards called a good fall out with that fellow, who seemed to make him metaphorically set up his feathers all round his neck and go at him as a strange young cockerel of a different breed who had suddenly appeared in the poultry-yard where he dwelt.

So Rodd stayed on deck, thrust his hands into his pockets, ignored the presence of the middy, and with something of a strut marched up to the two marines in the gangway, whistling softly the while, gave each a friendly nod, examined their grounded arms and their stiff uniform with its abundant pipe-clay, and ended by spreading his legs a little, swinging himself slowly toe and heel, and saying patronisingly—

"Rather hot toggery that, my lads, for weather like this."

" No, puppy, I have not gone below."

"Well, of all the impudence!" cried the young officer hotly; and he took a step towards where Rodd was standing.

Rodd faced slowly round, looked at the boy superciliously, then said as coolly as could be—

"Hullo, midshipmite! Not gone below?"

"No, puppy, I have not gone below," and as he spoke the lad pressed the hilt of his dirk involuntarily and sharply downward.

"Ha, ha!" laughed Rodd. "Why, that looks like wagging your tail like a moorhen. I say, why didn't you draw that skewer just now? My word, you did look fierce!"

One of the marines tittered, and the other spread his mouth into a broad grin, while, convulsed with rage, the young officer turned upon both furiously, making them draw themselves up as stiff as their muskets.

"How dare you!" cried the middy, turning back to Rodd, and now becoming fully conscious of the fact that the schooner's crew gathered forward were gazing at the scene with intense enjoyment.

"What's the matter, reefer?" said Rodd, whose face was scarlet, but whose words sounded as cool and indifferent as if he were calm in the extreme.

"Matter, you insolent blackguard!" cried the midshipman. "If I were not on duty, and too much of a gentleman to soil my hands with a schooner's loblolly boy, I would give you a sound thrashing with my belt."

"Would you?" said Rodd coolly. "That's the worst of you reefers. You are nearly all of you like that when you come ashore at Plymouth. It's your uniform and the wearing of a skewer that makes you all so cocky. Now, do you know you have said what a fellow just your age once said to me at Saltash—but he didn't. He had an accident, and then we shook hands, and I took him home to my uncle's and helped him to bathe his face. It was such a hot day that his nose bled a good deal. But we stopped it. Nice fellow he was too, afterwards. So I dare say you'd be if I had taken you in tow a bit."

"I understand you, sir," panted the middy; "and look here, I shall not forget this."

"Pooh! Yes you will," said Rodd, with a mocking laugh. "I wish you were going to stop on board. We have got a spare cot here. Get your old man to give you leave when your lieutenant has done smelling in all the lockers below. You come while the two vessels are in company, and I'll teach you how to use the gloves."

"Oh, if I wasn't on duty!" panted the middy furiously. "I haven't got a card with me, but give me yours. We may meet again."

"Hope we shall, I'm sure," said Rodd. "I say, reefer, don't be so jolly disappointed because you won't have the price of half a nigger for prize-money."

"Pah!" ejaculated the middy furiously; and turning his back upon Rodd he stepped to the side and looked over into the boat, to run his eye furiously over her crew, who were all sitting upon the alert, ready for any order that might be given.

But as he turned away and faced inboard, to his annoyance he found Rodd close up, smiling carelessly in his face.

"I say, reefer," he said, "you do look hot."

"Sir!" snapped out the middy, trying to look the boy down.

"I say, don't be so waxy because you are disappointed."

"I beg, sir, that you will not address your remarks to me; and please recollect that you and yours are not out of the wood yet."

"All right; only look here; your lads have had a long row, and you have got another one back. Let's give the poor fellows a bucket of water, and I'll pour a bottle of our lime-juice in and some syrup. It makes a splendid drink. Look there; those two red herrings of yours have begun licking their dry lips at the very thought of it."

The midshipman seemed to give himself a snatch, but he glanced at the two marines, and then turned and looked over into the boat, for he was horribly thirsty himself.

"Dry, my lads?" he said. "Like some water?"

"Thankye, sir!" came in chorus, and Rodd called out at once—

"Joe Cross! Bucket of fresh water—two pannikins! And is the steward there?"

"Ay, ay, sir!"

"Two bottles of lime-juice and some syrup for the boat's crew and marines."

Just then Uncle Paul's head appeared above the cabin hatch, and he stepped on deck, coming forward to where the two lads were, Rodd smiling and good-humoured, the middy wearing the aspect of the celebrated dog which had been pelted with big marrow-bones, upon each of which reposed a thick juicy bit of beef.

"Lieutenant Branscombe says will you step down and join us for a few minutes, Mr Lindon."

"Does he want me, sir?"

"Only to partake of a little refreshment this thirsty night."

"That's right," cried. Rodd. "You go on down with uncle. I'll see that your lads have plenty."

"Er—er—no grog, please," said the middy hastily.

"Not a drop, honour bright," said Rodd, laughing. "You shan't be mastheaded for that;" and he clapped the young officer merrily on the back.

The stay would have been longer, but the darkness was coming on fast; still it had been long enough for all to become the best of friends, and when the two officers came on deck it was to find the two crews engaged in a hearty game of repartee, the schooner's men casting jokes down into the boat, and the man-of-war's men hurling them back.

"Yes, a very smart crew, Captain Chubb," said the lieutenant, "but if it hadn't been for the doctor's papers here, we should have been obliged to lighten you of about half-a-dozen, for you know you have no business to have such men as this whilst his Majesty runs short."

Just then the two lads were talking together hard.

"Oh, don't you take any notice of that, Harding. Cocky, you called it. You should drop that; it's too schoolboy-like. You know a fellow may be only a midshipman, still the ship's roll does call him a man, and when a fellow's an officer in command of a lot of sailors, he's obliged to put it on a bit, else he'd never be able to keep them in their places."

"Yes, I see," said Rodd.

"That's right; and before I go I just want to say it was very thoughtful of you to promise that the lads shouldn't have any drink. I got into several rows when I was young and green, and went ashore with boats' crews. They used to try on all sorts of dodges to get away to the public-house. I say, get that uncle of yours to stop about here fishing for a bit. I want to get you aboard the *Di* and spend an evening with us at the mess. Do. I shall get to like you."

"All right; I will try," said Rodd. "It wouldn't be the first time I've been aboard a man-of-war."

"Eh? Where?"

"Plymouth harbour."

"Oh yes, I forgot. That's where you live when you are at home. Why don't you join altogether? You are just cut out for a middy."

"Couldn't leave uncle. Going to be a naturalist."

"A what?"

"Scientific gentleman."

"But serve the King!"

"What, and be sent down here hunting after the blackbirding blackguards?"

"Pshaw! That's not really what we are here for; only if we see a suspicious-looking craft we board her."

"Then what are you here for?"

"King's business. Mum. Mustn't say."

"Now, Mr Lindon! Good-evening, Captain Chubb; and good-evening, doctor. Glad to have met you, sir, and I hope you won't put me down in your black books as *homo durissimus*, or some other scientific name. Give way, my lads. Mr Lindon! Do you want to be left behind?"

"All right, sir," cried the middy, springing into the boat and coming down into the arms of a couple of the men. "Good-night, Harding! We shall expect you on board the *Di*."

Down dropped the oars on either side, and then splash, splash, in regular movement the blades tossed up the beautiful pale lambent water, while here and there they broke up the reflection of the stars that were gradually appearing in the soft violet sky, while the boat glided on farther and farther from the schooner, making its way towards the lights of the sloop, from which all of a sudden there was a sharp flash, followed at a perceptible interval by the report of a musket.

This was answered a few seconds later by a flash and smart crack from the sloop's cutter, whose course Rodd leaned over the side to watch till it was invisible, when he turned from the side, to find Joe Cross waiting and evidently watching him.

"Rather close shave, sir," he said. "I began to feel as if some of us was going to have our 'oliday come to an end. Wouldn't have been so bad, though, for there are some very jolly fellows there, and it aren't half a dusty life aboard a man-of-war when you have got over the first few days, and being what they calls homesick. Aren't no fear of their coming back for us, is there?"

"Not the least, Joe. You are all safe enough."

"We are a-going to give the doctor, sir, such a cheer when he comes on deck again—three times three, and one in for you. My word, sir, the lads did laugh to see you take the starch out of that there young reefer! It was fine!"

"Oh, never mind about that, Joe. But I say, you have been aboard a man-of-war. What would a sloop like that be doing down here?"

"Why, you know, sir; looking after the blackbird catchers—the slavers."

"Oh no; they are not on this station for that."

"Must be, sir."

"No, Joe."

"Well, but, sir, you heard what the lufftenant said to our old man. That's what they were after, sir, and a bit disappointed too, until you and the doctor made them so friendly. They thought they'd got hold of this fine craft, nice little prize, for she'd sell well just as she stands after being condemned. Handy little bit of pocket-money for them in these days when the war is over. Rather a puzzler to them at first. The second luff—that's what he was—had never tackled a natural history craft before, and he wouldn't believe it. That's what they are here for, sir, trying to put a stop to the slave trade. We come upon one in the *Naaera* once—the nearer and dearer we used to call her, sir. Just about such a sloop as that is. It wasn't our business, but we boarded her, the slave ship, I mean, in a calm, and the blackguards aboard of her showed fight and beat our boat off in trying to get away with their sweeps. They were making for one of these swampy rivers out eastward, rowing as hard as they could, and bringing up a lot of the poor niggers from below to help pull at the sweeps. Sweeps, indeed! Nice sweeps they were! And if they once got into the river we should have lost them."

"Well?" said Rodd. "And they beat you back?"

"That they did, sir. Took us quite by surprise. We never thought they would have the cheek to resist; and we lay off, rubbing our sore ears and growling and spitting like angry cats, not knowing what to do, feeling that we should get worse off if we pursued, and ashamed to go back to face our old man; and just as we were feeling at our worst we knew that our skipper had been watching us all the time with his glass, and there was our launch coming full swing, chock-full of men showing their teeth. That set us all up again, and we were like new men. Round went our boat's head, and we were off in full pursuit of the slaver, the lads pulling so hard that we got alongside before the launch could overtake us, swarmed over her low gunwale, and went at the slaver's crew tooth and nail, so savage that every man of us showed them the cutlass practice in fine style, driving them back step by step till if we had had strength enough we should have driven them overboard or down below; but they were too strong for us. Put half-a-pound weight in a scale, sir, if there's a pound in t'other it is too much for it, and so it was here, sir. We boarded her from the starn, and had driven them right up into the bows, but being a bit india-rubbery, when they could get no farther they bounced back on us and we were being driven step by step along the deck, farther and farther aft, till they gathered theirselves together with a rush, yelling like demons, and the next thing would have been that such of us as could stand would have been driven over into our boat again. But there was a regular hearty British cheer when we least expected it, for we had forgotten all about our other boat, and there were the launchers swarming over her bows and taking them in the rear. That made our lads take heart again. We cheered back, and charged, and there were the slavers, blacks, half-breeds and Portuguese, took, as you might say, between the jaws of a big rat-trap, every one of whose teeth was a British sailor; and to save being chopped in two, down they all tumbled into the slaver's hold, trapped themselves like the poor wretches the hold was packed with. My word, Mr Rodd, sir, there are some things as a fellow never can forget, and that was one of them. It was just awful, sir!"

"What, did you kill them all?" cried Rodd, horror-stricken.

"Nay, sir, not one. We might have killed some of them if they had kept on showing fight; and I don't say, mind you, as some of them hadn't got some very awkward cuts, for when a British tar's fighting in a good cause, and been knocked about till his monkey's well up, his habit is to hit hard; but there, as soon as we had driven that lot below they chucked their knives and axes and pikes away and began to howl for mercy. What I meant was so awful was that place down below—that there hold with the slaver's crew trampling about and trying to hide themselves amongst the chained-up cargo. Awful aren't the word for it, sir! The lads couldn't stand it: let alone the sick and dying, there were some there that must have been dead for days, and that in a close hold in a sea like this! But I believe it was much hotter. Even the slaver's crew themselves begged to be let out—and there, I won't say any more about it. It was quite time even then that our old country began to put a stop to the slave trade, and I am sorry to say they aren't done it yet. That's what made us chaps to-night so free-and-easy with that there boat's crew. You see, you can't help liking fellows who are trying to put a stop to things like that."

"No, Joe, of course not. But that's not what they are down here for."

"Who says so, sir?"

"Why, that midshipman, Mr Lindon, told me so."

"Well, he ought to know, sir. What did he say they were here for, then?"

"He didn't say, only that it was private and he couldn't speak."

"Well, I don't know, then, only a man-of-war wouldn't be down here for nothing; that's pretty sure. Maybe we shall run into company with them again some day, and then I dare say we shall know. They gave us lads a fright, but I aren't sorry we met them, sir, for it was a bit of a change. Yes, Mr Rodd, sir, they are down here on some business pertickler secret and sealed orders; but you wait a bit, sir, and I dare say one of these days you'll find out."

Chapter Twenty Five
Oh, Murther!

Rodd was early on deck next morning for his bath, which consisted of so many buckets of water fresh fished up and dashed upon him by the men as a makeshift, consequent upon Captain Chubb telling him that he could not have any swims on account of the sharks. "Can't spare you, my lad," he had said. "But I haven't seen a shark," grumbled Rodd. "No, my lad, but they would very soon see you. You never know where those gentlemen are."

So Rodd went on deck when sea and sky looked dim and a faint mist lay low upon the surface of the ocean, making everything indistinct. "She's gone, sir; she's gone!"

"Who's she, and where has she gone?" said Rodd, rather sleepily.

"The *Diadem*, sir."

"What, the sloop of war? Not she! You will see her come peeping out of the fog yonder before long."

"Nay, sir; she's gone right off, and it's all right. My word, I wish we had got a fiddle here!"

"A fiddle! What for?"

"Hornpipe, sir. The boys are all bubbling over and don't know how to bear themselves. Nothing like a few kicks up and down the deck to a well-played old tune, to get rid of it all."

"Why, what are you talking about?" cried Rodd.

"Talking about, sir? Ah, you never knowed what it was to be a sailor, and when you are free never knowing for a moment how soon you may be pressed. Why, I don't believe there was a man Jack on us as slept a wink last night with thinking about this morning."

"What, for fear you would be pressed, after what uncle said?"

"Ay, ay, sir. Your uncle meant right enough, and he believed what he said, and that there lieutenant was civil enough; but a second lieutenant aren't a first lieutenant, sir, and a first lieutenant aren't a post-captain. We all talked a bit last night, and put that and that together, and Isaac Gregg, who aren't a very wise chap—you see, sir, he's got too much fat about him to leave room for anything else—but he said something smart last night. 'Yes,' he says, 'my lads, that all sounds right enough, but suppose when that boat got back the captain says, Yes, he says, it's all very well, and I dare say that there gent got leave from Government to man his schooner and come down here bottling sea-leeches and other insects of that kind; but I am short of men for the King's ship, and that's more consequence than what he's doing of. So you just start back at daybreak in the boat with my compliments to Dr Robson, saying I'm very sorry, but he must please hand over six of the best lads he's got.'"

"Oh, nonsense, Joe! The captain would be too much of a gentleman."

"Being a gentleman, sir, is being a gentleman, but duty's duty, and officers and sailors have to give up everything to that. Last night, whether we was on the watch, or turned in to our hot bunks, every man Jack of us felt that the Bun was right, and a bit envious of him, because, poor chap, he would have been safe. They wouldn't have took him; but we all of us fully expected to see that boat coming back for us this morning. But not only aren't there no boat, but the sloop's slipped away in the night and gone."

"Where's she gone, then?"

"Well, that's what we don't know, sir, and we don't care."

"But are you sure, Joe? She may be lying off yonder in the mist."

"Oh no, she aren't, sir. Two on us have been up right aloft till we could lay our hands on the main truck; and when you are up there you are looking right over the fog. It's wonderful how close it lies to the water. It's all right, sir, and I believe we are safe. Aren't you glad?"

"Of course I am, Joe."

"I know you are, sir. But just you think what we must be, just about five hundred times as glad as you are, and we are all ready for anything you like. What's it to be to-day?"

"Well, I don't think we shall do much. Uncle will consider it too hot."

"Hot, sir? Not it! Just right. We shan't mind. Fishing, netting, rowing. You tell him not to think about us. It will just warm us up, for most on us had the shivers all night."

The low mist began to lift soon after Rodd had had his bath, for the level rays of the sun began to pierce the grey haze as the great orange orb slowly rolled up from the depths of ocean, investing it with the loveliest of pearly tints and iridescent hues, while not a speck of sail or the clearly marked lines of topmasts could be seen upon the horizon line.

"Well," said the doctor, at breakfast, as Rodd told him what the men had said, "the heat will be very great, but I shouldn't spare myself. If I gave up my researches to-day it would be for the sake of the men."

"You needn't consider them that way, sir," said Captain Chubb. "They would rather you didn't. But couldn't you do something that would spare my deck a little?"

"Well, I am afraid that's impossible, Captain Chubb," said the doctor.

"Ah, well, sir," said the captain, with a sigh, "I suppose you must go on; but it seems a pity when everything's so white and clean."

So the captain's decks suffered all day, and were swabbed clean again, while that evening before the mists began to gather there was a fresh surprise.

Rodd took it into his head to go up to the main cross-trees with the glass. He had said nothing, but he had some idea as to the possibility of the sloop coming into sight again, and he had made up his mind if he could see her in the distance to give Captain Chubb a broad hint, and urge him to press on full sail right through the night.

It was very glorious, Rodd thought, as he perched himself up aloft on the cross-trees, after finding the heavy glass very much in his way as he climbed.

"It's beautiful up here; but—"

He did not finish his remark to himself, but got his left arm well round the mast, adjusted the glass, and began slowly to sweep the horizon.

He felt in a state of doubt and suspicion, fully expecting that at any moment the tapering masts of the sloop might slowly creep into the field ready to damp his hopes, for his feelings were completely on the side of the men. But as slowly and carefully he ran the glass along what seemed to be the very edge of the world, his spirits rose.

"Nothing—nothing," he kept on muttering to himself. "Oh, how big the world is, after all! Here we are, just like a speck on the ocean, quite alone, and though there must be thousands of ships and boats sailing about, not one in sight, and in about another ten minutes all will be bright starlight again—and let's see, I began here, and I've swept the sea right round, and just in time, for before I could go round again or half-way it will be quite dark—and— What's that?" he cried excitedly.

He started violently, and his hands trembled so that he had great difficulty in steadying the glass to fix it upon that which had suddenly caught his eye.

"Nothing!" he muttered impatiently. "It was my fancy. I made as sure as possible, just as I was going to lower the glass, that I could see the three masts of the sloop standing right out yonder towards the west. All rubbish and imagination," he muttered. "I pictured that because it was what I was afraid of seeing when— Oh–h–h! It wasn't fancy! There she is! Oh, there she is, after all!"

He looked sharply down at the deck, which was occupied only by four of the men, the skipper and Uncle Paul being in the cabin. But one of these men was Joe Cross, and Rodd chirruped faintly to attract's the sailor's attention.

"Make out anything, sir?"

"Come up here, Joe," replied Rodd, in a low tone, and the man sprang to the ratlines and began rapidly to ascend till he was nearly on a level with the occupant of the cross-trees.

"See a whale spouting, sir? I should have thought it was getting too dark."

"No, Joe; but I have just made out the sloop with the glass."

"Nay, sir! Don't say that!" cried the man, in a startled tone.

"Take the glass, Joe. I am afraid it's true."

"Oh, murther! as Pat says," groaned the sailor, as he hurriedly adjusted the glass and began to sweep the horizon in the direction Rodd pointed out, a few points on the starboard bow. "Can't see nothing, sir. Were you sure?"

"Yes, Joe; quite."

"But it's getting dark too fast, sir. I can make nothing out. If you are right, though, she mayn't have seen us and may be out of sight again by morning.—Ah, I've got her!"

"There, I knew I was right, Joe."

"Not quite, sir. Yes, I've got her quite plain now, but she's dying out fast. It aren't a man-of-war. It's a two-master of some kind. A big schooner or a brig. It's all right, sir. There's life in a mussel, after all. My word, though, didn't it bring my heart up into my mouth!"

"Are you sure it's not a three-master, Joe?" cried Rodd joyously.

"Sartin sure, sir. Why, you talk as frightened like as we poor lads were."

"What vessel was it, then?"

"Oh, I don't know what she was, sir. I only know what she warn't. That's enough for us, eh, sir? I say, sir; what weather! Rather different to what we had in the French port. Looks settled too. Nice and cool the air feels. There, it's only fancy, but it's just as if I could sniff the land."

"How far are we away, Joe?" asked Rodd.

"Long way, sir. But I say, Mr Rodd, sir, I wouldn't say anything down below. It'd only skeer the lads and set them thinking all night."

"But wouldn't you say anything about having seen that ship?"

"Oh, if you like, sir. The skipper ought to know. But I can swear she warn't a man-of-war, and that's enough for us. Oh, there is the skipper. My word, though, you can hardly see him! Curus, isn't it, how the mist begins to gather? Pretty good sign we are not so very far off the shore. Will you hail him, sir, or shall I?"

"You, Joe."

A brief conversation ensued, question and answer ending by Joe's declaration that he believed it was a brig; and then they descended to the deck.

Chapter Twenty Six
Dreamy

Very curious incidents are sometimes invented, but the most extravagant can be matched by others that have really occurred.

One of the last things that had been talked about that evening had been the vessel of which Rodd had caught a glimpse in the short tropic twilight just as it was being swallowed up by the darkness and mist of night. Joe Cross had incidentally said that he believed it was a brig, and that night as Rodd lay half asleep, half wakeful, in his cot, kept from finding the customary repose of a tired lad by the heat of the narrow cabin below, the word brig brought to mind the vessel that had so nearly run upon them in Havre-de-Grace, and in a drowsy stupid way he had pictured her tall tapering spars, the flapping of her stay-sail, and the rush of the storm.

Then all was blank, till all at once it seemed as if time had elapsed and he was picturing the French brig once more, knowing that it was the *Jeanne d'Arc*, though all was darkness and he only caught sight of the vessel now and then, by the flashing of the fort guns, while the roar of their reports echoed loudly above the rush of the wind as the brave vessel tacked from side to side of the harbour, striving to reach the mouth and escape out to sea.

It was all very vivid as in a dream.

Flash went the fort gun, there was the roar of the report, and all was darkness, again and again, while somehow—he could not tell how it was—the heat was intense, and Rodd threw up one hand, which came in contact with the top of his cot with a sharp rap.

"Bah! It hurts," muttered the boy; and then dream and reality merged in one, for there was another flash and the roar as if of half-a-dozen guns.

But the boy was awake now to the fact that he was not dreaming of the escape of the French brig, but far south of the Equator, lying half stifled in his cot, listening to the roar of a tropic storm, while every now and then the cabin which he shared with his uncle was lit up by the vivid flashes, which were succeeded by fresh roars.

"What a storm," thought Rodd, "and how hot!"

He slipped out of his cot to go and thrust open the cabin window.

"Hear the thunder, uncle?" he said.

But it had ceased for the moment, the last peal dying softly away, and for answer to his question he had only the deep regular breathing of a sound sleeper.

"He must have been tired," thought the boy, and creeping closer to the cabin window he thrust out his hand to let in more air, but found the window wide open as it could be.

"He must have found out how hot it was and done that himself," thought Rodd, as he knelt softly upon the bulkhead to try and breathe the fresh air; but it was hot and half suffocating, while the blackness was intense. One moment there was a faint quivering somewhere above, and just enough to show him the murkiness of the sea which spread out from beneath him far away like so much blackened oil touched for a few brief instants with streaks of gold.

"Why, there isn't a breath of air," thought Rodd, and then he started back, dazzled by the brilliant glare of the lightning, which made him involuntarily close his eyes and keep them shut till the terrific crash of thunder, which seemed to burst exactly over his head, had gone rolling away as if its echoes were composed of gigantic cannon balls passing slowly down metallic tunnels right away into space.

"That was a startler," said the boy to himself. "How awful, but how grand! It's rather hard to think that the danger's in the lightning, and that there is nothing in the thunder to hurt."

Then once more all was black silence above and below, and all beyond the cabin window seemed to be solid.

"I never saw a storm like this at home," thought the boy. "Uncle can sleep!"

There was another brilliant flash, but this time Rodd felt prepared and did not shrink. He only knelt, gazing out of the stern window, impressed by the grandeur of that which he had seen.

Behind him he felt that everything in the cabin had been as light as day, but away from him all around he had looked upon a vivid picture, a gloriously wondrous cloudscape stretching far above and reflected far beneath in the smooth, oily, gently heaving sea—a grand vision of mountains of blue and gold and purple, which quivered before his eyes for a few moments in such vivid intensity that his eyeballs ached; then all was black again for a few moments, and then came the deep-toned roar as of hundreds of distant mighty cannons; not a sudden, sharp, metallic crash as in the last instance, but a deep murmurous intonation which made the woodwork of the schooner tremble.

Rodd felt no fear—nothing but a sense of awe at the grandeur of the storm, and it was with a feeling of eagerness that he waited for the next flash. But a minute passed before there was a faint quivering which slightly lit up the sea, to give place to blackness, silence and darkness. Then there was another faint quivering light that seemed to come from somewhere behind where he stood, and again he waited for one of those vivid flashes that should show up the configuration of the clouds shaped in mountain and valley and distant cave.

And many minutes must have passed, during which time Rodd listened in the appalling silence for the distant soft and increasing rushing sound of the coming rain, even as he had listened before in far-off Devon to the coming of some summer storm.

"There will be wind too," he thought. "I wonder whether all is made fast aloft; for a storm like this," he continued, in his ignorance, "can't come without a tremendous wind and a rush of rain."

His next thought was that he would go on deck and see what the watch were about; but he hesitated to stir, for the thought of the gorgeous cloudscape he had seen fascinated him and held him to his place.

"I needn't worry about that," he thought. "Captain Chubb's sure to be on deck. He wouldn't sleep like we do. If I go and open the cabin door it will wake uncle up. Hah! It's quivering again. The storm can't be over like this. Now there's another big flash coming."

He had hardly formed the thought when from quite up in the zenith down into the depths of the sea the arch of heaven seemed to open out in a sharp jagged line of vivid blue light, shutting again instantaneously, and the boy knelt gazing before him in wonder, for there, about a mile away, with every spar and yard and rope standing out black against the blue light, was the picture—the model, it seemed to him to be—of a tall-masted brig sitting motionless upon the water; and then it was gone.

"Why, that must have been the one we saw," thought Rodd, and he strained his eyes again as he listened for the roar of the thunder that should have succeeded the vivid zigzag flash of electricity; but it did not come, and he waited and waited in the darkness in vain, trying to grasp how it could be that a storm should come to an end in so strange and unsatisfactory a way according to his lights, and why there should be neither rain nor wind.

He waited, trying hard now to pierce the black darkness, but trying in vain.

There was nothing to see, nothing to hear, and in spite of the wonder and awe that had pervaded him, Rodd Harding now behaved like a very ordinary human being, for he yawned, felt sleepy and that he was not so hot as he was before, and thinking that it was no use to stop there any longer, and that he might as well dress, he crept softly back to his cot and stood thinking again.

"Can't be anything like morning," he said to himself, "and I shall be able to see that brig then. Why, I remember now; I was dreaming about the storm at Havre, and that vessel—what was it? The *Jeanne d'Arc*—escaping, and the forts firing at her; and I saw the flashes from the guns. Of course; how absurd! That was the thunder and lightning, and—"

Rodd slipped slowly on to his pillow, yawned again, muttered something about how sleepy he felt, and the next moment he was off as soundly as his uncle; but only, it seemed to him, to begin dreaming directly after about the escaping of the brig, and the storm, mingled with the noise and the shouting of people ashore, and a heavy bump from somewhere close at hand; and then the boy was wide awake again, springing up so suddenly in his cot that it was not his hand but his head that struck with a rap against the woodwork, as a voice that he hardly recognised in the confusion shouted—

"Rodd, boy! Quick—on deck! The schooner's going down!"

Chapter Twenty Seven
Strange Proceedings

"Is it a wreck, uncle?" panted Rodd.

"I thought so, boy," cried Uncle Paul; "but don't talk. Slip on two or three things."

He was still speaking, when there was a rush down the cabin stairs, and the captain shouted—

"Quick, doctor! Your pistols and a gun! We are attacked!"

The words thrilled through Rodd, and the next minute he had seized a double gun and was ready to follow his uncle and the skipper on deck, where in the faint light of morning he found nearly the whole of the crew gathered across the after part of the deck, armed with capstan bars for the moment, while the mate and Joe Cross were rapidly handing round cutlasses and pikes. The forward part of the schooner was in the hands of strangers, all well-armed; others were climbing over the bows from a boat which was made fast alongside, while hurried orders were being given to them in French by a tall, dark, grey-haired man, sword in one hand, pistol in the other.

"What's the meaning of this?" panted Uncle Paul to the skipper, while Rodd felt as if he were not yet awake, and suddenly recalled the fact that he had armed himself with a perfectly useless weapon, for in his excitement he had forgotten powder flask and bullets, having instead of the latter brought a belt containing small shot.

"Pirates or privateers, sir," replied the skipper hotly, "but just give us time. Be smart, my lads. Pikes and cutlasses, and then all together with a will!"

"For heaven's sake let's have no bloodshed, Captain Chubb!" cried Uncle Paul, catching the skipper by the arm.

"Not my wish, sir," said the captain shortly; "but this is my schooner while I command her, and I'm going to clear this deck."

"Ay, ay, sir!" came in a low, eager murmur from the men.

"There, sir," said the skipper; "you and the lad stand back. Ready, my lads?"

"No, no!" cried Uncle Paul, who saw that the strangers forward, all as well-armed as the schooner's crew, were eagerly waiting for the order to advance from their leader, each party being ready to be let slip for what might prove to be a desperate encounter.

Rodd grasped this, and then felt puzzled as he saw a youth of about his own age suddenly elbow his way to the front to stand beside the leader.

Suddenly awakened as he had been from sleep, Rodd felt more confused than ever, for the sight of the youth, who from his dress seemed to be the second officer, added to his confusion, though for the moment he could hardly tell why.

And this just as Uncle Paul was grasping the skipper's arm and saying—

"Don't be hasty. These cannot be pirates. There must be some mistake."

"Maybe, sir, but these fellows who have boarded us have made it. Now, sir, once more, stand back and let us clear the deck. They can talk when they are back in their boats."

There was a few moments' silence, each side seeming unwilling to begin, and taking advantage of an apparent hesitancy on the part of the strange leader, Uncle Paul instead of stepping back raised his hand and advanced, Rodd springing to his side, while their movement was exactly followed by the chief intruder and the youth who stepped to his side.

"Now, sir," cried Uncle Paul firmly, in French.

"I understand English," was the reply.

"I am very glad," said Uncle Paul. "Now, sir, you see that we are well-armed and prepared. What is the meaning of this attack?"

"Ah, I am glad, sir," said the stranger courteously. "Pray keep your men back, and I will mine."

"Tell them to clear off the deck, then, doctor. There must be no talk here."

"Be silent, Captain Chubb!" cried Uncle Paul sternly. "We must have no bloodshed."

"No, sir," cried his opponent quickly, and in very excellent English. "We are no pirates. I am the captain of that brig, and in urgent need of help."

"And this is a very strange way of asking for it, sir."

"Yes, yes, I know, my friend," cried the other hotly, "but it was forced upon me by circumstances. I have need of your vessel, and I must have it at all costs—peacefully if you will, and I am ready to recompense you, the owner, for any loss of cargo at your destination which you may incur; but I must have the use of this little ship."

"Indeed, sir!" said Uncle Paul, with a peculiar smile. "And if I say you cannot have it; what then?"

"Then, sir," said the stranger haughtily, "you see we are prepared. I shall be compelled to take it from you by force."

"Ah–h–h!" came like a low growl of satisfaction from the schooner's crew, and Rodd was conscious of a rather ominous movement on the part of the men, who began moistening their hands and taking a firmer grip of their weapons.

Rodd was drinking in this colloquy, which filled him with wild excitement; but all the time he kept glancing from the young officer who stood sword in hand to the brig he had seen over-night and again thrown up by the storm, still lying about the same distance away from the schooner, and then with his head suddenly seeming to become clearer he cried out aloud—

"Uncle, those are the officers we saw at Havre, and that's the brig that escaped."

"You—you were at Havre!" cried the elder officer excitedly; and he stepped closer to Rodd, his young companion, watchful and on the alert, following his example and keeping close as if to defend him from any attempted seizure.

"Yes, yes, of course," cried Rodd, without looking at the speaker, his eyes being fixed upon the young man.

"Then this is a French vessel?" cried the officer.

"No, sir," replied Uncle Paul. "It is my schooner, and I am not in pursuit of your brig."

"Why, it is!" cried Rodd suddenly, as he dropped the butt of his unloaded gun with a thud upon the deck. "I thought I knew you again!— Uncle, this is the young French prisoner I helped to escape from Dartmoor."

Before he could say another word the sword the young Frenchman held dropped from his hand to the extent of its gold-laced knot, and to Rodd's confusion a pair of thin arms were flung about his neck and he was held tightly to the young stranger's breast.

"Oh, *mon ami*! *mon ami*! My dear friend!" he cried. "Do we meet once more like this? *Mon père, c'est le jeune Anglais qui nous a sauvés dans cet affreux temps.*"

"Moray!" cried the officer, looking stunned. "Is this true?"

"True? Oh yes! Oh yes!" cried the lad, speaking now in English. "You, young angler, fisherman, this is my dear father."

To Rodd's false shame and confusion, he had to submit to another embrace, for before he could realise what was about to happen the officer had followed his son's example and not only embraced him, but kissed him on both cheeks.

"Well, this is a queer set out," said Uncle Paul. "Then you are the two fellows who broke into my bedroom and helped yourselves to my purse?"

"Ha, ha! Yes, my friend," cried the officer, laughing; "but you and your brave son will forgive. We were poor exiles and prisoners fighting for our liberty, and you will let us make amends."

"Oh, well, you did," said Uncle Paul bluffly; "but that is no excuse for turning pirates and trying to rob me of my ship at the point of the sword."

"No, no," cried the officer hastily, "but you are a brave Englishman, and you and your son—"

"No, sir, my nephew."

"—will forgive. One moment; let me think!" cried the officer, as he dragged his hand from out of his sword-knot and thrust the blade into its sheath. "Yes, yes, let me think. I have it, Morny," and turning to his followers he uttered a short sharp command which resulted in his men swinging themselves over the side and entering the two boats in which they had effected the surprise of the schooner.

At their first movement in retreat the skipper's crew burst into a loud jeering laugh, and made as if to rush forward; but at a word from Captain Chubb they were silenced and held back.

"I thank you, sir," said the French officer, raising his hat to the skipper. "It was well done. Now let me speak; let me explain," and he looked from Rodd to his uncle and back, and then gave a glance at the skipper, while the two lads stood hand in hand.

"It was like this," he said; "you saw us at Havre that stormy day, and of course my brig nearly crushed into your vessel. Then we lay at anchor close together till that order came down from a vile insensate Government to seize upon my vessel and my crew. It was the work of enemies, and I had to set sail at once, or once more my son and I would have had to pass years in the inside of a prison, not as culprits, monsieur, but as honourable gentlemen, French nobles, whose only crime was fidelity to one," —and as he spoke he stopped short, uttering the word *one* with grave reverence, as he took off his hat—an example followed by his son. "Well, gentlemen, I cannot explain to you. There is not time. Only this—you saw that I made what you English call a dash for it—for freedom. It was like madness, but we said we would rather trust the storm than the French Government. They sent boats full of soldiers to seize us, but we kept on. They opened fire upon us from the forts, but we did not shrink."

"Yes, yes, we saw all," cried Uncle Paul, "and a very brave dash you made."

Captain Chubb, who had listened, frowning heavily the while, uttered a low grunt.

"And a very fine bit of seamanship, sir," he said, and the officer turned to him and raised his hat.

"It was desperate, sir," he said gravely, "and I knew that I was risking the lives of my dear son and all on board; but no man there shrank. Well, sir, my story is long, but I must excuse myself for my conduct here. It is enough. We battled with the storm, as you saw, and escaped."

"I always said you had gone down," grunted Captain Chubb.

"No, sir. We escaped with but one wound, and that was to my poor vessel; and since the night when we left Havre-de-Grace upon my mission it has been one long struggle, as you would say, for life."

"Indeed, sir?"

"Yes," said the officer sadly, and he pointed over the side towards where the beautiful duck-like brig with its taper spars sat the smooth sea, but with a steady stream of water trickling down her side. "My chief officer and my men have worked in every way they knew long days and weeks; but it is of no use. I would not give up the great object upon which I have come, but it is forced upon us at last that before many days have gone over our heads that vessel will lie far down in the depths of the ocean. Do you not see how low she is in the water?"

"Eh?" cried the skipper eagerly. "Eh? I thought she was low down with cargo. You've sprung a leak?"

"A cannon ball crashed through her, sir, and we have never been able to master that leak."

"Then why in the name of thunder didn't you put into port?" cried the skipper contemptuously.

The officer smiled.

"I cannot explain," he said. "There was not time. I had work to do—a task that I had promised to fulfil, and we held on till it was forced upon me that I must get another vessel or stand with my men upon the deck and let our brave *Roi Dagobert* sink beneath our feet."

"That wasn't her name at Havre," said the downright skipper.

"No, sir," said the officer, smiling; "but were we not pursued? Would not news of our escape be sent far and wide? We were obliged to assume another disguise. The *Jeanne d'Arc*, we said, sank at Havre. That is the *Roi Dagobert* floating still; but for how long?"

"I don't quite see that," said the skipper bluntly.

"No?" said the officer. "Monsieur has never passed long years as a prisoner of war."

"Well, no," grunted the skipper. "Maybe that might have made me a bit shifty."

"There, sir," said the officer, turning now to Uncle Paul; "that is my excuse for this desperate venture—this attempt to seize your vessel. My business is urgent. I am a nobleman, a count of the French Empire, and I offer you any recompense you like to name if you will give up to me your vessel, leaving me full command for a week—a month—such time as I may need."

"And if I say, sir, that I cannot accede to what you must own are wild demands," said Uncle Paul, "what then?"

"What then?" said the officer slowly.

"You mean that you will attack us, and the strongest wins?"

The officer was silent, and he turned his eyes upon his son, who left Rodd and took his extended hands, both standing silent for a few moments.

"No, sir," he said at last, slowly and gravely. "Neither my son nor I can raise our hands against those who gave us liberty, almost life. Morny, my boy, we will do our duty to the last, and try to keep the poor *Roi Dagobert* afloat. She may live long enough, even as she has kept afloat so long. If she sinks with us—well, my boy, we shall have done our duty to him we serve, and our names may not be forgotten in our country's rolls."

There was silence for a few moments, which was broken at last by Rodd.

"But I say, uncle," he cried eagerly, "you always said you had plenty of time, and—"

The young officer turned quickly upon the speaker with an eager questioning look, but before Uncle Paul could speak, Captain Chubb took off his cap and stood scratching his head in the now bright morning sunshine.

"Look here, Mr Count," he said; "I am only a rough Englishman, and a lot of what you have been saying about mission and that sort of thing is just so much Greek to me. But do you mean to tell me that you got a ball through the bottom of your smart brig that night in Havre, and have never been able to stop the leak?"

"Yes, yes; that is so, my friend. My chief officer has tried everything that he could do, but we could not get at the place. And look yonder! The pump has been kept going ever since."

"Well, sir," continued Captain Chubb, "I don't know your first mate, and I don't want to say hard things of a man who could take that there smart craft out of the French harbour as he did that night. He is a very fine sailor, sir. But if I aren't got a carpenter on board this schooner as would give him ninety out of a hundred and then beat him, without bringing to work the little bit I knows myself, why, I'm a Dutchman, and that I aren't."

"Ah!" cried the Count excitedly. "You think—"

"No, sir; I don't say I think anything without having a look. But as there don't seem to be any fighting going on, and you and the doctor here turns out to be old friends, why, before you talk of throwing up your job and taking to your boats—which would be a much more sensible thing to do than going down with colours flying when there warn't no need, and setting aside getting some fresh water and provisions into your boats and making for a place on the West Afric coast—I should just like to come on board your craft with my man and see what mightn't be done by stopping that there leak."

"My friend!" cried the Count excitedly, and he caught the skipper by the hands.

"Well, sir," said the skipper, with a grim smile, "if you are Mr Rodd's and the doctor's friend and wants to be friends with me, why, Tom Chubb aren't the man to say no and want to keep enemies. So there's my fin. But look 'ere, you know," he continued, as he gave the Count's thin white hand a tremendous grip, "yours was a very queer way of coming upon us, and might have meant some nasty marks on my white decks. You can't help being a Frenchman, but do you know what an Englishman would have done? He'd have just come here civil like and said, 'Look here, strangers, we have sprung a leak, and we are going down. Come and lend us a hand at the pumps.'"

"Ah, yes, of course," said the Count warmly. "It is what I should have done."

"And you would like me to come aboard and see if there's anything we can do?"

"Yes, yes!" cried the Count eagerly.

"All right, then, sir," said the skipper coolly; "I am sailing under the doctor's orders, and if he's willing, I'm your man."

Chapter Twenty Eight
A Ship Surgeon

"Well, Mr Rodd, sir," said Captain Chubb, as he and the lad stood watching the regular dip of oars in the brig's two boats as they glided back over the tranquil sea to where their vessel lay motionless in the calm. "Well, Mr Rodd, sir, don't you wish you'd been born a Frenchman?"

"No," cried the boy sharply. "I am thankful I was born English."

"And so you ought to be, my lad. Of all the crackbrained, sentimental, outrageous chaps I ever met there's none of them comes up to a Frenchman."

"Oh, you are too bad, Captain Chubb."

"Too bad, eh? Why, aren't they always kicking up a dust and making revolutions, cutting off their kings' and queens' heads, and then going to war with all the world, with their Napoleons and Bonapartes and all the rest of them? Call themselves men!"

"Why, you are as bad as uncle," cried Rodd merrily. "You and he ought to be always the best of friends. But, if you speak fairly you must own that they are very gallant men."

"Gallant men!" cried the skipper scornfully. "I don't call them men. I call them monkeys! Men! Butchers, as cut off the head of their beautiful Queen Mary What-you-may-call-it, and then after shedding blood like that, sending no end of poor women who never did them a bit of harm to that guillotine. I'd be ashamed of myself, Mr Rodd, to take their part."

"Oh, nonsense!" cried Rodd warmly. "I say that the Count and his son have proved themselves to be very brave fellows. Why, you owned as much yourself about the way in which they escaped with the brig."

"Oh, that was right enough," grumbled the skipper.

"I am not going to deny," continued Rodd, "that there are plenty of horrible wretches amongst the French. And that Revolution was awful; but haven't we plenty of bad men amongst the English?"

The skipper chuckled.

"Well, yes, we have had some pretty tidy ones, if you come to read your histories. But I don't know so much about those chaps being brave. It was a very clever bit of seamanship, mind you, that taking the brig out in the teeth of the storm with hardly room to tack. I am not a bad pilot in my way when I like to try, but I will be honest over it; I daren't have tried that job. It was a very clean thing. But look here, my lad. It's no use for you to try and crack that up, because him who did it must have been as mad as a hatter, and between ourselves, that's what I think that Count is."

"Oh, fudge, captain!" cried Rodd. "No more mad than you or I."

"Well, I can answer for myself, my lad," said the skipper, with a chuckle, "but that's more than I'd do for you, for you do some precious outrageous things sometimes."

"I?" cried Rodd.

"Yes, you, my lad."

"What a shame!" cried Rodd indignantly. "I defy you to prove that I have done anything that you could call mad. Now tell me something. What have you ever known me do that wasn't sensible?"

"Oh, that's soon done," cried the skipper. "Didn't you go and gammon the soldiers when they were after the escaped French prisoners? Don't you call that a mad act? Fighting against the laws of your country like that!"

"Ah, well, I suppose I oughtn't to have helped them, captain; but I couldn't help it."

"No, sir, and that's what the Frenchmen would say. Now, what in the world is that chap after, with his mission, as he calls it? What does he mean by coming rampaging out south with a hole in the bottom of his brig and the pumps going straight on to keep the water down? Would any one but a lunatic go risking his crew and his vessel like that?"

"Well, it does seem rather wild," replied Rodd thoughtfully.

"Wild? Well, that's only your way of saying he's stick, stark, staring mad. And here he's been out weeks and weeks, knowing as he says that his brig was sinking, when he could have put in at Gib, or the Azores, or Las Palmas, or brought up in one of the West Coast rivers, where he could run up on the tidal mud, careened his vessel, and set his ship's carpenter to work to clap patches upon her bottom outside and in. Don't you call that mad?"

"No. He might have had reasons for not doing so."

"Ah, that's right, sir; argufy. You young scholarly chaps who have been to big schools and got your heads chock-full of Latin and Greek, you are beggars to argufy—chopping logic, I suppose you calls it—and I give in. You could easily beat me at that; just as easily as I could turn you round my little finger at navigation. But I'll have one more go at you; I says that there French Count is mad."

"And I say he is not," said Rodd, "only a brave, eccentric nobleman who may have a good many more reasons for what he does than we know."

"All right, youngster. I give you my side. Now that's yours. Now, just answer me this. Warn't it the crack-brainedest bit of ask-you-to-go-and-borrow-a-new-strait-waistcoat-to-put-me-in sort of a job for him to bring his two boat-loads of men, like a black-flag-and-cross-boned Paul Jones sort of a pirate, aboard our schooner in the dark, thinking he's going to take possession of it to use instead of his own brig, when if he'd had any gumption he might have managed to patch her up, and— Here, I say, I can't go on talking like this before breakfast, my lad. I must have my bowl of coffee and a bit of salt pork and biscuit before I say another word."

"Oh, very well," cried Rodd merrily. "I see we shan't agree; and we don't want to quarrel, do we, captain?"

"Quarrel? Not us, my lad! It takes two to do that, and we knows one another too well."

"Then look here," cried Rodd, "you are taking it very coolly and talking about breakfast; aren't you going to order the boat out and go aboard the brig at once?"

"I aren't a-going to do anything till I have had my breakfast," said the captain. "They've spoilt my morning snooze, but I aren't going to let them spoil my morning meal, nor my lads' neither."

"But it's urgent," cried Rodd. "Suppose while you are thinking of eating and drinking the brig goes down?"

"Yah! She won't go down. If she's floated for weeks like that she'll keep her nose above water while I swallow two bowls of coffee. I can't work without something to keep me going. Let them pump for another half-hour, and then we'll go."

"We!" said Rodd sharply. "That means me too?"

"Oh, ah, if you like to come; only we shall have to keep a sharp look-out."

"What, for fear it should sink under us?"

"Nay, I didn't mean that, my lad. I mean, you see, we are dealing with a lunatic."

"Captain!" cried Rodd indignantly.

"Ay, but we are, and there's no knowing what sort of games fellows like that will be up to. I mean to give the mate strict orders to load all three guns, and if he sees the Count coming off again with his two boats full of men to take possession while he's got us tight, to sink them without mercy. Ah, here's the stooard, welcome, as you might say, as the flowers in spring. Come along, my lad, and let's lay in stores."

In spite of his words and deliberate way of proceeding, Captain Chubb had made his arrangements so that within half-an-hour of going down to breakfast he had the schooner's boat lowered down with Joe Cross, five men, and the carpenter, who had already handed into the boat what he called his bag of tricks, the said tricks being composed of an adze, saws, chisels, augers, and nails, and very shortly afterwards the oars were dipping, and with Uncle Paul and Rodd in the stern-sheets they were gliding over the glittering sea and rapidly shortening the distance between them and the beautiful brig, which won a string of encomiums from the skipper as they drew near.

"Yes, she is a beauty," he said. "It would be a pity to let her go down. Look at her lines, and the way she's rigged. If I wanted to sail a brig I wouldn't wish for a better; but then, you see, I don't. She's a bit low in the water, though, and no mistake. Well, we shall see; we shall see."

The Count and his son were eagerly awaiting their coming, and welcomed them warmly as they mounted the side, while, casting off his show of indifference, the skipper cast an admiring glance round the deck of the brig, and then gruffly exclaimed—

"Now then, sir, I want your bo'sun. But look here, can he parley English?"

"No," said the Count, "but my son and I will interpret everything you wish to hear."

"I don't know as I want to hear anything, sir," growled the skipper. "I want to see for myself, and after that mebbe I shall want to give a few orders, which I will ask you to have carried out."

"Yes; everything you wish shall be done directly."

"Umph!" grunted the skipper, looking round. "Pump rigged, and two men trying to keep the water under. Ought to be four."

"Yes, of course," cried the Count, and he turned to give an order; but Captain Chubb clapped his hand upon his arm.

"Hold hard," he said. "They'll do for a bit. Now then, I want to go below and sound the well."

The Count and his son led the way below, the French crew standing aloof and displaying the discipline of a man-of-war, no man leaving his place while the skipper made all the investigations he required, and then came up on deck with his mahogany face more deeply lined with wrinkles than before.

"Well, captain," said Uncle Paul, while Rodd, who had kept close to his young friend of the Dartmoor stream, eagerly listened for what their expert had to say.

"Well, sir," he said, at last, as he took out a little seal-skin bag and deliberately helped himself to a little ready-cut scrap of pigtail tobacco, "your craft's in a bad way, and if something isn't done pretty smart she'll be down at the bottom before long."

"Yes, yes," cried the Count impatiently, "but we have tried everything, and it is impossible to get at the leak."

"Hah! Tried everything, have you, sir?"

"Yes, yes," cried the Count. "Some of my brave fellows have been half-drowned in diving, trying to plug from inside, using yards to force bags of oakum into the holes."

"Yes," said the skipper. "The ball went right through, I suppose?"

"Yes, yes," cried the Count, and Rodd noted that he was having hard work to master his impatience and annoyance at the skipper's annoyingly deliberate treatment of their urgent needs.

"So I suppose," said the skipper coolly, "but mebbe you haven't done quite all; leastwise I should like to try my little plan, and if it don't answer, why, you won't be any worse off than you are now; and when I give it up as a bad job, why, you will have to take to your boats and we shall have to find room for you aboard the schooner. Now then, please, you will just order two more men at that pump, and four more ready to take their places so as to keep on pumping hard."

"Yes, yes," cried the Count eagerly. "What next?"

"Order up what spare sails you've got from the store-room, and a few coils of new line."

The Count gave his orders quickly, and his men went off to carry them out.

"Good," said the skipper coolly. "That's smart."

"What next?" cried the Count.

"Well, sir, as quickly as I can, I want to do something to lighten the ship."

"No; I must protest!" cried the Count excitedly. "You are going to throw the guns overboard?"

"Humph!" grunted the captain. "Who said so? I didn't. Nay, that'd be a pity. I wouldn't do that till the very last."

"Ah!" sighed the Count, as if deeply relieved.

"Well, the next thing is, sir, just you leave me and my men alone and let yours look on till I want their help."

The Count was silent, and all looked on whilst in obedience to the skipper's orders the English sailors, led by the carpenter, set busily to work, seized upon the new spare sails that were brought up on deck, and cast loose the coils of fresh hemp line that were placed ready. Then with the skipper putting in a word here and there, resulting in the lines being attached to the corners of the largest square-sail, these latter were seized by a couple of the men, who dragged the sail forward as the brig glided very gently along, for it was nearly calm, and then passing the new sail deftly beneath the bowsprit, two of the men climbing out and seeming to cling with their feet to the bobstay until little by little they had got the edge right beneath the stay. Then while their mates at the corners helped at the lines, they passed down the sail right into the sea till they had lowered it to its full extent and they could do no more, save once or twice when they hung down from the stay and gave the canvas, which was slowly growing saturated, a thrust or two with the foot where it seemed disposed to hitch against the brig's keel.

And now the skipper took his post upon the bowsprit and gave his orders by word or sign to the men who governed the movement of the great square of canvas by means of the lines attached to the corners, the two at the fore corners of the sail getting outside the bulwarks, barefooted, to walk along the streak, and hauling just as much as was necessary to drag the sail right beneath the keel, their two messmates preparing to follow, and under the captain's guidance keeping all square and exact in the effort to get the keel to act as the dividing line to mark the oblong into two exact portions.

It was very slow work, for the canvas was stiff and moved unwillingly downward beneath the keel; but after a time it began to yield to the steady drag of the ropes upon the two fore corners, and, once started, progress began to be faster. For, so to speak, the brig began to help, sailing as it were gently more and more over the canvas, till at the end of about half-an-hour it was in the position at which the skipper had aimed, having while below in the hold pretty well marked down the position of the two holes made by the shot from the fort. These were about amidships, some few feet, as far as he could make out, on either side of the keel, one naturally being much higher than the other in the diagonal course taken by the heavy ball.

At last he called to his men to halt, and took off his cap, to stand thinking, the position now being that the sail was drawn right under the brig, and the sailors at the four corners were holding on tight to prevent the vessel from sailing clear.

So far not a word had been uttered by the Frenchmen, all of whom had stood clear or mounted the rigging or deck-house, so as to give the Englishmen ample room; but now in the silence Rodd advanced to the skipper eagerly, to say —

"Are you sure you have got the canvas well over the holes?"

Captain Chubb made no reply, but stood with his cap in his left hand gazing aft, and then he moved his right arm two or three times, as if forming an imaginary line through the brig's hull.

"Did you hear me, captain?" said Rodd eagerly. "Are you sure you have got the sail over the holes?"

"No," granted the skipper. "Are you?"

"No; but I thought —"

"Yes, my lad; so did I. You thought we ought to get the sail in the right place."

"Yes," said Rodd.

"Well, then, now, my lad, I should be much obliged to you if you'd tell me which is exactly the right place."

Rodd looked at him in despair.

"Thank you, my lad," said the skipper dryly. "I am much obliged. But all right, Mr Rodd; you can't tell, and I can't tell. We know that the ball that came from the fort must have gone downwards a bit, so that it went out from lower than where it went in; but there's no knowing whether she was hit from starboard or from larboard, and that's where I'm bothered. But never say die. I think we will make this bit of canvas fast now, for I'm pretty sure of one thing; it will be a plaister for one hole if it isn't for the other."

"But look here, captain," cried Rodd.

"What now?"

"Won't the water run under the canvas just the same as it did before?"

"No, my lad, it won't; and I'll tell you the reason why when we have done. Of course you know I am not going to stop all the water from coming in below, but if I can get it checked a bit so that they can keep it down easy with one man at the pump instead of two, she won't go to the bottom just yet, and they will have time enough to get into port to set the carpenter at work."

"Then you won't let our carpenter try to stop the holes?"

"No, my lad. You see, he never learned to be a fish, so that he could work under water; and though he's a bit of a crab in his way, I don't think he could manage it for all that. Now I'm ready to go on. Come, my lads, put your backs into it and haul them sheets tight. Here, master, let two of your men go to each corner and help my lads. All together as hard as they can!" shouted the skipper, and the Count quickly translated his order.

"That's right! Haul away, my lads!" shouted the skipper. "That new canvas won't give. Harder! Harder! Now then, one more—all you know!— Make fast!"

"Excellent! Superb!" cried the Count, as the men ceased from making fast the ropes, which were brought over the bulwarks and passed round the belaying pins. "Do you think that will stop the leak?"

"Maybe yes, sir; maybe no. If it don't do it we will put another plaister on, and another, and another. You have got plenty of spare sails and rope, and when we have used all yours I dare say we can find some more in the schooner. Now then, set your men going at that pump, and rig up another as quick as you can."

One pump began to clank heavily at once, and a short time after another was at work, and the clear bright water began to sparkle out of the scuppers, while, moved as it were by the same spirit, the French crew burst into a shrill involuntary cheer.

"How can I ever thank you, captain?" cried the Count, while his son snatched at Rodd's hand.

"Ah, I haven't done yet, sir," said the skipper coolly. "This is only a try."

"Oh, it's grand," cried the French lad, clinging to Rodd's arm. "You have saved our ship."

"Don't you holloa till you are out of the wood, young fellow," said the skipper, as he heard the words. "Now, Mr Rodd, sir, what was it you wanted to know?"

"Why the water will not still rim in underneath the canvas."

"Only because of this, my lad. Aren't they pumping the water out now as fast as ever they can?"

"Yes," cried Rodd; "but more will run in."

"Yes, my lad, and as it runs in won't the weight of the water outside push the canvas closer and closer in round the leak?"

"Yes, of course," cried Rodd. "I didn't think of that. And as there gets less inside it will seem to suck the canvas closer to."

"Quite right, my lad. That's about the way it works; and now we have got to wait for about an hour before we can know whether we have got both holes covered, or only one."

"Wait for an hour?" cried Rodd.

"Well, perhaps, before we are sure; but I dare say I shall be going down and sounding the well a time or two before that."

But long before the hour had elapsed the skipper found that though the water in the brig had subsided to a certain extent, one of the holes must be still uncovered, and he began at once to repeat his proceedings, coming to the conclusion that one of the bullet-holes was beyond the reach of the canvas. This time, after all was drawn tight, half-an-hour's pumping proved that his surmises were correct, and the skipper smiled with satisfaction as the Count and his men cheered them in delight on finding after a good deal of pumping that there was a very perceptible diminution of the water in the hold.

"It is superb, and so simple," cried the Count to Uncle Paul; "but I feel humbled, sir. Why could not our French sailors have been able to do this?"

"Well," said Uncle Paul good-humouredly, "the only reason I can give is that they were not English."

"That's it, sir," said the skipper. "You have hit the right nail on the head. But look here, Mr Count—I don't know your name."

"Des Saix," said the Count, smiling.

"Look here, sir; this is nothing to make a fuss about. It will keep you afloat while the weather's fine, but just come a rough time, those sails will be ripped off as easily as pocket-handkerchiefs. Besides, they will hinder your sailing no end."

"Ah, that is bad," said the Count, changing countenance.

"Oh no, not it. There's worse disasters than that at sea."

"But will it not be possible for the carpenters to stop the leaks?"

"No, sir; not unless you do what I say."

"Ah! What is that?"

"Run your craft up one of the rivers to where you can careen on the mad, and then a few hours between tides will be enough to put everything straight."

"Is there no other way?" asked the Count.

"Only downwards, sir," cried the skipper; and the French lad glanced questioningly at Rodd, who shook his head.

"No," said the boy, almost in a whisper. "I don't think there is any other way. He is quite right."

After another hour's pumping, the skipper gave out his intention of going back to the schooner; but the Count would not hear of it. He begged and implored Uncle Paul to give him their company at the breakfast he was having prepared, and after a little hesitation the doctor gave way, and suggested to the skipper that they should leave their departure till late in the afternoon, when a far better opinion could be given of the state of the brig.

"What do you say, squire?" said the skipper, looking at Rodd.

"Oh yes, let's stay!" And his impulsive young French friend grasped him by the wrist.

"Very well, gentlemen, I have only one thing to say, for I don't suppose the schooner will sail away and leave us behind. Let them call it dinner, and I'll stop. I aren't been in the habit of eating my breakfast at two o'clock in the day."

Chapter Twenty Nine
The Count can't find Words

That afternoon, after what had proved to be a very friendly, pleasant breakfast, through which nothing could have been more courteous and hospitable than the conduct of the Count and his son towards those with whom they had become so strangely intimate, the skipper hurried the end of the meal by suggesting that he should once more sound the well.

They went on deck at once, to find both pumps were being kept energetically going, the half-dozen men from the schooner taking their turns in the heartiest way, a general fraternisation having taken place, while on seeing the result of the skipper's examination, the delight of the Count and his son seemed unbounded.

"There you are, then, sir," said the skipper, in answer to a look from the doctor, "and now we will leave you to it."

"And I suppose," said Uncle Paul, "that you will have no hesitation, sir, in following Captain Chubb's advice?"

"And making for the mouth of some river," said the Count, glancing at his son, "to get the brig ashore, so as to repair her?"

"Exactly," said Uncle Paul. "You must see that there is nothing else that you can do."

"Nothing else that I can do," said the Count slowly, and Rodd gave him a wondering glance, for the skipper's remarks about the brig's owner being out of his mind came to his memory. "You intend to cruise about here, then, Dr Robson?"

"Here or anywhere," was the reply. "Probably here until I seem to have exhausted the natural history specimens that I can collect."

"Yes," said the Count, gazing fixedly at his son, "until you have exhausted the natural history specimens that you can collect."

He spoke in a curious dreamy way as if he were thinking hard, while Rodd coloured a little as he saw that the young Frenchman was gazing at him fixedly, for once more he could not help thinking of the skipper's words.

"Do you know of a place that would be likely, doctor?" said the Count. "I mean a river that we could sail up into shallow water, if we were so fortunate as to reach one without sinking first."

"Not I," said the doctor, "but my captain here has cruised along this coast in by-gone days, and he tells me that it would be easy enough to find inlet after inlet, and deltas with streams, running up through the muddy mangrove swamps."

"But then we might never reach the shore," said the Count slowly— "not with the brig—in spite of your kindly, I may say brotherly aid."

Rodd felt that the Count's son was still gazing at him searchingly, but he did not turn his head, for the doctor began speaking at once.

"Really, my dear sir," he said almost curtly, "national dislike seems to exist to a great extent amongst your countrymen. Do you really think we English should be such barbarians as to sail away and leave a crippled ship to its fate?"

"No, no, no, doctor!" cried the Count warmly. "But how could I be so grasping as to ask you, full of your scientific pursuits as you are, to stand by us till we can reach the shore in safety?"

"You would not ask it, sir," said the doctor warmly. "There would be no need. Of course my schooner will stand by you, ready to give you help until your brig is once more fit for sea."

"Forgive me, doctor!" cried the Count eagerly.

"There is nothing to forgive, sir," replied the doctor, "only I think I may say that saving in times of war there is no such thing as nationality amongst those who go to sea. My experience is that they are always brethren in times of distress."

The Count held out his hand, which was warmly grasped, while the young French ex-prisoner looked at Rodd with eyes that seemed to speak volumes.

At this moment the skipper gave a grunt of satisfaction and broke in.

"There's plenty of choice, gentlemen," he said. "I'd venture to say I could find you the mouths of a dozen sluggish rivers up which you could go with the tide as far as you liked, and then moor our vessels to the forest trees, easily finding places close in shore where the tide as it went out would leave the brig here softly in the mud ready for careening over in a cradle where she wouldn't strain or open a single seam; and the doctor here being willing, I'll promise to take the job in hand and make the brig's bottom as sound as ever it was, even if we have to strip off a little copper from along the top streak, where it isn't so much wanted, so as to put new plates where the damaged ones have been."

"I shall be only too glad, Count," said the doctor; "and now I think we will get back to the schooner, and Captain Chubb here will shape his course somewhere to the south-east, till within the next few days we near the coast, when he will select a suitable place for his purpose."

"I cannot find words," said the Count, in a husky voice.

"Don't try," said the doctor.

"No, but—er,"—continued the Count, in rather a hesitating tone, "you do mean to keep cruising about here—and farther south or west?"

"Don't you give that another thought," said the doctor frankly. "The schooner is my own, and almost any portion of the ocean or the shore offers attractions to me and my nephew. We can find interest anywhere. I only hope that you will not find our society dull."

The Count made a gesture, and then, after a word or two to the skipper, the latter gave his men orders, and they took their places in the boat.

It was then that the Count's son, who had been very silent for some time, looking at Rodd as if longing to speak, suddenly turned and whispered something to his father, who replied with a comprehensive gesture, and the lad immediately approached the doctor.

"It will be hours yet, sir, before it is dark, and I have so much I should like to say to your nephew. Can he not stay till evening, and then our boat shall bring him to your vessel? You will not," he continued playfully, turning to Rodd, "be afraid of going down?"

"My nephew is at liberty to do as he pleases," replied the doctor frankly. "What do you say, Rodd?"

"Oh, I want to stay, uncle. I should like to hear all about the escape."

A few minutes later the two lads were leaning together over the rail watching the departing boat, and chatting together as if they were old schoolfellows who had met again after a long separation, Rodd delighted with his companion, and disposed to feel disappointed in himself lest the refined, polished young officer—one, evidently, of the *haute noblesse*— should look down upon him as a rough, rather boorish young Englishman.

Somehow that evening, with its rapid change from glowing sunset light to purple violet darkness, seemed wonderfully quick in coming, and as the brig's well-manned boat grazed against the schooner's stern and Rodd turned in climbing up the side to hang by his left hand and extend his right, the feeling of inferiority melted away in the young Frenchman's warm grasp, as the latter said—

"I suppose we shall be sailing very slowly till we reach the shore, and I want to see more of you. I shall come and fetch you first thing in the morning. Don't say anything; you must come. *Au revoir!*"

The brig's boat pushed off as soon as Rodd had swung himself on deck, and as it glided away into the soft darkness with the regularly handled oars dipping up from the surface of the sea what seemed to be like so much lambent liquid gold, suggesting to Rodd as he gazed after his new friend that the stars might have been melting all day in the torrid sun, and that this was their pale golden light floating upon the sea, a hand was laid upon his shoulder.

Chapter Thirty
The Doctor paints Pictures

"Back again, then, Rodd!"

"Oh yes, uncle. Did you think me long?"

"So long, my boy, that I was thinking of sending the boat to fetch you, for fear you should be converted into a Frenchman. Hang them all! How I do hate them and their nasty, smooth, polished ways!"

"Oh, uncle, you don't!" cried the boy indignantly. "I do, sir. How dare you contradict me! And I won't have you getting too fond of that French boy. He and his father set me thinking about old Bony, and as soon as I begin thinking about Bony I have a nasty taste in my mouth. — Well, how did you get on?"

"I had a most delightful afternoon, uncle. Young Morny — let's see, he's Viscount Morny —"

"Viscount grandmother!" snapped out the doctor. "Anybody can be a viscount in France if he's got an income of a few hundred francs — francs in France of common silver. They rank with golden guineas in your grand old home."

"Oh, well, I don't know, uncle I only know that he's the nicest fellow I ever met."

"Gush!" cried the doctor. "I won't have it, Rodd. I won't have you making too much of these French people. I don't like them."

"But you don't know them, uncle. Both the Count and his son are the most gentlemanly men I ever met."

"The most gentlemanly men you ever met!" cried Uncle Paul mockingly. "Nice puppy you are to set yourself up for a judge! Very gentlemanly, to come in the dark with two boat-loads of savage-looking buccaneers to seize our schooner! And they would, too, if it hadn't been for Captain Chubb's courage."

"Oh, uncle, don't be unreasonable. The poor fellows were desperate. Suppose you had been in such a position as they were."

"I am not going to suppose anything of the sort, sir," cried the doctor indignantly; "and look here, Rodney, I will not have you setting up your feathers like the miserable young cockerel you are, and beginning to crow at me, just as if you were full grown. It's growing unbearable, Rodney, and I won't have it, sir. I am very much displeased with you, and you had better be off to your bunk at once before we come to an open quarrel. It is too much, sir, and if your poor mother were alive and could hear you talking like this she'd—she'd—she'd—there, I don't know what she wouldn't say."

"I do," said the boy.

"What would she say, sir?" snapped out the doctor.

Rodd stood silent in the darkness for a few moments as he stole his hand under the irate doctor's arm.

"She'd say that dear Uncle Paul had been thinking about old Bony, and that it had made him very cross with me about nothing at all."

Uncle Paul made a sound like the beginning of a speech that would not come, and the silence seemed deeper than ever, nothing being heard but the soft lapping of the water under the vessel's counter, as she glided slowly through the sea.

But Rodd felt the warm arm under which his hand nestled press it closer and closer to the old man's side, and that he was urged along the deck to keep pace with his elder slowly up and down, up and down, from stem to stern, for some minutes before that speech came—one which was quite different from that which Rodd fully expected to hear, for it was in Uncle Paul's natural tones once more, as he said very thoughtfully and in quite a confidential manner—

"Yes, very gentlemanly, Pickle, my boy; quite the nobleman, I might say, and I am not at all surprised that you helped that poor lad to escape. A little effeminate, but certainly a very nice lad. But I have been thinking about them ever since I came on board this afternoon, and I can't quite make out that Count. What's he doing here, my boy? On some mission, and connected with some jealousy and a stop being put to his cruise. I am not quite sure, Pickle."

"Rodney, uncle," said the boy mischievously.

"Pickle, you dog! Be quiet. I am talking sense. But I think I have worked it out. He betrayed himself. He's a naturalist, boy. He betrayed it in his looks and words as soon as he learned what I was about. Didn't you notice how eager he was to know about our pursuits?"

"Yes, uncle; I noticed that directly."

"Ah, I thought so. A naturalist—a born naturalist, Pickle, and in spite of his being a Frenchman I shall begin to feel a brotherly respect for a follower of the only pursuit worthy of a gentleman. Well, we had a very short sleep last night, so we have got a long one due to our credit to-night, and on the strength of that Captain Chubb has arranged to have supper quite early. This has been a queer day, Pickle, a very queer day, and I am not at all displeased, for I am beginning to think that we have got a very good time before us."

"What time, uncle?"

"Ashore, my boy. What do you say to having a couple of the sailors with guns to keep us company while the rest are new-bottoming that brig? Walks in the primeval forest, Rodd, wonderful botanical rambles, shooting birds of glorious plumage, most likely coming across the great man-ape, the chimpanzee. What do you say to that, my boy? Won't that be a grand change from fishing and dredging and bottling specimens?"

"Uncle Paul, don't!" cried the boy.

"Don't? What do you mean, sir?"

"You were talking just now of our having a good long sleep to-night to make up for all we lost since we went to bed last."

"Well, sir, what of that?"

"How's a fellow to sleep, uncle, with such things as that to think of? Why, I shan't get a wink for thinking of the big chimpanzees; and as for eating any supper now, why, my appetite has completely gone."

"Stuff!" cried Uncle Paul, pressing the lad's arm to his side. "Rodd, my boy, we must cork a bottle or two and throw them overboard to-morrow, and then have a little practice with bullets in our guns. We may come across dangerous beasts there, leopards and the like, while that there are great man-apes in those forests of the West Coast there is not a doubt."

"Well, I think I could shoot at one of those great spotted cats, uncle, all tooth and claw; but wouldn't it be rather queer to shoot one of those big monkeys which look so much like human beings? I mean those big ones with ears like ours, and no tails."

"Humph! Ha! Well, I— Yes, all right, captain! We are coming down."

Chapter Thirty One
Great Friends

The days that followed the attempt to salve the brig after so strange an introduction to her commander and his son, fell calm all through the hot sunny time, and only that a pleasant cool breeze ushered in the evening and continued till the sun rose again, very little progress would have been made by the schooner and its consort, sailing east and south.

But nobody seemed troubled. When the French and English sailors were together they were the best of friends; while long conversations and arguments often took place between the doctor and his new friend, the skipper generally letting them have the cabin to themselves.

Sometimes they drifted into political questions and came very near to losing their tempers; but each mastered and kept down his opinions, for a genuine feeling of liking had arisen between them, and the Count seemed never weary of listening to Uncle Paul's disquisitions upon the marvels of natural history, nor of studying with him the wonders of creation which he had collected and had to show. Then day by day the brig, which was freed every day from as much water as she had gained during the night, sailed steadily on in the schooner's wake in full charge of her stern fierce-looking French mate—one of the most silent of men.

And while the Count was mostly with the doctor, literally taking lessons in pelagic lore, the two lads had become inseparable.

"Look here," said Rodd, almost hotly, one day, "if ever you say a word again about my helping you to escape at Dartmoor, you and I are going to leave off being friends."

Morny laughed, a pleasant, almost girlish smile lighting up his well-cut Gallic features.

"Why, Rodd," he cried, "isn't that rather hard? I used to think that was the most horrible time in my life, but I feel now that one part of it was the most delightful."

"There you go again," cried Rodd. "You are beginning."

"No, no, I wasn't. But I can't forget being a prisoner in England, and about all that I went through there with my father when he was bad so long with his wound."

"Bad so long with his wound?" said Rodd eagerly. "Ah! You may talk about that. Yes, I should like to hear. Tell me all about your being taken prisoners, and how it happened."

"For you never to be friends with me any more?" said the French lad maliciously.

"No, no, no. But I hate for you to be what you call grateful. You are quite a good sort of chap, and you speak our language so well that I forget you are not English sometimes, till you begin to be grateful to me for saving you, and then I feel that you are French. There, now you may tell me all about it—I mean about before you met me fishing."

The two lads were under the awning upon this particular day just amidships. It was a hot and breathless time, but both were pretty well inured to the weather, and were so interested in the subjects supplied to them by Nature in the way of floating wonders that they never troubled themselves about the heat.

Upon this occasion they were lying together upon the deck, suffering to a certain extent from lassitude consequent upon the heat. There was a man at the wheel, and Joe Cross was seated upon the main cross-trees with a spy-glass across his legs, ready to raise it from time to time and direct it eastward to try and pierce the faint silvery haze that lay low upon the horizon. The boys had grown very silent and thoughtful, Moray trying to recall memories of the past so that he might respond to his English friend's demand upon him that he should relate something of his old experiences in connection with the war and his being brought over to England, and so deep in thought that he paid no heed to his companion. Meantime, Rodd, without any desire to play the eavesdropper, lay listening to the scraps of conversation which came up through the cabin skylight, growing a little louder than usual, for, as was occasionally the case, an argument was afloat respecting the late war, the doctor according to his wont growing wroth upon an allusion being made by his guest to the ex-Emperor Napoleon; and there were evidently threatenings of a storm, which was, however, suppressed by the grave dignity of the Count and a feeling of annoyance which attacked Uncle Paul upon realising that he had ventured upon dangerous ground.

"Oh, Uncle Paul," said Rodd to himself, and he lay and laughed softly, making Morny start.

"Was I talking aloud?" said the French lad, flushing.

"You? No! Didn't you hear? It was Uncle Paul. Your father was talking about Napoleon, and directly his name is mentioned uncle begins to boil over."

"Ah, yes, so you have told me, and I gathered something of the kind. My father should not have spoken about the Emperor, though he venerates his name."

"Do you?" said Rodd.

"I?" replied Morny proudly. "Of course. He is the greatest man who ever lived."

"I say; I'm not Uncle Paul."

"Of course not. But why do you say that?"

"Because it seems as if you were trying to lead me on, like your father did with uncle."

"Ah, no, no, don't think that. Better to let such things rest."

"Yes," said Rodd. "I didn't hear much of what they were saying, only they talked loudly sometimes about the way the French and English hate one another. It seems so stupid. Why should they? I don't hate you; and I suppose you don't hate me."

"Of course not! You have given me plenty of cause."

"Whoa!" shouted Rodd. "You are getting on dangerous ground again. Now, look here; why should the French hate the English?"

"Because the English never did us anything but harm."

"Nonsense!" said Rodd coolly. "Now, look here, suppose you and I had a good fight, and I got the best of it—gave you an unlucky crack on the bridge of your nose, and made both your eyes swell up so that you couldn't see."

"Well, it would be very brutal," said Morny. "Gentlemen should fight with the small sword."

"Oh, I like that!" said Rodd merrily. "And then one of them sticks it in the other's corpus and makes him bleed, if he does nothing worse. Why, people have been killed."

"Yes, in the cause of honour," said Morny, slowly and thoughtfully.

"But that wouldn't have happened if they had been fighting with their fists."

"It's of no use to argue a matter like this with an Englishman," said Morny. "He cannot see such things with the eyes of a Frenchman."

"And a jolly good job too," said Rodd. "But we are running away from what we have been talking about. I was saying, suppose you and I were fighting and I hit you on the bridge of the nose and made your eyes swell up so that you couldn't see; that would be no reason why you should always hate me afterwards. Wouldn't it be much better if the one who was beaten owned it and shook hands so as to be good friends again?"

"Hah!" said Morny, giving vent to a long deep sigh.

"Uncle Paul always says that there is so much good to do in the world that there is no room for animosity or hatred, especially as life is so very short. Here, I don't see that we English have done anything worse to you French than conquering you now and then."

"What!" cried Morny. "What have you to say to the way in which you treated your prisoners? You were never taken captive with your father—I mean your uncle, and shut up in a great cheerless building right out upon a cold, bleak, dreary moor."

"No," said Rodd gravely.

"My father and I were, after a sea-fight in which one of your great bullying ships battered our little sloop of war almost to pieces and took us into Plymouth, not conquered, for our brave fellows fought till nearly all were killed or wounded."

"I say," cried Rodd earnestly, "I didn't know about this! Were you wounded?"

For answer Morny with flashing eyes literally snatched up his shirt-sleeve, baring his thin white left arm and displaying in the fleshy part a curious puckering and discoloration, evidently the scar of a bad wound.

"Poor old chap!" said Rodd softly. "I say, how was that done?"

"Grape-shot," replied Morny, drawing himself up proudly and deliberately beginning to draw down and button his sleeve.

"Did it hurt much?"

"Yes," said Morny rather contemptuously. "My father was wounded too, so that he had to be carried below, or else we should never have struck, but he would have gone down as a brave captain should with colours flying, fighting for the Emperor to the very last."

"Then I am precious glad that the Count was taken below," said Rodd.

"Why?" snapped out the French lad fiercely.

"Because of course you would have sunk with him, for you couldn't have swum for your life with a wounded arm."

"No; but shouldn't I have had my name written in history?"

"Perhaps. But you and I would never have met and become such good friends; for you know we are precious good friends when we can agree."

Morny laughed.

"Yes," he said pleasantly, "when we can agree. But do you think it was good treatment to keep us shut up there as prisoners on that dreary moor?"

"Let's see," said Rodd; "Dartmoor—all amongst the streams and tors, as they call them?"

"Yes; a great granite desert."

"Oh, but it was very jolly there," said Rodd.

"I don't know what you mean by jolly," said Morny contemptuously.

"Why, they didn't keep you shut up. They let you roam about as you liked, didn't they, as long as you didn't try to escape?"

"Well—yes; but it was a long time before I went out at all," replied Morny sadly. "For months I never left my father's side, and for a long time I never expected that he'd recover; and as I used to sit there by his bedside, watching, I began to get to hate the English more and more, and long to get away so as to begin righting for my country again. But of course I couldn't leave my wounded father's side."

"No," said Rodd slowly and in a low voice, as if repeating the words to himself. "Of course you couldn't leave your father's side."

"No," repeated Morny softly, "I couldn't leave my father's side. But after a time he made me go. He said my wound would never heal—for the surgeon had told him so—if he kept me shut up day after day, and that I must go out with the other prisoners and roam about on the moor; but I said I wouldn't leave him, and I didn't till he told me one day that I was growing white and thin and weak, and that he could see how I was suffering from the pain in my wound."

"Ah, yes," said Rodd, in a low tone full of earnestness. "It must have given you terrible pain."

"And at last he said," continued Morny, "that if he saw me getting well it would be the best cure for his injuries, but that if I were obstinate and refused to obey him now that he was lying there weak and helpless, it would surely send him to his grave."

"And then of course you went?" replied Rodd excitedly.

"Yes, I went then," replied Morny, "for at last I had begun to see that he was right. And then every morning after we had been all mustered, as you call it, and were free to go outside the gates, I went out with a lot more right on to the wild desert. But I wanted to be alone, and as soon as I could I wandered away up amongst the great stones, and sat down to think and rage against myself for feeling so happy when I wanted to be miserable and in despair about our fate. For it was as if something within me was mocking at my sufferings and trying to make me laugh and feel bright and joyous, for— Oh, how well I can remember it all up there! The sun was shining brightly, and the great block of stone upon which I sat down felt hot and so different to the cold cheerless prison inside. Every here and there amongst the stones there was the beautiful soft green grass, and little low shrubs were in full blossom, some a of rich purple, and some of the brightest gold, while in two or three places far up in the blue sky the *alouettes* were singing like they do in France; and every puff of soft warm wind that floated by was scented with the sweet fragrance of that little herb—I forget its name—that which the bees buzz about."

"Wild thyme?" said Rodd quickly.

"Ah, yes; wild thyme. And there for a long time I sat nursing my left arm, fighting against what seemed to be a feeling of happiness, and trying to think of all the evil that the English had done us, and what I would do as soon as I got free. But it was too much for me. I couldn't do it, and what I had looked upon from the prison windows from between the bars would not seem to be the same wild stony desert, but beautiful and full of hope and joy."

"Ah!" cried Rodd. "That's because you were getting better. I know what you felt. I was like that once after a bad fever, and when I was taken out one fine morning for the first time, though I was weak as a rat I felt as if I must run and jump and shout all about nothing; but it was because everything looked so beautiful, and I knew that I must be getting well."

The boys' eyes met for a few moments, and then Morny bowed his head slowly and went on.

"Yes," he said quietly, "I suppose it was a beautiful healthy place, and it began to make me feel like that; and as I looked round—for I had climbed very high—I could see right down into parts of a valley that was all full of sunshine and flashing light, for there was a little dancing stream running swiftly along, and as I looked down into it and saw how it widened here and narrowed there as it flashed amongst the great rocks of granite, it set me thinking about home, and instead of going on planning how I would revenge myself upon the English, I began to wonder whether there would be trout there too, and soon afterwards I began to creep slowly down so as to see. And then I remember that I burst out laughing at myself, for it seemed so droll. My legs would keep on bending under me, and I had to sit down and rest every now and then."

"You were so weak," said Rodd earnestly.

"Yes, that was it," cried Morny; "but I didn't understand at first, and somehow I didn't seem to mind a bit, but sat down and rested time after time, till at last I got right down to the edge of the little river, all shallow and dotted with blocks of stone; and there at first were the little trout darting about to hide themselves, scared away by my shadow upon the water. But as I sat down to watch they soon came out again, and began leaping at the little gnats that were flitting about the surface. Then do you know how that made me feel?"

"Well," said Rodd, "I know how it would make an English boy feel— myself, for instance."

"How?"

"As if he'd like to have my namesake with only one *d* in his hand, and begin whipping the stream."

"Yes, that's how I felt," said Morny softly.

"I know about those trout on Dartmoor," cried Rodd, "right up on the moor. I know somebody who used to go and fish there, and he told me that he could go and catch dozens and dozens and dozens of them whenever he liked. But they were so very small."

"Yes," said Morny, speaking dreamily now, with his eyes so lit up, that as Rodd watched his thin delicate face, he thought how handsome and well-bred he looked.

"Too good-looking for a boy, but more fitted for a girl," he mused.

"And did you go and fish?" he cried, as he suddenly caught Morny's eyes gazing at him questioningly.

"Oh yes. I went back to the prison and spoke to one of our guards—a frowning, fierce-looking fellow—and I told him how ill my father was, and that he never seemed as if he could eat the prison rations, as they called them, and that I wanted to try and catch some of the little fish on the moor and cook them, and try if I could tempt him with them."

"And what did he say?" cried Rodd, for Morny had stopped.

"He made my heart feel on fire at first, for he growled out 'Bah! Rubbish! There, go on in.' 'Savage!' I said to myself. 'Just like an Englishman!'"

"What a brute!" cried Rodd. "But I say, old chap, our fellows are not all like that."

"No," said Morny. "But I hadn't done. Next minute he shouted after me, 'Halt!' and when I stopped and looked round he called out, 'Ahoy! Jim!' and another of the guards with his piece over his shoulder marched up to where we stood, and the man I had first spoken to turned to me and said, 'Here, you tell him what you said to me.'"

"And did you?" cried Rodd.

"I felt as if the words would choke me at first, but just then I seemed to see the trout hot and brown upon a dish and my father, sick and pale, looking at them longingly, and that made me speak to the other guard, who was scowling at me. And as I spoke a grim smile came over his face, and his eyes twinkled, and he showed his teeth. 'All right, youngster,' he said. 'Got a rod?' I shook my head. 'No line? No flies?' I shook my head again and again. 'All right, young 'un,' he said. 'You come to me two hours before sundown; I shall be on duty then. I'll set you up with a bit of tackle. But I say, you Frenchies don't know how to throw a fly!' 'I used to,' I replied, 'at home, in France.' 'Lor', did you?' he said. 'Hear that, Billy? I never knew as a Frenchman knew how to fish. But that's all right, youngster—only my ignorance. A fisherman's a fisherman the wide world round.'"

"Well?" said Rodd, for his companion had stopped.

"Well?" said Morny.

"Go on."

"What about?"

"Well, you are a chap! Don't you know I was always very fond of fishing?"

"I know you like fishing, for I saw you enjoying it that day when—"

"Steady!" cried Rodd.

"I've done," said Morny.

"But I don't want you to have done."

"Why, you forbade me to touch upon what you call dangerous ground."

"Bah! That's another thing. I don't want you to be grateful. But of course I like to hear about you going fishing. I could almost wish that you and I could go and have a few hours together on Dartmoor now."

"And we cannot," said Morny quietly.

"No; but we might try for bonito or dolphins. But go on. I want you to tell me about how you got on. Did you go to that prison guard two hours before sundown?"

"Oh yes. He was as friendly as ever he could be, just because he found that I was fond of fishing, and lent me his rod and line and flies that he made himself, and told me the best places to go to, and he was as pleased as I was when I came back to the prison with a dozen and a half of little trout. Oh, I remember so well almost every word he said."

"Well, what did he say?" cried Rodd eagerly.

"Oh, he was a good-humoured droll fellow, though he looked so gruff, for when I showed him my fish he slapped me on the shoulder and said, 'Well done, young 'un! You are one of the right sort after all.' And then he told me to take the fish into his quarters, and his missus, as he called her, would cook them for me so that I could take them to my sick father; and when I thanked him he said it was all right, and that he and his 'missus' had been talking together about how bad the French captain looked, and that I had better get him a nice little dish like that as often as I could."

Morny stopped again, and Rodd gazed at him impatiently.

"Here, I say," he cried, "what a tantalising sort of chap you are! Why, I could tell a story better than you."

"Why, I have told you the story," said Morny.

"No, you haven't. You keep stopping short when you come to what interests me most."

"Nonsense! You don't want me to go on telling you about catching more fish and getting them fried day after day, and about taking them up to my father."

"What do you know about it?" cried Rodd. "It's just what I do want you to tell me. Did he like them and eat them, and did they do him good? Those are the best bits."

"You are a droll of boy," said Morny, laughing.

"I'm a what?" cried Rodd.

"Droll of boy—*drôle de garçon. C'est juste, n'est-ce pas?*"

"Oh, if you like," cried Rodd merrily; "but if you don't think those are the best parts of the story, which are?"

"Ah!" said Morny thoughtfully. "The part that I remember most is feeling that somehow things are not always so black as they look, that Dartmoor was not such a dreary desert, and that the fierce frowning guards were not so hard and unpleasant as they seemed. There were times after that when I was very happy there, for my father's wound began to get better, and I found myself strong and well again. But after a time there was a new governor there, who behaved very harshly to the prisoners, and as we got well the great longing for freedom used to grow within us, and some of the men tried to escape. This made the governor more harsh and stern. We were kept more shut up—"

"And I suppose that made you long all the more to get free?"

"Of course," replied Morny; "and at last there came a time when we heard a little news from across the sea—news which seemed to make my father the Count half wild with longing, and one day he told me that he had had a lot of napoleons sent to him to help him to escape, and that the first fine day we were allowed out for exercise upon the moor we would make a dash for liberty."

"You should have done it when you were out fishing," said Rodd.

"Oh no. The fishing had been stopped for a long time—ever since the first attempts had been made to escape."

"Oh, I see," said Rodd.

"And at last the day came," continued Morny, "and we made our attempt, but only to find that we were very closely guarded, and that soldiers were on the look-out in all directions; and in the attempt my father and I became separated, and I should have been taken if it had not been that—"

"Look here," cried Rodd, springing up, "there's Joe Cross signalling to me from the maintop. He can see something. I say, that happened luckily for you, young fellow, for you were just getting on to dangerous ground."

Chapter Thirty Two
Land Ho!

"What is it, Joe?" cried Rodd.

"Easy, sir!" said the man softly. "Not too loud," he continued, from where he was seated upon the cross-trees. "I don't want to give the skipper a false alarm, else he won't believe me next time."

"What about?"

"Easy, my lad! Just in a whisper like. I aren't sure, but to you I says, Land ho!"

"Whereabouts, Joe?" cried Rodd excitedly.

"Ah!" cried Morny, springing up. "Land!" And he faced round to gaze towards the brig that was sailing very slowly after them some three hundred yards away—sailing, but doing little more than forge her way through the water.

"Nay, not that way, sir," said Joe softly, "but doo east. You can't see anything from down there, Mr Rodd, sir. I can't even make certain with the glass."

"Hold hard, Joe! I am coming up," cried Rodd. "All right, sir; but you will be disappointed when you do."

"I won't be long, Morny," said Rodd eagerly.

"No; be quick," whispered Morny excitedly. "I want for my father to know. He is so anxious about the brig."

Rodd gave him a quick jerk of the head as he went on climbing the ratlines as quickly as he could, forgetting all about the heat and the silvery glare of the piercing sunshine.

He was not long mounting to the sailor's side, seating himself on the opposite side of the mast.

"Now then," he cried, as he shuffled into his place; "let me look."

"All right, sir. Ketch hold," replied the sailor stolidly. "You'll do it; your eyes are so much younger and sharper than mine."

"None of your gammon, Joe!" cried the boy sharply, as he focussed the glass to suit his eyes, while with one arm embracing the butt of the main-topgallant-mast he held the tube steadily to his eye, asking for guidance the while.

"Now then," he said; "whereabouts?"

"Right straight ahead, sir. You can't miss it if it's there, for it stretches away as far as you like to left and right!"

"Why, there's no land, Joe."

"Not looking down low enough, sir, perhaps. It aren't right up in the sky."

"Well, who's looking up in the sky?" cried Rodd irritably.—"I am looking right down to the horizon line."

"Well, that's right, sir. Take a good long look. Now then, can't you see it?"

There was silence for a few moments, and Morny, who was gazing upwards, seemed to be all eyes and ears.

"Can't you see it, Master Rodd?" repeated Joe.

"No."

"Perhaps 'tarn't land, then, sir."

"No. It was all your fancy. There's nothing to be seen."

"Where are you looking, sir?"

"At a little low bank of pale misty cloud. That's all, Joe. Your eyes want a good rub."

"Dessay they do, sir. They aren't much account," said the man; "but that caps what I saw," and putting his hands to the sides of his mouth he yelled out in stentorian tones, "Land ho!"—a signal that was followed by the hurried shuffling sound of feet ascending to the deck.

"Here, what are you doing?" cried Rodd angrily. "Spreading a false alarm like that!"

"Oh, it's right enough, sir."

"But there's nothing but a cloud there, Joe."

"Looks like it, sir, but land it is all the same."

"Where away?" came in the skipper's hoarse voice.

"Dead ahead, sir," replied the sailor, and Rodd steadied the glass again, bringing it to bear upon what looked more than ever like the faintest of faint hazes upon the surface of the distant sea.

"Can you make it out, Rodd?" cried Uncle Paul, who had hurried on deck with the Count.

"Well, I can just see something, uncle, and I suppose it's land."

"Oh, that's right enough, my lad," cried the captain. "Can't be anything else."

"Not clouds?"

"Ah, I don't say that," cried the skipper. "You may see a bit of haze too, but there's solid land beneath. There, sir," continued the skipper, "that's what we are looking for. Now the next thing we want to see is water."

"Well, we can see that plainly enough, Joe," said Rodd, speaking with his eyes still to the glass.

"Ay, but he means dirty water, sir."

"What do you want to see dirty water for?"

"Muddy, then, sir, showing as there's a river coming out there. I say, sir, wouldn't t'other young gent like to come up and have a squint?"

"Oh, of course. I forgot. Below there! Morny! Come on up and have a look."

The lad sprang to the main shrouds and began to hurry up, while Joe Cross, who had finished the task to achieve which he had been sent, began to lower himself down, leaving space for the young Frenchman, to whom the glass was handed in turn, ready for him to declare that he could make out the distant land.

"Ah," he panted, as he handed back the glass, "how I have longed to see that! Now, Rodd, we shall soon get the brig careened over and the leaks repaired, and then—"

"Well," said Rodd, "what then?"

"Be off to sea again," cried Morny excitedly.

"Well, you seem in a precious hurry," grumbled Rodd.

"Wouldn't you be if your schooner was like our brig?"

"No. Uncle and I are reckoning upon making a lot of discoveries ashore. If you are on a scientific expedition, wouldn't that do as well for you?"

"No," replied the French lad shortly. "We must follow out our researches by sea."

"Then what is it you are looking for? I thought you were going to tell me the other day."

"Yes, my father," cried Morny, answering a hail from below. "I am coming down."

When the two lads descended it was to find that the Count had been speaking to the skipper, who had given orders for the schooner's boat to be lowered so that the two visitors could return at once to the brig, with the understanding that both vessels were to send up studding sails and use every possible speed now to get within touch of the shore, before making south and keeping a bright look-out for some estuary or river mouth.

"You will follow me, sir," said the skipper; "but do you know what this coast line will be like?"

"I cannot say I do," replied the Count. "Cliff and hill, with mountains farther in?"

"Nay, sir; all muddy shore, covered with dark green mangrove forest. I don't suppose we shall be long before I send you up a signal; and then we can sail right in. There will be nothing to mind in the way of rocks, for where I lead it will be all mud."

Very shortly afterwards the lads parted, and as Rodd stood looking after the boat that was bearing their two visitors to the brig, Uncle Paul came up close behind him.

"Pity those two were born Frenchmen, Rodd, my boy," said the doctor, "for there is something very gentlemanly about the Count, and I like that lad Morny too. There is something about him, Rodney, that you might very well copy."

"Is there, uncle?"

"Yes, sir, there is. Certainly. I am not your father, but I am your uncle, and it gratifies me very much to see the polished, almost reverent way in which that lad behaves towards the Count. It's polite, and it's respectful, and it's—er—it's—er—"

"Why, you wouldn't like it, uncle, if I were to behave to you just as he does to the Count."

"Well, not exactly, Rodney, but there's something very nice about it. Great pity, though, that they are French, and so corroded, so crusted over, as I may call it, with a sort of hero-worship for that tyrannical usurper. There, I won't mention his name."

"That's right, uncle; don't, please."

"Why, sir?"

"Because it always makes you so cross, uncle."

"Now, Rodney, that's what I don't like. If I have an antipathy to a scoundrel, and speak out firmly as an Englishman should, it is not for a boy like you to say I am cross; and I am quite sure that young Morny would have had too much common-sense to speak out like that to his father. It is a great pity, though, that they are both, as I say, so eaten up with that hero-worship, and I am very much afraid that I spoke a little too plainly to the Count to-day. It was rather unfortunate too. It was just when we had been having a very interesting conversation upon the medusae, especially those of a phosphorescent nature. By the way, has Morny said much to you about the object of their research?"

"No, uncle. He always seems disinclined to speak."

"Humph! Yes, he does seem very reticent. His father as good as said, as I think I told you, that this was a voyage of discovery, a search for something he wanted to take back, and which was to make his country very great. But he has never said what, and it would be so very ungentlemanly to seem curious."

"But you do feel curious to know, don't you, uncle?"

"Well, I must confess, my boy, that I do—a little jealous, perhaps, of another man's success, for I did learn as much as this, that he felt pretty sure of being successful if he could get the brig sound again. Well, I suppose we shall know some day."

"I don't like to say any more to Morny, uncle. It would seem so small; and besides, he never questions me anything about what we are doing—only seems very much interested."

"You are quite right, Rodd. It would be mean and petty. Leave it to them, and if they like to take us into their confidence, well and good. If they do not, well, it is no business of ours."

"Why, uncle," cried Rodd suddenly, and then he stopped. "It isn't because—"

Rodd stopped short again, looking straight away over the sea, as if in deep thought.

"Well, my boy? It isn't because what?"

"Oh, I don't like to say, uncle. You would laugh at me."

"How do you know that? Wait and see," cried Uncle Paul. "Now then, what were you thinking?"

"I was wondering whether they could be trying to discover that which we found quite by accident."

"That which we found quite by accident, Pickle?"

"Yes, uncle, and that may be the reason why they don't like to talk about it. You see, all ships' captains and people have been so laughed at, and told that they are inventing fables, that they are very quiet and like to keep things to themselves, just the same as Captain Chubb was when we saw that thing. You see, uncle—"

"Go on, Pickle! Go on!" cried Uncle Paul.

"Oh, I haven't much more to say, uncle, only this—if ordinary captains are so particular about speaking, and so afraid of ridicule, wouldn't a big scientific man like the Count, who has fitted out an expedition for the discovery, be very careful too, lest the object of his voyage should get about? But oh, nonsense! It's ridiculous. It can't be that. Don't laugh at me, uncle. It's only what I thought."

"I was not going to laugh at you, Rodney, my boy," said the doctor quietly, "for the simple reason that I do not see anything to laugh at. It's a very clever, good idea, and quite possible. Yes, my boy, it's more than possible. I don't say that you are right, but very likely to be. The Count and his son are French, and, like their countrymen, very touchy and sensitive and afraid of ridicule. I shouldn't be at all surprised, my boy, if that really is the reason for their being so secretive in their ways."

"I am glad you think so, uncle," cried the boy.

"No, no, no; don't take it like that. It may be after all only a fancy of yours."

"Yes, uncle, but if that's what they are searching for, to prove that there are such—such—er—what-you-may-call-'ems in the sea—"

"Phenomena, boy—phenomena," said the doctor shortly.

"Yes, uncle; phenomena—wouldn't it be an act of kindness to tell them that we have already made the discovery, and try to show them the part of the ocean where such creatures are to be found?"

"Hum! No, my boy. No. We should be making matters worse. Not only should we be showing the Count and his son that we have found out what they want to keep secret, but we should be robbing them of the honour of their discovery as well. No; let them take us into their confidence if they like, and if they do, so much the better. If they do not—well, the loss is theirs."

Chapter Thirty Three
Coast Land

"Our skipper's as right as can be, Morny," said Rodd the next evening, as the lad was once more on board the schooner, and they were sailing gently along about a mile from shore, the brig following pretty close behind with the water streaming down from her scuppers as the work at one of the pumps was still kept up.

For there was the coast, much as he had described, an undulating line of the singular dark green mangrove forest that looked low and dwarfed, and, now that the tide was low, showed to full advantage, the singular ramification of its roots giving the bushy forest the appearance of standing up upon a wilderness of jagged and tangled scaffolding through which the sea washed over the muddy shore.

"Not pleasant-looking, gentlemen," said the skipper, coming up to them. "Not the sort of place where you would like to settle down and build a country house."

"Why, it's horrible," cried Rodd. "But why should it be so muddy here, instead of being all nice clean sand?"

"Because it's the edge of a low swampy country, my lad, where great rivers come from inland and bring down the soil of thousands of miles."

"But I always thought Africa was a sandy desert place where lions were roving about, and where Mungo Park went travelling to Timbuctoo and places like that."

"Yes, my lad," said the skipper; "but that's the Africa of the old books, and there's plenty of it like that on the east side and up in the north and where old Mungo Park went to, no doubt; but all along this coast it isn't a dry and thirsty land, but as soon as you get through the mangroves, full of great forests and big rivers. Why, look at the sea here. Right away out it was all as clear as crystal; now here there's mud enough for anything."

"But we shan't want to stop long in a muddy river with banks like this, captain," said Morny.

"Don't you be in too great a hurry to judge, sir," said the skipper. "I have sailed up one or two of these rivers in my time, and when you get higher up you will find it very different: big forests with grand trees, rivers with fine water, and places beautiful enough for anything, such as will satisfy travellers who don't want ports and towns. You and the doctor, Mr Rodd, will be able to get some fine shooting up there, if you like, and fine fishing too. Do you want to get any birds of all the colours of the rainbow?"

"Why, of course!" cried Rodd eagerly.

"Well, there you'll find them, sir—singing birds too, green and gold and scarlet and grey, and some with long tails, and some with short. Only," continued the skipper dryly, and with a grim smile at the two lads, "they don't sing like our birds at home, but in a foreign lingo, all squeak and scream and squawk, through their having crooked hook beaks. They are what people at home call parrots and parakeets."

"Oh, that's what you mean!" cried Rodd, laughing.

"Of course, sir—them as you teaches to talk. Wicked 'uns, some of them, ready enough to learn anything the sailors teach them, but sulky as slugs when you want them to learn anything good."

"But there are plenty of them, captain?" said Rodd.

"Thicker than crows at home, sir. Then what do you say to monkeys?"

"That I should like to see them alive in the forest."

"Well, there you have them, sir; and you could come across plenty, if you went far enough, big as boys."

"Ah, now you are telling travellers' tales, captain," said Rodd.

"Nay, my lad, not I. I have seen them as big as boys, only not so tall, because their legs have all gone into arms. Little, short, crooked legs, they have got, as makes them squatty. But when they stand up their arms are so long that they nearly touch the ground. Big as boys? Why, they are bigger! I never saw boys with such big heads. And they all look as if they had been born old; wrinkled faces and long shaggy black hair."

"Now, look here, captain, I don't mind you joking me, but don't play tricks with the Viscount here."

"Not I, my lad. I am just telling you the honest truth, and you may believe me."

"But where's the river where these things are?"

"We shall come across one of them before long, sir," said the skipper. "I expected to have found one that suited my book hours ago. I was very nearly going up that one just about dinner-time."

"Oh, but that was only a little inlet," said Rodd.

"Looked so to you, sir, but all along here the shore's full of inlets, as you call them; but they are deep water and go winding in and out, and perhaps open out into big sheets of water like lagoons, as they call them. But I am of opinion that if we don't turn into one to-night we shall do so some time to-morrow, and perhaps find just the sort of spot we want. It we don't we will go a bit farther south."

"But take us up beyond all this horrible mangrove swamp," said Rodd.

"You leave that to me, sir," said the skipper. "We have got a good bit of work to do with that brig, and I want to bring my lads out again, and the Count's too, well and hearty, not half of them eaten up with fever and t'other half sucked into dry skins by the mosquitoes. No, we shall have to sail right up to where it gets to be a forest and park-like country."

"There'll be no towns?" said Rodd.

"No, sir, but we might come across a blacks' village, and if we do we can anchor somewhere on the other shore."

Another afternoon had come before the mangrove forest seemed to turn inland and run right up the country, just as if they had come to the end of that portion of the land; but miles away the skipper pointed out that the forest began again and also swept inland, while by using the glass the lads were able to trace the configuration of the coast, and saw that the two lines of coast north and south came together away east.

"There," said the skipper, "what do you say to this for the mouth of a big river?"

"River?" said the doctor, coming up.

"Yes, sir—or estuary, which you like. This is the sort of one that will suit us, though as far as I can make out it is not down in my chart. So all the more likely to suit our book."

"But do you think it's a river, and not a bend of the coast?" asked the doctor.

"If it was a bend of the coast, sir, the tide wouldn't be flowing in like that. It's a good-sized tidal river, sir, and we are going to sail in as far as we can get before dark, and if all turns out as I expect, we shall be carried in past the mangroves and be able to moor to-night perhaps to forest trees."

"And if we don't?" said Rodd.

"Why, then we shall anchor, and find plenty of good holding ground."

The tide carried them in rapidly, and a nice soft breeze filled the sails, bearing them onward till the mangrove swamp on either hand began to close in rapidly, while towards evening they were gliding where the banks were about a mile apart, and just at sunset muddy patches began to make their appearance, upon which Rodd noticed three times over, portions of the rugged trunks of trees that had been denuded of every branch as they floated down with the stream.

All at once, just where the mud glistened ruddily in the rays of the setting sun, Rodd started, for a thick stumpy tree trunk suddenly began to move gently, then glided a few feet over the mud, and finally went into the river with a tremendous splash.

"Why, what's that?" cried Rodd excitedly.

"Croc," grunted the skipper gruffly. "Thousands of them along here."

Chapter Thirty Four
How to get back?

"Almost as bad as you tacking out of the harbour, Morny," said Rodd that evening, as the two vessels glided up the rapidly narrowing and greatly winding river.

"Oh no," replied the French lad. "There is no tremendous storm of wind blowing, threatening to tear the sails to ribbons, no soldiers in boats using their muskets, no big guns sending heavy balls from the forts."

"No," said the skipper, who had overheard the remarks; "not a bit like it, Mr Rodd. It is rather awkward work, though, and we have to be always on the dodge, else the next thing would be we should go ramming our noses right in the muddy banks and getting stuck fast; and that wouldn't do."

"Oh, you would get off again next tide," said Rodd carelessly.

"Mebbe," said the skipper. "As the old country chaps at home say, we mought and we moughtn't."

"Look, Morny," cried Rodd. "There's another of those great crocs. What a thick one! Why, that one must be five-and-twenty feet long."

"Fourteen," grunted the skipper.

"No, no; it must have been twenty," cried Rodd.

"Fourteen, outside," growled the skipper. "How can you tell when you only catch sight of them on the move?"

"Well, it was a tremendous thickness," said Rodd.

"Ay, it was thick enough, and heavy enough; and they are stronger than horses. And just you look here, youngster, while we are up this river, where I dare say they swarm, you had better keep your eyes open, for those chaps will pull a deer or a bullock into the water before the poor brute knows where it is, and as to human natur', they lie waiting close to the banks for the poor niggers, men, women or children, who come down to get water, and they nip them off in a moment."

"Ugh! Horrible!" cried Rodd.

"Yes, and what made me speak to you was that we are going to settle down for a bit up here in the forest where the sun will be very hot, and where there'll be no end of great shady trees hanging over the river side and seeming to ask folks to jump in and have a nice cooling swim."

"I say, captain!"

"Oh, I'm not laughing at you, my lads," said the skipper sharply. "When we are lying moored or at anchor up here it's just the sort of thing that you might make up your minds to do without saying a word to anybody. I know I should have done so when I was your age. But I just say to you now solemn like—don't you do it. For if there's anything one of these great reptiles likes it's a nice clean French or English boy."

"Oh, come now," cried Rodd merrily, "you don't call that talking solemn like, captain?"

A grim smile dawned upon the old sailor's countenance.

"Well, no," he said; "but I mean it solemn like. I don't suppose one of they crocs would study about what colour it was, but they go for anything that's alive and moving, hold on with those great teeth of theirs, and whatever it is they catch, it's soon drowned when it's pulled below, and never heard of again.—Starboard, my lads! Starboard!" he shouted, with both hands to his mouth, and the schooner curved round and went off on another tack in obedience to the helm.—"It's rather an awkward job, my lads," continued the skipper. "You see, we have to sail to all points of the compass, and one minute you have got the wind blowing gently fair and free from right ahead or dead astern, and the next you are going into shelter and got no wind at all."

"But we keep on going steadily up the river, captain," said Rodd.

"Yes, my lad; we have got this strong tide in our favour. I am reckoning that if we drop anchor soon we shall be able to get as far as we want next tide."

"But how far do you mean to go?" asked Morny anxiously.

"Oh, a good way up yet," replied the skipper.

"But why not keep on now?" asked Rodd.

"Because I want to pick a good berth before the dark comes down and catches and leaves us nohow. Got any more questions to ask?"

"Hundreds," cried Rodd merrily.

"Humph! Then I think I ought to have my pay raised. I joined the *Maid of Salcombe* to sail her, not to give you lessons in jography, etymology, syntax, and prosody, as it used to say in my lesson book when I was a little 'un."

"Ah, well, I won't bother you any more to-day, captain," said Rodd; "only one always wants to know what things are when they are quite fresh."

Captain Chubb did not answer for the moment, for he had to shout another order to the steersman and make two or three signals with his hand to those on board the brig, which was following in the schooner's track, keeping as close as it could to be safe.

At the end of five minutes, though, he had returned to his old position, and grunted out with a look as if he wanted to be questioned more—

"Well, I suppose such youngsters as you like to know."

Then all at once he shouted out a fresh order, which was followed by the rattling out of the cable through the hawse-hole as the anchor splashed and went down to a pretty good depth before the rope was stopped, one order having acted for both vessels, and just before dark they swung round head to stream, with the water lapping loudly against their bows.

"That's enough for one day," grunted the captain. "Safe and snug a harbour as any one could wish to be in, and there's the trees, you see, on both sides, good, sound, solid forest trees such as would cut up into fine timber, and all the mangroves left far enough behind."

In a remarkably short time, as the two lads stood watching the shores, the forest on either side grew intensely black, and though the steward announced that the evening meal was ready, no one seemed disposed to go below, for, succeeding to the solemn evening silence, they seemed to be surrounded by strange sounds from the depths of the forest as well as from the river, whose current began to grow sluggish, suggesting that before long the tide would be at its height, and ready to turn with the rushing of the water outward to the sea.

"Why, it's awful," said Morny, in a subdued tone, as he stood with Rodd gazing at the nearest shore.

"Yes, not very nice," replied Rodd. "You and your father had better stop on board here to-night."

"Oh no. Our boat is hanging astern. We shall go back."

Rodd thought that he should not like to attempt to row from vessel to vessel in the darkness of such a night, for something seemed to suggest to him the possibility of being swept out to sea; but he did not say so, for fear of making his companion nervous, and they stood listening and whispering together, trying to give names to some of the uncouth noises which floated to their ears.

Many were sharp quick splashes as if some great fish had sprung out of the water in pursuit of prey, or in a desperate effort to escape a pursuer. Then every now and then there would be a resounding slap, as if one of the great reptiles that haunted the river had struck the surface a tremendous blow with its tail.

"What's that?" asked Rodd, directly after, as a low, deep, mournful sound came from amongst the trees upon the shore, sounding like a piteous cry for help from some woman in distress.

This was succeeded by a painful silence, and then Rodd raised his voice—

"Captain! Captain Chubb! Do you hear that? Are you there?"

"Oh yes, here I am, my lad," came from out of the darkness. "And I should be precious deaf if I hadn't heard it."

"Well, ought we to take the boat and try and save her?" cried the boy passionately.

"How do you know it's a *her*, my lad? I should say it was a *him*. It's the cock birds and not the hens that shout like that."

"Bird!" cried Morny. "It was a human being."

"Ah, it do sound something like it, my lad, but that aren't a human. It's one of them great long-legged storky chaps with the big bills, calling to his wife to say he's found frogs, or something of that kind. You wait a minute, and if she don't come you will hear him call 'Quanko!'—There, what did I say?" said the skipper, with a chuckle, as in trumpet tones came the cry of the great long-legged creature in a sonorous *Quang, quang, quang, quang*!

"Why, the captain seems to know everything," said Morny admiringly. "I say, how did you know that, sir?"

"Oh," said the skipper modestly, "one just picks up these sort of things a little bit at a time. Now then, do you hear that?"

The two lads did hear it—a peculiar musical (?) wailing cry which was repeated again and again and then died out, half-smothered by a chorus of croaking from the swampy river banks.

"Oh yes, we can hear," cried Rodd. "We can do nothing else but listen. But what was it made that cry?"

"Ah! That's one of the things I don't know," said the skipper, chuckling. "What should you think it was?"

"Oh, I don't want to be laughed at again," cried Rodd, "for making another mistake. Perhaps it's some other kind of stork."

"Nay, you don't think it is," said the skipper. "You think different to that. Come, have a guess."

"Well," said Rodd, "I should say it was some kind of great cat."

"Right, my lad; not much doubt about that. I don't know what sort it is, but it's one of them spotted gentlemen. I should say there'd be plenty of them here. Well, I have had about enough of it for to-day. I am just going to see about the watch, and to say a few words below to your father about having a good look-out kept, and then it won't be very long before I turn in to my cot, for I am tired. This has been a rather anxious day."

"You are going to speak to my father about having a good look-out kept?"

"Well, yes, my lad, and with our men well-armed. I don't say as it's likely, and we are too near the sea for any villages of blacks; but it wouldn't be very nice to have two or three big canoes come and make fast to us in the night, and find the decks swarming with niggers who might think that we were made on purpose for them to kill."

"Why, you don't think that's likely, do you?" cried Rodd.

"Not at all, my lad. But safe bind, safe find. What I have always found is this—that when you keep a very strict look-out nothing happens, and when you don't something does. Are you lads coming down?"

"Not yet," said Rodd.

"I suppose you will be going soon, won't you, Mr Morny?" said the skipper, who somehow always forgot their visitor's title.

"I am expecting my father will be coming up soon to say it is time."

"Yes; I shouldn't leave it much longer," said the skipper. "I'll tell him.— Joe Cross, there!"

"Ay, ay, sir!"

"You and four men stand by with the gig to take the Count aboard his vessel. You will just drop down head to stream ready to pull hard if the tide seems a bit too heavy; and you, my lad, be ready forward with the end of the line made fast to the thwart and the grapnel clear, ready to drop overboard to get hold of the mud if you find the current too strong."

"Ay, ay, sir!" cried the man; and the skipper went below.

"I am glad of that, Joe," said Rodd eagerly. "I was thinking whether there was any risk of the boat being swept away."

"So was I, sir; but it's always the same. Whenever I think of something that ought to be done I always find that our old man has thought of it before. Did you see that we have swung round to our anchor?"

"No," said Rodd.

"We have, sir, and the tide's running out like five hundred million mill-streams. You come for'ard here and feel how the cable's all of a jigger, just as if the river had made up its mind to pull it right out of the mud."

The two lads followed, and it was exactly as the man had said, for the great Manilla rope literally thrilled as if with life, while the river glided by the schooner's cutwater with a loud hiss.

"Why, Joe," cried Rodd, as he gazed in the sailor's dimly-seen face, "how are you going to manage to row back?"

"Well, sir, that's one of the things I have been asking myself."

"Well, you had better speak to the skipper."

"Not me, sir. I'm not going to try to teach him. If I was to say a word he'd jump down my throat bang. Oh, he knows what he's about, or he wouldn't have told me to stand by with that there grapnel."

"Yes, of course he'd know," said Rodd quietly. "I should like to know how you'd got on."

The two lads stood listening to the weird sounds from the shore, every now and then being puzzled by something that was entirely fresh, while the swiftly running water gleamed dimly with the faintly seen reflection of the stars, showing that a mist was gathering overhead, while Joe Cross and the men lowered down the boat and hauled her up to the gangway, ready to convey the visitors to the brig.

They had hardly finished preparations before the voices that had come before in murmurs from the cabin were heard ascending to the deck, and the Count cried out of the darkness—

"Are you ready there, Morny, my son?"

"Yes, my father," replied the lad, and Rodd walked with him to the side.

The men were in their places, with their oars ready to hand to lower at once, Joe Cross holding on in front with his boat-hook through a ring-bolt. A few more words passed between the Count and Uncle Paul, and then the former bade his son descend into his place, following slowly directly after.

"Good-night," he said.

"Good-night, Rodd!" cried Morny. "We shan't be long getting to the brig."

"No," cried Rodd. "Good-night! Here, one moment; I'll slip down and come back with the gig."

Before any one else could speak he had dropped into the boat, his feet touching the nearest thwart as the skipper cried "Let go!" and almost the next moment the men were pulling hard, while Joe Cross dropped upon his knees to feel for the grapnel so as to make sure it was at hand, while to Rodd it seemed that the boat was motionless in the rapid river and that the schooner had been suddenly snatched away.

Chapter Thirty Five
Up a Tree

"Put your backs into it, my lads," cried Joe Cross, almost fiercely. "Steady! Steady all, and look out that you don't have a smash. Pull! Hard! Here, I shall be tugged out of the boat!"

For it seemed almost directly after that the dimly-seen hull of the brig rose up out of the darkness close at hand, while from where he knelt— fortunately for himself—the coxswain felt his arms being jerked out of their sockets as he caught with the boat-hook at the brig's main chains. "Stand by there!" he roared, as he held on. "Lend a hand here to help the gentlemen on board! Somebody say it in French! Up with you!"

There was no need for the use of another tongue, for a lantern shed its light down upon them, willing hands were ready, and the Count and Morny scrambled aboard.

The next moment the Count was giving orders for a rope to be passed down to the boat.

"Make fast, and come on board!" he shouted. "You'll never get back to-night."

The order came too late, for as he spoke another order was given out by Joe Cross, who had loosed the precarious hold he had with the boat-hook, as he shouted while giving the boat a thrust away—

"Now for it, my lads! Pull for all you know!"

Almost the next moment Rodd dimly saw that they were clear, and as the men tugged at their oars with all their might he dropped upon his knees in front of stroke, clapped his hands against the oar, and swinging with the man, thrust with all his force.

Five minutes of desperate tugging at the oars in the midst of darkness which seemed to rapidly increase. The men had rowed with all their force— not to get back to the schooner, but to reach the brig and one of her ropes that they knew would be thrown to their help; but to Rodd, as he strained his eyes from where he knelt striving to give force to the stroke oar, it was like catching so many glimpses, first of the brig's side, then of its stern, and then once more it was as if they were standing still in the water and the brig was rushing away.

"Steady, my lads! Don't break your hearts!" cried Joe Cross firmly, his voice ringing clearer out of the black silence. "It aren't to be done. Midstream's our game. If we try to get ashore we shall be among the branches, capsized in a moment, and—"

The sailor did not finish his speech then, but Rodd did to himself, and hot though he was with his exertions, a cold shiver seemed to run through him, as he mentally said—

"The crocodiles!"

"That's better, my lads. Just a steady pull, and I'll keep as I am with the boat-hook. We mustn't have a capsize."

"What are you going to do, Joe?" cried Rodd.

"Don't know, sir," said the man gruffly. "Perhaps you can tell me."

"I? No," cried Rodd.

"Ah! That's awkward," said the man. "I don't know what the skipper was about to set us on this job. That's the worst of being a sailor. They trains us up to 'bey orders directly they're guv, and we does them, but one never knows how to be right. I oughter ha' told the old man as this was more'n men could do; 'cause I half thought it were. But then I says to myself, the skipper knows best; and here we are in a nice hole."

"A nice hole!" cried Rodd angrily. "Why, we shall be swept out to sea."

"Looks like it, sir—I mean seems."

"But why not make for the shore, where we could catch hold of some of the overhanging branches?"

"I told you, sir. 'Cause we should be capsized before we had time to wink. Steady, my lads—steady! It's no use to pull, Mr Rodd; four times as many of us couldn't stem a stream like this."

"Will they come down after us? Yes, my uncle is sure to."

"Not he, sir. It would be just about mad to try it, and our old man will be so wild at being caught like this that he won't let him stir. 'Sides that, sir, what are you talking about? How are they to know we have been swept away?"

"Because we don't come back, of course," cried Rodd angrily.

"That won't do, sir. Skipper knows, of course, after the way we went off, that it's just impossible."

"But the Count will tell him."

"Too far off for shouting, sir. You take my word for it that the skipper will make up his mind that we are stopping on board the brig till the tide runs slack again. If anything's done it will be by the Frenchies, and I don't believe they'll try."

"Oh, but the Count would. His son would make him."

"No, sir. The Count's a fine naval officer who has seen service, and he knows too well what he's about to send a boat's crew swirling down this river to go nobody knows where. The only folks as can help us is—"

"Yes—who?" cried Rodd, for the man broke off in his speech.

"Ourselves, sir; and we shall find it precious hard."

"That's right, Joe," said one of the other sailors. "Better speak out, mate, and say the worst on it."

"Say it yourselves," cried Joe Cross roughly.

"Yes, speak out," cried Rodd. "What do you think?"

"We can do nothing, sir, but keep her head straight and go down with the tide, doing all we can to keep from being sucked into the shore among the trees."

"But look here, Joe, aren't we very close in now?" cried Rodd, who had just noticed in the darkness that the sailor he addressed was leaning over the bows and straining his eyes in one particular direction.

For answer the man yelled to his messmates to pull with all their might.

The oars dipped, but at the second stroke there was a crashing rustling sound of twigs, followed by a sharp crackling and snapping, as they were swept in amongst the pendant branches of some huge forest tree, one bough striking Rodd across the shoulders and holding him as it were fast, so that the boat was being dragged from beneath him.

Then there was more grinding of the gunwale of the boat amongst the boughs, the water came swishing in over the side, and directly after the frail vessel partly turned over, with her keel lying sideways to the rushing tide.

Then more crackling and rustling amongst the boughs, mingled with shouting from the boat's crew, and from out of the confusion, and somewhere above him in the pitchy darkness and low-lying night mist, came the voice of Joe Cross—

"Now then, all of you! Where away?"

"Here!"

"Here!"

"All right, mate!"

"Lend a hand, some one!"

"Are you all here?" cried Joe Cross again.

"Ay, ay, ay, ay!" came in chorus.

"But I don't hear the young guvnor."

There was silence.

"Where's Mr Rodd?"

A moment's pause, and then—

"Mr Rodd! Ahoy!"

"Here, Joe, here!" came in half-suffocated tones.

"Wheer, my lad?" cried the man excitedly.

"Here! Here! Help!"

"But where's yer *here*, lad? I can't see you.—Can any of you? Oh, look alive, some on you! Get hold of the boy anywhere—arms or legs or anything—and hold on like grim death."

There was a sharp rustling of leaves and twigs which pretty well drowned Rodd's answer—

"I'm down here."

"Where's *down here*, my lad? Are you under the boat?"

"No, no. Hanging to a bough, with the water up to my chest, and something's tugging at me to drag me away."

"Oh, a-mussy me!" groaned the sailor. "Why aren't it to-morrow morning and sun up? Can't any of you see him?"

"No, no, no, no!" came back, almost as dismally as groans.

"Well, can't you feel him, then?"

"No."

"I am here, Joe—here!" panted the lad. "Higher up the river than you are. A big branch swept me out of the boat."

"Ah, yes, we went under it," groaned Joe. "Well, lads, he must be the other side of the tree. Here, where's that there boat? Can any of you see it?"

"No; we are all on us in the tree?"

"Well, I don't suppose you are swimming," roared Cross savagely. "Do something, some on you! Thinking of nothing but saving your own blessed lives! Are you going to let the poor lad drown?"

"Here, coxswain, why don't you tell us what to do?" snarled one of the men.

"How can I," yelled Joe, "when I don't know what to do mysen? Oh, don't I wish that I had got the skipper here! I'd let him have it warm!"

"Joe! Joe!" came out of the darkness. "I can't hold on! I can't hold on!"

"Yah, you young idgit!" roared the sailor. "You must!"

"I can't, Joe—I can't!" cried Rodd faintly, and there was a gurgling sputtering sound as if the water had washed over him.

"Oh–h!" groaned Joe. "Don't I tell you you must! Hold on by your arms and legs—your eyelids. Stick your teeth into the branch. We are a-coming, my lad.—Oh my! what a lie!" he muttered. Then aloud, and in a despairing tone, "Can any one of you get up again' the stream to where he is?"

"No!" came in a deep murmur. "If we go down we shall be washed away."

"Same here," groaned Joe. "I'm a-holding on with the water right up to the middle, and just about ready to be washed off. I can't stir. Oh, do one of you try and save the poor dear lad! I wish I was dead, I do!"

"Joe!" came faintly.

"Ay, ay, my lad!"

"Tell Uncle Paul—"

The words ended in a half-suffocated wailing cry, and almost the next moment there was a tremendous splashing of water, and the snapping of a good-sized branch, followed by sounds as of a struggle going on upon the surface of the rushing stream as it lapped and hissed amongst the tangled boughs and twigs.

"Hold hard!" yelled Joe. "Anywhere.—Got him, boys—*urrrrr!*—"

It was as if some savage beast had suddenly seized its prey. Then there was a loud panting and more crackling as of branches giving way, and directly after, in answer to a volley of inquiries, Joe Cross panted out—

"Yes, I've got him, my lads, and he's got his teeth into me; but I don't know how long we can hold on."

"You must hold on, Joe!" shouted a voice.

"Stick to him, messmate! I'm a-trying to get to you."

There was more crackling in the darkness, and a peculiar subdued sound as of men panting after running hard; but it was only the hard breathing of excitement.

"Have you got him still, Joe?" came in gasps.

"Yes, my lad, but he's awful still and I don't know that he aren't drowned.—No, he aren't, for he's got his teeth into my shoulder, and he's gripping hard. But the water keeps washing right up into my ear."

"Hoist him up a little higher," panted the other speaker.

"How can I? I've got my arm round him, but if I stir it means let go. What are you doing, mate?"

"Trying to get down to you, but as soon as I stir the bough begins to crack."

"Steady, mate, steady! I can't see you, but I can hear, and if you come down on us we are gone. Here, I say, it will be hours before it's morning, won't it?"

There was a groan in reply—a big groan formed by several voices in unison.

"But how long will it be before, the tide goes down and leaves us?"

There was no reply, and a dead silence fell upon the occupants clinging to different portions of the tree, all of whom had managed with the strength and activity of sailors to drag themselves up beyond the reach of the water and at varying distances from where Joe Cross clung with one messmate hanging just above his head.

"Well, look here, messmates," said Joe at last, "it's no use to make the worst on it. I've got the young skipper all right, and he's growing more lively, for he just give a kick. Now who's this 'ere? It's you, Harry Briggs, aren't it?"

"Ay, ay, mate; me and water, for I swallowed a lot before I got out of it."

"Now, look here; how are you holding on?"

"Hanging down'ards, my lad, with my hind legs tied in a knot round a big bough; and I keep on trying to get hold of you by the scruff, but I can't quite reach."

"Why, that's a-hinging like the bees used to do outside my old mother's skep. Well, you mustn't let go, my lad, else down you come."

"Well, I know that, mate," growled the man. "But I say, can't you reach up to my hands?"

"Yah! No!" growled Joe. "I've only got two. Can't you reach down a little further and get hold of my ears, or something?"

"My arms aren't spy-glasses, and they won't reach within a foot of you. Can any of you swarm out above us here?"

"No—no—no!" came in voice after voice, from points that were evidently fairly distant.

"Oh!" groaned the sailor addressed as Harry. "Fust time in my blessed life I ever wished I was a 'Merican monkey."

"What for, mate?" panted Joe.

"So as to make fast round this 'ere branch with my tail."

"Joe! Joe!" came in a low hoarse tone. "Where am I!"

"Well, you are here, my lad; but don't let go with your teeth. Take another good fast hold, but more outside like. Keep to the wool of the jumper—if you can."

"Hah! I recollect now. We are in the water, and I have got hold of you."

"That's right, my lad, and I'd say take a good fast holt of my hair, only Ikey Gregg scissored it off so short when it turned so hot that there's nothing to hold. But can you hyste yourself up a bit higher?"

"I'll try, Joe; but the water drags at me so. But, Joe, what are you holding on to?"

"What they'd call a arm of the tree, sir."

"But if I try to climb up you shan't I drag you loose?"

"Oh, I'm no consequence, my lad. If I'm washed off I shall get hold again somewheres. Never you mind me. There's Harry Briggs up aloft a-reaching down a couple of his hands. If you feel you've got stuff enough in you.—Take your time over it, my lad—you see if you can't swarm a bit up me and then stretch up and think you are at home trying to pick apples, till Harry gets a big grip of your wristies; and then you ought to be able to swarm up him. Now then, do you think you can try?"

"Yes, Joe; I think so," panted the boy. "That's right, my lad. I'd give you a lift, only I can't, for I'm in rotten anchorage, and we mustn't get adrift."

About a minute passed, in which little was heard but the whishing of the water through the leaves and twigs, and the sound of hard breathing. Then Joe spoke again—

"I don't want to hurry you, my lad, but if you think you can manage it I'd say, begin."

"I'm ready now, Joe," said the boy faintly. "But do you think you can hold on?"

"Aren't got time to think, my lad. You go on and do it. That's your job, and don't you think as it's a hard 'un. Just you fancy the doctor's yonder getting anxious about you, and then—up you goes."

"Yes, Joe," panted Rodd.

"And once you get hold of Harry Briggs' hands he'll draw you up a bit. He's a-hinging down like one of them there baboons, tail up'ards. Then, once he hystes you a bit, you get a good grip of him with your teeth anywhere that comes first. He won't mind. That'll set your hands free, and then up you goes bit by bit till you gets right into the tree."

"Yes, Joe; and then?"

"Well, my lad, then I'd set down striddling and have a rest."

"Below there! Ready!" cried Briggs. "I can't reach no further, youngster, but I think if you can climb up and grip we might manage it."

"Yes! Coming!" cried Rodd.

And then no one saw, and afterwards Rodd could hardly tell how he managed it, but with the water pressing him closer as he clung face to face with the partially submerged coxswain, he managed to scramble higher, clinging with arms and legs, till he occupied a hazardous position astride of the sailor's shoulder, holding on with his left hand and reaching up with his right, snatching for a few moments at nothing.

"Where are you, my lad?" came from above.

"Here! Here!" panted Rodd, and then, "Ah, it's of no use!"

As he spoke he felt himself going over, but at that moment his fingers touched the sleeve of a soft clinging jersey, a set of fingers gripped hard at his arm, and in a supreme effort he loosened his other hand, made a snatch, and then began swinging gently to and fro till another hand from above closed upon his jacket and lightened the strain.

"Got you, my lad!" came from overhead. "Now look here; I'm not going to hyste you up, 'cause I can't, but I am going to swing you back'ards and for'ards like a pendulo till you can touch this 'ere bough where I am hanging, and then go on till you can get your legs round it and hold fast. Understand?"

"Yes," panted Rodd.

"Now then. Belay, and when you get hold you shout."

It was the work of an acrobat, such as he would have achieved in doubt and despair.

The sailor began swinging the boy to and fro, to and fro, with more and more force, till Rodd felt his legs go crashing in amongst the thick twigs of the great bough that was drawn down by the weight of the two upon it a good deal below the horizontal.

"Harder!" he cried, as he swung back, and then as his legs went well in again he felt that a thick portion was passing between his knees, and thrusting forward his feet with all his might he forced them upwards and directly afterwards passed them one across the other in a desperate grip which left him dragging on the sailor's hands.

"Fast, my lad?"

"Yes."

"Can you hold on?"

"Yes."

"Then good luck to you!" cried the sailor, as, relieved of the boy's weight, he too swung head downwards for a moment or two, then with a quick effort wrenched himself upwards, got hold of the branch with both hands, and after hanging like a sloth for a few moments, succeeded in dragging himself upon the bough, which all the while was swaying heavily up and down and threatening to shake Rodd from where he hung, but at the same time inciting him so to fresh desperate action, that with all a boy's activity he too had succeeded in perching himself astride of the branch.

"All right, my lad?" cried Briggs.

"Ye–es!" came gaspingly.

"Then you wait a bit and get your wind, my lad.—Joe Cross! Ahoy!" he yelled, as if his messmate were half-a-mile away.

"Right ho!" came from below. "Where's the boy?"

"Here, Joe—here!" shouted Rodd, the sound of the man's voice seeming to send energy through him.

"Hah–h–h!" came from the sailor, and directly after from different parts of the tree there was a cheer.

"Now then, what about you, matey?" shouted Briggs.

"Well, I dunno yet, my lad; I'm just going to try and shape it round. I want to know where some of the others are, and whether if I let go I couldn't manage to make a scramble and swim so as to join a mate."

"No, no, no!" came in chorus. "Don't try it, lad. Aren't you safe where you are?"

"Well, I don't know about being safe," replied the sailor. "Mebbe I could hold on, but here's the water up to my chesty; and don't make a row, or you'll be letting some of those crocs know where I am. Look here, Mr Rodd, sir; are you all right?"

"Yes, Joe; I can sit here as long as I like.—That is," he added to himself, "if the branch doesn't break."

"Well, that's a comfort, sir. And what about you, Harry Briggs?"

"Well, I'm all right, mate; only a bit wet."

"Wet! You should feel me!" cried Cross, quite jocularly. "How about the rest on you?"

"Oh, we are up aloft here in the dark, mate," said one of the men. "I dunno as we should hurt so long as we didn't fall asleep."

"Oh, I wouldn't do that, mates," said Cross. "You might catch cold. You hang yourselves out as wide as you can, so as to get dry."

"But look here, Joe Cross," shouted Rodd, who was rapidly recovering his spirits, "you mustn't sit there in the water. Can't you manage to climb up?"

"Oh yes, sir, I can climb up easy enough, only it don't seem to me as there's anything to climb."

"But doesn't the branch you are sitting on go right up to the tree?"

"No, sir; it goes right down into it, and I'm sitting in a sort of fork, like a dicky bird as has been picking out a handy place for its nest."

"Then what are you going to try to do?"

"Nothing, sir, but think."

"Think?"

"Yes, sir—about what I'm going to say to the skipper if ever we gets back."

"Why, what can you say?"

"That's what I want to know, sir. I know what he'll say to me. He'll say, Look here, my lad, you were coxswain; I want to know what you have done with my gig."

"Ah, the boat!" said Rodd. "Do any of you know what's become of the boat?"

"I don't," said Briggs.

"Oh, she's half-way to South Ameriky by this time, sir," said Joe, "and I shall get all the credit of having lost her."

"Never mind about the boat, Joe."

"Well, sir, if you talk like that, I don't. But it's the skipper who will mind."

"It's nothing to do with him, Joe. It's uncle's boat; and it wasn't your fault."

"Thank you, sir. That's a bit comforting like, and warms one up a bit; but if it's all the same to you I'd raither not talk quite so much, for I don't know as crocs can hear, but if they can it mightn't be pleasant. Well, my lads, just another word; we have got to make the best of it and wait for daylight, and I suppose by that time the tide will have gone right down, and some on you will be getting dry."

There was silence then, and the men sat holding on to their precarious perches, listening to an occasional sound from the river or the shore, loud splashings right away out in the direction of what they supposed to be the main current, and an occasional trumpeting wail or shriek from the forest— sounds that chilled and produced blood-curdling sensations at the first, but to which the men became more and more accustomed as the hours slowly glided on.

"Look here," said Joe Cross, at last, "because I said I didn't want to talk, that wasn't meant for you who are all right up above the water. It's bad enough to be keeping a watch like this on a dark night, but that is no reason why you chaps shouldn't tell stories and talk and say something to cheer Mr Rodd up a bit. He had about the worst of it, swep' out of the boat as he was. So let go, some on you. You've got to do something, as you can't go to sleep. But I tell you one thing; you chaps are all much better off than I am. I shan't fall out of my bunk on the top of any of you. But look here, Harry Briggs, you always want a lot of stirring up before one can get you to move. Now then; you have got a bit of pipe of your own. Sing us a song. Good cheery one, with a chorus—one that Mr Rodd can pick up and chime in. Now then, let go."

"Who's a-going to sing with the water dripping down out of his toes?"

"Why, you, mate," cried Joe. "There, get on with you. You chaps as knows the best songs always wants the most stirring up, pretending to be bashful, when you want to begin all the time!"

"I tell you I don't, mate. I'm too cold."

"Then heave ahead, and that'll warm you up. You tell him he is to sing, Mr Rodd, sir. You're skipper now, and he must obey orders. It'll do us all good."

"Well," said Rodd, "it doesn't seem a very cheerful time to ask people to sing in the dark; but perhaps it will brighten us all up."

"Ay, ay, sir!" came from the rest.

"Am I to, Mr Rodd?" said the man appealingly; and after a little more pressing he struck up in a good musical tenor the old-fashioned sea song of "The Mermaid," with its refrain of—

"We jolly sailor boys were up, up aloft,
And the land lubbers lying down below, below, below,
And the land lubbers lying down below!"

right on through the several verses, telling of the sailors' superstition regarding its being unlucky to see a mermaid with a comb and a glass in her hand, when starting upon a voyage, right on to the piteous cry of the sailor boy about his mother in Portsmouth town, and how that night she would weep for him, till the song ended with the account of how the ship went down and was sunk in the bottom of the sea.

It was a wild sad air, sung there in the branches of that tree amidst the darkness and night mist, and in spite of a certain beauty in the melody the singer's voice assumed a more and more saddened tone, till he finished with the water seeming to hiss more loudly through the lower branches and the inundated trunks around, and then there was a sharp slapping noise on the surface of the stream that might very well have been taken for plaudits.

Then there was a strange braying sound like a weirdly discordant fit of laughter; and then perfect silence, with the darkness more profound than ever.

"I'm blessed!" came at last from Joe. "Hark at him, Mr Rodd. He calls hisself a messmate! Ast him, I did, to sing us a song to cheer us up. Why, it was bad enough to play for a monkey's funeral march. It's all very well for you others to join in your chorus about jolly sailor boys sitting up aloft, but what about poor me sitting all the time in a cold hipsy bath, as they calls it in hospitals, expecting every moment to feel the young crocs a-tackling my toes? Why, it's enough to make a fellow call out for a clean pocket-handkerchy. Here, some on you, set to and spin us a yarn to take the taste of that out of our mouths."

Chapter Thirty Six
The Doctor prescribes

And so that awful night wore on, one story bringing forth another, and the spinning of one yarn being followed by the spinning of one perhaps longer.

It was anything to relieve the terrible tedium and beguile their thoughts from the peril in which they were placed. The lapse of time was discussed, and the possibility of the slackening of the furious flow of the falling river so that a boat might come down in search of the unfortunates, but to a man all came to the conclusion that nothing could be expected until daylight, and that they must bear their fate as best they might.

The most cheerful thing that fell to their lot during the weary hours was the announcement made from time to time by Joe Cross, that the water was sinking a little lower and a little lower, so that he had room to hope that after a while he too would be able to, as he put it, drip himself dry.

But the monotony was terrible, and the morning seemed as if it would never come. For it was far different from being in the temperate region of the world, where in the summer months the darkness was slow to come and was succeeded by a very early dawn. There in that tropical southern land they were where the twenty-four-hours day was pretty equally divided into light and darkness, with scarcely any twilight to soften down the division.

But still as everything comes to those who wait, so it was there, and Joe Cross announced at last that he was sitting quite clear of the water, and therefore, as he judged it, they had not very much longer to wait before it would be day.

But he was wrong. What seemed to be an interminable time elapsed before the watchers could see for certain that a faint light seemed to be piercing the dense grey mist that covered the river. But this did at last become a certainty.

Before long, on one side, grey and grim-looking beneath a heavy mist, the great river could be seen gliding steadily along, while away to their right rose the primeval forest, rising as it were out of a sea of shadow.

The change came quickly then through a rapid twilight to the bright rays of the sunshine, which seemed to attack the river mist, piercing it through and through, routing it, and sending it in clouds rolling along the stream, while, now glistening and muddy, the banks showed out beyond the trees amidst which the huge monarch in which they had taken refuge stood towering almost alone.

"Why, we must have come inshore for some distance last night," cried Rodd, in wonder.

"Ay, my lad. Banks flooded. High tide perhaps," said Joe bluffly. "Well, the sooner we gets down into this mud and stretches our legs the better; and if they don't come down in the boats, how we are going to get back is more than I know."

"Look! Look yonder!" cried Rodd, as, sweeping the park-like stretch around him, he suddenly caught sight of an object that filled his breast with joy.

"Three cheers, my lads," shouted Joe, waving his hand, "and— Oh, hold hard! Avast there! Gig's safe to have a hole through her bottom."

For there, about a hundred yards away, between the trees, lay something gleaming amongst the mud.

He could only see a portion, but that was enough, and one by one, stiff and cold, the unfortunate party lowered themselves down from their perches to drop into a thin surface of soft mud, the swift rush of the tide preventing it from accumulating to any depth.

Their fortune was better than they anticipated, for on reaching the boat's side it was to find that, though bottom upward, she had escaped any serious injury, the yielding boughs into which she had been swept having checked the force of the concussion and left her to glide from tangle of boughs to tangle, until she had been wedged into a huge fork and had from there slowly settled down.

But there was neither oar nor boat-hook, and the line fastened to her foremost thwart had been snapped in two.

"All her tackle gone," said Joe grimly. "Well, we must try and find and hack off some big bamboo canes with our jack-knives, and then try if we can't punt her up against the tide, which ought to be pretty slack by now—that is, if they don't come to find us."

"But look here, Joe," cried Rodd, as he stood shading his eyes from the horizontal sunbeams; "there's the river, and the mist's rolling along with the tide. Here, I'm puzzled. Which way did we come?"

"Why, that's plain enough, Mr Rodd, sir. Down with the stream yon way."

"But that must be down-stream."

"Nay, not it, my lad. The river winds, and so did my head. Here, I'm all of a maze still. No, I aren't. Here, I'm blest! Why, you are right, sir. That is up-stream, and— Hooray, my lads! One pole will do, to steer. We are going to be carried back again, for the tide's turned and running up steady."

A very little search resulted in their coming upon a bed of canes, out of which four were cut and trimmed, supplying them with good stout poles twelve or fourteen feet long, and laying these along the thwarts the men, glad now of the exercise to drive out the chill, insisted upon Rodd getting into the boat while they waded through the mud by her side, half lifting, half thrusting, and succeeded at last in getting her to where a sloping portion of the bank ran down to the river.

"Now all together, my lads," cried Joe. "Keep step, and hold her well in hand, for she'll soon begin to slide; and as soon as she reaches the water, jump in. Make ready. I'll give the word."

"Stop!" shouted Rodd. "What about the crocodiles?"

"Oh, murder!" cried Joe. "I forgot all about them. Well, never mind. This aren't no time to be nice. It's got to be done, so here goes."

Rodd seized one of the poles, and going right to the bows knelt down in the bottom, and holding the pole lance fashion, prepared to try and use it.

"That won't be no good, my lad," cried Joe. "Now, my lads—one, two, three! Off she goes!"

They ran the gig quickly down the muddy slope, and as they touched the water and the foremost part began to float they took another step or two, gave her a final thrust, and sprang in, just as Rodd realised the truth of the sailor's words, for as they glided out with tremendous force, before they were a dozen yards from the water's edge the gig's stem collided just behind two muddy-looking prominences that appeared above the surface of the water, and as the shock sent the boy backwards over the next thwart the boat, which was bounding up and down with the result of the men springing in, received another shock from something dark which rose out of the water, and then they glided on past a tremendous ebullition and were carried onward by the rising tide.

"Here, let me come, Mr Rodd," cried Joe Cross, as he scrambled forward. "Here, catch hold, sir, and help me drag my jersey over my head. The brute's stove us in, and if I don't look sharp— Pull, sir, pull—right over my head! That's got it," he cried, and he set to work thrusting the woollen knitted shirt bit by bit along between the edges of two of the planks, through which the water was rapidly gurgling in. "There," he said; "that'll keep some on it out; but don't all on you stand looking at me as if I was playing a conjuring trick. Get a couple of those poles over the sides. Nay, nay, it's no use to try to punt. Dessay the water's fathoms deep. Just keep her head straight, and let the tide carry us on. Look out, my lads! There's another of them up yonder. See, Mr Rodd, sir—them two nubbles? Them's his eyes. He just keeps his beautiful muddy carcase all hid under water and squints along the top with them pretty peepers of hisn to look out for his breakfast. Keep back, sir; I believe he's coming on at us, big as the boat is. Oh, this is a pretty place, upon my word! He means me, because he can see my white skin."

Instead of answering, Rodd picked up the bamboo pole, which had been jerked from his hands when they encountered the other reptile.

Three of the men followed his example of holding them ready to strike at what they could see of the crocodile, and as they were carried closer by the tide and Rodd could just make out below the muddy surface that the water was being stirred by the undulation of the tail of the monster, which was apparently fourteen or fifteen feet long, three poles were sharply thrust together, two of them coming in contact with the creature's head just behind its eyes.

The blows were heavy, having behind them the weight and impetus of the loaded boat, and once more there was a tremendous swirl in the water, as the crocodile raised its head right out, turned completely over, displaying its pallid buff under portion, and then curved itself over, and in the act of diving down threw up its tail and struck the surface of the water with a blow that deluged the occupants of the cutter with spray.

"Well," cried Joe, as the boat glided on, "I don't know what you chaps think of it, but I am getting warm again, and I call this 'ere sport. But I say, Mr Rodd, I am beginning to wish you was aboard the *Maid of Salcombe*, and you'd took me with you."

"Same 'ere, sir," cried the men, in chorus.

"See any more, Mr Rodd?"

"No, not yet, Joe."

"Well, there's no hurry, sir. Let's get our breath. But do you call this 'ere fishing or shooting?"

"There's another," cried Rodd excitedly; "but it's going the other way."

"Got to know perhaps, sir, how we upset t'other. But we can spare him, for I'll be bound to say there's plenty more of them. Now I wonder what they are all for—pretty creatures!"

"What they are for, Joe?" cried Rodd, without taking his eyes from the surface of the muddy stream which was carrying them onward.

"Yes, sir; I don't see as they are much good. I say, there's another one! No, he's ducked his head down. Ah, he's coming up again. Look out, my lads!" cried the man. "I wish there was another pole. There's nothing left for me but my knife, and they are as hard as shoehorns, I know. I don't want to break my whittle against his skin. No, he's going to let us go by. Ah! Look out!"

For as they drew nearer the sun flashed off the reptile's muddy skin, and they could see it glide round rapidly and strike two tremendous blows on the surface with its serrated tail—blows that had been probably directed at the boat, but which fell short, while in its blind stupidity it kept on thrashing the water several times after the vessel had passed.

"Ahoy! Ahoy!" came from somewhere, seeming to echo from the trees that covered the bank.

"Ahoy! Ahoy!" shouted Joe Cross back. "Why, that means help, sir. The brig must be lying there, just round that bend beyond the trees."

"Oh no," cried Rodd excitedly. "We must have gone down miles with the tide."

"Ahoy! Ahoy!" came again. "Boat ahoy!" from somewhere out of sight; and glancing back Rodd made out that they were passing along what seemed to be a rapid bend.

"Ahoy!" was shouted back, and then all at once, to the astonishment of the sufferers, a couple of boats came into sight from right astern, their occupants sending the spray flying as they bent to their oars and seemed to be racing to overtake the gig.

For the moment the boats, quite a quarter of a mile behind, took up all their attention, and Rodd stood up in the bows waving his hand wildly.

"There's Uncle Paul, and the skipper, in one!" he cried.

"Ay, ay, my lad; that's our old man," shouted Joe.

"And there's the Count, and eight men rowing hard, in the other, but—but—oh, I say, Morny isn't there!"

"Oh, he's being skipper and taking care of the brig, sir," cried Joe sharply, as he noted the boy's disappointed tone of voice.

"No, he isn't," shouted Rodd, signalling with his pole, as he saw one of the rowers rise up in the brig's boat and begin waving an oar; "he's pulling with the men!" And his voice sounded hoarse and choking, while, realising this fact, the boy coughed loudly and forcibly, as if to clear his throat.

"Here, you've ketched a cold, Mr Rodd, sir," cried Joe. "But never mind them behind in the boats. They'll ketch us up soon. There's another of them beauties coming at us. The beggars do seem hungry this morning. We hardly seed any of them when we were coming up yesterday. Why, of course, this is their breakfast-time, and the sight of us has made them peckish. Now then, all together, lads! Let him have it."

Four poles were thrust together, with somewhat similar effects to those on the last occasion, for the onset of the great reptile was diverted, the boat's head turned aside, and the blows aimed at them by the creature's tail fell short, though to the men's dismay their efforts had driven them towards another of the monsters, which was gliding towards them from their left.

But here again they successfully turned the creature aside, and Rodd exclaimed—

"Suppose we missed!"

"Oh, the beggars are too big to miss, sir," cried Briggs. "But suppose we did; what then, sir?"

"I don't know," cried Rodd excitedly. "What do you say, Joe?"

Frontispiece.] The hideous jaws snapped to.

"I don't know, sir. I never learned crocodile at school, though there was one in my spelling-book, and I 'member I couldn't understand why a four-legged chap like him, as lived in the water, should make a nest and lay eggs like a bird. Here, Harry, let me handle that pole for a few minutes. I should like to have a turn. Thank you, lad," he continued. "Yes, they're rum beasts, Mr Rodd, sir, and I dare say they are very slippery; but I don't suppose I shall miss the next one— Ah! Would yer!" he shouted as one of the reptiles rose suddenly, open-mouthed, close to the boat's head.

As the man spoke he made a heavy thrust with his pole, his companions having no time to take aim, and the next moment the hideous jaws snapped to, there was a fresh swirl, the bamboo pole was jerked out of Joe's hand,

and he would have overbalanced himself and gone overboard had not those nearest to him seized him and snatched him back.

"Well, now," he cried, "just look at that!" For about half of the bamboo remained visible and went sailing up the stream.

Just then there was the sharp report of a gun from behind, followed by another, while before there was time for re-loading there was the loud *crack, crack* of a double fowling-piece.

"Hurrah! That's uncle!" cried Rodd. "They are firing at the crocodiles, and it will be with bullets."

"And sarve them jolly well right, Mr Rodd, say I," cried Joe, "for I call it taking a mean advantage of a man to sneak off like that with his pole. Why, look at him, sir. He's having a regular lark with it—picking his teeth, or something. Look how he's waggling the top of it about. What do you say to try and steer after him and get it back?"

"Ugh! No!" cried Rodd. "It would be madness."

"Well, not quite so bad as that, sir. Say about half-cracked; and that's about what I'm beginning to think. I say, they are getting all the fun behind there."

"Look out; here comes another!" cried Rodd, for there was a pair of eyes in front gliding rapidly towards them just above the water, but apparently not satisfied with the appearance of the boat, or perhaps less ravenous, the two prominences softly disappeared before they were close up, and Joe Cross, evidently divining what might happen, suddenly caught Rodd round the waist and forced him down into the bottom of the boat.

"Look out, my lads!" he yelled.

As he spoke the hinder part of the boat began slowly to rise, showing that they were gliding right over a reptile's back. Then it was turned to starboard, the water coming almost to the edge; but as it glided on it began to sink to the level again, just as it received a heavy shock from below and was driven forward with a jerk just far enough to escape a blow from a serrated tail which rose astern and showered the water over them in so much blinding spray.

"Here, ahoy there!" shouted Joe. "Look alive, and bring up them guns! There's more sport up here than we want. I wouldn't care, Mr Rodd, if we had got our oars and my boat-hook. Nay, I don't know, though. It's just as well I haven't, for I should be getting it stuck perhaps, and never see that no more."

A few minutes after, while the firing was kept up from astern, the two boats came up on either side, and amidst the heartiest of congratulations Rodd cried —

"Ah, uncle, you have overtaken us at last! I am glad you have come!"

"Overtaken you, my boy! Why, we have been miles down the river towards the mouth. We started as soon as the tide was slack enough for us to leave the vessels. We must have passed you in the fog, and we were beginning to despair. But we came upon one of the sailors' caps hanging in a bough, when, thinking that perhaps we had gone too far, and Captain Chubb feeling sure that you had run ashore somewhere in the darkness, perhaps been carried right into the flooded forest, we came back and —"

He ceased speaking, took a quick aim over the side of the boat, and discharged the contents of his double gun into the head of a reptile which rose three or four yards away.

"The brutes!" he went on. "But there don't appear to be so many here. We seem to have been coming through quite a shoal."

"There's plenty of them," growled the skipper, "but three boats together scares them a bit. Here, my lads, lay hold of this line and make fast, and we will give you a tow back to the schooner. We shan't be long getting up to it with this tide. Why, hallo here! Not content with losing the oars and boat-hook, you've been and got the gig stove in! And the grapnel gone too! Here, you Joe Cross, what's the meaning of all this?"

"I'll tell you about that, captain, by and by," said Rodd quickly. "What's that? You want to come aboard, Morny? No, you had better not. It's all muddy, and we shall have to begin baling. Pitch us in a couple of tins."

"I'll bring them," cried the young Frenchman, rising in the boat. — "Yes, my father, I wish to go. Hook on, and let me get aboard," he continued to the French coxswain.

Half-an-hour later, with the men taking it in turns to bale, and with the crocodiles seeming to have become more scarce, they ran up alongside of the two anchored vessels, cheering and being cheered from the moment they came into sight.

"Now, my lads," cried the doctor, "every one of you take what I'll mix up for you directly, and have a good bathe and rub down. I am not going to have you all down with fever if I can stave it off."

Chapter Thirty Seven
Talking like a Boy

Perhaps it was nearly all weariness and the result of the excitement, but it may have been due to Uncle Paul's potion; at any rate Rodd went off fast asleep, and when he awoke it was to find Morny sitting by his cot. "Hullo!" he cried. "You here!"

"Yes, I am here," was the reply. "How are you?"

"Oh, I am all right. Have I been to sleep?"

"Well, yes, you have been to sleep," said Morny, smiling at him in a rather peculiar way.

"What are you laughing at?"

"Oh, I was only smiling at you."

"What, am I scratched and knocked about?"

"Oh, very slightly."

"But I say, I am so precious hungry. What time is it?"

"Just upon six. Some bells or another, as you call it."

"Get out! Why, it was seven o'clock this morning when I lay down to sleep after my bath; so how can it be six o'clock? You don't mean to say that it is six o'clock in the evening?"

"Indeed, but I do. You had better jump up, or it will soon be dark."

"What a nuisance! Why, I must have slept twelve hours."

"Oh, you think so, do you? Yes, a good deal more than that. I was getting quite alarmed about you, only your uncle said you were quite right and you were to have your sleep out."

"I say, look here," cried Rodd; "am I dreaming, or are you playing tricks? I am getting muddled over this. I lay down this morning, and as soon as my head was on the pillow I must have gone off fast asleep."

"Yes, but it was yesterday morning."

Rodd sat up quickly in his cot and screwed himself round to stare hard in his companion's face.

"Look here," he cried, "you are playing tricks!"

"Indeed I'm not! You've been sleeping for about a day and a half."

"Well!" cried Rodd, beginning to dress hurriedly. "But never mind. I will make up for it by not going to sleep for a whole day. Look here, you know what's been going on. Where are we? Going up farther so as to get a mooring-place?"

"We came up yesterday, miles higher up the river, and the brig's moored close by an open part of the shore. There, make haste and finish dressing and come and look."

The lad dressed himself probably more quickly than he had ever achieved the performance before in his life, and in the process he learned that his uncle and Captain Chubb were on board the brig with several of the men, the skipper superintending the moorings and the arranging of cables from the brig to a couple of great forest trees, with tackle so ordered that the vessel could be careened over to any extent desired, and that the next morning she was to be allowed to sink with the tide so as to be bedded in the mud and laid over until the bottom was so exposed that the carpenter and his mates could get to work.

As soon as Rodd had hurried on deck he found all as his companion had described, while he had just mastered these facts when there was the sharp report of a gun.

"What's that?" he cried.

"Oh, only your uncle having a shot at a crocodile. Both he and my father have been at it all day, sending bullets into them whenever a head appeared on the surface of the water."

"But I say, look here, Morny; why didn't this wake me?"

"Oh, you were shut up down here and too fast asleep."

"Then that would be uncle's dose," cried Rodd. "He must have given me too much. Why, he might have killed me."

"Oh no. I expect he knew too well what he was about. He seems to have kept off the fever."

"Fever, yes! Has anybody else got it?"

"No. Your men are quite well."

"But they didn't sleep as long as I have?" cried Rodd anxiously.

"Not quite; but they all had very long sleeps, and my father says that they would have been longer if their messmates had not disturbed them. Now then, you had better go back to your cabin again. The steward told me that he was keeping some breakfast ready for you to have at any time."

"Wait a bit," cried Rodd, and he hailed his uncle and Captain Chubb before having a good look round at their position, and finding that they were in a beautiful open reach of the river, with the forest overhanging the stream on one side, while on that where the brig was seated close in shore there were only a few scattered trees, and those of large size, for the main portion of the forest had retired back nearly a quarter of a mile.

The next morning, as arrangements had been made to begin work at daylight, Captain Chubb and certain of the men, including Joe Cross, had their breakfasts by lamplight, and were on board the brig long before the sun rose.

Then came a busy time, with everybody anxiously watching for the success of Captain Chubb's plans.

He took his place upon the brig with the schooner's carpenter, the two lads bargaining that they might stay too, and as the tide sank the brig, which had been hauled in close to the bank at high water, soon touched bottom, her keel settling down steadily into the mud, and in due time began to careen over more and more, her progress being governed by a couple of capstans that had been arranged upon the shore. This went on until long before low water she was lying so much over on her side away from the shore that the sail that had been used as a plaister, as Rodd called it, was slackened off, and one of the holes made by the cannon ball fully exposed to view.

Then followed a busy time, the carpenter and his mates stripping off the copper and using their saws hour after hour as long as the tide left the leak bare, while after working as long as was possible, pieces of new thin plank were temporarily nailed on over the now much-enlarged opening, which was carefully caulked and all made as secure as possible.

This done, the capstans were manned again, and with the rising tide the brig raised to her proper position, and secured for the night, but hauled in as close to the shore as was possible, with the consequence that though the water rose through the untouched leak considerably, it never reached so high within as the point it had occupied with the pumps hard at work.

It proved to be a much longer job than had been anticipated, though the men worked as hard as was possible while the tide was low.

But the time passed very pleasantly for Rodd and his uncle, for they took their stations on board the anchored schooner, firing at every crocodile that showed itself, the presence of the men at work upon the muddy exposed shore proving an irresistible attraction during the first part of the time. But so many had been sent writhing and lashing the water, to float downstream, that at last they began to grow shy, and the sportsmen were enabled to direct some of their charges of small shot at specimens of beautiful birds that came within range, as well as at the abundant waterfowl—ducks and geese—that gathered morning and evening to feed, but often to become food for the hideous reptiles that lurked beneath the trees close in shore.

This latter sport proved highly welcome to the crews of both vessels, providing as it did a pleasant change of diet after so much salt provision, for very few fish were caught, consequent upon the way in which they were persecuted by the reptiles.

"I wish you would join in. I am sure you can shoot well," said Rodd; but Morny shook his head.

"No," he said; "my father is so anxious to see the brig repaired."

"Yes, I suppose so," said Rodd, "but that wouldn't make any difference. You can't help."

"No, I cannot help," replied the lad, "and I should like to be with you all the time, but I can't leave his side. It would seem so hard if I didn't stay with him to share his anxiety."

"Well, but you might have a few shots at the crocodiles. That's helping to protect the men who are at work."

"True," replied Morny, smiling. "But you two are such clever shots. You can do all that. Don't ask me again, please."

Rodd was silent.

But during the long dark evenings in that grand and solitary reach of the river, which looked as if it had never been visited by human beings before, there would have been most enjoyable times had not the Count seemed so preoccupied and thoughtful. Still it had become the custom that there should be a constant interchange of courtesies between the occupants of the two vessels, the sailors thoroughly fraternising, while their superiors alternately dined together upon schooner or brig, and a thorough rivalry sprang up between the English and French cooks as to who should provide the best meals for officers and men.

"I should like for us to make an excursion right up the river as far as we could go in the boats," said Rodd one evening, to his French companion. "Uncle wants to go."

"Then why don't you?" said Morny. "You have plenty of time," he added, with a sigh, "for the repairs go on very slowly. One of the leaks is not stopped yet."

"They are not going on slowly," retorted Rodd. "I talked to Captain Chubb about it, and he said the work must be thoroughly done, so as to make the brig as good as ever she was."

"Yes, they are doing it well," said Morny sadly.

"He said—" continued Rodd, with a laugh; and then he stopped short.

"Well, why don't you go on?"

"Oh, never mind. You wouldn't like it. You are sensitive, and it might hurt your feelings."

"I promise you it shall not. Tell me what the captain said."

"Well, he said he wasn't going to have any Frenchmen throw it in his teeth that he hadn't done his best because it was a French boat, and that he was taking more pains over it than he should have done if it had been ours."

Morny laughed.

"Oh yes," he said, "I know he is doing his best, and I wouldn't care, only my father is so anxious to get to sea again."

"Well, all in good time," cried Rodd. "They are fitting the copper sheathing on again, and to-morrow they will begin careening the brig over so as to get at the other side."

"Ha! Yes," said the French lad, with a sigh of satisfaction. "Well, you take your boat to-morrow, and plenty of men and ammunition, and go on a good long excursion."

"Shan't," said Rodd gruffly.

"But why not?"

"Aren't going without you."

"What nonsense! I'm busy. You are free."

"I am not. If we went away leaving you alone with a brig that won't swim, who knows what would happen? The crocs would send the news all up and down the river that we were gone away, and come on at you with a rush."

"That's absurd! You talk like a boy."

"Well, I am one. Yes, that is nonsense. But suppose a whole tribe of niggers came down out of the forest to attack you."

"They couldn't. You know yourself that the forest is impassable except to wild beasts."

"Well, then, perhaps they would come down, or up—yes, up; they wouldn't come down, and find you helpless, because we should meet them and come back to help you."

"We could fight," said Morny coolly, "and sink their canoes with the big guns."

"What, when they are fast lashed to one side, and your deck all of a slope? No, we are not going, so don't bother about it any more. Who knows but what there may be towns of savages right up inland, or up some other river farther along the coast? I dare say it's a beautiful country—and there, I won't hear another word. We are not going away to leave you in the lurch. Uncle said as much. He likes the Count too well."

Morny laughed merrily.

"Why," he said, "he's always quarrelling with my father and hurting his feelings by the way in which he speaks about our great Emperor."

"Stuff!" cried Rodd indignantly. "That's only Uncle Paul's way. He always talks like that when he gets on to politics. Why, I have a sham quarrel with him sometimes about Napoleon. I pretend that I admire him very much."

"Pretend!" cried Morny eagerly.

"Well, I tell uncle that he was a very great general and soldier."

"Yes, yes! Grand!" said the French lad, flushing.

"And that I shouldn't have wondered at all if he had conquered the whole world."

"Yes, yes!" cried Morny excitedly. "That was brave of you! And what did your uncle say?"

"Said I was a young scoundrel, and that if I wasn't so big, and that he disliked corporal punishment, he'd give me a good thrashing to bring me to my senses."

"And you—you—" cried Morny, grasping him by the arm, "what did you say to that?"

"Nothing at all. Only burst out laughing."

"Burst out laughing?"

"Yes, and then Uncle Paul would grunt out 'Humbug!' and we were good friends again."

The young Frenchman shrugged his shoulders and shook his head.

"Ah, yes," he said. "Even those who worshipped him mock at the Emperor now that he is in misfortune—even you, Rodd. But I can forgive you, because you are English and the natural enemies of our great Emperor. But those of our countrymen—cowards and slaves—parasites of the new King. *Lâches!* Cowards! But let us talk of something else. You make me like you, Rodd. You always did, and—"

"Ah–h–h! Getting on dangerous ground. Now look here; will you come with us shooting?"

"No. I have told you why."

"Well, I am horribly disappointed. But I like you for it all the more, Morny. You are a regular trump to your father."

"I!" cried the young man fiercely. "I play the trumpet to my father! Never! If I praise him it is all the truth, because he is so honest and brave and good."

"Why, what's the matter now?" cried Rodd in astonishment. "Oh, I see—trump! You don't know all our English expressions yet. Where's your dictionary?"

"There was no such word in it that I do not understand," cried the lad.

"Then it isn't a good one," said Rodd merrily.

Explanations followed, and the two lads parted that evening, both eager for the coming of the following day and the attack that was to be made upon the second leak where the ball from the fort had made its exit on the other side nearer the keel.

Chapter Thirty Eight
A Proposed Adventure

It was a busy and an anxious day. The brig's guns had been carefully ran to starboard and firmly lashed, and the yards lowered down, her topmasts struck, and all made ready for laying her right over in the mud at low water, so that her spars should be upon the shore.

"It wouldn't do to lay her over like this," said the skipper gruffly, "if she were full of cargo. It would mean a bad shifting. But I think we can manage, and I'll risk it. We can easily start her water casks."

There was no question of shooting that day, Rodd preferring to stay with his French friend; and the doctor seemed to quite share the Count's anxiety as they watched the proceedings of the sailors while the tide went down.

But everything went on admirably. As the water sank a steady strain was kept upon the cables, and by slow degrees the brig careened over towards the land till the newly-repaired side sank lower and lower, and she lay more and more over, till at last the water that had flooded the hold began to flow out with the tide till the beautiful vessel lay perfectly helpless upon her side, with the whole of her keel visible upon the long stretch of mud. Then Captain Chubb, taking hold of a rope which he had made fast to the larboard rail, climbed over on to the brig's side, and steadying himself by the cord, walked right down and stood shaking his head at the ghastly wound which the vessel had received.

For after passing right through the hold, the cannon ball had struck upon and shattered one of what are technically called the ship's knees, ripping off a great patch of the planking and tearing through the copper sheathing, which was turned back upon the keel, making a ragged hole several times the size of the fairly clean-cut orifice by which the shot had entered.

"You had better come and have a look here, Count," cried the captain— an invitation which was accepted by several of those interested, and in a very short time an anxious group was gathered round the vessel's injury.

"Well, sir," said the skipper, in his rough, brusque way; "what do you say to that?"

"Horrible!" groaned the Count. "My poor vessel!" And he looked at the captain in despair.

"Well, sir," said the latter, "if anybody had told me that I could make a patch with sails over the bottom of your brig so as to keep her afloat as I have, I should have felt ready to call him a fool. It's a wonder to me that you kept her afloat as you did, before you came to us for help."

"But now, captain," cried the Count, as his son looked anxiously on, "is it possible, away from a shipyard, to mend this as well as you have done the other injury?"

"Well, sir, if we were close to some port I should say, no, certainly not; but seeing where we are, there's only one thing to be done."

"Yes? And that—?" cried the Count.

"Do it, sir. But it will take some time."

The Count made an impatient gesticulation, and then threw his hands apart in a deprecating way, as if he accepted the position in despair.

"Yes," he said; "you brave Englishmen, you never give up. You will do it, then?"

"Oh yes, sir; we've got to do it; and what do they say? Time and tide wait for no man; so I'll thank you all to clear off and let me and my lads get to work. Only look here, sir; there's going to be no hoisting and lowering here. We shall have to keep the brig lying on her side without any temporary patches, and the tide will have to flow in and out, even if it does some damage to your stores. So while my lads are stripping off the copper, you will keep your men busy with your hatches open to make a pretty good clearance inside, so that we can work in there as well as out here."

"Yes, yes," said the Count, who seemed to quite resign himself in full obedience to the skipper's wishes. "But you will use all the speed you can?"

"You may trust me for that, sir," said Captain Chubb; for after two or three attempts in the early parts of the proceedings connected with the repairs, and saying Monsieur le Count, the blunt Englishman gave it up in favour of plain straightforward "sir," and stuck to it; while the titled captain seemed to like the Englishman none the less.

"Now," said the captain, as he climbed back on to the sloping deck, following the others, "I didn't know that your brig would be so bad as this, but I had my suspicions, and when I have not been busy here I have been casting my eye round for a good crooked bit of timber that would make a ship's knee if I wanted one."

"And do you know where there is one?"

"Yes," said the skipper; "and I think it will make a very good makeshift, for the wood's as hard as hard. But what wouldn't I give for a good old crooked piece of Devon oak from out of Dartmoor Forest!"

Shortly afterwards he had set the carpenter and his mates to strip off the copper sheathing, while he led off Joe Cross and another man about a quarter of a mile away from the river bank to where a huge pollard-like tree was growing at the edge of the forest, all gnarled and twisted in the most extraordinary way.

The two lads had followed them, and Rodd looked at the selected tree aghast.

"Why, you are never going to set the men to cut down that tree, captain?" he cried.

"Why not, my lad? Do you know a better bit?"

"Better bit!" cried Rodd. "Why, the men can hardly get through that with those axes. Most likely take them a fortnight—I might say a month."

"Ah, well, I don't want it all. I am not going to load up the brig with a cargo of timber. I only want that big dwarf branch from low down there where it starts from close to the root; and you will mind and get that big elbow-like piece as long as you can, Joe Cross."

"Ay, ay, sir! Just you mark out what you want, and we'll cut accordin'. Better take all the top off first, hadn't us?"

"Why, of course, my lad. One of you use the saw while the other works away with an axe. You quite understand?"

"Ay, ay, sir; me and my mate has seen a ship's knee afore now;" and rolling up their sleeves, they soon made the place echo with the blows of the axe, while the rasping harsh sound of the saw seemed to excite a flock of beautifully-plumaged parrots, which began to circle round the head of the tree, before finally settling amongst the branches uttering their sharp screeching cries, and giving vent to croaking barks, as if resenting this attack upon their domain.

The carpenter and his men were meanwhile hard at work at the copper sheathing, making such progress that they were busy with their saws, dividing plank and trenail and working their way round the hole by the time the tide had risen sufficiently to drive them back, and then the Count and his party grouped themselves as best they could about their old quarters, looking despondently at what seemed like the beginning of a very hopeless wreck, a good deal of confidence being needed on their part to feel that all would come right in the end.

Fortunately the tide during the next two or three days did not rise so high, and good progress was made, while, thanks to the way in which the French crew had worked, the damage done by the water as it flowed in through the gap that was made was principally confined to its leaving a thick deposit of mud.

The doctor tried all he could to persuade the Count to take up his abode upon the schooner, and offered to accommodate as many men as he liked to bring with him, but he would not hear of it, and, as Rodd said laughingly to Morny, insisted upon living all upon one side and climbing instead of walking about the deck.

Then all at once there was a surprise. It was on the third day, when Joe Cross and his mate had called in the aid of a couple more to help drag the ponderous roughed-out piece of crooked timber to the waterside ready for the carpenter and his men to work into shape with their adzes, and while the latter were slaving away at high pressure to get all possible done before they were stopped by the tide, that, in obedience to a shout from Captain Chubb, all the men of the schooner's crew hurried to their boat to get on board, while those of the brig hurried to their arms ready for any emergency. For coming up with the tide and round a bend of the river, a large three-masted schooner made its appearance with what seemed to be quite a large crew of well-armed men clustering forward, and apparently surprised at seeing that the river had its occupants already there.

"What do you make of them, sir?" shouted the skipper through his speaking trumpet.

"A foreigner—Spanish, I think," shouted back the Count, after lowering his spy-glass. "Same here, sir. Slaver, I think." The fact of her proving to be a slaver did not mean that an attack was looming in the future, but slaving vessels upon the West Coast of Africa bore a very bad reputation, and the preparations that were rapidly made did not promise much of a welcome.

As the stranger drew near it was evident that busy preparations were being made there too, but in his brief colloquy with Uncle Paul the skipper grunted out that he did not think the foreign vessel meant to attack, but to be ready to take care of herself in case the English schooner tried to surprise her and make her a prize.

"We ought to have taken the boat," he said, "and gone up. It seems to me that there must be a town up there somewhere—savage town, of course, belonging to some chief, for it aren't likely that there can be three of us all coming out here into this river on a scientific cruise. Two's curious enough, English and French, but a Spaniel won't do at all. For that's what she is, sir, plain enough. Well, if she means fight, sir, you mean business, I suppose?"

"Of course," said the doctor sternly; "and I am quite sure that we can depend upon the Count's help."

"Ay, ay, sir; but it's a bad job the brig can't manoeuvre at all."

"But I should say," said the doctor, "that when these men see how firm we are and well prepared, they will prove peaceable enough."

As it proved in a short time after colours had been hoisted, those of the French brig being raised upon a spare spar, the stranger came steadily on in the most peaceable way till the tide had carried her within reasonable distance of the schooner's anchorage, when an order rang out, an anchor was lowered with a splash, and as she swung slowly round, a light boat was dropped from the davits, and a swarthy-looking Spaniard, who seemed to be an officer if not the skipper of the swift-looking raking craft, had himself rowed alongside the schooner. A brief colloquy took place in which questions and answers freely passed, Captain Chubb speaking out frankly as to the object of their mission there, an avowal hardly necessary, for the appearance of the brig with the newly-cut hole, and her position, told its own story.

The Spanish skipper, for so he proved to be, was just as free in his announcements as soon as he found that the brig and schooner were friendly vessels, and began to explain that he was on a trading expedition, that there was a king of the country up there, a great black chief, who had a large town, and that he came from time to time with stores to barter, which he always did with great advantage, going away afterwards pretty well laden with palm-oil and sundries, which the blacks always had waiting for his annual visit, these sundries including, he said, with a meaning laugh, ostrich feathers, choice dye woods, ivory, and a little gold.

He spoke strongly accented but very fair English, and made no scruple about coming on board the schooner and examining her critically as he talked.

"I thought at first, captain, that you had found out my private trading port and were going to be a rival;" whereupon the doctor began chatting freely with him and asking questions about the natural products of the place; and Rodd listened eagerly, drinking in the replies made by the Spanish captain as soon as he thoroughly realised the object of the schooner's visit and the bearing of the doctor's questions.

He soon became eagerly communicative regarding the wild beasts that haunted the forests, the serpents that were found of great size, the leopards and other wild cats that might be shot for their skins, the beauty of the plumage of the birds, and above all the wondrous size of the apes that haunted the trees.

"There's gold too to be washed out of the soil," he said, looking hard at Rodd; "but don't you touch it. Leave that to the blacks."

"Why?" said Rodd.

"Because," said the man, shaking a fore-finger at him, upon which was a thick gold ring, "the white men who turn up the wet earth to wash it out get fever."

"But," said the doctor, "we have not come gold-hunting. And so there are great apes in these forests? Have you seen them?"

"Oh, yes," said the Spanish captain. "I have been coming here for ten years, and never saw another vessel up here before—only the big canoes of the blacks. Why, I could take you into the forest and show you plenty of beautiful birds and flowers, and all kinds of wonders."

"But the forest seems to be impassable," put in Rodd.

"Yes," said the Spaniard, with a laugh—"to those who don't know their way. Higher up there are small rivers which run into this, where boats can go up and get to where the trees are not all crowded together, but more open like this patch here," he continued, waving his hand to where the forest retired back. "There are sluggish streams where you can wander for days, and camp ashore, and shoot all kinds of things. I used to at one time, when it was all new to me; and I collected skins and sent them to Cadiz and other European cities, where they sold well. But I have given all that up long enough. The black king—bah!—chief—he's only a savage. He makes his people collect the palm-oil and other things for me, and I load up and take them back."

"Then you would make a good guide," said the doctor.

"I, captain?" said the man eagerly. "Oh yes. A man could not come here for ten years, and stay a month or two each time, without getting to know the country well."

"I suppose not. But this is the captain. I am only a doctor, travelling to make discoveries."

"Ah, a doctor!" cried the Spaniard eagerly. "Then you will help me and one or two of my men! Yes? I will pay you well."

"Oh," said the doctor quietly, "if I can help you, or any one with you who needs assistance, I will do so, of course. I want no pay, but I might ask you to guide me and my nephew here in a little expedition or two into the forest."

"Uncle," said Rodd quickly, "we mustn't leave the Count and Morny."

"Well, well," said the doctor, "we'll see about that."

"I am glad to know you, Señor Medico," said the Spaniard, patting on the stiffness of the formal Don and bowing profoundly, "and I will gladly help you in any way I can. But I am only a poor trader, and glad to do any business I can when I meet a strange ship that has needs. Do you want powder? I see you have guns," he said sharply.

"Oh yes," said the doctor. "One never knows what enemies one may meet with among savage people; so we are well-armed, and as you see have a good crew."

"Yes, yes," said the Spaniard, looking sharply round.

"But I thank you. We have plenty of powder."

"So have I," said the Spaniard. "The black chief is always glad to buy it, and guns too. That is my money—that and rum. Those will always buy palm-oil. But I have plenty of ship stores; canvas, oakum, and pitch. You are mending the other ship, I see. Can I sell you some?"

"I thank you, no," said the doctor. "We are well supplied, I think, with everything; and in reply, if there is anything you want that we can supply to you I shall be pleased."

"Then I should like a few canisters of your good English powder."

"Thought you said you'd plenty," said Captain Chubb gruffly.

The Spaniard closed his eyes slowly till they were like two narrow slits, and he gave the skipper a meaning nod.

"Yes," he said significantly, "I have plenty. It is good for the black man's guns. But if you fired it from yours—pff! It makes much smoke, and the barrel very wet, and the shot do not go too far. But the black men know no better. I do. Ha, ha! You will let me have a few pounds for my own pistols?"

"And that long gun of yours too?" said the skipper.

"Yes," said the Spaniard. "As your medico says, one never knows what savage people one may meet. It is good too behind a bullet for our friends here in the river. You have seen them?"

He put his wrists together with his palms closed, and then slowly opened them widely in imitation of a crocodile's jaws, and closed them with a snap.

"Oh yes," said Rodd, "we have met them, and found out how horny their skins are."

"Ugh! Beasts!" said the Spaniard. "Last time I was here they swept two of my men out of a boat, and I never saw them more. We caught some fish as we came up the river, at the mouth. *Adios, señores*; I will send you some. We shall meet again. I do not hurry for some days, for I am before my time."

"How far is it up to the town?" asked Captain Chubb.

"Three days' journey. This is a great river, and the water is deep right up into the country till you reach the mountains, far beyond the town."

"Well," said the doctor, "let's go ashore, Rodd, and tell the Count. We didn't bargain for this, eh, captain?"

"No," said the skipper gruffly, as he watched the departing boat, after ordering the crew back into their own so as to row the doctor and his nephew to the brig.

"Well, Rodd," continued the doctor, "it would be a grand chance for us to have some expeditions with a good guide. What do you think of the Spanish captain?"

"Don't like him at all, uncle. There's a nasty, catty, foxy look about him."

"A mixture of the feline and the canine, eh, my boy? Well, he must be a bad one! Ah! British prejudice is as strong in you as it is in me."

Chapter Thirty Nine
Spanish Liquorice

There was quite a discussion when the doctor joined those waiting by the brig, the Count being bitterly annoyed and displaying more excitement than the others had seen in him before, while Morny kept close to his side, and whispered to him from time to time, as if trying to calm him down.

"Yes, yes, my son," he cried passionately, and speaking to him in French; "but you are a boy, and do not think. Look here," and he pointed to the helpless brig, "how do we know but that he may be an enemy? And we are in this helpless state, quite at his mercy."

The doctor was listening attentively, and understood every word.

"I know," he said soothingly, "this must be very painful for you; but Captain Chubb believes that before many days are over the brig will be as strong as ever. I answer for him that he is making every effort to finish what he has undertaken."

Uncle Paul directed a glance at the skipper, who stood scowling close by.

"Thank you, doctor," he granted, as he gave a nod. "And I feel sure that this Spanish captain, who is evidently an ordinary trader, will prove perfectly inoffensive; and besides, my dear sir, we are not at war now, and what enemies can you have to fear?"

"Ah, yes," said the Count bitterly, as he made a deprecating gesture with his hands, turning and directing his words at his son; "what enemies can we have to fear?"

"Well, I am glad you look upon it in that light," said the doctor. "Now, if it had been years ago, with your smart little craft, and you had been followed up here by a small sloop of war, or an English letter of marque, you might have expected to be made a prize. But this is an ordinary Spanish schooner, and though I suspected it at first, I don't think she is tainted by the slave trade, but engaged in traffic with the natives for the sake of palm-oil."

"Perhaps you are right, sir," said the Count.

"I feel sure I am," said the doctor, "and I must confess to having hailed this man's coming, from the help he will be to me in a little expedition I propose to make when we have seen the brig restored and all set right."

"I thank you," said the Count, "but I am so anxious for the success of my own scientific search that I have got into the habit of seeing enemies in every one, even as I did, doctor, in you and your men. And you see this is an armed vessel with a very strong crew."

"Well," said the doctor good-humouredly, "we have armed vessels with very strong crews. Anxiety has made you nervous, Count. Here's your doctor," he said, turning to Captain Chubb, "and before many days have passed he will have cured all your trouble, and we can get to sea again."

"Ah, yes, that will be better," said the Count, wiping his moist brow. "You must forgive me, doctor—and you too, Captain Chubb. I am impatient, I know. But I see now all will be well. One moment, though: you said we can get to sea again. We? You will sail with me?"

"My dear sir," said the doctor, "you need have no fear. Captain Chubb will make your brig as sound as ever. You will need to look for no further assistance from me."

"I did not mean that," said the Count hastily. "I meant brotherly help— the help that one devoted to research could give to another."

"But," said the doctor, laughing, "you have never confided to me what particular form of research yours is."

"No, I have not," said the Count hurriedly, "and I ask you to spare me from explanation. Be satisfied if I say that we are both bound upon great missions, and that you, a brother scientist, can give me enormous help by working in company with me for the next few weeks at most. Is this too much to ask of a learned doctor like you?"

"Oh no," said Uncle Paul good-humouredly; "I do not see that it is. You are not going to ask me to help you to escape from an English prison."

The Count gave an involuntary start.

"Of course not," said the doctor, "for I am thankful that all that kind of trouble is at an end, and that France and England are at peace; and besides, you are free to come and go where you please. Well, as your son and my nephew have become such inseparable friends, and my time is my own, I will ask no questions, but sail where you sail, and pick up what I can to complete my specimens while you continue your research; and believe me, I wish you every success."

"Ah," said the Count, with a sigh of satisfaction; and with all a Frenchman's effusiveness he laid his hands on the doctor's shoulders and said, with some little show of emotion, "I thank you. You are making me as great a friend as my son is to your nephew."

Watch was mounted on both vessels at night as if they were in the presence of a dangerous enemy; but there in the great solitude of that forest through which the river ran, there was nothing human to disturb the night.

Savage nature was as busy as ever during the dark hours through which the creatures of land and water fled for their lives or pursued their prey. Otherwise everything was wondrously still, and those upon schooner or brig who might have felt doubtful about the Spanish craft saw or heard nothing save the low murmur of voices in conversation and the occasional opening or shutting of a dull lantern, whose use was explained by the sudden glow cast upon the face of some swarthy sailor as he lit a fresh cigarette, after which a couple of faint points of glowing light rising and falling might have been seen passing to and fro upon the Spaniard's deck.

Then as daylight came again there was the busy sound of the saw, chipping of the adze, the creak of auger, and the loud echoing rap of the mallet, as some tree-nail was driven home.

On the previous evening the conversation that had gone on between the doctor and the Count had hardly ended before the Spaniard's boat, rowed by a couple of men, came as near as they could get to the brig, and one of the bare-legged men, after giving a sharp look round into the shallow water, as if in search of danger from one of the hideous reptiles on the look-out for prey, stepped over into the mud, and came up, bearing a basket of large, freshly-caught fish, which he placed in the hands of a couple of the sailors, and then stood waiting.

"Ah!" cried the doctor. "The fish the Spanish captain promised me. Our thanks to your master, and I will not forget what he wanted."

The man answered him in Spanish.

"Ah, now you are taking me out of my depth," said the doctor. "Do you speak French?"

The man shook his head.

"English, then?"

"*No comprende, señor,*" replied the man hurriedly—or what sounded like it.

"Never mind, then," said the doctor. "I'll send your skipper some powder to-morrow."

The man shook his head and made signs, repeating them persistently, frowning and shaking his head.

"I think he means, uncle," cried Rodd, "that he won't go away until you have paid him in powder for the fish."

"Hang the fellow!" cried the doctor petulantly. "Why hasn't he been taught English? I don't carry canisters of gunpowder about in my pockets. Can any one make him understand that the powder is in the little magazine on the schooner?"

"What does he want? Some gunpowder?" said the Count.

"Yes. I promised him a present of a few pound canisters."

"We can get at ours," said the Count quietly, and giving an order to the French sailor who acted as his mate, the latter mounted into the brig, disappeared down the cabin hatchway, and returned in a few minutes with half-a-dozen canisters, with which the man smilingly departed, after distributing a few elaborate Spanish bows.

The weather was glorious, and all that next day good steady progress was made with the brig repairs, while Rodd and his uncle spent most of the time keeping guard over the workmen and sending crocodile after crocodile floating with the tide, to the great delight of the grinning crew of the Spaniard, who lined the new-comer's bulwarks as if they were spectators of some exhibition, and clapped their hands and shouted loud *vivas* at every successful shot, while all the time tiny little curls of smoke rose at intervals into the sunny air as the men kept on making fresh cigarettes as each stump was thrown with a *ciss* into the gliding stream.

"Quiet and lazy enough set, Pickle," said the doctor. "How they can bask and sleep in the sunshine! It's an easy-going life, that of theirs. Ah, there's the skipper! Fierce-looking fellow. He looks like a man who could use a knife. But you don't half read your Shakespeare, my boy."

"What's Shakespeare got to do with that fierce-looking Spaniard using his knife, uncle?"

"Only this, my boy," said the doctor, drawing the ramrod out of his double gun and trying whether the wads were well down upon the bullets, for a couple of the ugly prominences that arched over a big crocodile's eyes came slowly gliding down the stream; "I mean that a Shakespeare-reading boy clever at giving nicknames—and that you can do when you like—would have called that fellow Bottom the Weaver."

"I don't see why, uncle. Bottom the Weaver?" said the boy musingly, as he slowly raised his gun.

"No, no; stop there, Rodd! That's my shot. I saw the brute first."

"All right, uncle; only don't miss;" and the boy lowered his gun. "But who was Bottom the Weaver?"

"Tut, tut, tut!" ejaculated the doctor. "I say, this is a big one, Rodd — a monster."

"Here, I recollect, uncle. He was the man who was going to play lion."

"Good boy, Pickle; not so ignorant as I thought you were. Well, didn't he say he'd roar him as gently as any sucking dove, so as not to frighten the ladies?"

"Yes, uncle."

"Well, didn't our knife-armed Spaniard roar to us as gently as —"

Bang.

"Got him!" cried the doctor.

"No, no; a miss," cried Rodd.

Bang, again.

"That wasn't," said the doctor, and as the smoke drifted away there was a burst of *vivas* again from the Spaniards as they saw their dangerous enemy writhing upon the surface with the contortions of an eel, as it turned and twined, and then lashed the water up into foam, till in a spasmodic effort it dived out of sight and was seen no more.

"Poor fellow!" said Joe Cross from the brig, in the most sympathetic of tones. "Such a fine handsome one too, Mr Rodd, sir! Talk about a smile, when he put his head out of the water, why, a tiger couldn't touch it! It must have been three times as long."

So the work went on, and the tyrants of the river perished slowly, but did not seem to shrink in numbers. But the carpentering party were able to do their work in safety, and when, after the interval for dinner had ended, Uncle Paul and his nephew carried on what Rodd called a reptilian execution, the Spaniard's crew were lying about in the sunshine asleep upon their deck. They were too idle to take any interest in the shooting, while their captain, a rather marked object in the sunshine from the bright scarlet scarf about his waist, worn to keep up his snowy white duck trousers, lay upon the top of the big three-masted schooner's deck-house with his face turned to the glowing sun, and with a cigarette always in his mouth.

"I believe he goes on smoking when he's asleep, uncle," said Rodd.

"Yes, Pickle, and if I were an artist and wanted to paint a representation of idleness, there's just the model I should select. They are a lazy lot."

"Yes, uncle, and twice over to-day I saw them talking together, and I feel sure that they were laughing at our men because they worked."

No communication whatever took place between the strangers and the first occupants of the anchorage till after dark, when, as Rodd was leaning over the taffrail talking to Joe Cross, who said he was cooling himself down after a hot day's work, the Spaniard's boat was dimly seen putting off from the big schooner, and was rowed across, to come close alongside as Joe hailed her.

The Spanish skipper looked up, cigarette in mouth, and nodded to Rodd.

"You tell your ship-master," he said, "that I have been thinking about the birds and the spotted leopards and the big monkeys. I know a place where they swarm. Good-night!" And at a word his boat was thrust off again and rowed back towards the gangway from which they came.

"Well, let 'em swarm," said Joe Cross, as if talking to himself. "I don't mind. This 'ere's a savage country, and 'tis their nature to. He seems a rum sort of a buffer, Mr Rodd, sir. What does he mean by that? Was it Spanish chaff?"

"Oh no, Joe. My uncle was asking him about what curiosities there are in the country. That's why he said he had been thinking about them."

"Oh, I see. But how rum things is, and how easy a man can make mistakes! Now, if I had been asked my opinion I should have said that that there was a chap as couldn't think even in Spanish; sort of a fellow as could eat, sleep and smoke, and then begin again, day after day and year after year. This is a rum sort of a world, Mr Rodd, sir, and there's all sorts of people in it. Now look at that there skipper. He fancies hisself, he does, pretty creature! White trousers, clean shirt every morning, and a red scarf round his waist. 'Andsome he calls hisself, I suppose. He don't know that even a respectable dog as went to drink in a river and saw hisself, like that there other dog in the fable, would go and drown hisself on the spot if he found he'd a great set of brown teeth like his!"

"Ah, Joe, Spaniards are not like Englishmen."

"Oh, but I don't call him a Spaniard, sir. I've seen Spaniards—regular grand Dons, officers and gentlemen, with nothing the matter with them at all, only what they couldn't help, and that's being Spaniards instead of Englishmen. These are sort of mongrels. Some of this 'ere crew are what people call mollottoes. They are supposed to be painted white men, but payed over with a dirty tar-brush. Talk about a easy-going lot! Why, I aren't seen one of them do a stroke of work to-day. They are in the ile trade, aren't they, sir? Palm-oil."

"Yes, Joe; I suppose so."

"Ah, that accounts for it, sir. Handling so much ile that it makes them go so easy."

The sailor burst into a long soft laugh, "What are you laughing at, Joe?"

"That warn't laughing, sir; that was smiling. When I laugh hearty you can hear me a long way off."

"Well, what were you smiling at?"

"I was thinking, sir, about how it would be if our old man had that lot under him. My word, how he'd wake them up! Poor, simple, sleepy beggars! It would set them thinking that they hadn't took a skipper aboard, but a human hurricane. I wonder who owns that there craft, and whether he gets anything out of the oil trade. *Viva*, indeed! Yes, our old man would give them something to *viva* about. Their skipper too—nice way of coming up a river to get a cargo. Well, I suppose they get their tobacco pretty cheap; and that's how the world turns round."

Another day glided by, with steady visible progress in the brig's repairs; and the Count seemed in better spirits, and said a few complimentary words to the skipper.

On board the schooner Captain Chubb appeared to be setting an example to the Spaniards, for those of his crew who were not helping the carpenters at the brig were kept busy holystoning, polishing, and coiling down ropes into accurate concentric rings, till the *Maid of Salcombe* was as smart as any yacht.

Meanwhile the Spaniards lined the bulwarks of their vessel, smoked and yawned, and watched the reptile shooting, and then stared in sleepy wonderment at the busy smartening up of the English schooner.

The evening came, and this time the Spanish captain had himself rowed across again, to find that it was the doctor who was leaning over the side with his nephew, and, cigarette in mouth still, the man said slowly—

"He tell you about the birds and the monkeys up the little river?"

"Yes," said the doctor, "and I've been thinking about it."

"Ah, yes," said the Spaniard. "I am going to stop a fortnight yet before it's time to go up with my cargo. I'll make my men row you up to the mouth of that little river; and I could show you something you'd like, but you would have to take your guns—you and him too. But maybe the boy would be afraid."

"That I shouldn't!" cried Rodd hotly.

"Oh! Then you could come," said the Spaniard. "But you'd be in the way if you were afraid. Think about it. Good-night."

The doctor was ready to enter into conversation, and question him; but the boat went off back at once, leaving Uncle Paul mentally troubled, for the idea of an excursion into the depths of the forest wilds was exciting in the extreme.

"He needn't have been in such a hurry, Pickle," said the doctor. "I should have liked to have questioned him a little."

"Yes, uncle. I should like to hear about such things; but it was like his impudence to say that I should be afraid!"

"Yes, my boy; it was rude," replied the doctor thoughtfully, "Ah! It's such a chance as might never occur again. A guide like that isn't always to be picked up."

"No, uncle," replied the boy; "and it must be very wonderful in the depths of the forest, where you can get through, because you would be able to row."

"Yes, my boy; wonderfully interesting," said the doctor eagerly.

"But we couldn't go, uncle."

"Why, Pickle? Why?"

"Because we couldn't go away and leave the brig like that."

"No; of course not, my boy. It would be too bad, wouldn't it? And of course we couldn't go and trust ourselves to a pack of strangers, eh?"

"We shouldn't be afraid, should we, uncle?"

"Well, no, my boy; no. But I don't think it would be prudent. But there, there, we mustn't think of it. We can't do everything we like."

Chapter Forty
The Doctor's Charge

It was very tempting, and, like most lovers of natural history, the deeper he plunged into his pursuit, with its wonders upon wonders, the more infatuated Uncle Paul grew. The nephew was quite as bad, though, boy-like, his was more the natural love of novelty than that of science.

Who among you is there who has not revelled in the thought of something new, the eager desire to see something fresh? The country boy to see vast London with all its greatness and littleness, its splendour and its squalor, its many cares and too often false joys—the town boy to plunge into that home of mystery and wonder, the country. And though as a rule the country boy is disappointed, he of the town, when once he has tasted the true joys of the country and seen Nature at her best, is never satiated. But that love of the novel and the fresh is in us all—the desire for that which in Saint Paul's days the men of Athens longed for: something new.

Hence then it was no wonder that Rodd, as he paced the schooner's deck and looked across to either side of the river where the primeval forest commenced, felt the strange longing to go and see, to hunt and find the myriads of fresh things upon which he had never set eyes before—wonders that might be more than wonderful—dangers which would be exciting, possibly without danger; in short, all the boy's natural love of adventure was stirring within him—that intense longing to cast away culture in every shape and to become, if for ever so short a time, something of the natural savage once more; and he was ready to urge on his uncle to go for just one expedition, only there was a sense of duty to hold him back.

And as the time went on, and the brig was rapidly approaching completion, Uncle Paul more than once angrily exclaimed to his nephew—

"Pickle, I wish that abominable Spaniard was on the other side of the world!"

"So do I, uncle," cried the boy. "We were getting on as nicely as could be, with plenty to interest us, and fresh adventures, and then he comes here setting us longing to go off into the wilds."

"Yes, my boy, and if it wasn't for the Count and the sense of duty we feel towards him? we would be off to-morrow morning."

"Well, why not go?" said a voice just behind them.

Rodd and his uncle started round in astonishment, for they were both so intent upon their conversation, as they leaned over the rail talking together, that they had not heard anybody approach, and for a moment they were utterly speechless as they stood staring at the Count, who had just come on board, while Morny was climbing up the side to join him.

"I—I didn't know you were here," said the doctor confusedly.

"Why, you asked me to come on board and dine and spend the evening with you," replied the Count good-humouredly. "Had you forgotten?"

"Well—well," said the doctor, "I— Really, I'm afraid I had. What—what have you been about?" he continued, turning angrily upon Rodd. "It's a strange thing, Rodney, that when you know of some engagement that I have made, and it slips my memory, you never remind me of it."

"Well, uncle—I—"

"Well, uncle—you! I remember now well enough. You were there this morning when I asked the Count and— Ah, Morny, my lad! How are you? Glad you have come.—But, as I was saying, what were you thinking about?"

"Expedition into the forest, uncle," said the boy frankly.

"Expedition into the forest, sir! Um—ah! Well.—Yes, I'm afraid I was thinking about it too. I am so sorry, Des Saix. But welcome all the same, if you will forgive me."

"Forgive you, yes!" said the Count warmly. "That and a great deal more. But I am very glad that you have so strangely led up to the subject upon which I wish to talk to you."

"What, my forgetfulness?"

"No, no! That expedition into the forest."

"No, no; don't talk about it. I have thought about it too much, and it worries me."

"Well, I want to put a stop to its worrying you. Morny here has been telling me how anxious you both are to go."

"Morny! Why, what did he know about it? He couldn't tell. Here, you, Rodney, have you been letting your tongue run, sir, exposing all my weaknesses?"

"No, sir, that he has not," replied the French lad eagerly; "but I have gathered from your remarks, and words that Rodd has more than once let drop, how anxious you both are to have a run up country and see something of what the wilds are like."

"Oh, fudge! Stuff! Nonsense!" cried the doctor petulantly. "That's quite out of the question."

"Why?" said the Count.

"Why?" cried the doctor. "Oh, because it's—that is—er—I feel—"

"Bound by a sense of imaginary duty," said the Count, smiling. "You think it would be unfriendly to me and my son here to leave us in what you English people call the lurch; and therefore you are depriving yourself of what would be a great pleasure as naturalists and hunters in which you would indulge if we were not here."

"My dear Des Saix, I do wish you would not talk about it," cried the doctor. "There, I confess that if we were alone I should probably take advantage of the Spanish captain's knowledge of the country, and go a little way up with him; but as matters are, with your brig still unfinished, and so much to do, I consider it would be an act of disgraceful selfishness to go away and leave you alone here."

"Absurd!" said the Count. "You would be going into wilder parts while we should be quite at home here, in the nearly finished brig, and have her in the best of trim by the time you came back."

"Impossible!" snapped out the doctor. "Nothing of the sort."

"What do you say, Morny?" continued the Count. "You feel that they are both eager to go?"

"Yes, father; and I am sure that Rodd is burning with desire."

"You don't know anything about it," cried Rodd.

"Well," said the Count, "ever since we met I have given way, and taken your advice, doctor, in all things; but we have come to a time now when I think I have a right to assert myself. Captain Chubb thinks that he will have finished in two days more. He is certain that he will have all done, caulked, tarred, and the copper replaced, in three days; so I have come to the conclusion that you people, who have been quite slaves in the way of sharing my troubles, thoroughly deserve a holiday. So I set you free—you too, Morny."

"Me, father!" cried the lad in astonishment.

"Yes; I am sure you would enjoy a trip with Rodd as much as he would like you to go with him."

"Yes, that I should," cried Rodd; "but—"

"Yes," said Morny gravely; "but—you would not wish me to leave my father like this. Thank you, my father. I could not go, and I will stay."

"No, Morny; you will obey my wishes. You have your young life saddened enough with disappointments, so that when there is an opportunity to keep one away I call upon you to accompany young Harding here as his companion, and I wish you both a very enjoyable trip."

"That's very nice of you—very nice indeed," cried the doctor; "but I cannot sanction it. I think we should be doing very wrong if we let those boys go alone."

"But they would not go alone. You would have full charge of your nephew."

"Now, Des Saix!" snorted the doctor.

"Let me finish," said the Count good-humouredly; "and as a man in whom I place full confidence I entrust you with the care of my son. Now, doctor, please, no more excuses. I will not deprive you of the pleasures a naturalist would enjoy in such an excursion. Your preparations could be soon made; so send over for the Spaniard to-night and tell him you will be ready to start at the turn of the tide to-morrow, so that it may bear you up into these unknown regions—unknown to us—and a pleasant trip to you!"

"No," said the doctor, "I shall certainly not think of trusting ourselves to that man and his crew."

"There I agree with you," said the Count; "with a good crew of your own trusted men."

"And if he could be spared," cried Rodd, "I should like for us to have Joe Cross."

"Now, look here," cried Uncle Paul, "this is taking a weak man at his weakest time. Really, Count, we ought not to go. Look at what your position would be in case anything should happen."

"Nothing is likely to happen," said the Count, "and if it did, though my brig is still helpless I should have your vessel, with about half your crew, and my own. So now not another word."

"There," said the doctor, "I am afraid I am beaten."

Chapter Forty One
Reptilian

It was just about the same time as the Spaniard had chosen for his other visits, after dark, that his boat was again rowed across to the schooner's anchorage, the man asking for the doctor.

"I'm here," said Uncle Paul, going to the side, from where he had been talking to the Count. "What's the matter?"

"Matter?" said the Spaniard wonderingly. "Oh, there's nothing the matter. I thought I'd tell you that those two men of mine you gave the physic to are quite well again, and don't want any more. That's all. Go on shooting the crocodiles. Good-night!"

He gave an order to his men, and the boat's head was turned, but as soon as they had proceeded a little way back the Spaniard gave another order, and his men checked the boat and kept on gently dipping their oars to keep her in the same place. "Doctor there?" shouted the Spaniard. "Yes."

"Haven't thought any more about going up the river, have you?"

There was dead silence for a few moments, and then Uncle Paul said sharply, as if making an effort—

"Yes; I shall start as soon as the tide turns to-morrow morning."

"Very well," said the man carelessly. "I will come across with my long-boat and eight of my men. They want a job to keep them awake."

Then he grumbled out some words in Spanish to those who were with him, while, as if annoyed at what he had heard, Captain Chubb uttered a low growl.

"No, you needn't do that," cried Uncle Paul. "Our men would like to go up the river. If you will come across to act as guide I will use my own boat, and take all provisions that are necessary."

"Very well," said the Spaniard. "Perhaps that will be best. Your boat's lighter than mine. Take plenty of powder and shot. Like some of my men to come and help?"

"Oh no; it will not be necessary," replied the captain.

"Bring blankets," shouted the Spaniard. "Dew's heavy. Good-night!" Then the boat was rowed away.

"You mean to go?" grunted the skipper.

"Yes; I don't like to lose this opportunity, and our friends here would like us to go."

"Well," grunted the skipper, after a few moments' thought, "he's only one, and you'll be how many?"

"I was taking eight of the men to row; that is to say, four rowers, and their relief; Cross for coxswain—nine; and our three selves."

"Nay, I'm not going till that brig's finished," said the skipper angrily.

"I felt assured of that," said the doctor. "The young Count is going to join us."

"Ah, that's better," said the skipper. "But look here, gentlemen, I only look upon myself as a servant."

"Not as mine," said the Count gravely. "I shall always look upon you, Captain Chubb, as one of my most valued friends."

"And I am sure Captain Chubb knows that I do," said the doctor, "and that I have ever since he set me down as a scoundrelly slaver."

"Oh, don't bring that up again, sir," grunted the skipper. "That was a blunder, and every man makes them. Well, that's very nice of you, gentlemen—very nice indeed; and I was going to speak out a bit nervously,—as I consider it to be my duty to do as Dr Robson's servant; but as you both speak of me as you do, I hope you won't be offended when I say outright that I don't like that Spanish chap at all."

"Well, I don't know that I particularly like him," said the doctor; "but he will be very useful to me, and show me what I want. I shall pay him for his services, and there'll be an end of it."

"Yes, gentlemen, that's right enough, but I wouldn't trust him a bit. The doctor will say that it is British prejudice. Perhaps it is; but here's my crew; there isn't a man among them as I'd say was perfect, but same time I'd lie down and go to sleep quite comfortable and feeling safe, if I knew any one of them was on the watch; and it did me good when I heerd you say, sir, that you wouldn't have any of the mongrel crew. If it had been the other way on, and you'd said you were going to take Mr Rodd and the young French gentleman and trust yourselves up the country in their boat, I'll tell you outright, sir, I should have struck against it, and if you'd held out and rode the high horse as master, why, there'd have been a mutiny. The men would have took my side, and we wouldn't have let you go."

"And quite right too, Chubb," said the doctor, clapping him on the shoulder. "It would have been a good proof that I had done wisely in making you my friend. What do you say, Count?"

"Quite right," was the reply. "Well, captain," continued the Count, "I don't see that the party can come to much harm with nine of your stout men to act as bodyguard, if this Spanish captain is used as a guide."

"No, sir, I don't see as they can; and as the doctor's come out on purpose to collect all kinds of curious things and see some of the wonders of the world, I suppose it is right that he should make use of a chance like this. But I wouldn't trust that man, gentlemen, farther than I could see him, and that's what, with your leave, I am going to say to my lads. I am just going to tell 'em that they have got to bring the three gentlemen back safe and sound, even if it means that some of them is going to lose the number of their mess, and that means this too, that if Mr Spanish skipper don't play his game fair—well then—"

The skipper ceased speaking, and screwed up his lips very tightly just in the light shed by the swinging lantern.

"Well, captain," put in Rodd, who felt rather amused at what he called the fuss the skipper was making, "why don't you finish what you were going to say?"

"Because I didn't think it was needed, my lad," was the reply. "What I meant was, that if the doctor here didn't think it was his duty to give that yellow chap a very strong dose, one of my lads would."

The doctor was in as high glee the next morning as the two lads, and, it might be added with justice, the nine sailors who were to form their crew, for to a man they were bubbling over with excitement and delight.

The moment they had heard that they were to go they began making their preparations; all their weapons were already in a perfect state of cleanliness, and shone as much as hands could make them, but every pistol and gun-lock was carefully re-oiled, every flint taken out and tightly replaced, while the blades of their cutlasses, that literally glittered, had a final touch given to them and the edges passed along the grindstone, which was sent spinning round in the little armoury as hard as it could go.

The skipper himself spent half the night with the steward, packing provisions, Joe Cross helping, for though he was to be coxswain of the boat, he said he came in there, for after the cook he held that he knew more about cooking "wittles" than any fellow in the ship, and this was acknowledged without dissent, though one of the men did say that Joe Cross took more than his share, since in addition to other duties he had the canisters of gunpowder in charge.

The morning was glorious, the sun and the early breeze soon chasing away the river mist, and before the tide had turned, everything was ready, the well-stored boat alongside, and an awning rigged up over the after-part big enough not merely to act as a screen for the gentlemen, but to shade those who were not rowing, while they were having their rest, while by a little addition the boat's sail could be spread over the little unshipped mast and used as a covering from the night dews when the boat was moored somewhere to the bank after the day's work was done.

"There, gentlemen," said the skipper, "I think that's about as near as we can get it; but I don't see no sign of your Spanish guide as yet. It seems to me as if every one yonder is asleep. Here, you, Joe Cross, I knowed there'd be something. You've forgotten that screwdriver and the little bottle of oil."

"That I aren't, sir! They're in the fore-locker in the little bag of tools."

"Good," grunted the skipper; "and I suppose you'll help the doctor and young Mr Rodd skin the birds they shoot?"

"That's right, sir, and Mr Rodd's been laying down the law to me to take care and keep that there soapy stuff covered over as he dresses the inside of the skins with, 'cause he says it's pison."

The skipper grunted again as he stood at the side and scowled down into the boat.

"Spun yarn?" he said sharply.

"Plenty, sir."

"But you lads never thought to give your jack-knives a whet, I'll be bound."

Joe Cross turned to the crew.

"Show knives, lads!" he shouted. "The skipper wants to try them all on his beard."

"Steady!" growled the skipper. "That's right, then. Well, Mr Rodd," he continued, "I suppose everything's all right. No; where's that there extra coil of new signal line?"

"Starn locker, sir," said Joe.

"And an extra line with new grapnel?"

"Fore-locker, sir," said Joe.

The captain grunted.

"Here, get the grapnel out of the jolly-boat and lash it under one of the thwarts. You might lose one again."

"There it is, sir," said Joe—"lashed just amidships out of the way."

"Come, come, captain," said the doctor good-humouredly as he took off his straw hat and wiped his moist brow, for he too had been as busy as the rest, "you have had your innings; I want to have mine. You, Rodney, you never thought to see that the quinine bottle in the little leather medicine chest was re-filled."

"Rammed it in tight, uncle," said the boy triumphantly, "and saw to all the other bottles."

"Then," said the doctor, "we'll say all is ready. Only look here, my lads; I'll give you half-an-hour before we start, so you had better go down below and have some more breakfast, for it will be a good many hours before we have another meal."

No one stirred.

"Well," said the doctor impatiently, "did you hear what I said?"

This time a low murmur ran through the crew, and Joe Cross took a step forward and touched his hat.

"Beg pardon, sir," he said; "the lads' respects, and they says they're all tight, cargo well stowed."

"Then you don't want the extra half-hour?" said the doctor, looking at his watch. "So there's nothing to do, then, my dear Count, and you, Captain Chubb, but for us to shake hands and say good-bye."

"Where's your guide?" grunted the captain.

"Ah, where's our guide?" said the doctor, looking in the direction of the Spanish three-master. "He said at the turn of the tide. I ought to have asked him to come here to breakfast."

"Here he comes, uncle," cried Rodd, for at that moment the head of the Spaniard's boat was rowed out from the other side of the anchored vessel, which might have been quite deserted, for not a head was to be seen.

"Hah!" cried the doctor. "I like that. It tells well for his being a trustworthy guide. So now good-bye, Count. Your son's mine till we come back."

The Count mastered his desire to embrace the doctor, and grasped his hand in regular English fashion, and by the time the Spaniard's little gig, rowed by two men, had come alongside, the last farewell had taken place with the captain, who then looked over the rail and grunted out—

"Coming aboard, señor?"

"No, no; but just one word. I have been talking to my crew, and told them they are to take their orders from you till I come back. They won't give you any trouble. Let them smoke and sleep as much as they like."

"All right," growled the skipper. "When shall we see you back?"

"When your señor likes," said the Spaniard, lighting a fresh cigarette from the one which had threatened to burn his moustache. "I take the boat as far up into the forest along the little rivers till he tells me to turn back, and then we will begin to row or sail the other way."

A few minutes later the French crew of the brig, and the men of the schooner who were to stay and help the carpenter and his mate, stood ready to give a farewell cheer. The travellers were on the boat, the rowers in their places, with their oars held upright ready to drop into the rowlocks, the little sail rolled round the mast was lying ready for use if a breeze sprang up, and Joe Cross stood right forward, boat-hook in hand, looking as smart as the rest of the crew, that is to say, just as if they had stepped off a man-of-war's deck, and then every one well-armed, ready for the attack upon any wild creatures they encountered, or for the defence of their lives against an enemy, waited for the skipper to give the signal to start, which he did at last by raising his hand.

Then, as the boat was pushed off into the now rising tide, a mingled French and English cheer arose, full of good wishes, while of the Spaniard's crew not a man was visible save the two in the captain's boat, who had just reached the three-master's stern and had begun to make fast.

The cheer was repeated as the Devon boat, in obedience to the dipping of the oars, glided farther out into mid-stream, while directly after there was a heavy swirl just beneath her bows, followed by the sudden protrusion of the huge grinning head of a fierce crocodile, the monster bent on mischief, and receiving a most unexpected salute, for Joe Cross was standing balancing his boat-hook in his hands, ready to lay it down along the thwart, but, quick almost as lightning, he gave it a twirl as he rested one foot upon the gunwale and drove it, harpoon fashion, crash into the reptile's head.

"He's got it!" cried the man, as he started back; but he did not escape the shower of water that was sent flying over the boat, the crocodile vigorously lashing the surface with its serrated tail as it floated astern.

"Yes," said the Spanish captain quietly, "but you had better shoot them, *señores*, and keep a little back from the side. There's plenty of them up the river, and one of you might get swept out of the boat."

Chapter Forty Two
Night in the Jungle

In spite of the risks run from the ravenous reptiles, whose daring proved that they had a hard struggle for existence, familiarity soon bred contempt, and the sailors laughed, as they proceeded up the beautiful river, at perils which not many days before would have made them turn pale.

For they were enjoying an excursion that seemed to present fresh beauties at every yard. As a rule the forest came down to the flowing water on both sides in waves of verdure, with grand trees which every now and then presented the aspect of some gorgeous flower garden, here red, there blue, at other times in lovely wreaths of white, while it seemed, Joe Cross said to the lads, as if one of the blossoming trees took flight every now and then and came skimming over the boat, filling the sky with flowers, so beautiful were the flocks of parrots and other birds that, apparently attracted by the strangers, flew screaming and whistling overhead.

There was no question about getting a shot at some beautiful green and orange long-tailed paroquet, or at one of the soft grey scarlet-tailed parrots which, as they flew across the river, shrieking at those who had interrupted their solitude, gave place to others of a delicate pink; but upon seeing Rodd raise his gun, the Spaniard laughed and said —

"Never mind them. I could fill my schooner with those things at any time. You wait till we get up into the little side river. There will be something better worth shooting then; or perhaps you would like to kill a few as you are coming back."

"Yes, Rodd," said the doctor; "that would be wiser, my lad."

"But suppose we don't see them as we come back," said the lad.

"Not see them?" said the Spaniard, laughing. "Why, the country's alive with them!"

Then as the party sated their eyes upon the various objects they passed, a light soft breeze arose when they turned into a bend of the river, and the Spaniard expressed his satisfaction, and suggested that the sail should be hoisted.

This was rapidly done, the oars were laid in, and Joe Cross came aft to preside at the newly-shipped rudder, while all through the rest of the day, and after the tide had run its course and become adverse, they tacked from side to side, or glided onward with the wind astern, the men only having at very rare intervals to take to their oars.

It was soon after mid-day that the doctor proposed that the boat should be run ashore and that they should land to dine at a lovely park-like opening where the dense portion of the forest had receded farther from the bank; but the Spaniard shook his head.

"No," he said, "don't do that. It looks very nice, but it isn't safe. There are the crocodiles basking about the bank, snakes and serpents nearly everywhere, and the leopards and other great cats hanging about among the trees. Keep aboard. It's safer here."

"He means to take care of us, Morny," said Rodd, in French, and directly after he gave his companion a meaning look, for the Spanish skipper turned to the doctor and said—

"Tell your men to have their guns handy."

"What for?" said the doctor. "Do you scent danger?"

"Nothing particular," replied the man, "but up here in these parts you never know what may happen next. Something may come just when you think you are safe, and it's best to be always ready."

So that and the following meal were eaten in the boat, which just before dark was at the Spaniard's suggestion run up into a calm reach where the forest had become very distant, while the river seemed to have widened out to double its former size.

Here he proposed that they should anchor for the night and wait for the morning before continuing their journey.

This was disappointing to the lads, who looked longingly at the shore, while Rodd suggested that there were several places that looked level, and where it would be easy to rig up a tent where they might sleep.

The Spaniard laughed, and with a grim smile said—

"You wanted a guide for coming up here, young man. If we did what you say we shouldn't all be ready to go on again in the morning."

"What, because of the wild beasts?" said Rodd eagerly.

The Spaniard nodded.

"He is quite right, Rodd," said the doctor. "And I suppose we might catch fever here?" he continued.

"Bad," said the Spaniard laconically. "Keep to the boat."

The night came down dark and beautiful; the great purple velvet arch that spread from side to side of the river was gloriously spangled with stars, for in the day's ascent the little party seemed to have left the river mists behind, and as they sat together the doctor and his young companions revelled in the loveliness of the scene, while they listened to the strange sounds from forest and river which constantly smote upon their ears and now seemed wondrously near.

"It seems very different," whispered Rodd to Morny, for something preyed upon his spirits and stayed him from speaking aloud.

"Yes," said Morny, in the same subdued tone; "it is very different from being aboard the vessels. I shan't go to sleep to-night; shall you?"

"No. Who could go to sleep? Why, as soon as one lay down I should expect to see the great slimy snout of a crocodile thrust over the boat's gunwale, and then—"

"I say," said Morny, "don't!"

But nothing worse than sounds troubled the party that night, as not long after this conversation the two lads obeyed the doctor's suggestion that they should creep under the awning, whose canvas sides were tightly belayed to the gunwale; and though both declared that they would never close their eyes, they and the watches into which the little crew was divided followed the Spanish skipper's example, and in turn slept heavily till sunrise, the great orange globe slowly rolling up over the edge of the forest and shining brilliantly down upon the glittering river, for as over-night there was not a sign of mist.

About half the day passed with plenty of favouring gales to help the boat along, and spare the men's arms, and Rodd commented on this to their guide.

"Wait a bit," he said. "A little farther on, and we shall turn into one of the little rivers where the high trees are close together at the sides. There won't be much wind there, and the men will have to row."

Everything was as he said, for as they passed out of the main stream the banks were but a little way apart, and in place of the full flow of the great river the stream grew sluggish; but everything being so close at hand the beauties of the forest became far enhanced.

"You said rivers," said the doctor suddenly. "Are there more than this one?"

"Plenty," replied the man, and he made himself a fresh cigarette as he sat back in the boat, to go on smoking. "Not so many crocodiles here," he said, "and they are smaller. More birds too. Look!" And as the men dipped their oars to row slowly up the winding stream, which often seemed to turn back upon itself, the Spaniard pointed now to tiny bee-like sunbirds with their dazzling metallic casques and gorgets—the brilliant little creatures that take the place of the humming-birds of the New World.

At another time, though the two lads, eagerly observant and with the doctor to back them, needed no showing, their guide pointed to the many brilliantly-tinted birds of the thrush family, at the barbets and trogons, not so brilliant as those of the Western world, but each lovely in itself, while as they went on and on along their meandering river path, the birds that struck them as being most novel and at the same time tame in the way in which they came down the overhanging branches of the great forest trees, as if their curiosity had been excited by the strangers, were the many-tinted plantain eaters, with their crested heads, and the lovely green and crimson touracoos, which, while their violet and crimson relatives wore, as it were, a feather casque, displayed on their part a vivid green ornamentation that passed from beak to nape, which when they were excited looked more like a plume.

They had come thus far without firing a shot, for the doctor had said—

"Let us leave the shooting till our return, and be contented with charging our memories and feasting our eyes, for no dried skins, however carefully they are preserved, will ever display the beauties of these birds' nature as we watch them here in life. But we must have a skin or two of these touracoos, for I want to show you lads the wonders of that vivid crimson upon their underparts."

"Oh, I can see it plainly enough, uncle," said Rodd.

"Yes," said Uncle Paul, "but you don't notice what I mean. Instead of that crimson being a beautiful dye fixed in the feathers, it is a soft red pigment which can be washed out into water and— I saw something moving up that creek," he added, in a low voice.

"Niggers perhaps," said the Spaniard, without turning his head.

"Likely to attack?" asked Rodd.

"Pish!" said the Spaniard contemptuously. "Harmless. Fishing perhaps. We shall see more, I expect, farther on."

He did not trouble himself to turn his head, though the rest in the boat kept a sharp look-out for what had attracted the doctor's attention up a narrow inlet arched over by the overhanging trees, but it was not until close upon evening that, as they pursued their winding way, this side stream opened out more into a reach, and then for the first time a movement some hundreds of yards behind brought forth a warning from Joe Cross, who was seated with the tiller in his hand.

"Just cast your eye back, Mr Rodd, sir," he said; "yonder there where the stream opened out it seems to me there's a canoe with a couple of Indians in it. Nay, I mean blacks."

"Yes; look, captain," said Rodd eagerly; and the Spaniard slowly raised himself up from where he was leaning back, took his cigarette from his lips, shaded his eyes, and then after a cursory glance replaced the cigarette and sank back.

"Niggers," he said. "Fishing."

Then they rowed on, leaving the two occupants of the canoe behind, till, coming to what he considered to be a suitable place, the Spaniard suggested that they should stay there for their meal upon an open sandy little beach some fifty yards across, beyond which the forest rose dark and thick again.

"We can land and light a fire," he said, "and make coffee and stretch our legs."

"It would not be safe," said the doctor, "to rig up a tent here, would it?"

"Oh yes," said the captain. "The only thing to trouble us here might be a leopard or two; but a shot would scare them away."

This was good news, and heartily welcomed by the whole party, and in a short time cooking was going on in the glowing embers of a fire, for which there was abundant fuel close at hand, while a canvas tent, strengthened by branches thrust deep in the sand, was cleverly contrived by the sailors.

"I say, Morny, this is something like!" cried Rodd, as they sat together watching the men finishing their meal, with their jovial contented faces lit up by the glowing fire which flashed and cast shadows and sent up golden clouds dotted with tiny spark-like embers, as it was made up from time to time, according to the Spanish captain's suggestion that it would keep away all wild beasts and clear off the snakes.

"Yes; my legs were beginning to feel cramped. I wonder how my father is."

"Oh, he's happy enough," said Rodd, "and enjoying himself with the thought that Skipper Chubb has had a good day's work getting on a new outer skin over the hole."

"Ah, yes, I hope so," cried Morny eagerly, his friend's suggestion seeming to brighten him up.

"And I say," cried Rodd, "shan't we sleep to-night! How I shall stretch! I don't think I should much mind a great spotted cat coming and sniffing round the tent. Of course it would be very horrid to be clawed or bitten, but there's something natural about that. The idea of being grabbed by one of those great slimy reptiles and dragged under water, and before you have had time to squeak—"

"Rodd, don't, please!" cried Morny, with a shudder. "It makes my flesh creep."

"Yes; I was going to say it's time you lads changed your conversation," said the doctor quietly, "for none of the forest creatures are likely to disturb us to-night with a watch-fire kept up like this."

"But I say, uncle," said Rodd mischievously, later on—when the watch had been set, with a big pile of dead firewood laid ready to replenish the fire, and Uncle Paul was about to follow the example of the Spanish captain and select his patch of dry sand covered with canvas, beneath the extemporised tent.

"Well, what, my boy?" said the doctor drowsily. "Don't talk now. I am sure every one wants to go to sleep."

"Yes, uncle; I am sure I do," said the boy, who was already fitting the projecting bones of his back into the yielding sand; "but do you think it's likely—"

Rodd stopped to give Morny, who was beside him, a nudge with his elbow.

"Do I think what's likely, Pickle?" replied the doctor.

"That those two black fellows we saw in the canoe will sneak ashore to come and do anything to us with their spears?"

"Rodney!" cried the doctor indignantly.

"But they are sure to have spears, uncle, or else they couldn't be sticking the fish."

"Go to sleep, sir!" said the doctor angrily.

Rodd went at once, and did not stir again, till an extra loud crackling of burning wood made him start up in wonder and alarm.

But it was only the morning watch, in the persons of Joe Cross and the appointed cook, making up the fire afresh in view of what Joe called boiling the billy and to give the cook some good broiling embers, for it was the break of day once more.

Chapter Forty Three
The Strangers

Rodd's toilet did not take him long, for though the water was clear and tempting as it rippled on the sand, the recollection of what might possibly be there in the way of ravenous fish, if even there were no reptiles, kept him from venturing for a swim, while when he suggested to the Spaniard the possibility of bathing in safety, the man looked at him in surprise, and his words were tinged with contempt as he said—

"Bathe! What for?"

Rodd did not answer, but turned his back quickly and hurried away to where Morny was questioning Joe Cross and the cook about whether the men they had succeeded in the watch had heard anything in the night.

"Here, catch hold of me, you two," Rodd gasped out, "and help me away there among the trees."

"Hah! What's the matter?" cried Morny. "Are you taken bad?"

"Horrid. Don't talk to me. Get me out of sight. I am going off."

Morny and Joe each caught him by an arm and hurried him in amongst the trees.

"Don't be frightened," gasped out Rodd. "Oh, that Spanish chap! He'll be the death of me!"

"Why, you are laughing!" cried Morny angrily. "How dare you frighten us like this!"

"I—I—I—I—" gasped out Rodd—"couldn't help it, old fellow. Oh, that Spaniard!"

Morny was really angry, but Joe Cross's frank face had expanded into a grim smile.

"What game's he been up to, Mr Rodd, sir?"

"Oh, it was very stupid of me," said Rodd, wiping his eyes; "but I was afraid of laughing in his face, and the more I tried to look serious the more it would come; and I didn't want to offend him."

"Just like 'em, sir," said Joe, as Rodd explained himself more fully. "'Tis their natur' to; and besides, it's what an old woman I used to know called being codimical. Yes, sir, I've watched 'em aboard that there three-masted schooner. Them there mongrel chaps, they must save a wonderful lot of money every year in soap."

"There," said Rodd, wiping his eyes again, "I am all right now; but it's very comic. The more you feel you mustn't laugh, the worse you are. I suppose laughing must do one good. I always feel so much better after having a good grin."

"Do you good, Mr Rodd, sir! I should just think it does! Why, it's natur'. Does you good to have a long talk sometimes, don't it; eh, Mr Morny, sir?"

"Oh yes, I suppose so," replied the lad.

"And you know it does you a lot of good to get your teeth to work when you are hungry, Mr Rodd."

"Yes, Joe," cried the lad eagerly. "What's for breakfast?"

"Ah, you wait a bit, sir, and you will see. But as I was saying about laughing, what's your smiling tackle for, and your grinning kit for, if they aren't to use and set you right when otherwise you would be all in the dumps? Yes, sir; give me a good laugh. But one don't always get one's share along with our old man. Still we like him, for he always means right by us. Ay, there's worse chaps in the world than old Chubb, and I'm just ready and waiting to drink his health and long life to him in a pannikin of the finest coffee a coxswain ever brewed; and as for the frizzled ham that cookie's got thriddled on sticks over them embers to eat with the dough-cakes he's baking in the ashes— Here, let's get back, for fear there's an accident."

"Accident?" said Morny. "Why, what accident could happen?"

"Out of sight, sir, out of mind; and that aren't a French proverb, but you might like to turn it into one as your countrymen could use. They might forget, sir, as we are here."

Well rested, in high spirits, and with a good breakfast waiting, the morning meal was eaten with the greatest of gusto, while to every one the expedition wore more and more the appearance of a delightful holiday.

There was an exception, though, and that was in the person of the Spanish captain, who looked grim and sombre, and ate little, but smoked a great deal.

Just as the tent was being struck and a clearance being made of the remains of the breakfast, Rodd suddenly called out—

"There they are again!" And he called attention to the two nearly nude blacks, who were creeping along the edge of the bank opposite to them in their canoe.

"Why, they are watching us," said Uncle Paul.

"Hungry," said the Spanish skipper laconically.

"Yes, that's it," cried Rodd, and after a glance at his uncle he tore down a wild banana leaf, turned it into a natural green dish, heaped upon it some of the remains of the breakfast, and carried it a short distance along the bank, where he placed it close to the water's edge, signed to the blacks, and then joined his companions, who were about to enter the boat.

Very soon afterwards they were gliding along the stream again, after the sailors, by Uncle Paul's orders, had carefully extinguished the remains of the fire.

"We don't want to start a conflagration, my boys," he said.

As the men slowly dipped their oars, for there was not a breath of wind, the two lads had to make an effort to, as it were, drag their eyes from the lovely floral scene on either side of the little river, while they watched the proceedings of the blacks.

"Well, they are a pair of stupids," said Rodd. "What is it—ignorance or suspicion?"

For the two dark objects remained on the farther bank, one seated with a paddle, the other upright, spear in hand, holding on by an overhanging bough to keep their boat from drifting on with the current.

"Suspicion," said Morny quietly.

"Miserable wretches! Do they think I want to poison them?"

"No. I'll tell you," said Morny. "Poor creatures, they have been so ill-used by the white people with black hearts who come to these shores that they think the food you have put there is the bait of a trap."

"To catch blackbirds! Why, of course! They think we want to carry them off for slaves. They're as bad as old Captain Chubb; eh, uncle? He took us for slavers, Morny, when uncle wanted to engage him. Well, I forgive them, poor chaps.—Ah, they think it's safe now. They're going to risk taking the bait."

For all at once the two negroes began to paddle themselves slowly across the river to where the bright green banana leaf lay glistening upon the sand, and the last the two lads saw then of those they had tried to benefit, as the boat glided on with four oars dipping and making the water flash like silver, was with the canoe drawn up on to the sands, the two savage-looking blacks squatting on their heels, eagerly devouring the remains of the breakfast. "Oh, never mind the sun being hot, uncle," cried Rodd, as they went on and on. "I don't mind if I'm half roasted. Look, Morny; did you ever see anything so lovely? Look at the flowers on that great tree. Why, it seems to blaze with scarlet."

"Yes, and look at the birds," was the reply. "I wish my father were here, with his mind at rest, to enjoy all this as I do, or should if he were with us. There, quick! What's that—running in there among the leaves on that tree?"

"Snake," cried Rodd, who just caught sight of the movement. "No. Who ever saw a snake with four legs? Why, it's a great lizard of a thing! Why, uncle, that must be one of those queer chaps that turn all sorts of colours."

"Yes," said the doctor, "you are right, Pickle," and he focussed upon it a little old-fashioned single opera-glass which he carried in his pocket. "That's a chameleon, sure enough; and a big one too, I should say, though it's the first one I ever saw alive."

"What's he after?" said Rodd.

"Having a game, catching butterflies, I think, sir," suggested Joe Cross. "So he is, Joe."

"Why, Master Rodd, it makes us chaps wish we was boys again and ashore there running after them butterflies with our caps; only one couldn't run among the trees, and they fly too high. I never see flutterbies, as we used to call them, with colours like these, though. We used to catch white 'uns, and yaller ones, and sometimes what we used to call tortoiseshells. But I call all this 'ere— Look there, sir; there's one as big as my hand—two—lots on 'em! Yes, I do call this 'ere dead waste both of the butterflies and the birds."

"Why, my man?" said the doctor quietly.

"Why, sir, everything you see flying about in the air is as lovely as lovely, and no one to look at them. Why, if I had my way I'd have all these sort of things flying about in old England. Yes, sir, they are all wasted here."

"That they aren't, Joe," cried Rodd. "We are looking at them, and enjoying them; and I say, uncle, isn't it time we began to get some specimens?"

"Plenty of time yet, my boy. Why, captain, the country here on either side is very beautiful."

"Satisfied, then?" said the Spaniard coolly.

"Thoroughly," replied the doctor, "and very glad to have met with such a guide."

"But I say, captain," cried Rodd, "don't forget the big monkeys and the leopards."

"Oh no," said the Spaniard. "Farther on yet; and I can't be sure. There are plenty in the woods one day, and the next they are gone. But we shall come across some of them." And he sank back smoking again.

"Just look at him," said Rodd. "He doesn't seem to take notice of anything."

"These things have grown common to him," replied Morny quietly; "but don't look only at the trees on the banks. Cast your eyes down sometimes into the clear water."

"Don't say there are any of those great reptiles here," said Rodd hurriedly.

"No, I have not seen one to-day; but look at the fish we disturb. They go gliding away to right and left like so many flashes of silver and gold."

"Now, boys, there's something," said the doctor. "Right across the river." For there was a rush and a splash as some animal that had evidently been wading close in under the bank sprang out of the water with a rush, and disappeared amongst the low growth.

"What's that, captain?" cried Rodd, making a snatch at his gun.

"Hog," said the Spaniard quietly. "Did you see it?" asked Rodd. "No; I know the noise they make. Plenty here." And then it was birds, anon flowers, and some two or three miles farther on Joe Cross, who sat just behind the boys, tiller in hand, glanced at the doctor and asked—"Which way?"

For the river forked into two of equal size, and at his question the Spaniard raised his eyelids a little and made a sign with his left hand.

This branch proved to be if anything more rich in its objects of beauty than the winding stream they had left, for there was enough to sate even the most exacting lover of nature, while there always seemed to be something fresh. One minute a sailor would be pointing out a brilliantly-scaled thin green serpent gliding along the surface of the water, eel-like in motion, but with its back quite exposed to the sunshine, giving it the look of frosted silver, while before long another man made his discovery, the whole party being eagerly on the watch for fresh objects of interest, and at this, without waiting for orders, the rowers ceased dipping their oars, to let the boat drift slowly by a lovely curtain of fine strands and leaves dotted with flowers which hung down from some fifty feet up, till the tips of the twigs touched the water.

In amongst these vine-like branches a vividly-coloured serpent that appeared to be some six or eight feet long, and but little thicker than a man's thumb, was deliberately climbing and twining, its eyes having first attracted attention by sparkling in the sunshine.

"Don't seem afraid of tumbling into the water," suggested Joe.

"Wouldn't matter if it did," said Rodd. "You saw that one a little while ago, how it could swim."

"So, I did, sir; so I did," replied the man, who was as much interested as the naturalists of the party. "But there are such a lot of good things to see that one seems to shove the other out of your head. Now, what will that chap be doing there, slithering about over the water? Out for a walk?"

"Trying to catch one of those bright little sunbirds, I suppose," said Rodd.

"No," said the doctor, who was watching the serpent through his glass. "I should say that one is after birds' nests."

"Think of that!" cried Joe. "But he wouldn't blow the eggs, sir, would he, and make a string?"

"No, my man," said the doctor, smiling, "but swallow them, I should say, or the young birds that he might find in the nest. Why, Rodd, my boy, one wants three or four lives here, and then one wouldn't see half the wonders of this paradise. Here's world within world of wonder and beauty."

"Row away, my lads," said the Spaniard, who seemed to have only one object in life, and that the re-lighting of cigarettes.

"Ay, ay, sir!" cried the men, and they dipped their oars again.

Then on turning a bend of the stream there was a waft of warm wind to fan their cheeks, when the sailors forward stepped the mast, and hoisted the yard of the lug-sail, which filled out at once, the rowers laid in their dripping oars, which seemed to shed diamonds and pearls back into the stream, and away they glided among the glories of the low flat land, through which streams seemed to run like veins, forming a perfect maze of waterways, each if possible more beautiful than the other, while proving wonderfully similar in width and depth, so much so that at last, after winding round bend after bend of the last stream they had entered, the doctor turned suddenly to their guide and said—

"Why, captain, how are we going to find the way back again?"

The captain opened his eyes slightly and smiled, as he took a little compass from his pocket.

"With this," he said; "but—pah! I could find my way here with my eyes shut. Look; there's a good place for a fire, and the boys here can get plenty of good fish, if you have a line, for the men to cook."

At this suggestion Joe Cross handed the tiller to Rodd and made his way forward to the locker, from which he produced a couple of fishing-lines.

The boat was run ashore at a similar patch of sand to that where they had made their previous halt, and while some of the men were collecting dead wood from beneath the trees, there was a sudden rush, and something yellowish dropped with a thud from the nearest great fork, made four or five great bounds through the low bushes, and disappeared.

"Leopard," said the Spanish captain quietly. "Get out your gun, sir. His mate will not be far away."

He had hardly spoken before another of the great cats leaped from bough to bough of the huge forest tree they had approached, and disappeared in turn, escaping unscathed.

"You are keeping your word, sir," said Rodd. The Spaniard smiled, and remained in his place, while Joe Cross and the lads paddled the boat out again to a spot the Spaniard pointed out, and there dropped the grapnel, before beginning to fish, using small pieces of fat pork for their bait.

Long before the fire had burnt up enough for cooking purposes or the great kettle had boiled in the shade of the huge tree that had been chosen for kitchen, bites had become frequent, and fine carp-like fish, whose golden scales glittered in the light, were being hauled into the boat; but eager though the lads were, and full of enjoyment of their sport, it was hot out there in the sun, and arms were beginning to ache, while hunger asserted itself more and more.

"I say, Morny," cried Rodd, "enough's as good as a feast."

"Yes, sir," cried Joe, "and we have got enough and the feast to come, for these look as if they'd be good. Shall we put ashore?"

Rodd nodded assent, and soon after Joe and a couple of his mates had been busy with their knives on the sandy river bank, the unwonted sound made by a frying-pan arose from the fire, with the result that there was no doubt about the carp-like fish being good, and the *al fresco* dinner proving a success.

The afternoon was wearing on when the preparations for a fresh start were made, the Spaniard promising the doctor that he would point out another good resting-place for the night before it was dark.

"All aboard!" cried Joe just then. "Why, look at that now! Well, there's plenty of fish left, Mr Rodd, and in this 'ere hot country we had better have it fresh."

"Why, I didn't expect to see them again, uncle," cried Rodd, and he pointed across the river to where the two blacks with their canoe had suddenly appeared, as if they had been in hiding and watching the cooking going on till it seemed to them that their time had come, when they lay there with their boat just as before, apparently waiting till the strangers had gone on.

"Do they mean to keep on following us like this, captain?" asked Rodd.

"*Quien sabe*?" he said. "It is a free country, and you will not mind?"

"Mind! No," cried Rodd. "But they will have to cook what are left for themselves. I say, uncle, can we trust them to put the fire out afterwards?"

"Oh yes, my lad. I suppose we must."

"That's right, Mr Rodd, sir. They'll take care not to fry themselves. But here, cookie, don't you leave them our pan."

Once more as the boat swept round a bend a glimpse was caught of the two blacks, who had no hesitation now about paddling across to the deserted halting-place.

The Spaniard was as good as his word that evening in guiding them to another bivouac, and that night, feeling perfectly secure, the lads lay down to sleep, looking forward to another day of intense enjoyment in the wondrous labyrinth of Nature's beauties, far from feeling satisfied with what had gone before.

Three more days passed, and halt after halt had been made at spots which always presented just the right facilities required, the Spaniard proving how great was his knowledge of the geography of the country through which they rowed or sailed, while the two blacks, who over and over again seemed to have disappeared, always turned up again ready for the departure of the travellers, who now took it as a matter of course to leave plenty of fish or flesh collected by the guns for the poor savages' support.

More than once the lads had made advances to these men, to try and get them to approach, but their shyness and suspicion were most marked, and they never came near till the departing boat was some distance off.

"Now," said the doctor, one evening, "I have been mentally marking down such birds and insects as I wish for us to collect, so to-morrow morning all this pleasure-seeking must come to an end, and we'll all work hard, shooting, skinning, and boxing a few butterflies as well."

"What a pity!" said Rodd. "I should like to go on yet for weeks."

"So should I, Pickle, but we must get back to the schooner."

"And the brig," cried Morny eagerly.

"Yes, my lad," said the doctor, "and I am afraid the Count will think we have exceeded our time; but we shall be going steadily back from to-morrow morning, collecting as we go, and I am sure you will agree that we have had a grand excursion, everything having been most successful."

The following morning broke as gloriously fine as ever. The fire was crackling, and Joe Cross announced that it was not fish that morning, but fried bacon, and soon after the pleasant aromatic scent of the coffee was rising in the morning air as they took their seats in the shade of a great fig-like tree whose boughs seemed to be full of twittering and whistling love-birds gathered in a huge flock to feed upon the saccharine embedded seeds of the little fruit.

"Hullo!" said the doctor suddenly, turning to Rodd. "Where's the Don?"

"Having another cigarette somewhere, I suppose, uncle," said Rodd, laughing. "I thought he was along with you."

"No, my boy," replied Uncle Paul. "I thought he went with you this morning when you made the men row a little farther along the stream."

"That was only to take a last look upward and see what it was like farther on before we turned back; and it is so beautiful up there—better than anything we have seen. I say, uncle, let's have another day."

"No, no, Rodd," cried Morny, catching him by the arm. "I couldn't bear it. We must go back now."

"Quite right, Morny, my boy," said the doctor quietly. "Yes, we have come to the end of our tether. Let's get back to the Count and Captain Chubb."

"Well, all right," said Rodd. "Never mind what I said, Morny, old chap. I always was a pig when I was getting anything I liked. Let's have breakfast, and then—

"Huzza! We're homeward bound—ound—ound!
Huzza! We're homeward bound!"

he trolled out merrily; and then, clapping his hands to his lips, "*Español* ahoy!" he shouted.

"Ahoy!" came back from the bank of trees across the little river.

"*Español* ahoy!" shouted the boy again, and there was the answering echo.

"Well, I hear you!" cried Rodd merrily. "But how did you get there without the boat?"

There was no answer to this.

"Coffee and fried ham!" roared Rodd.

"'Am!" came back.

"Yes, but it's only bacon!" shouted Rodd.

"'Acon!"

"Well, why don't you come?"

"Don't be stupid, Rodney," cried the doctor shortly. "Here, Cross—cook—any of you; have you seen the Spanish skipper?"

"No, sir!" came in chorus.

"Dear me," said the doctor thoughtfully; "now I come to think of it I don't remember seeing him this morning."

"No, uncle; nor I neither. Did you see him, Morny?"

"No, not this morning. I saw him talking with you last night, sir."

"Yes; that was when I was saying that we should start back for certain, and he went and lay down in his usual place, close to the side of the tent, directly afterwards."

"Oh yes; he was there when we lay down, wasn't he, Morny?"

"Yes; I remember that."

"But we have not seen him since, uncle."

"Very strange," said the doctor, and turning to the men he questioned them in turn, with the result that all were sure that they had not seen the Spaniard since over-night.

The doctor and the two lads stood gazing at one another for some minutes in silence.

"Do you think anything could have happened to him?" said Morny at last.

"Oh no," cried the doctor sharply. "He's too much at home here in these wild parts for that."

"But I was thinking, uncle—" said Rodd, in a hesitating way.

"Thinking of what, my boy?"

The Ocean Cat's Paw | 313

"That there might be some few crocodiles up here in this narrow part of the river, after all."

"Absurd, Rodney! Don't jump at conclusions like that!" cried the doctor.

"But they are such horribly fierce creatures, uncle."

"Don't be absurd, sir! Is it likely that one of those reptiles could have come up out of the river, crawled into the tent, and dragged him out again, without some one knowing it? No; he must have got up early and gone off by himself somewhere, as this is as far as we were to go, meaning to see if he could find the traces of a chimpanzee, so as to show us one or more before we start back."

"Yes, that's possible, uncle," said Rodd. "And perhaps he has found one."

"Very likely; and if he has he'll soon be back to take us on the trail."

"Perhaps so, uncle," said Rodd meaningly.

"Why do you speak like that, sir?"

"Because I say he may have found one, uncle."

"Well—and then?"

"The chimpanzee won't let him come back."

"Really, Rodney, you make me very angry sometimes," cried the doctor. "If ever there happens to be a little hitch of any kind you immediately clap it under your mental microscope and try to make it as large as you possibly can. That's it for certain, Morny. He wants to keep perfect faith with us, and so he has gone to see whether he can find any signs of these great apes. Well, we won't let the breakfast spoil, and it would be a sort of madness to go hunting about in the forest for his tracks; so come along. I dare say he'll be back long before we have done."

But the breakfast was eaten without any sign of the Spaniard, and now the doctor began to be thoroughly uneasy, for the time was there when they ought to be starting on their backward journey, and minute by minute he grew more impatient.

His excitement was shared by the two lads, and the men were questioned again and again, while all joined in searching round the little encampment as far as was possible; and that was a very short distance, for almost directly after the stretch of sand was passed they came upon dense shrubby growth, and beyond this there were the huge forest trees matted together by vines and lianas into an impassable wall, while as far as could be made out there was no trace of any one having tried to force his way through.

"Most singular thing," said the doctor. "We can't go away and leave him alone in these wilds. But have everything ready for an immediate start, and we must wait."

"I say, Morny," said Rodd, "what do you make of this? Here, stop a minute, though. Can you think of any way by which he could go?"

Morny shook his head.

"There's no path into the forest," he said, "and it's just as dense on the other side if any one ventured to swim across the river to go from there."

"To go where?" said Rodd sharply.

"I don't know. I was only thinking of what any one might try to do."

"And then," said Rodd, "there's only up the river and down the river, and he had no boat. But it's no use to bother; we have got to wait and see; and we mustn't forget those two poor niggers. I wonder whether they will follow us back?"

"Sure to," said Morny; "right back to the vessels."

"Hi! Joe Cross!" cried Rodd. "Put what's left of the breakfast in a wild banana leaf again and leave it on the bank."

"Got it all ready here, sir," was the reply.

"Why, Morny," cried Rodd, catching his companion sharply by the arm, "where are the niggers?"

"Where are the niggers?" said the young Frenchman, staring.

"Yes; they have always been ready waiting till we finished our meals. They were there last night."

"Yes," said Morny; "they were there last night."

"Then where are they this morning?"

Morny looked across the river and back at his companion, while the doctor, who had been conversing with the men, came hurriedly up and joined them.

"What are you two talking about?" he said.

"About those two blacks, uncle," said Rodd, whose voice sounded rather husky.

"What about them, sir?"

"They have always been hanging about, uncle, till we had done our meals, and then waited for what was left."

"Yes. True. I saw them paddle across last night in the dark and fetch what was put for them, in a curious animal-like way."

"But you didn't see them go back, uncle?"

"Yes, I did, sir, and I remember thinking how cat-like they were in their actions, pouncing upon the food and eating it there and then. I watched them till they had done, so as to see them steal off again with their boat, and I meant to write a note about it in my paper regarding this trip."

"Well, they are not waiting this morning, uncle," said the boy meaningly.

"No," said the doctor, glancing in the direction of the wild banana leaf.

"Well, uncle, what do you make of that?"

"I don't know, my lad. What do you make of it?"

"I don't quite know, uncle. They are savages."

"Yes, boy, they are savages."

"And they've got spears, uncle," said the boy meaningly.

"There you go again, sir!" cried Uncle Paul, irascibly now. "You know perfectly well, Rodney, how this sort of thing annoys me. I suppose the next thing you will be telling me is that one of them came with his spear and behaved as one of Captain Cook's friends says the Australian blacks behaved to the girls they wanted to steal for their wives."

"No, I don't, uncle," cried the boy ill-humouredly. "I don't know what Captain Cook's friends say. I hardly know who Captain Cook is— Yes, I do: he's the man who sailed round the world."

"Well, then, I'll tell you, sir. He said the blacks come in the dark, twist their spears in the girls' hair, and carry them away. And I suppose you mean to infer that that's what has become of the Spanish captain?"

"I don't, uncle," cried Rodd.

"But if you do, sir, you are wrong; for the Don, as you two lads nicknamed him, had hardly a bit of hair on his head. There, there, there; being cross won't make any better of it. Hope to goodness that nothing has happened to the poor fellow. Can't have got up in the night and walked away in his sleep, can he?"

"Well, but if he had, uncle, he must have woke up by this time, and then he'd walk back again."

"Well, we can't go without him, my dear lads. He has been a very faithful servant to us, and it would be a mean, cowardly, despicable act for us to leave him in the lurch. Oh, it's impossible. It would be little better than murder to leave a man here without a boat."

Rodd looked hard at Morny, as if questioning him with his eyes; and so the French lad took it to be, for he made a deprecating gesture with his hands.

The doctor was watching his nephew keenly, and now clapped him sharply on the shoulder.

"What are you thinking about, sir?" he cried.

"About what you said, uncle," said the lad, rather confusedly.

"I didn't say anything, sir. I was listening to you."

"Yes, you did, Uncle Paul," said the boy sternly. "You said that it would be murder to leave a man here without a boat."

"Oh, of course. So I did. And so it would be, sir. But now look here, Rodd. I haven't known you, sir, since you were little more than a baby without being able to read some of the changes which come over your face. What were you thinking about that boat?"

"I was thinking, uncle, suppose he had one."

"But he hadn't one. Look here, sir; you are thinking something, and suspecting something."

"Yes, uncle, I am; but I don't know what."

"I suppose that's because you were prejudiced against the Spaniard by what Chubb said."

"I suppose so, uncle. You know how he said he wouldn't trust that man a bit?"

"Yes, yes."

"Well, I always felt that I couldn't trust him a bit."

"Prejudice, boy—prejudice."

"I dare say it was, uncle; and when I found how he showed us everything we wanted I tried to believe in him; but my head felt as if it wouldn't go."

"He hadn't got a boat; he hadn't got a boat," said the doctor, as if to himself.

"No, uncle; but suppose he had got a canoe?"

"That's it," cried Morny excitedly. "You are right, Rodd. You think those were his two men?"

"Yes," said Rodd. "Two black fellows out of his schooner."

"And—and—" panted Morny, as the doctor's jaw fell and he stood staring at the two lads, utterly speechless—"you believe that he has led us right out here in this wild maze of a place to lose us, while he goes back to—to—"

The poor fellow broke down, and Rodd caught him by the hand; but Morny in the passion of his emotion snatched his away.

"Don't—don't say it!" he cried.—"While he has gone back for who knows what? Oh, father, father, why did I come away?"

"Stop, boys, stop!" cried Uncle Paul; and to the surprise of both he plumped himself down upon the sand, drawing up his knees, planting his elbows upon them, and resting his burning head upon his hands. "Wait a bit," he said. "I want to think; I want to think; I want to think. Ah–h–h!" he groaned, at last. "Who could have imagined it? Who could have thought it? A trick—a ruse!"

Then springing up he looked sharply round, to see that the boat's crew were grouped together watching him wonderingly, and that seemed to bring him to himself at once. He turned sharply upon Rodd and gave him a grave nod of the head, and said quietly —

"I am afraid you are right, my boy. Morny, my lad, I told your father that in this expedition you should be to me as my son. Let me play the father to you now, and tell you that it is your duty to act as a man."

"Act as a man, sir—" began Morny.

"Yes, my boy; act and not talk. Aboard, every one of you, my lads," he continued, to the sailors. "I am afraid we have been wiled away here by a cunning trick, for what reason remains to be proved. But whatever it means, we are twelve staunch men with our duty before us, and that is, to get back as quickly as possible to the schooner and the brig. I may be deceived, but I believe we are the victims of a plot, and if so I am afraid it will go hard with that Spaniard when we meet. Now, then, I don't know how long it will take, but we have got to do it, and when we get back to our schooner, no matter what has happened, there's ten guineas apiece as a sort of prize-money for the brave lads who have helped to pull us through."

A loud excited cheer burst from the crew, and several voices broke in afterwards with something indistinguishable amidst the noise.

"What's that? What's that I hear?" cried the doctor sharply to Joe Cross.

"The lads say they don't want no ten guineases, sir, but they'd all give as much as that to get hold of that dirty Spaniel by the neck."

"Hah!" ejaculated the doctor. "Now then, not ten guineas, but twenty, for the man among you who can guide us through this wilderness of waters back to our stout Devon boat. Now then, who's the one among you who can act as guide?"

A dead silence fell upon the group, and for the first time since their start a black storm-cloud began to spread slowly over the sky.

Chapter Forty Four
Wet Dust in the Eye

It was the precursor of a terrible tropic tempest, with bluish lightning that was blinding, while the roar of heaven's artillery was incessant. But not a man blenched as the rowers bent to their oars, gladdened by the feeling that the current was with them, as they sent the boat rapidly along for their last halting-place. But a mile had hardly been covered when, with a wild shriek and roar, down came the rain, not in showers or in drops, but in sheets so heavy that before a minute had elapsed every one was drenched, and soon after two of the men had to begin to bale.

To proceed was impossible, and braving the risk, the boat was rowed beneath the overhanging branches of one of the monarchs of the primeval forest which reached its limbs far out over the stream, and there, somewhat protected, the boat was moored. For quite a couple of hours the little party crouched in the bottom, aiding the shelter by spreading the sail over the awning, the men holding on to keep the canvas from being swept off by the howling gale, while the rain poured off in buckets-full, as the men said.

Then a new danger attacked them. The stream swelled and swelled till the boat rose feet higher and was forced in among the low-hanging branches, while the great risk now was that they might be swept out and along the furious torrent into which the sluggish river had been turned.

But just as it seemed impossible to hold on any longer, and when the forest on either side had become river too, the rain ceased as suddenly as it had begun, the wind dropped, and the clouds began to pass away, while in less than an hour the sun was shining brightly down, and huge clouds of steam floated over the flooded land.

It was impossible to cast off from their mooring, for every man agreed that to follow the course of the rushing water would mean that they would be swept away from the river and in all probability be capsized before they had gone many hundred yards.

There was nothing for it, then, but to bale hard and free the boat from water, wring out and try to dry their saturated garments, and do what they could in the way of drying the sail and awning, in the hope that the flood would soon pass away.

Fortunately Cross was soon able to announce that the water was sinking, and this continued so rapidly that before many hours had passed they were able to put off once more into the stream, which had pretty well returned to the limits of its banks; and the drying of their clothes and of such stores as had suffered followed in rapid course.

But it was a disheartening commencement of their journey back to the main river, and darkness fell upon a desolate and terribly depressed company, who passed the night of solitude and despair wondering what had happened at the anchorage where the brig had been left careened.

Rodd had tried to whisper comfort to his comrade, but only to be met with imploring words, the lad begging to be allowed to sit and think; and Rodd respected his prayer.

No better fortune attended him with Uncle Paul, who sternly bade him be silent.

"I too must think, my lad," he said—"and pray."

The silence was shared by the sailors, who only indulged in a whisper now and then.

And how the rest of that night passed away Rodd hardly knew. Of one thing only was he quite certain, and that was that sleep never visited the occupants of that boat.

Daylight at last, when such provisions as were absolutely necessary were partaken of as the boat went steadily down-stream, for there was water enough in the river still to have completely changed its sluggish character, while this was hailed by the men with delight, seeing that it helped their course, while wherever the wind was available the sail was hoisted and they sped along, every one keeping a sharp look-out for their last bivouac but one, it having been decided amongst them that they must have been swept by that one, which was hidden by the swollen stream.

But in spite of the keen observation of the sailors and the sharp look-out by the doctor and the two lads, that day passed without the familiar sandy embayment among the trees being sighted, and before long it became a certainty that they were gliding along a different channel to any they had passed before.

The flood might have altered the stream to a certain extent, but they passed banks that were certainly different, and just at dusk when a brisk breeze was blowing they glided through an opening among the trees which did not seem familiar, and the question arose, should they turn back?

But before it was settled, darkness fell, and another dismal night was passed.

The next day broke bright and fine, and encouraged thereby, every man was keenly on the alert to try and sight one of the Spaniard's halting-places; but it was long before such an opening was found, and then when it was hailed with delight as their resting-place at the end of that day's work, it was forced upon them that they had never been there before.

Fortunately, though their stores were diminished in quantity, fish were plentiful, and every now and then a bird fell to Rodd's or the doctor's gun, for it was felt to be a necessity, as more and more all realised that they were involved in a perfect labyrinth or network of watery ways, and that their stores should be supplemented. For opening after opening in the great walls of verdure kept presenting itself, nearly always involving the party in a dispute as to whether they had been there before, till their mental confusion became greater, their ideas more sadly confused, and the tract of low-lying water-netted country, far from seeming the paradise through which they had glided on their way up, now seemed the dwelling-place of despair.

"Isn't there one of you who can guide us aright?" cried the doctor despairingly. "Is it possible that what seemed so easy to that treacherous Spanish wretch should prove such a horrible problem to us all?"

For a time no one spoke, the men hanging their heads, and by way of showing their earnestness tugging harder at their oars. But at the next appeal Joe Cross was egged on to make some answer.

"You see, sir," he said, "there isn't anything we wouldn't do for you. The lads here are sharp enough, but they wants a handle to work them. We are only sailors, used to having an officer over us, and without him we aren't much account."

"Oh," groaned the doctor to Rodd, "and I cannot direct them! Rodd, boy, my brain feels as if it were giving way."

"Don't be down-hearted, sir. Don't chuck up your pluck, young gentlemen," continued the poor fellow earnestly. "We must get out at last. It all seemed so easy as we come up; but without that Spanish chap, and now that it seems to be all turned upside down like, as we are coming back'ards, it's like looking for a needle in a bottle of hay. You see, me and my messmates have turned it all over in our heads, and it always comes to this, that that storm either made us take a wrong turning, or else that that

Spaniard took us into a tangle of watercourses out of which no one but him and them niggers could find the way."

"Yes, yes," said the doctor; "we were thoroughly trapped into what has proved to be a horrible maze."

"Ay, ay, sir!" cried Joe. "And amazing it is; but we are not going to give up, sir. Wish we may all die if we do; for you see, it must all come right at last. We have a lot of provisions, plenty of powder and shot; we can't fail for fresh water, which is a great thing for sailors; there's wood enough to make fires for five hundred years; and as for good fish to eat, why, you could almost catch them with your hands."

"No, my men," said the doctor, more firmly, "we are not going to despair, for if we keep going down-stream we must reach the main river at last."

"That's what I keep thinking, uncle," cried Rodd; "but every time we turn out of one of these rivers we seem to get into another, and I want to know why it is that we have never yet come upon a sandy patch where we made a fire."

Embayments of this kind they found again and again during the next few days of their, so to speak, imprisonment in this labyrinth, and in which they were fain to halt for food and sleep; but whether the flood had obliterated all signs of their occupation, or whether the places were absolutely fresh, they never knew.

One thing was determined on, and that to keep on with dogged British obstinacy till the problem was solved, and after losing count of the days that they had spent in the forest, and after vain usage of the compass, which had only seemed to lead them more and more astray, they had their reward one noon, when the boat was run up on to the sand of a forest nook which seemed strikingly familiar, and Rodd and Morny both sprang out, gun in hand, followed by Joe Cross, who excitedly cried—

"All right, gentlemen! Here we are at last! I'd just swear to this tree and that other big one right across the river."

"Yes," cried the doctor; "this, I am quite certain, is where we set up our tent the night we missed our guide."

"The morning, uncle," cried Rodd. "Yes, boy; I should have said the morning. Look, Morny! You do not speak. Isn't this our last halting-place on our way up?"

The French lad gave his hands a despairing wave in the air.

"Yes," he said; "that's what I feel, sir. Why, we have been all these weary, weary days trying to get back to the river so that we might row away to the brig, and this is the spot from which we started!"

"Well, gentlemen," cried Joe Cross, "I say hooray to that. Yes, this is the place, aren't it, messmates?"

"Yes, yes," came in an excited chorus, for the discovery seemed to have sent a thrill of joy through all the men.

"That's right, messmates," cried Joe. "Then all we have got to do now, gentlemen, is to try and take our bearings right, rub the wet dust out of all our eyes, and make a fresh start."

"The wet dust, Joe!" cried Rodd, with the nearest approach to a smile which had appeared upon his face for many days. "Here, uncle, get out the compass, and let's see what we can do with that."

"No," said the doctor quietly. "We must make a fresh start, but it must be calmly and well, and after food and a good night's rest. Collect wood, my lads, to make a fire. Boys, take your guns and go up-stream a little higher where we have never been before, and shoot what birds you can. Two or three of you men do what you can from the shore with the fishing-lines. To-morrow morning we will start calmly and trustingly to the river once again. Be of good heart, Morny, my lad, for the end of our awful struggle must be coming near, and every one of us must do all he can to help his brother for the one great end."

A cheer rose at the doctor's words, and the change in the whole party was wonderful.

All worked with such energy that long before darkness set in the tent was rigged up for the night, a good meal had been prepared, and almost as full of hope as on the night when they had last encamped there for their rest, a couple of hours were pleasantly passed before the fire was once more made up and the watch set. Very soon afterwards all were plunged in a deep and restful sleep, one from which Rodd and Morny were startled by a terrific clap of thunder. Then the interior of their tent was lit up by a vivid blue flash of lightning, by which they saw the watch—Joe Cross and one of the sailors leaning over them, the former saying—

"There's going to be an awful—"

"Storm," he would have said, but his words were drowned by another crash which came instantly upon a sheet of lightning, and pretty well stunned them with its roar.

Chapter Forty Five
Storm Waters

In the intervals between the almost incessant peals of thunder Joe Cross informed the lads that the storm had been coming on for the last three hours, faint and distant at first, the merest mutterings, and gradually increasing till it was the terrific tempest now raging.

"They must have had it horrid, sir, somewhere, only I don't suppose there's no people. What we had before was nothing to it."

"There," cried the doctor, "something must be done to the boat in the way of making it thoroughly secure."

"Can't be no securer, sir. We've got her moored head and stern to a tree, and two grapnels down as well."

"Capital," cried the doctor. "Well thought of! But we must have the sail and some of the canvas that we have got here spread over the boat to keep the water out."

"That's done, sir, as far as the stuff would go, and now I want what we have got up here, before the rain comes."

"Down with it at once," said the doctor; and in an incredibly short space of time the tent was struck, what they had ashore was transferred to the boat, and she was covered in as much as was possible.

And none too soon, for the party had only just embarked when a few heavy drops of rain came pattering down upon the tightened canvas, soon increasing to quite a deluge, but, with the peculiarity of a tropic storm, just when it was beginning to try the canvas and threatening to soak the interior of the boat, it ceased almost instantaneously, and they sat listening to the rushing sound of the rain as it swept over the forest, rapidly growing more distant till it died away.

"Gone!" cried Rodd excitedly. "We didn't want any more troubles, and it would have been dreadful to have been wet through again."

"Don't be too hopeful, my boy," said Uncle Paul. "That may only be the advance guard of a far worse storm. It seems too much to think this is the end."

"It might be all, sir," said Joe Cross, "for it's been an awful bad 'un, going on for hours in the distance."

"Then we shall be having the water rise again," cried Uncle Paul.

"Yes, sir; that's what I thought," replied the man, "and why I moored the boat so fast."

"Quite right," cried the doctor, "for likely enough we shall be having the water coming down from far away, and we must hold on here at any cost, or we shall be lost again."

"What time do you suppose it is, Joe?" asked Rodd.

"Wants about a couple of hours to daylight, sir."

"Morning!" cried the lads together. "Ah, then it will be easier to bear!"

During the rest of the darkness it was evident that the storm had passed over them. There were a few distant mutterings of thunder and little flickerings of lightning which grew fainter and fainter, to die away in the west.

The sailors crept out from beneath their awning on to the sand, and were able to announce that the river had only risen a few inches, and the rain that had fallen had rapidly soaked in and drained off, while a pleasant cool air swept briskly over them from the east, heralding a fresh bright dawn, which came at last with all the promise of a glorious day.

With some difficulty a fire was started, but once begun the men soon contrived to get up sufficient for the hurried breakfast; the canvas was struck where necessary, and the rest spread to dry in the coming sunshine; and then all being ready for their next start, the doctor consulted with the coxswain, who after a little pressing gave his opinion as to what would be the best course to take.

"You see, sir," he said, "I have been thinking that I could get us back to our last camping-place; I mean, before we came here."

"Well, that's what we all thought before, Joe," cried Rodd pettishly.

"Wait, Rodney, my boy, and let Cross finish," said the doctor.

"I've about done, sir," said the man. "What Mr Rodd says is quite true, but he aren't quite got what I mean. You see, sir, when we come up here with the Spanish skipper aboard I sat astern steering, and when we went away again I had hold of the tiller once more, same as before."

"Well, we know that," said Rodd shortly. "Be silent, Rodney!" cried the doctor. "Go on, Cross."

"Well, sir, when we come I was looking this 'ere way; when we started back I was looking t'other way. Now it seems to me, now we are going to start again, if instead of sitting astern and looking straight forward, if I was to go and sit right in the bows and left somebody else to steer while I looked over his head, I should be looking up both sides of the river just as it was when we were coming, and I should see the landmarks again as I saw them when we were coming here, and consekently I should know my way better, and I don't think I should miss the next landing-place again."

"Yes, I see what you mean," cried Rodd excitedly. "Why, to be sure, Joe! Don't you see, uncle?"

"Yes," cried the doctor. "Quite right, Cross. We will start at once, going as slowly as we can, and we will, all but the steersman, ride backwards, keep a sharp look-out, and help. — What's the matter, Morny?"

For the young Frenchman had suddenly started up in the boat, to stand peering in the direction that they were about to take, and held up his hand as if to command silence.

"What's that?" cried Rodd, leaping up too.

"What?" asked the doctor.

"Sounds like distant roaring of some kind of wild beast, sir," said one of the men.

"That it aren't, messmate," said Joe, who had also risen to his feet, and stood with his hand behind his ear. "It's another storm coming. Nay, it aren't. It's all bright and clear that way. Why, it's water, gentlemen, coming with a rush from just the way we want to go."

"Impossible!" cried the doctor. "Why, it would be against the stream."

"I don't care, sir, begging your pardon. I've been in the Trent and the Severn and the Wye. It was only when I was a boy, but I recollect right enough. It's what they used to call a bore, with a great wave of water coming up the river like a flood and washing all before it."

"Had we better land?" cried the doctor.

"And lose our boat, sir? No. Be smart, my lads. It can't be very far away. All eight of you, oars out, and we must keep our head to it so as we can ride over the big wave and let it pass under us. I don't suppose there will be much of it. It's a sort of flood water coming down from yonder after the storm, and it will soon be over. Don't you worry about it, gentlemen. It will be nothing to a big wave at sea."

The men made ready with all the discipline of a trained crew, and heads were turned in the direction of the increasing sound, while it seemed hard to believe, in the midst of the brilliant sunshine, with the smooth river gliding onwards as if to meet the supposed wave, that there could be anything wrong.

The expected danger had seemed to be close at hand, but it had been far more distant than the party had supposed, for the roar went on steadily increasing, but with no other suggestion of peril save the noise, though that was enough to make the stoutest-hearted there quail.

It seemed an age, but was certainly less than an hour, before the dull heavy roar began to be mingled with a strange crashing and breaking sound which puzzled all, till the coxswain, who was standing up in the bows, boat-hook in hand, announced that it was the breaking of trees and crashing together of their branches as they were being torn up by the roots.

"Impossible!" said the doctor impatiently.

"Nay, sir, it aren't," said the man. "I don't mean the big trees, but the little 'uns along the banks; and it's getting close here, sir. It's a big flood, that's what it is, coming down from the mountains, for there must be some inland. There! Look yonder. Can't you see the trees beginning to wave? It's just as if a lake had broke loose and was coming sweeping over the country. You, Harry Briggs, hold fast to that tiller. You others, look at your work, and pull. Turn your heads, you lubbers! I'll do all the looking out. And when I say row, every mother's son of you pull for his life."

Joe Cross's words were beginning to sound indistinct before he had finished, half-smothered as they were by the increasing roar, as from far down the river a dark line of something could be seen rising some six or eight feet like a huge bank extending right across the river and apparently into the forest on both sides.

For as far as eye could reach the trees seemed to be in a strange state of agitation, the lower branches bending towards the party in the boat, as if beneath the blast of a tremendous gale.

"Sit fast, boys, every one!" yelled Joe; but he stood upright himself, and the next minute with a wild rush a great bank of water was upon them, seeming to come with a leap and dash, to plunge beneath the boat's bows as if to toss her on high and roll her over and over in the flood. But as it struck them the trained men sat for a moment or two, till in little more than a whisper above the roar of water, Joe Cross's voice was heard to give the order "Pull," when seven balanced oars dipped together, and the bows began to sink.

The men got well hold of the water, and after three or four rapid tugs the boat sat level once more upon the surface of the flood, obeyed her helm, and though being carried rapidly along stern on, she shipped very little water, and in a very few minutes the greater peril was passed.

The crashing roar and rush of the water was almost deafening, but Joe retained his upright position and signalled with one hand to the steersman, while he followed suit to the rowers, who kept up a steady pull against the furious stream, with the result that now the boat sped on stern foremost at the same rate as the flood.

But the frail craft was exposed to endless risks as the water rushed along between the two great walls of verdure which marked out the devious winding course of the river. Time after time they were within an ace of being swept amidst the boughs of some towering tree; at others they were brushing over the tops of the shrub-like growth; and yet amidst the many dangers the crew never flinched, but kept on for hour after hour, head to stream, with the boat always being borne onward along straight reaches and round winding curves which looped and almost doubled back, till at last the violence of the flood grew less, leaving them more and more behind, till the greatest danger was over and the speed at which they glided was reduced to nearly half that of the first rush of the flood.

Another hour passed, and they were still gliding on, and now as they were swept into a wider reach, it was plain to see how the whole forest was flooded on either side, apparently to the depth of some six or eight feet, as near as the coxswain could judge.

Four times over he had drawn attention to the fact that they were passing the entrances to similar rivers to that down which they sped, one of them being remarkable for the fact that a portion of their stream set right into it, while from the others it glided out in the opposite way. Soon afterwards, with a little clever scheming, the boat was guided into an eddy where the water swirled round comparatively slack; and here her head was turned and she resumed her strange journey onward in the normal way.

The men's labour too now had pretty well ceased, only a dip or two of the oars being required occasionally to keep the boat's head straight and make her answer her helm.

And now conversation became more general. The danger being evidently over, one man hazarded a joke, something about a near shave, while another said it was a pity because they would have all this 'ere work to go over again.

Joe Cross heard the remark, and this started him talking, as he laid down his boat-hook and wiped his streaming face.

"Yes, Mr Rodd," he said, "you wanted to come farther up the river, and here you have had it. Well, I suppose when the flood's spread all over it will do same as they always does, begin to drain off again and carry us back. But I am afraid, Dr Robson, sir, that I must give up what I undertook to do."

"What?" cried the doctor.

"Ride back'ards, sir, and find the way out of this wet cat's-cradle of a place. I am very sorry, sir."

"Sorry!" cried the doctor cheerily. "My good fellow, what you have done during the last few hours has earned the lasting gratitude of us all."

"Has it, sir?" said the man, staring. "Why?"

"Haven't you saved all our lives," cried the doctor, "by your clever management of the boat?"

"Oh, that's what you mean, sir! But you must play fair, sir. You mustn't blame me for that. Part on it's my being on board a man-of-war; part on it's due to Captain Chubb. So you must thank him."

The doctor smiled, and noting this absence of anxiety, Rodd broke out with—

"I say, uncle, Morny's starving. Isn't it time we had something to eat?"

"Oh, Rodd!" cried Morny.

"Yes, of course," replied the doctor. "See what you can do, cook, at once. But surely, Cross, some of the men might lay in their oars?"

"Yes, sir, and if it goes on like this I don't see that we need let this flood keep on carrying us farther away. There's a nice wind, and not so much washed-out wood afloat. I am thinking I might have the sail hoisted and begin to sail back. But my word, look here: how we are widening out, sir! Look ahead yonder. It's getting 'most like a lake. Perhaps it is one."

"No," cried Rodd; "it's the river still. Look yonder at the forest right along the bank."

"Yes, sir, but I was looking at the forest on both sides here where we are. Why, we are running into another river. It aren't a lake, but it's ten times as big as this one that we've been spinning along, and— Well! it's a rum 'un! No; it's unpossible."

"What's impossible?" cried Rodd sharply, and all gazed at the sailor, who sat looking forward, holding on by one ear and scratching the other.

"Why, this 'ere, Mr Rodd, sir. Just you look, Dr Robson, and see what you think on it."

"Of what, my man?"

"Why, this 'ere, sir, what I am asking you of. Can't you see, Mr Rodd, sir?"

"I can see that we are gliding out of a muddy stream covered with green twigs and great tufts of jungle grass, into a big river flowing right across us and all thick with what seems to be a different-coloured mud."

"That's right, sir; and didn't you see that splash, just as far off as you could look?"

"No, Joe."

"Would you mind lending me that there glass of yourn, sir?" said Joe to the doctor, who passed the little field-glass to the man, whose hands trembled as he focussed it to suit his eye, and he once more stood up in the boat and swept the water as far as he could see.

"Thank you, sir," he said, handing it back. "Perhaps you would like to have a look yourself. But it's all right, gentlemen, and my lads. Them's crocs out yonder, and we have been washed out into the big river again with no more trouble; and if we don't see our brig and our schooner again before many hours, why, my name aren't Joe!"

Chapter Forty Six
A Knot in the Network

Incredulity was impossible, although at first it was very hard to believe. But there was the fact. They had been wandering through the sluggish network of streams of a vast tropic, marshy forest, until a tremendous storm in the hinterland had flooded the low country and they had been swept out again far away from the spot where the Spanish captain had guided them in, and, as they were soon to learn, for reasons of his own.

Without question they had descended some miles along the main river, which ran swiftly, burdened as it was by the waters of the flood, but not sufficiently to do more than raise it to a rather abnormal height. Still it was not safe to continue their journey downward by night, and in spite of the anxiety of all, the boat was moored to a huge tree up which the water had risen some three or four feet, and all anxiously watched for the coming of the next day. They slept but little, for there was so much to discuss, the doctor feeling now sure that when they missed the Spanish captain it must have been because when all were asleep he had stolen down to where the two blacks would be waiting for him with their canoe, and then gone on up the river beyond their camp.

"But I don't see quite what for, uncle," said Rodd.

"I do," cried Moray. "He knew the country so well, and our ignorance, which would make us go wandering helplessly about, while he knew of a nearer way out into this river again, through which we seem to have been providentially swept."

"That's right—quite right, Moray," said the doctor. "You see now, Rodd?"

"Yes, uncle, it's quite clear now. I wish I wasn't so dense. Do you see, Joe?"

"I didn't afore, sir; but it's all as clear as crystal now, and I should just like to explain it to the lads. My word, gentlemen! That chap's been running up a big bill again hisself, and when we get hold of him he'll have to pay!"

"What are you thinking of, Moray?" said Rodd, a little while after, while they were sitting listening in the darkness to the murmur of Joe's voice forward as he was explaining matters to the men.

"I was thinking," said Moray gravely, "of how long it would be before it is day."

The longest night comes to an end, and the breaking of that next day showed the river much sunken and pretty well at its normal tidal height; and with four men rowing steadily the boat glided downward, with the sun when it rose showing first one and then another landmark which seemed familiar; but after their one journey upward no one present could recall how far they were above the careening place.

Again and again as they passed round some great bend Moray rose from his seat, and, as Rodd afterwards told him, made them all miserable by gazing wildly downwards in the expectation of catching sight of the brig, or of seeing his father in his boat coming upward in search of the missing ones, who had quite outstepped the time that their stay was to last.

It was always the same; the poor fellow sank back into his place wearily, his countenance drawn and a look of despair in his eyes. At such times Rodd would watch his opportunity, steal his hand quietly along, and give Morny's arm a long and friendly grip, with the result that the dim eyes would brighten a little and dart a grateful glance in the English lad's direction.

The journey downwards seemed endless, and proved to be far longer than any one there anticipated. But just as the longest and darkest watch nights come to their end, so it was here, when, skimming along under sail, taking long reaches, for the wind was abeam, all at once Joe Cross, who was the first to see, sang out a loud and hearty—

"Ship ahoy!"

"Hah!" cried Morny. "Do you see the brig?"

"No, sir," replied the man, as Morny, the doctor and Rodd shaded their eyes and gazed down-stream; "I can't make out the brig."

"Oh, you don't half look," cried Rodd. "There's the Spanish schooner, and ours, and just beyond them, half hidden by the trees and land, there are the tops of the masts of the brig. Hurrah, Morny! She's all right, afloat, and— Here, what are you looking that way for?"

"Because I can't see her," said the French lad despairingly. "There is something wrong."

"Why, my dear old chap," cried Rodd, "you can't see well, because of the trees, but as we get farther out, there she lies, to the left, with her two masts as plain as plain."

"I can see those two masts you mean," said Morny sternly, "but they are low-down raking masts; the *Dagobert's* are much higher, and stand up stiffer than those. Do you forget she's square-rigged? Why, that's a schooner."

"So it is," cried Rodd. "I was deceived by the two yards on her foremast. But look here, it can't be another schooner. Captain Chubb may have been altering her rig when he got her upright again. Why, of course! It must be so. There can't be three schooners there. They must have had some accident to the brig's mainmast when they raised her again. Broke her topgallant, perhaps, and rigged her fore and aft."

"Not they, Mr Rodd, sir. Our old man would have cut a spar somewhere from the forest and rigged her square, if it was only a jury-mast. 'Sides, they'd got spare spars on board, same as we. That's another schooner. You can see her clearer now — a long low one, with masts that rake more than the Spanish skipper's vessel. Strikes me as we shall find that for some reason or another they haven't got the brig afloat."

"Another schooner, Joe?" cried Morny passionately. "The brig not finished? For some reason or another! What reason? What does it all mean?"

"Be calm, my lad; be calm," cried the doctor. "In a very little while we shall know the worst, or the best. Mind, we know nothing as yet. It is all suspicion. For aught we can say to the contrary, that man whom we have condemned may be innocent, misjudged by us, and now be lying at the bottom of the river where we missed him in that mysterious way."

Morny bowed his head and tried to look gratefully at the doctor; but his agony was too great, and he stood there till their boat had got to the end of its tack and swung round in the other direction, when with shaded eyes he gazed before him wildly, trying to get a view beyond where the three schooners could now be plainly seen, anchored in mid-stream.

But for some time the curvature of the river put this out of the question, and to break the painful silence the doctor said quietly —

"Another long low schooner, with raking masts. But it may be only another trader, anchored in company with the rest."

"Ah," cried Morny to Joe Cross, "you see something more than we do!" For the man, who was looking out from beyond the sail, suddenly gave a start and angrily slapped his thigh.

"Well, I'm very sorry, sir; but yes, I do. The brig's lying careened right over, just as she was when we started on our trip."

"But look here, Morny," cried the doctor; "that may mean nothing more than that she is not finished yet. Remember, to those we left we are missing, and in their anxiety about our lengthened stay they may have started upstream to find us."

"You are saying this to comfort me," cried Morny passionately. "No, doctor; we have got to face the worst. It is not so."

It seemed cruelty to prolong the conversation, and soon after the order was given to lower the sail and unstep the mast, for the wind had pretty well dropped as they swept in towards where the vessels were anchored, and the distance being short, the men took to their oars once more, while, with no impediment to their view, the doctor took out his glass and offered it to Morny. But the lad made a quick gesture, and sat back looking straight before him, while the doctor used the glass himself, gazing with it first at the brig, about whose hull no one was visible, while all seemed still on board the three schooners.

"Take a look, Rodney," said the doctor aloud, as he handed the glass. "I can see nothing wrong."

Rodd eagerly took the glass, raised it to his eyes, and said quietly—

"Why, I can't see a soul on board the *Sally*, uncle, and the people on the other schooners must be asleep. They haven't seen us yet— Yes, they have!" he cried. "The men are hurrying up on our vessel from below, but—"

"But what, my boy?"

"I—I don't quite know, uncle. Something isn't right. Oh, Morny, what have I said?"

As the boy spoke he let the glass drop to the full length of his arm, and in all probability it would have fallen to the bottom of the boat had not Joe Cross caught it in his hand.

"May I look, sir?" he said sharply, and without waiting for consent, he raised it to his eyes and quickly scanned all three of the schooners in turn.

"It's no use beating about, gentlemen," he said sharply. "Something is wrong, for all three decks are swarming now with men like bees—wasps, I ought to say," he muttered, as he concentrated his gaze upon the *Maid of Salcombe*. "Our vessel, doctor, is in the hands of pirates, or slavers, and they are making ready the long gun. Now, my lads, look alive. Every man buckle on his arms and then load."

The oars were allowed to swing from the tholes, and the boat was left to glide slowly downwards, while in their smart orderly way her crew prepared for action.

"You will load too, gentlemen—with ball. Now, doctor, will you take command and lead us?"

"What to do?" asked the doctor.

"Why, to take our schooner again, sir. She's in the hands of an enemy."

"But is it possible that we can do this, Cross?" cried the doctor.

"I don't know, sir, for she's got a lot of men on board; but we have got to try."

"Stop. Let me think," said the doctor. "I am no man of war, and this is not in my way. If any unfortunate fellow were wounded I could do my best. But look here, my lads; you are nearly all men-of-war's men, and you, Morny, you are a naval officer. Seeing the odds before us, what is our duty here?"

"To fight," cried the young man passionately, through his clenched teeth.

"Ay, ay, sir!" came heartily from the men; and as the doctor turned his eyes inquiringly upon Rodd, who was fiercely ramming the second bullet upon the small shot already in the two barrels of his gun, he saw a look in the lad's face that he had never seen there before, and in spite of the pain of the situation, he felt a thrill of satisfaction running through his breast at the thought that, young as his nephew was, he was English to the core.

"Yes," said the doctor, "we must fight; but with such odds against us we must bring cunning to bear."

"Ay, ay, sir! That's right," cried Cross. "But perhaps, as we've got right on our side and only a set of mongrels before us, a good bold dash to board them will make us as strong as they. I say, sir, if you will let me lead, we will try and take our schooner, give them a broadside of bullets when we get close up, and then out steel and board her like men. Once over her side, there won't be many of them left on deck at the end of five minutes; and as soon as we have got her and the use of her guns, if we don't sink them other two pirates I have never been to sea."

"That's right, Joe," came in chorus, as, standing in the bows with one hand upon his gun, the other upon his right hip, he looked the very perfection of a British man-of-war's man, ready to lead or be led, wherever duty called.

Then, as if inspired by his appearance, the crew burst out into a ringing cheer, helped by the two lads, while the doctor took off and waved his straw hat as he joined in. *Bang—thud!*

A great grey puff of smoke started from the schooner's deck and a ball came skipping in their direction over the smooth stream.

"Well, I do call that too bad," cried Joe, as the men uttered a deep-toned "Yah–h–h!"

"Arter the way in which I cared for you and kept you clean, to go and behave like that!"

"Well, poor dumb beast," growled Briggs, "she don't know no better."

"Do you call that dumb?" cried Joe, merrily enough. "Well, I s'pose she was obliged; but I don't think much of their gunnery, messmates," continued the man, as he made use of the glass again. "Oh, they're all at work, sir, re-loading, and it will soon be our turn. I propose, sir, that we let them give us another shot, and then dash in before they have time to re-load. They won't hit us; will they, boys?"

"Not they!" came in chorus; but the next moment there was another report, and a smaller ball struck the water so near the boat that the spray was sent flying over them.

"They've got the two small guns to bear, sir," said Joe quietly, "and there's somebody aboard as knows how to aim."

He had hardly ceased speaking when there was another puff of smoke from the schooner's deck, accompanied by a whizzing, shrieking sound through the air just above their heads, while before they had glided with the stream another dozen yards there was a puff of smoke from the three-master's deck, followed directly after by a puff from the strange schooner, and as the reports of the two heavy guns were echoed from the great walls of verdure upon the river's bank, the air over their heads seemed full of shrieking missiles.

"Grape and broken iron," growled Joe Cross. "Take the tiller, Harry Briggs. Step the mast, my lads, and run up the sail. Don't take no notice of their shot. It don't do to go mad, even if we do want to fight. Don't go to sleep over it, boys. We are in the breeze again, and we must run into shelter and think."

A low growl came from the men as they rapidly obeyed orders, and not a man seemed to flinch as the long gun of the English schooner sent forth its heavy missile again, this time to strike the water some distance ahead and then rise and go crashing amongst the trees, whose leaves could be seen to come pattering down.

Three more shots came skipping over the river before the boat began to glide swiftly, under the pressure of her sail, and yells of derision came ringing from the enemy as they saw the effect of their fire and the effort being made to escape.

"Ah!" half sighed Rodd. "They've left off."

"Ay, sir," said the coxswain. "They know they can't hit us now we are flying through the water; and the worst of it is, they think we are afraid and that we English dogs are running away as hard as we can, with our tails between our legs. But they aren't, sir; they're a-standing up stiff and at right angles, as our old man calls it, to our backs; eh, messmates?"

"Ay, ay, Joe!" came from the crew, with a roar of laughter.

"And as for my teeth—our teeth, I mean—they are about as sharp as sharp. But we have got the wind with us, gentlemen, and we will just run up-stream and round the bend yonder, so as to get behind the trees just somewhere where we can keep watch with that there little spy-glass, and by and by we will have another try. This go they a'n't played fair, but next time we'll make 'em."

"How, Joe?" cried Rodd.

"Well, sir, my idea is to tackle 'em man to man when they can't use their guns. I mean when it's too dark for them to aim; and then we can drop down upon them, or sail up to them fore or aft or either side, and them not know where to have us. It won't be shooting then, but cold steel, as we know how to use. Well, think of that now!" cried the man, as the boat was now literally skimming over the surface. "Call myself a leader! Why, as true as I am here, I never once thought of firing a shot. Why, we might have given them one volley, messmates. I don't suppose we should have hit, with them behind the bulwarks, but we might have startled the beggars at the guns. Never mind; we have saved our gunpowder. A man must miss sometimes, and this has been a bad 'un. Next time, though, my lads, we must make it a hit."

The sailor ceased speaking, for his eyes had suddenly lighted upon Morny's face, and, as he afterwards said to Rodd, "Blest, sir, it sent a regular chill through me, for in all the hooroar of that job I forgot all about his father and our old man. But never say die, sir. They may have got away in one of the boats and be coasting along out to sea."

Chapter Forty Seven
Fireworks

The boat was well run up out of reach and sight of the enemy, a spot being selected where by a little manoeuvring beneath the shade of an overhanging tree a few boughs could be pressed aside and a watch kept upon the movements of those on board the schooners, in case of their boats coming in pursuit, or, what was quite probable, one or other of the vessels heaving anchor and coming up with the tide.

But the time wore on without any sign being made, and as far as could be made out through the glass, the Spaniards seemed to be quite content with beating off the attack, and from their movements they had apparently come to the conclusion that they had seen the last of the occupants of the boat.

But they did not know the temper of those on board, nor that a quiet little council of war had been going on, till, feeling the necessity for the men being properly prepared ready for any fresh attempt, the doctor suggested that a substantial meal should be made; and this was partaken of with a far better appetite than could have been expected. More than one plan had been suggested regarding the next proceedings. One was that they should steal down the river under cover of the darkness and go in search of their friends; another, that an attempt should be made, when the tide was flowing most swiftly, to cut the cables, in the hope that the vessels might drift ashore; but Joe Cross disposed of this directly as not likely to be of any permanent advantage, and declared that there was only one thing to be done, and that was, to follow up with another bold attempt to board.

"You see, gentlemen," he said, "we never had a chance to get within touch of the Spanish mongrels. I don't want to brag, but with a fair start there aren't one of our chaps here as wouldn't take a good grip of his cutlass and go for any three of them; eh, messmates?"

"In an or'nary way, Joe," said Harry Briggs.

"Well, this is an or'nary way, messmate."

"Nay; I call this a 'stror'nary one."

"Well, speak out, messmate, and say what you mean."

"Well, same as you do, Joe, only I put it a little different. Win or lose, I'd go in for tackling three of them in an or'nary way, but I says this is a 'stror'nary one, and you may put me down for six, and if I get the worst of it, well, that'll be a bit of bad luck. But anyhow I'd try."

"And so say all of us," came from the rest.

"Well," said Joe, laughing, "I never knew afore that I was the most modest chap in our crew."

"Oh, I have no doubt about your courage, my lads," said the doctor, "nor that my nephew here, though he is a boy, will fight like a man; but if we are to do any good we must work with method against such great odds. So now, Cross, let us hear what you propose to do."

"Try again, sir—in the dark—and play a bit artful."

"But how?" cried Rodd eagerly.

"Well, I'll tell you, Mr Rodd. I proposes that we just show ourselves once or twice towards evening, and then make a dash right across the river to hide again among the trees. That'll set 'em all thinking and asking one another what our game's going to be. Then we will lie up till it's dark, up with the grapnel, and steal quietly down the river, keeping pretty close to the trees, till we are about opposite the enemy, and then we'll make a mistake."

"Make a mistake?" said Rodd. "I don't understand you."

"Well, sir, I aren't done yet. What I mean is, have an accident like; one of us sneeze, or burst out a-coughing, and me break out into a regular passion, calling him as coughed a stoopid lubber and a fool for showing the enemy where we are. It will be best for me to be him as coughs or sneezes, and do it all myself so as not to have any muddle over it. Then I shouts out, 'Pull for your lives, boys—pull!' And we makes no end of splashing as we goes on down the river, and all the time as supposing that it's going to be dark enough so as they can't fire at us. Then it seems to me, Dr Robson, sir, that the enemy will say to theirselves, 'They want to get out to sea, and they are gone,' while as soon as we have got a bit lower down we'll lie up under the trees and wait till about an hour before daylight, and all as quiet and snug as so many rats. They'll think they have got rid of us, and all the while we shall be waiting our time to steal up again right by 'em and begin to come down once more from where they don't expect; and then—board."

"Hah!" cried Rodd. "Capital!"

"You see, gentlemen, it'll all have to be done as quiet as quiet, for they're sure to have a watch set. I know what out-and-outers they are to sleep, but it's too much to expect that they will have both eyes shut at a time like this. One way or t'other we shall have the tide with us, but even if we don't I think it might be managed, and anyhow we shall have no big guns at work upon us, and watch or no watch we'll manage to lay this 'ere boat alongside of our schooner, and if any one says anything again' our getting aboard, I should like to know why, and if we do get aboard I don't think it's in the schooner's new crew to drive us back again into the boat. There, gentlemen, that's all I know, and if some one else—the doctor here, or Mr Rodd, or Mr Morny, who is a French naval officer—can give us a better way, I'll follow anywhere, and I know the lads will come after me like men."

There was silence for about a minute, and then the doctor coughed, drawing all eyes upon him.

"There is no better way," he said. "It's a splendid plan."

A murmur of assent arose, and Joe Cross looked quite modest.

"But it will be some time yet before we can make our attempt," said the doctor; "and how are we to pass the weary time till then?"

"Oh," said Joe cheerily, "we can watch these 'ere great smiling efts till then. They seem to be sailing about and watching us as if they'd got some sort of an idea that they were to have us to eat by and by, which I don't mean that they shall. And then there'll be making the false starts. I think, sir, as we'll make one or two, as if we was half afraid to make a dash for it, and that'll draw their fire."

"But suppose they hit us, Joe," cried Rodd.

"Oh, we must chance that, sir. They can't hit us. They couldn't hit a hay-stack in a ten-acre field; let alone a boat being pulled hard across stream. That'll be all right."

And so it proved when Joe Cross put his tactics into force, making the men row out into the river, and then ordering them to lie on their oars, while Rodd watched the schooner's decks and announced that some of the men were busy about the guns and all crowding to the bulwarks to watch the proceedings of the boat.

Then a feint was made in one direction, then in another, and at last Joe stood up in the stern, to begin gesticulating to the men, as if bullying them into making a bold dash to row swiftly down as near the farther shore as they could go.

A minute later two puffs of smoke from different vessels shot out into the clear evening air, the balls ricochetting from the water in each case a few yards away. Then, with the men pulling as hard as ever they could, the boat's head was swung round, and rowing diagonally across the stream they made for the shelter of the shore from which they had come, the sail was hoisted, filled, and away they went till they were right round the bend and the anchored schooners were out of sight.

"There, Mr Rodd, sir, what did I tell you?" cried Joe triumphantly. "I knew they couldn't hit us. Chaps like them ought never to be allowed to handle a gun."

"Well, my man," said the doctor, "if the rest of your plan will only succeed like this we shall achieve a victory."

"Nay, nay, sir; only a little boat action. There, my lads, now we'll have a rest. They're sure to think we have gone right up the river."

"But they may send boats to follow us," suggested Rodd.

"Certainly, sir, they may; but I don't think they will. They won't come to close quarters so long as they have got bulwarks to fight from behind and the guns to tackle us when we show. They think that we can't face the pieces. Well, I don't say as we are very ready to when there's another way round, but we haven't got long to wait before we must make another move, for the sun's down behind the trees, and I shouldn't be sorry if it was to come on a fog."

But no fog came, only darkness the blackest of the black, and the few stars that peered out only looking strangely dim.

The wind had fallen soon after the sail had been lowered and the mast laid well out of their way. One of the balls of spun yarn they had in the locker had been brought into use, cut into lengths, and the oars secured so that they could not slip away when they were left to swing, and at last under cover of the night the next part of Joe's programme was begun.

It was harder work than had been anticipated, for though the current close in shore was slack, it was very difficult to keep at a respectable distance from the bank as they glided down-stream, while every now and then there was a swirl in the water suggesting that one of the great reptiles had been disturbed.

But still the adventurers progressed, and their leader was keenly on the alert, looking out for the lights of the anchored vessels, ready to raise his false alarm as soon as he got abreast.

But he looked in vain; the Spaniards had taken the precaution to cover their riding lights, and Joe Cross was about to draw his bow at a venture, when a sharp shock which made the boat thrill suggested that they had struck upon a floating tree trunk, washed probably out of the bank during the past flood.

But the next moment they were aware that the boat's stem had come in contact with one of the crocodiles, which gave a tremendous plunge and began to send the water flying in all directions as it beat heavily upon the surface with its tail.

"Starn all!" roared Joe Cross involuntarily, and then recollecting himself, he roared out, "Pull, lads! Pull for your lives!" For a light suddenly appeared some thirty or forty yards to their left, followed by another lower down the river.

There was the buzz of voices upon the anchored vessels' decks, and Joe kept on yelling wildly to the men to pull, the noise and excitement being increased by the reports of muskets fired at them in a hurried ungoverned way, the flashes of light giving them faint instantaneous glimpses of the vessels and the faces of the men on board.

"Steady, my lads, steady! Ease off," said Joe, "gently. We have got to come back again, you know, so we needn't go too far. Two or three cables' lengths is plenty. How do you think we're getting on, sir?"

"Is it possible they may come in pursuit?" whispered the doctor.

"Nay, sir, I don't think it's likely. If it was us aboard those schooners we should think that we—meaning us—there, sir—you know what I mean—we should think t'other side was making for the sea. Well, that's what they think, and now, sir, if they'll only show their lights for the rest of the night, why, so much the better for we."

"I don't see why, Joe," said Rodd, after a few minutes' thought.

"Well, I'll tell you, my lad," whispered Joe.—"Steady there—steady! I am going to lower down the grapnel, for I dursen't run in among the trees. They'd crackle too much if we tried to moor to a branch, and we don't want to capsize. Harry Briggs, look alive, and drop the flukes overboard; make fast, and let us swing."

This was all done almost without a sound, and just then a faint gleam of light as the boat swung round showed them that certainly one of the anchored vessels was still showing her light, while as it swung round a little farther there were a couple more gleams higher up, as of distant stars.

"That's all right, gentlemen. Now, Mr Rodd, sir, I haven't answered your question. Here's just enough breeze blowing to make me alter my plans, so after a bit we'll step the mast again and have the sail ready for hoisting, for we shall be able, with the lights to guide us, to sail close up under the farther shore and come down again from just the way they don't expect, run the boat alongside our schooner, and then one on us will hold on by the boat-hook, while with the rest it's all aboard, and the schooner's ours."

That night seemed to Rodd almost as long, at times longer than the one he had passed in the tree. But here it certainly was shorter, as he afterwards declared, for about a couple of hours before daylight Joe whispered his belief that they had none of them heard the slightest sound from the direction of the lights, that if any one on board the schooner's deck would be sleeping it would be then, and that they must start at once.

There was no question of all being ready, and at the whispered orders Harry Briggs hauled softly upon the grapnel line, while very slowly and silently the yard ran up the little mast, and the boat began to career over as the sail filled.

Then with Joe Cross at the tiller she began to glide up-stream, the grapnel was lifted on board without a sound, and silently and steadily they began to cross the river diagonally till they were as near as the steersman dared lay the little craft to the farther shore.

Under his skilful management all went well, and so silently that nothing but the faint pattering lap of the water against the bows could be heard.

To the two lads, though, that sounded unusually loud, as they crouched down involuntarily but quite unnecessarily lower and lower in the boat lest they should be seen, the light hoisted in each schooner seeming bound to show the white sail to the watch of each vessel in turn.

But no alarm was raised; not a sound reached the adventurers, and to Rodd it seemed as if, after terrible periods of agony, three heavy loads had been lifted from his breast. He wanted to whisper a few words to Morny, who all through had been seated by his side, but nothing but the pressure of hand upon arm passed between them, while they could hardly hear the doctor breathe.

At last, though, that period of the terrible suspense was at an end, and the third light they had passed, that of the *Maid of Salcombe*, was beginning to grow fainter, and being left behind.

"Now, what next?" thought Rodd. "How much longer shall we have to wait before the attack is made?"

The answer came very shortly after, for Joe Cross bore lightly upon the tiller, sent the boat gliding round in a wide circle which ended by bringing the three mooring lights they had left behind all in a line, and then as they began to glide down-stream he whispered—

"It's now or never, sir.—Cutlashes, my lads; in five minutes we shall be alongside. You, Harry Briggs, shy the grapnel on deck and make fast; we shall soon be all aboard. Then come and help us all you can."

There was a low deep breath like a thrill passing through the boat, a peculiar sound of movement which Rodd knew was the men drawing their cutlasses, and then as his heart went heavily thump, thump, thump within his breast, he felt that two hands were seeking for his, and as he raised it towards the right it was grasped firmly a moment by Uncle Paul's, and the next moment, as it was released, by that of Morny.

It was short work, for the boat was gliding steadily down, and directly after the lad felt Joe Cross bending over him.

"She's just right, sir," he whispered. "Ketch hold of the tiller, and keep her as she is. I must go for'ard now to lead."

The boat swayed a little as the man stepped between his mates to the front. Then as soon as the distance was considered right a light rattling sound was heard, and Rodd was conscious of the sail being lowered, though he could see nothing of it, while almost the next minute there was a faint shock as the boat glided against the side of the schooner.

Then Joe Cross's cry, "All aboard!" rang out, followed by a stentorian cheer, and amidst the rush and hurry the tiller slipped from the boy's hand and he was climbing over the thwarts to spring into the fore-chains. Then he tottered as if about to fall back into the boat, but a big hand grasped him by the shoulder, steadied him for a moment, and then he was with the little party dashing side by side into what seemed to be a chaos of savage yells and shrieks which rose in wild confusion from the gang of Spaniards who had sprung up from their sleep, where they lay scattered about the deck.

English shouts to come on, Spanish yells, wild mongrel cries, a shriek or two of despair, a heavy plunge followed by another and another, savage blows, and utterances such as fierce men make in the wild culmination of their rage; then plunge after plunge in the water alongside and astern, the splash of swimmers, strange lashings about in the river, followed by shrieks and gurgling cries, and then, heard over all, the combined voices of so many stout Englishmen in a fierce—

"*Hurrah!*"

"Now then, all of you," shouted Joe Cross. "There's a lot of them down below. Close that cabin hatch. Two on you to the fo'c'sle; serve that the same. If you run against anybody in the dark, tell the beggar he'll be safer overboard than here."

But there proved to be no one below in the men's quarters, and after making quite sure the two men returned to their comrades. Then—

"Where's Mr Rodd?" shouted Joe.

"Here, Joe," came out of the darkness.

"Mr Morny?"

"I'm here," came in a breathless voice.

"And the doctor?"

"Helpless, Joe. My ankle's sprained."

"Bad luck to it," cried the man. "Where's Harry Briggs?"

"All right, mate," came in a gruff surly voice; "but you needn't have been in such a hurry to get it done."

"Hurry?" cried Joe. "Why, it's only just in time. Later than we thought. It's getting light. Now then, who else is hurt?"

There was a growl or two, and Joe shouted again—

"Is any one killed? Bah! Won't say so if he is! What about that boat, Harry?"

"She's fast enough, messmate."

"Hah! That's right. Now then, hold hard a moment. Hear 'em aboard the other boats?"

The question was unnecessary, for shouts and yells for help were evidently rising from men who had swum down-stream to the sides of their consorts, and ceased as they were dragged on board. But a low buzzing murmur kept on, as from a couple of wildly-excited crowds.

Then a sharp shrill voice began giving orders in Spanish, one being followed up with a pistol shot, which was succeeded by a yell and a partial cessation of the buzz of excitement that sounded as if coming from a swarm of human hornets.

"That was the Spanish captain's voice, I am sure," cried Rodd.

"Eight, sir," shouted Joe. "I'd swear to it. Well, he's getting part of his dose. Oh, if it wasn't so dark! Big gun's crew!" he cried. "Is the tackle with her?"

"Ay, ay!" came in answer, after a short bustle of movement, in which trained men took their places.

"Here, run the rammer down her throat, my lads. She may be loaded."

There was the sound of the stout ash staff passing down the bore of the gun, and the answer came—

"Right!"

"Good," replied Joe. "Lower down that light. We must use that—if we fire. But we want fresh charges, and there will be no more here."

There was a quick search made, but without result, and Joe Cross stood silent for a few moments.

"Well," cried the doctor, "why don't you send below, to the magazine?"

"Cabin hatch is closed, sir, and some of the slavers are below. This way, my lads—cutlashes. We must have them out."

"Of course!" cried Rodd excitedly, and Morny uttered a suppressed hiss, as he pressed forward, sword in hand.

"Yes, gentlemen," said Joe; "it's their doing, and they must chance the crocs, for we must clear the vessel before it's broad day."

At that moment there was a crashing sound as if the cabin hatch was being forced open, and as Joe Cross, followed by the rest, dashed aft, there was a yell, a rush, and some eight or ten of the mongrel enemy forced their way on deck, to be met at once by the schooner's crew, who charged at them as men-of-war's men know how to charge.

There was a short encounter, the clash of steel against steel, and the fresh-comers who had taken refuge below began to give way, and in a couple of minutes more the deck was once more cleared, the splashing and plunging of swimming men making for the rapidly dimming light of the next schooner being followed by more blood-curdling yells and groans, mingled with cries for help, while a few minutes later a boat could be faintly seen and efforts were evidently being made to drag the swimmers on board.

"Now then for the gun!" cried Joe.

"What are you going to do?" asked Rodd, who with Morny kept close to the coxswain's side.

"Fight, sir," replied Cross fiercely, "before they begin to fight us. See to the other guns, my lads. The way's open to the magazine now. It'll be light directly, and that Spanish skipper won't leave us long before he begins.— There, what did I say?"

For all at once the meaning of the Spaniards' orders, enforced by a pistol shot, was explained by a bright flash, the roar of a heavy gun, and the whistle of a shot just over the speaker's head.

A dead silence now fell for a few moments upon the deck of the *Maid of Salcombe*. There was a little bustle of preparation, and then a period of waiting, during which Joe Cross carefully sighted the loaded gun, depressing her muzzle all he could, the two lads the while listening excitedly to the stir and orders which came from the Spanish three-master's deck.

"Oh, fire, Joe—fire!" whispered Rodd. "We shall have another shot from her directly."

"Yes, my lad, I know; but I want to make sure of a little more light.— *Fire!*" he said, directly afterwards.

A spark was seen to sink at once upon the touch-hole of the long gun, there was a deep roar as she seemed to leap from the deck, a heavy instantaneous crash, and then a return shot which went wide of their schooner.

"You've hit, Joe," cried Rodd excitedly, as he stood amidst the smoke, which began to spread about where they gathered.

"Yes, sir, I hit," said the man, with a half-laugh, as the crew of the gun busied themselves sponging out and preparing to re-load. "They pretty well filled her to the muzzle, but they got what they meant for us. But hallo! what's the meaning of this 'ere? What's the matter with us now?"

The Mulatto—cut down by Joe Cross, who had answered the boy's call.

Only this, that the *Maid of Salcombe* was adrift and threatening, if something were not done to bring her up, to drift ashore not far from where the faint morning light revealed the brig lying right over on her side as helpless as any hulk.

Joe Cross, closely followed by the lads, ran forward to the bows, Rodd one side, Joe and Morny the other.

"Why, the cable must have broke adrift," cried the coxswain, leaning over, to see that the great rope was hanging down straight from the starboard hawse-hole.

"Cut, Joe, cut," shouted Rodd. "Quick! Look out!" For as he had leaned over the bulwarks just above the larboard hawse-hole, a great swarthy mulatto, knife in hand, was climbing up, and as soon as he caught sight of the lad he made for him at once.

Rodd stood upon his guard and managed to strike aside the thrust made at him by the mulatto; but the latter was lithe and active as a monkey. He struck at the boy again, and as Rodd gave way the fellow threw himself on to the rail and sprang over, but only to be cut down by Joe Cross, who had answered the boy's call.

It was the saving of Rodd's life, but the mulatto was dangerous still, and recovering himself he made a dash at Morny, who stepped aside, while, with all the ferociousness of a Malay running amok, the man sprang aft, avoided two or three cuts made at him by the sailors, and then plunged over the side, to begin swimming towards the three-master, which was in the act of sending another shot at the doctor's vessel.

This one crashed through the bulwarks, sending the splinters flying in all directions, and making the coxswain shout to his men to stand firm, as, seeing their perilous position, he hurried to their help, for the big schooner had slipped her cable, a sail had been run up, and she was beginning to answer her helm, while the *Maid of Salcombe* was drifting helplessly towards the shore.

It was a choice between hoisting sail and letting go another anchor while the chance was there, as the two vessels forged slowly ahead preparing to send in another shot.

This latter in his excitement Joe Cross essayed to do, striking their enemy just at the water-line as she passed them, while now the slaver's sister craft began firing as she too, hoisting sail, was coming up-stream.

"Ah!" panted the sailor, as he turned to Uncle Paul. "Here's your peaceful schooner, sir, as trades in palm-oil! Why, they are pirates and slavers, sir, and I've done it now. Too late, my lads—too late!" he cried to the men, who had let go the other anchor. "Nothing can save us now. We are going ashore."

"Oh, don't give up, man," cried the doctor angrily.

"I won't, sir. None of us will; but— There, I said as much. We just touched bottom then. There she goes again! And in another minute we shall be fast in the mud, and they'll have nothing to do but powder away at us till we are a wreck. Slew that there gun round, boys, and let's give her another shot or two while there's a chance."

"No, no," cried Rodd. "Not at that! Fire at the other. Can't you see, Joe? Uncle! Morny! The three-master's going down!"

It was quite true, for the first shot from the *Maid of Salcombe*, that sent from the long gun, crammed as Joe had said almost to the muzzle, had torn into the slaver just below water-line. The second had been just as effective in its aim, the water had been pouring in ever since, and now, as she was evidently settling down by the head, her guns were forsaken, all discipline was at an end, and her crew had made a rush for the boats, which were soon after overcrowded and being pushed off by their occupants to make for the third schooner. This last, fairly well managed, came slowly on, firing from time to time at the English craft, which, had now swung round upon her heel and lay bowsprit to the shore in a falling tide.

As far as was possible her guns were slewed round, and a steady reply to the enemy's fire was kept up; but her doom seemed to be sealed, the Spaniard being able to choose her own position, while minute by minute the English vessel was getting more helpless.

"Well, gentlemen, what's it to be?" said Joe, as he stood coolly wiping the blackened perspiration from his forehead.

"Keep on firing to the last," said the doctor sternly. "Better die like men than surrender and be murdered, for after what has passed there can be no mercy here."

"That's right, sir," said the man, "but there's the young gentlemen, and we don't any of us want to die if we can help it."

"Why, you are not beaten, are you, Joe?" cried Rodd fiercely.

"Not a bit of it, sir, but here's our schooner, and there's Mr Morny's brig. It's no use to make an ugly face over a nasty dose. We are beaten, and nothing that we could do could keep that slaver from seeing that she's won."

"Go on firing, and sink her," cried Rodd. "Look at the other one," and he pointed to the three-master, whose decks looked as if they were awash.

"Well, sir, that's what we have been trying to do; but she won't sink. How so be, here goes, my lad, for another try, and— What's the meaning of that?"

For all at once through the smoke that rose from the schooner they could see that something fresh had taken place—what, they could not make out, but it was something important, and one of the enemy's smaller guns was fired in the other direction.

"Why, there must be help coming from down the river," cried the doctor excitedly. "Yes, hark at that!"

For in reply to the schooner's gun a desultory series of musket shots began to ring out, and encouraged by this and the knowledge that help must be at hand, the little English crew sent forth a cheer, dragged the long gun more and more round, and sent one of the most successful shots they had fired crash into the enemy's stern.

To the astonishment of all, the firing on board the enemy ceased; another sail was run up, and as it filled the schooner swung round upon another tack and began to sail steadily down the river, clearing the way for those on board the English vessel to see a couple of well-manned boats being rowed steadily up-stream, with men in the stern-sheets keeping up a musketry fire.

"Quick!" shouted Moray. "Another shot! Friends! Friends!"

"Yes, sir," said Joe quietly, "but I don't see how it's to be done. Yes, we might do it from a little gun;" and he ran with a part of the crew to try and slew her round.

"No good, gentlemen," he said. "By the time we can get a shot off we shall risk hitting those boats, whatever they are, and they are coming to our help. Here, hasn't anybody got a glass?"

"No," cried Rodd; "it was left in the boat."

"Well, there's one in the cabin. Here, one of you run down."

"No, no," cried Morny excitedly; "they're our boats. Look! That's my father in one," he cried hysterically.

"And if that aren't our old man in the other my name aren't Joe Cross!"

Chapter Forty Eight
The Help that came

In those brief few minutes despair and dogged determination were turned into the mingled emotions of triumph and delight, for the two boats, after giving two or three volleys at the schooner, whose crew contented themselves with hoisting a couple more sails to increase their speed, came on as hard as the men could row, their crews cheering in French and English with all their might, while in the stern of one the Count stood up waving his cap; in that of the other Captain Chubb, looking grim and stern, stood like a statue, his left foot on the thwart before him, his right resting upon the muzzle of a musket.

"Here, I don't feel as if I'd got a cheer left in me, lads," cried Joe Cross to his tired companions on board the stranded schooner; "but we must give them one, or they'll think we aren't much obliged to them for coming, and there's no gammon about it, we are, and no mistake."

"Cheer, yes!" cried Rodd. "With all your might, my lads. Take your time from me. Now then, as you never cheered before—Hooray!"

There was no want of heartiness either in that or in those which followed, to be returned as enthusiastically from the two boats, which were rapidly nearing, so that in a few minutes Rodd and his uncle were wringing the hands of the bluff old skipper, while it was observable that all three kept their backs to the French Count and his son till they came up together, when the three started round in surprise, going through a curious kind of pantomime as if they were astonished to see the Frenchmen there.

Meanwhile a regular fraternisation had gone on between the crews, and after a mere glance at the three masts of the schooner, which were standing out of the water about a couple of hundred yards away, the skipper's whole attention was directed to their own vessel, whose keel was now fast in the mud, and which was beginning to heel over slightly.

"Then I suppose you took her again, doctor?" he said gruffly.

"Well, hardly," said Uncle Paul. "It was Cross and the lads who did that."

"More shame to him, then," growled the skipper. "I should have thought you were seaman enough, Joe Cross, to have kept her afloat and not run her aground like this."

"Well, I do call that ungrateful," cried Rodd. "I say, uncle, oughtn't he to have saved the schooner from being taken?"

"That's one for me, doctor," said the skipper, with a grim smile and a twinkle in his eye. "The boys of this here generation seem to grow up pretty sharp. But he's quite right. They pretty well caught a weasel asleep that time."

"But how was it?" cried Rodd.

"How was it, my lad? Why, we was hard at work one morning, when up the river comes another of them nice respectable schooners in the oil trade. Oil trade, indeed! Rank slavers, that's what they were, carrying on trade with one of those murderous chiefs up country! Set of black Satans as attack villages and carry off the poor wretches to sell to your oil traders for sending off to the plantations. Well, one don't like killing fellow-creatures, or seeing them pulled down below by the crocs, but somehow I don't feel so very uncomfortable about them as we had to fight with and have got the worst of it. What are you smiling at, young Squire Rodd?"

"I was only thinking how you always hated the slave trade, captain."

"Right," said Captain Chubb, with a friendly nod. "Well, the schooner sends her skipper aboard the three-master. Then he comes to where I was busy at work with the men, putting the finishing touches to the brig, and tells me and the Count a long tale about his having come up to join his friend the Spanish captain, who he hears has gone up the river for a row. Then he goes back to his schooner, makes her snug, and it seemed as if him and his men had all gone to sleep, when it was me."

"You?" cried Rodd wonderingly.

"Well, what they call metyphorically, my boy, for I was wide awake enough; but I couldn't see anything beyond the *Dagobert*, nor the Count neither, for he wanted her afloat. Then the time went on, and all very quiet, till just in the middle of one of the hottest days when I was in full feather, thinking that I could tell the Count that night that the job was done, and we could let her sit the water again next day when the tide served, all at once we had a surprise. There were only four or five men aboard the schooner, and I suppose they were keeping their watch, but just all at once a couple of boats rowed up to them, one from one schooner, one from the other, and before any of us knew what was up, our fellows were swimming for the shore, and if it hadn't been for the Count, who was on the look-out for crocs, and let them have two barrels twice over, neither of the poor fellows would have joined their mates as had been working with me."

The speaker turned to the Count, who nodded his head quickly, and then looked at his son as much as to say, Yes, this is quite true.

"Well," continued the skipper, "I felt as if all the wind had been knocked out of me, and as soon as I could speak and quite understand that my schooner had been took, I began to bully-rag the poor lads who had just escaped with their lives, for, not having time to get a gun or a cutlass, they had been almost as helpless on board as they were in the water among them reptiles. I couldn't even believe it then, and began questioning the lads, and you might have knocked me down with a feather, as people say, and the Count there with another, when they all swore that our Spanish skipper had led the men from his three-master in one of the boats. Then we began to see the worst."

The skipper turned with a questioning look at the Count again, to receive a second grave nod, while this time the latter laid his hand upon his son's shoulder, and a long eager glance passed between them.

"Well, I don't know that I have much more to say," said the skipper, "only that it was a bad job, being a fresh one we had got to tackle and meant to do. The Count here fitted me and my lads up with some weepuns, and we settled that as soon as it was dark we'd man two of the brig's boats, and board first one and then the other of the two schooners. Well, we tried, but they were waiting for us, and I don't know how we escaped, for they met us with such a fire that if we had kept on both boats must have been sunk, and we never got within touch of either of the enemy, but drifted down with the tide; and somehow just then I suppose there must have been a flood somewhere up the river, down came the water in a way that we couldn't meet, and it was only by pretty good seamanship on the part of the Frenchmen more than ours, though we helped all we knew, that we were able to keep afloat; and since then we have been right down to the sea, and it's been very hard to get enough to eat. But somehow we managed to keep alive, shooting what we could and catching a fish or two now and then as we came up the river again. For of course we were not going to give up without finishing our job; and it seems to me that we got here just at the right time, and found that things weren't half so bad as we thought; eh, Count?"

"My friend," replied the latter, "how can I ever repay you?"

"Oh, let's talk about that, sir, when I have done something to keep the *Maid of Salcombe* upright and finished my other job and the brig's afloat, which it seems to me we can manage at high water; but I never bargained for having our schooner to set right too through the lubberly management of that chap Joe Cross. There," he cried angrily, "I can't and won't say another word till I have had something to eat, for we are all half starved."

"Get on board the schooner, then, every one," cried the doctor, "for I have got my work here."

It was a fact, for now the fight was over the men began to stiffen, and several unexpectedly turned faint, it proving that though not a single man was seriously wounded, nearly every one of those who had followed Joe Cross in his gallant achievement of boarding the schooner, and in beating down the slaver's crew when they forced their way out of the cabin, was more or less injured and had been doing his best to hide the knife stabs and contusions he had received.

It was during the next two or three days that the doctor proved that he was in his element, and that his knowledge of natural history was not confined to his ordinary scientific pursuits, for no surgeon could have been more skilful in his treatment of wounds, no physician more able in alleviating the fever which supervened.

It was a busy time for all, for not only was there the grounded schooner to guard from going over, but strict watch to keep for the return of enemies, and then, when the high tide served, all hands were at work, save the poor disappointed fellows whose injuries kept them to their bunks, in raising the brig to her old proud position. As she floated out, herself once more, and dropped anchor in the stream, the men literally yelled themselves hoarse, while on the following day at the Count's request both vessels were dropping down with the tide, all on board eager to leave behind the river, which in spite of its many beauties was too full of painful recollections for its waters to be recalled without horror and disgust.

Chapter Forty Nine
The Count's Appeal

The south-west coast of Africa was fading away in the distance as the two consorts with their natural history seekers rode over the dazzling silver sea. The lads were abaft the schooner's wheel, quite inseparable now, looking down through the eddying water at the fish, which seemed to have taken the swift vessel for some mighty companion of their own nature, in whose wake they could swim along in peace without fear of lesser enemies.

About an hour before, the brig's gig had brought the Count and his son alongside the schooner, and the former was below in the doctor's museum-like laboratory, listening to his learned friend's remarks upon some fresh object that, now they had returned to the ways of peace, had been fished up from just below the surface of the sea.

Four of the schooner's crew were under an awning, lying upon a couple of doubled-up spare sails which had been spread upon the deck, and the two lads had been seated with them chatting for some little time before they strolled aft.

"How well your men look," Morny said suddenly—"all except Joe Cross."

"Yes, he looks rather thin and pale, doesn't he?" said Rodd quickly; "but he isn't ill. You saw how full of fun he was, and ready to joke about having been bled too much. Uncle says he'll soon be well again, for he's in such good spirits. But uncle told me quietly that it was a wonder to him none of the poor fellows were killed. But oh, I say, isn't this nice!"

"Lazy," said Morny.

"Oh, I don't call it lazy. It's so jolly to be able to hang about in the sunshine without feeling that there's some great trouble coming on directly."

"Ah, yes," replied Morny, with a sigh, "and that perhaps you may not live to see me next day."

"Well," said Rodd, "I don't think it's lazy. Uncle says that after you have been at work very hard it's like unstringing the bow; and so it is. I want to begin fishing or dredging or sounding again. I don't want any more shooting. Now, do you know what I should like just now?"

"No."

"I'd soon show you then that I wasn't lazy. I should like to see one of those beautiful ripples two or three hundred yards off which show that there's a shoal of fish feeding on the transparent what-you-may-call-'ems—I forget Uncle Paul's name for them."

"Well, if that would give you any satisfaction," said Morny, laughing, "I wish that a shoal would rise."

"Don't you be in such a hurry; I hadn't finished. I was going to say I should then like to see one of those great sea-serpent-like creatures rise slowly from below, to begin feeding on the fish—one of those great scientific wonders that you and your father are trying to discover and capture; for that's it, I suppose, though you do keep so squat about it."

"Ah–h–h!" said Morny, with a sigh; and he glanced sidewise at his young English companion.

"It is quite a joke, that it is," continued Rodd. "It's just as if you were jealous and afraid that uncle and I would get beforehand with you, and win the credit of the discovery for old England, instead of you carrying it off for your *la belle France*."

"Ah!" sighed Morny again, with a sad smile upon his lips.

"You French chaps are so sentimental. *La belle France* indeed! Just as if old England or the British Isles weren't quite as beautiful! Only we don't go shouting about it everywhere. I say, Morny, you don't half believe in me."

"It is false!" cried the young Frenchman angrily. "Why, I believe in you more than in any one living—except my father."

"Oh, indeed!" cried Rodd banteringly. "And here since I have known you I have told you everything till I haven't a secret that I have kept from you."

"Why, you have had no secrets," said Morny.

"Well—no; I suppose you couldn't call them secrets. But you've got one, and you have never let it out to me."

"No," said Morny gravely, "because it was not mine to tell. You don't want me to be dishonourable, Rodd?"

"Why, of course I don't, old chap. I don't want you to tell me till you like, only it is rather a joke sometimes that you make such a mystery of what uncle and I know as well as can be."

"You know!" cried Morny sharply.

"Why, of course I do. It's what I say. You want—I mean, your father does—to carry off the honour of having solved the mystery of the great fish or reptile that has been talked about for the last hundred years. I say, though, there's that other great old-world thing that they find in the rocks. What's his name?"

Morny shook his head.

"Here, I've got it—the sea-sawyer! That isn't quite right, but it sounds something like it. Why, he must have been just like a great crocodile."

"Ugh! Don't talk about them," said Morny, with a shudder.

"Eh, why not? There are none of them here. I wish we could have caught one to dry or stuff, or keep in spirits. I mean quite a little one, you know. Ah, those were rather horrid times, though, and I shan't want a specimen reptile to make me remember them."

"No," said Morny musingly; "we want nothing to make us recollect them."

"But I suppose it is nearly all over now, for our voyages will soon come to an end."

"Oh no?" cried Morny eagerly. "Why should they, now that your uncle and my father have become such friends?"

The lads both started, for those of whom they were speaking just then strolled up behind them.

"Well, boys," said the Count gravely, "what are you two talking about?"

"Rodd was saying that he supposed our friendship would soon come to an end."

"Indeed?" cried the Count, raising his eyebrows and turning to give a meaning glance at Uncle Paul. "Why should it, eh, my lad? I thought you and Morny had become such fast friends."

"Yes, so we have, sir," cried Rodd, flushing; "but I didn't quite mean that, for I hope we shall often meet; but I thought that now we are out at sea again we should be separating. The brig will be going one way, and we shall be going another."

"Do you wish this to be so?" said the Count, after another glance at Uncle Paul.

"I? Oh no, sir."

"And you, Morny, my son?"

"I, my father? They should not go away if I could stop it."

"You hear, doctor? Is not this strange after what we have been saying in the cabin. I tell you again, before long I will be quite open with you about the object of my voyage. At present I ask you not to press me."

"I have told you," said the doctor, smiling, "that I will not. I have told you also that my object for the short time that I shall stay down here in the south is to keep close inshore, while you tell me that you wish to be able to sail right out to sea, and free to carry out your project, whatever it may be."

"Yes, yes, and I have told you too that you could be of the greatest service to me by following close at hand, and that I should always be most grateful if without injury to your own cruise you would keep in company with me for the present."

"Ready to help in case of further emergencies?"

"No," cried the Count warmly; "my ideas were not so selfish as that. But tell me this—is it urgent that we should part company now? I mean, would you suffer loss, or would your own researches be injured by keeping in company with us for say another month?"

"No–o," said the doctor carelessly; "I am just as likely to make discoveries far out to sea as close inshore."

"Then stay with us for the present. I ask it as a friend, while I guarantee that you shall not suffer by what you do for me."

"Well," said the doctor, slowly and thoughtfully, as he looked at the two lads, who were intently listening for his words, "what do you think, Rodd? Shall we sail in company with the brig for a little longer?"

"Am I to be judge, uncle?" said the boy merrily. "Yes, if you like."

"Well, then," said the lad, with a mischievous twinkle in his eyes, as he found that Morny with lips parted was gazing at him with a look of appeal, "you see, uncle, we have been together a good while now, and though we tried to help the brig we seem to have dragged it into a good deal of mischief."

"What are you saying, Rodd?" cried Morny passionately.

"Oh, I mean that we have helped you a bit, but you have been very unlucky since we have been together. Still, if Morny doesn't mind risking it, and doesn't mind putting up with my jokes about *la belle France*, and yours, uncle, about the Emperor Napoleon—"

Morny started, and looked sharply at his father.

"—though by this time," continued Rodd, "I suppose you, sir, have found out that at heart uncle is very fond of the Emperor, and admires him very much—"

"You impudent young scoundrel, how dare you!" growled the doctor. "Bah!" he muttered to himself, "Temper!" Then turning quickly to the Count, he said almost apologetically, "Don't take any notice. I have spoilt him, sir; I have spoilt him. Look here, my dear sir; I shall very much regret the day when we have to part, for my own sake and for my nephew's, for since he has had the advantage of your son's companionship I have been in hopes that he would acquire something of his refinement and polish, and that it might lead in time to his achieving to somewhat of the carriage of a gentleman. I regret to say that so far he is as rough and boorish as ever. Still, in the hope that every one of his opportunities may not be thrown away, I shall be glad to prolong the intimacy a little longer. There, sir," he snapped out, as he turned sharply upon Rodd, "what do you say to that?"

"It's all right, Morny," said the boy quietly. "Go on polishing. I'll be more attentive now, uncle."

Morny gave him a quick nod, and turned then to grasp Uncle Paul's hand, while the brig and the schooner went sailing on westward ho!

Chapter Fifty
The Doctor will not believe

It was about a fortnight later, during which time, in deliciously calm weather, the two vessels had been cruising here and there, to the great satisfaction of the doctor, who was in a high state of delight, for he had been harvesting, as he termed it—bottling, Joe Cross said—numberless specimens of the strange creatures that swarm upon the surface of the southern Atlantic. And as they had got out so far, the doctor had been sounding Captain Chubb as to the possibility and advisability of making for that strange volcanic island known as Trinidad—not the richly verdant island of the same name that seems as if it had been once a portion of the north-east shoulder of leg-of-mutton-like South America, but the solitary island right away south-east from Bahia, which stands lonely in the ocean, the remains of the great volcanic eminence swept by the terrific seas and tempests that come up from the South Polar Ocean—an island that is the habitat of strange sea-birds, the haunt of fish, and the home and empire of those most hideous of the crustaceans, the land crabs.

Captain Chubb grunted and said he would think about it and consult the chart. As for the brig, Rodd did not banter Morny upon the subject when he came aboard, as he did pretty well every day when Rodd and his uncle had not visited the brig; but it was a standing joke between the lad and Uncle Paul that King Dagobert had not sighted the sea-serpent as yet.

"And it's my belief, Pickle, that they are going the wrong way to work."

"Why, what would you do, then, uncle?"

"Well, I'll tell you, my boy. He's a very shy bird, and if he knows you are looking for him he won't show. If you and I take up the search I tell you what we'll do; we won't look for him; we'll let him look for us."

"According to that, then, uncle, we are more likely to find him than they are."

"Of course, my boy. Why, haven't we proved it?"

They were down in the laboratory, where Joe Cross had been helping them over the bottling, but he had gone up on deck, the day's task being over, and the skipper now came down, looked and snorted at the fresh regiment of bottles, and made some remark about the doctor seeming out of spirits. But he did not mean it for a joke. Captain Chubb never did joke, for he was one of those men who pass their lives looking out for squalls, and his allusion was to the emptiness of the doctor's set of kegs.

"Well, it doesn't matter," said the doctor. "Sit down and let's talk. I have got quite as many preparations in spirits as will last me for years. By the way, did you think any more about Trinidad?"

"Deal," said the skipper shortly, and he gave the fixed table a rap with a roll of paper which he had brought down tucked under his arm. "Here's the chart."

"Well?" said the doctor, wincing, as the skipper unrolled the map on the dresser-like table, and catching up first one specimen bottle and then another used them as paper-weights to keep the chart flat, while he began to operate with his big rough, brown, index finger.

"Here y'are," he said, "and its character written about it: currents, shoals, stormy seas, all kinds of dangers. Bad landing-place; very rocky— place if you go to you ought to stop away."

"Sounds hopeful; eh, Pickle?"

"Oh, but curious, uncle. I should like to go."

"Well, then, you won't," said the skipper gruffly, "because your uncle's too wise to tell me to risk the schooner in such a sea."

"Humph!" grunted the doctor.

"I'll obey your orders, sir, and sail anywhere," continued the skipper, frowning very heavily, "but it's my duty to tell you when you are going wrong."

"Of course," said the doctor, "and as you give the place such a bad character, captain, we'll disappoint Rodd and stay away."

"Right," cried the skipper. Then after drawing a deep breath he looked fiercely at Rodd, and then glared at the doctor, who opened his eyes a little, wonderingly.

"Do you know where you are now?" said the skipper.

"Well, not exactly, only that we have been on ground rich in objects such as I wish to collect, and—excuse me, captain—that bottle—your elbow. I wouldn't have an accident to that for the world."

"Well, then," continued the skipper, very gruffly, as he dabbed his big finger down in the middle of the chart, "you are here."

"Saint Helena," said Rodd, after a quick glance at the chart.

"Right," grunted the skipper. "Now, Dr Robson, am I to speak out, or will you send young Mr Rodd here up on deck first?"

The doctor stared.

"I see no reason for sending my nephew away," he said coldly. "He and I have the fullest confidence in one another."

Rodd, who was standing leaning over the map, moved very slightly, but somehow his left hand stole on to his uncle's shoulder.

"Right, then," said the skipper harshly. "It is my duty, Dr Robson, to tell you that you are in a false position."

"Then, Captain Chubb, as my navigator in whom I have the most perfect trust, it is my duty to tell you that you ought to be on deck sailing us out of it as soon as you can."

"Come down here on purpose," said the skipper shortly, "and here goes. Now then, doctor, you are such a busy man, and you are so wrapped up in your fads about natural history and that sort of thing, that anybody artful could take you in and cheat you as easy as swallowing a gooseberry."

"Well, you have a nice opinion of me, Captain Chubb!"

"I have, sir—a splendid opinion of you," cried the skipper, "and I'd say it before all the judges in the land—I mean at home—that there was never a more straightforward gentleman made than you. I'd do anything for you."

"Hear, hear! Bravo, Captain Chubb!" cried Rodd. "What about me?"

"You, youngster? Well, you aren't half a bad 'un as boys go. But look here, doctor; time's come for me to speak out. You are a bit too innocent."

"Am I? Well, captain, that's better than being a bit too guilty; eh, Rodd?"

"A deal, uncle. But what's the matter, captain?"

"Why, this here, my lad. I can't stand still no longer and see your uncle being made a cat's-paw of."

"Cat's-paw, eh, captain?" said the doctor. "Let's see, that means to fetch the roasted chestnuts out of the fire. This must apply to you, Master Rodd."

"To me, uncle?" cried the boy, aghast.

"Yes; I don't know anybody else whom Captain Chubb looks upon as a monkey."

"Nay–y–y! I mean that there French Count."

"Stop!" cried the doctor sternly. "Mind what you are saying, Captain Chubb. Count Des Saix is my friend—a gentleman, a nobleman."

"I dessay he may be at home," said the skipper, meeting Rodd's indignant eyes, "but he aren't a gentleman, or he wouldn't be making such a tool of you. Now, don't you put yourself in a fury, doctor, or you'll be saying words you'll be sorry for arter. A gentleman like you as thinks, and is scientific too, has no business to go in a passion. That's all very well for a skipper as has got to manage a lot of awkward sailor chaps; if he didn't use words sometimes there'd be no getting a ship along. But you have got to take it cool like a Ann Eliza, and hear it right through, and then set yourself down and judge according."

"But look here, Captain Chubb," said the doctor angrily, "I cannot be silent and let you malign my friend."

"He aren't your friend, sir; he's only a Frenchman, and though I've done my duty by him right through, I allers felt as if I couldn't trust him."

"Why not?" said the doctor hotly.

"Because he being a natural born enemy of an Englishman, it didn't seem right that he should pretend to be such a friend of yourn."

"Why not, sir?" cried the doctor warmly.

"Now, none of that, doctor. I did warn you about not getting put out. Don't you call me, *sir*, 'cause I don't like it."

"Look here, Captain Chubb," cried the doctor, "I am sure you mean well."

"Thankye, sir; I do."

"Then why have you taken this prejudice against the Count?"

"That's a straight question, sir. Now let me ask you one. What's he doing here?"

"Upon some kind of research."

"Not him, sir! That's what he's told you, and it aren't honest. He's carrying on a game of his own behind you; and the boy's as bad as the old man."

"How dare you!" flashed out Rodd.

"Silence, Rodney!"

"I can't be silent, uncle. I won't stand here and listen to such an outrageous charge against those two gentlemen. I don't know what has come to Captain Chubb, but he ought to be made to apologise before he leaves this place."

"Well, he aren't going to be made to, young pepper-caster," growled the captain. "Honest men don't apologise for telling the truth, even if it don't taste nice."

"Look here, Chubb," said the doctor, "we are having too many words. Let's have a clear understanding about what you think."

"Right, sir. Let's get to the bottom of it at once. You want an explanation. It's this now. I have been very suspicious from the first. What about this 'ere Count and his son? First you knowed of 'em was as they was prisoners at Dartmoor. Well, it sounds bad for a man to be a prisoner, but as he was took in war that don't count for much, so we'll let that go. Next thing is, you runs agen 'em at Havre, cutting their cable and running for it when Government gives orders for them to stop. Next thing is, they boards our schooner like a set of pirates, only we seem too many for them; and then they cackles up a cock-and-bull story about wanting help, when they see they couldn't seize the schooner."

"Look here, Captain Chubb—" began the doctor.

"Give me my chance, sir, and let me finish, and then have your say. Help they had, and plenty on it, and I will say that a nicer, more gentlemanly-tongued chap than the Count I never met, nor had to do with a pleasanter nor nicer young fellow than his son."

"Thank you," said Rodd sarcastically.

"Now, don't you sneer, youngster," growled the captain, "for it aren't clever, nor it aren't nice. Well, now, doctor, we all went through a deal all along of these Frenchies, for I don't see how it could have happened if it hadn't been for them."

"Why, you took us up the river, captain," cried Rodd indignantly.

"That's true, sir, but it was to do the best for their leaky brig, and I made her as good a craft as ever she was; so you needn't chuck that in my teeth."

"Be silent, Rodney, and let the captain speak."

Rodd gave himself a snatch and clenched his fists.

"Well, sir, to make a long story short, the Count gammoned you into keeping company with him, and brought you here—here, of all places in the world—here, to Saint Helena," and he thumped the chart just where the island was marked.

"Yes," said the doctor thoughtfully—"here, to the neighbourhood of Saint Helena; upon a scientific research."

"Scientific research!" growled the skipper scornfully. "Look here, sir, don't you be so innocent. You make me wild. What's this 'ere Count? A Frenchman, aren't he?"

"Well, plenty of clever Frenchmen have followed science," said the doctor indignantly.

"Chinese too, sir, though they can't dress like Christians," cried the skipper. "But just you tell me this 'ere, sir; who lives at Saint Helena? Don't old Bony? Him as we shut up like the warlike lunatic he is, to keep him out of mischief?"

"Well, yes," said the doctor, much more suavely; "there is something in that."

"I should think there is, sir! Haven't I heard you carry on dozens of times about what a bad 'un he's been to the whole world?"

"Yes, yes, Chubb; I certainly do entertain strong feelings against that tyrant and usurper."

"You do, sir. I've heard you say things at times as have sounded red-hot."

"And I'm not ashamed of them, Captain Chubb," cried the doctor warmly.

"'Shamed on 'em! Not you, sir! They're a honour to you as an English gentleman. Not much of the innocent in you about that."

"Thank you, Captain Chubb; thank you," said the doctor.

"Oh, uncle!" cried Rodd, between his teeth.

"You let your uncle alone, youngster; I aren't done with him yet. Now then, doctor, your eyes aren't quite open now, but you are beginning to peep. Now, just have the goodness to tell me what you are a-doing here at Saint Helena—a place that a gentleman with your sentiments ought to have kept clear of like pison."

"Well," cried the doctor, warming up again, "you know I have accompanied my friend the Count upon his scientific expedition."

"Your friend the Count, sir! His scientific expedition!" snarled the skipper. "Do you call old Bony a scientific expedition?"

"I don't understand you, captain."

The Ocean Cat's Paw | 367

"Then here you have it, sir, plain. Your friend the Count is a Bony party, and as the French Government knew what game he was on and tried to stop him from running out of Havre, when he come upon us and found out what we were doing, 'Here's my man,' he says; 'I will just creep under his cloak and carry on my little game to carry off Bony. No one will suspect me if I am in good company, and on what he calls scientific research.' Consekens, here's you, sir, off the island of Saint Helena in co and company with this 'ere Bony party come to carry off and set free the man of all others you hate most in the world. Now you understand what you have come to do."

"I'll be hanged if I have!" cried the doctor, bringing his fist down with a tremendous thump upon the table, making one of the bottles leap up, fall over upon its side, and discharge its stopper at Rodd, who fielded it cleverly, though the contents—gelatinous infusoria and spirit of wine— were scattered all over the map.

"That's spoke like you, sir," cried the skipper; "but you needn't have spoiled my chart."

"Confound your chart, man! Here, Rodney, you hear all this? Do you think it's true?"

"No, uncle, I can't."

"Neither can I, sir. I cannot. I will not. You, Captain Chubb, you mean well, I know, but— Oh, it's outrageous! That I, Paul Robson, a man of my sentiments, should come to do such a disloyal thing as this—this—this— this treachery against my country and my King! Here, Captain Chubb, are you mad, or—"

"Drunk, sir? Say it out. I don't mind. It does me good to see you come to your senses like this. Brayvo, sir! That's the way to take it."

"Oh, uncle!" panted Rodd.

"You let him alone, sir. He's all right," cried the skipper. "I've stuck the harpoon into him. You give him line, and you'll see we shall have him in his flurry directly."

"Stop, man! Where are your proofs?"

"Yes," cried Rodd, stamping excitedly about the cabin; "where are your proofs?"

"Proofs?" said the skipper. "I d'know. Yes, I do. You ask the Count to his face, and his boy with him, whether what I say aren't true."

"Yes," cried the doctor. "Go on deck, and take that confounded speaking trumpet of yours. Hail the brig, and ask the Count to come on board."

"Yes—with his son!" stormed Rodd. "How can I? They went off this afternoon on some game or another, and haven't been in sight since."

"Hah!" said the doctor, fanning himself with one hand, wiping his face with the other, and then shaking his bandanna silk handkerchief up and down to try and get cool. "There, I am not going to be in a passion, Rodney. I am not going to say angry words to you, Chubb, for you believe all this, while I—I—I can't believe it. The Count is too grand a gentleman to have made a—a—what you said, of me. But I will have this matter cleared up, and you will have to apologise to me and the Count."

"And to Viscount Morny des Saix," cried Rodd.

"Yes, my boy; exactly," said the doctor; and then to the skipper—"If you are wrong!"

Saying this, he literally stamped out of the cabin.

"Where are you going, uncle?" cried Rodd, following.

"Up on deck, my boy," cried the doctor, without turning his head. "I feel like a furnace, and if I speak any more words they'll be like the skipper said—red-hot."

"Well," said the captain, as he stood staring towards the cabin stairs, "I never see'd the doctor with his monkey up like that afore. Anyhow, he aren't afraid to trust me with his bag of tricks down here, and bottles of mixture. But he needn't have spoiled my chart!"

Chapter Fifty One
That's Saint Helena

Night, and no sign of the brig. Morning, and the doctor and his nephew both on deck, with a sail in sight upon the distant horizon, while just beyond it, looming up, was what seemed to be a dark cloud.

"There she is!" cried the doctor, glass in hand. "We will soon know the truth now, Rodd."

"That, sir?" said a voice close behind them. "That's Saint Helena."

The doctor started round as though he had been stung, to stare fiercely in the frank face of Joe Cross, who looked rather thin and hollow-cheeked, but had declared himself well enough to take the morning watch.

"It is, sir," said the man, who took the doctor's angry stare for a look of doubt. "That's right enough, though it don't look like an island. It's the big rock where they've got Bony shut up."

"Bah!" snapped the doctor, and he turned on his heel and walked away.

"Turned out of his bunk wrong side up'ards, sir?" asked the man, with a smile.

"Pah!" ejaculated Rodd, and he stamped off in the other direction.

"Old 'un's been giving it to him, I suppose," said Joe to himself. "Oh, I know; he'd been upsetting that bottle of fish soup as the skipper fetched me down to swab up last night—that as went all over the skipper's chart. Pore young chap! I'll go and smooth him down."

"What do you want?" cried Rodd angrily.

"Oh, nothing, sir. I only wanted to say I'm sorry I put your uncle out about the island. I'm a bit deaf in one ear since I got hurt over that fight, and I mis-underconstumbled him. He said, 'There she is,' and I thought he was talking about Bony's island, and he meant the brig."

"Well, suppose he did? There she is."

"Nay, sir; you take another look. That's a three-master, sir. Don't you see?"

"Oh yes, I see now, Joe," said Rodd, who was rather ashamed of his petulance to the man. "She was end on to us, and I didn't see the mizzen. Why, she's in full sail!"

"Yes, sir, a regular crowd of canvas, topgallants and stunsles all up, and if I haven't forgotten all about a man-of-war, that's what she is, as we used to say, by the cut of her jib, which is a very sensible remark, sir, as from here her jib's quite out of sight."

The doctor kept on deck till breakfast-time, sweeping the horizon with his glass, while the skipper walked up and down with his long mahogany-covered glass tucked under his left arm, and his hands very deep down in his pockets, while his shoulders were hitched up to his ears.

Then breakfast, with everything hot except the conduct of the occupants of the cabin. This was almost icy, and hardly a word was spoken.

Up on deck again, with the schooner careening over to the pleasant breeze, but no sign of the brig; but the three-masted vessel was overhauling them fast, and before long a gun said, Heave to, in the very emphatic monosyllable so well understood in the Royal Navy.

The skipper gave a glance at Uncle Paul with one eye, and that morning it seemed if as he had been suddenly afflicted with a cast, for the other eye turned outward and looked at Rodd.

Then he gave the order to the man at the wheel, who with a few turns of the spokes ran the swift little vessel well up into the wind, her sails began to flap, and she quietly settled down into a gentle rock upon the beautifully rippled heaving sea. Then time went on, with the man-of-war bearing down upon them rapidly, while the doctor stood scowling angrily at the rock which had so much to do with the fate of nations standing out more clearly in the sunlit air.

In due time a boat full of men was swung down from the davits of the cruiser, the oars dipped, and she came skimming along with a steady pull, and every stroke pulled clean and with hardly a splash, till she came alongside, when, to the delight of Rodd, there in the stern-sheets were the same officer and middy who had overhauled them off the African coast.

Rodd was all eagerness, and advanced ready to grasp hands with the reefer, but to his great surprise everything was coldly stern and formal. Two marines followed the officers on board, and the skipper, doctor, and Rodd were ordered down into the boat as prisoners, while a prize crew under the command of the middy, who looked more important than he did upon his first visit to the schooner, and stared at Rodd as if he had never seen him before, was left on board.

Uncle Paul spoke to the lieutenant, but his words were received almost in silence, while no explanation being forthcoming, he sat still and frowned.

The sloop of war, their old friend, was soon reached, and the prisoners were marched up to the quarter-deck where the captain stood waiting for them, scanning them sternly before beginning to question the skipper as to the name of the schooner and their object in those waters.

Questions were answered and explanations given in Captain Chubb's most blunt and straightforward way, before the captain turned his searching eyes upon Uncle Paul.

"Then you are Dr Robson, sir?" he said.

"Yes. May I ask—"

"You are here carrying out a scientific research?"

"Yes."

"In company with your consort, Count Des Saix, of the French brig *Dagobert*?"

"That's quite right, sir; but may I ask—"

"Why you are my prisoners? Certainly. But I will shorten matters by telling you that your scientific research was a plot to carry off the prisoner of the British Government, the ex-emperor Napoleon Bonaparte."

"No, sir, I'll be hanged if it was!" cried the doctor.

"Which plot has completely failed," added the captain. "As I have said, sir, you are my prisoner."

"And what about Captain Chubb, here, and my nephew?"

"They are prisoners too, of course."

"But my schooner—my pleasure yacht?" said the doctor.

The captain slightly shrugged his shoulders, as he smiled—

"That will be well taken care of, sir, you may depend."

"Ah, Rodd, my boy," said the doctor, shortly afterwards, "you are getting plenty of adventures; but you needn't be uncomfortable. This will all be cleared up. Well, Chubb, I am afraid you were right; at any rate the King's officer seems to be quite of your opinion."

"Yes, sir, but wait a bit," said the captain. "I suppose they'll get us close in, and I shouldn't be at all surprised if we find, when we get to the other side of the island, that they've got the brig snug in shelter there."

"What, captured too?" cried Rodd excitedly.

"Yes, sir. This sloop of war is kept here to cruise about the island and keep strangers off. That's what she's for."

Chapter Fifty Two
I have sinned—Forgive

That same afternoon the sloop of war was lying close inshore, with the brig and schooner near at hand, when a barge put off from the landing-place bearing the Governor and other officials, who were received at the gangway of the sloop with the customary salute, and shortly afterwards a little informal court was held, with the prisoners present, while the First Lieutenant of the sloop gave evidence to the effect that just after dark he had observed, from the anchorage where the sloop lay, a light, evidently intended for a signal, exhibited in a peculiar way from the masthead of some vessel.

He had noticed the brig now lying at anchor some distance in the offing early in the evening, but an adverse wind had prevented the sloop from going out. This light appeared at intervals during the next two hours, and on reporting the matter to the captain it was considered sufficiently suspicious for the brig from which it evidently came to be overhauled. This was done during the night; the prisoners brought in; and they were here to give an account of themselves.

Upon being asked if there was any difficulty in overhauling and seizing the brig, which appeared to be well manned and armed, the lieutenant smiled and said no, for the simple ruse of answering the brig's signal by the exhibition of lights in a similar way brought her close inshore, and then in the darkness the rest was easy, for it fell perfectly calm, and the sudden advance in the darkness of three well-armed boats made resistance vain.

"They offered no resistance, then?" asked the Governor.

"Oh yes," was the reply; "a very brave resistance; but they were overpowered by numbers and brought in."

As this evidence was given the Count and his son stood together, the former looking calm and dignified, the latter defiant, and when asked what defence he had to make for his clandestine approach to a place where it must have been well-known to him landing could be only allowed by the special permission of the Governor, and told that it was perfectly evident his coming could have but one intent, to aid in the escape of the prisoner who had been so long in the island—the Count spoke out at once bravely and earnestly in the defence of those who were there standing as fellow-prisoners.

He wished, he said, to exonerate the English doctor and the captain of the schooner from all participation in his attempt. They had met on the high seas quite by accident, and finding how carefully the prison of his august master was watched, he had led the doctor into the belief that he too was engaged upon a scientific expedition.

Just then the eyes of the two lads met, and as Rodd darted an angry indignant look at Morny, the latter made a deprecating gesture, while he seemed to say, Be merciful; you do not know all.

The Count went on, taking the whole blame of the proceedings upon himself, and asking for mercy for his son, who had acted entirely under his orders and had been perfectly obedient, as a son should be. As he spoke these words he looked hard at Rodd, and then at his uncle, who stood frowning there.

"I failed in my enterprise," continued the Count, "for I was growing desperate at the difficulties which surrounded me. Certain signals should have answered mine, and the lights which were shown from the direction of the shore were not exactly those which I anticipated. But, as I have said, I was growing desperate at my want of success, and in the hope that after all these signals might mean that my august master would be brought off in a fishing-boat, I risked all and allowed myself to be deluded, as it were, into what proved to be a trap. I have no more to say, gentlemen, save this, that I ask no mercy for myself. Whatever the English laws award to one who has acted as I have done, I accept. But my son, as I have said, was entirely under my orders, and as for my crew, they have only been my faithful servants, and tried to carry out my will. England must be too brave to wish to punish such as these. As to the doctor, his nephew, and the crew of the schooner, it would be absurd for England after my explanation to say more to them than 'Go in peace.'"

There was perfect silence for a minute or so, and then the Governor, one of his staff, an officer of foot who was the commander of the military force stationed in the island, and the captain of the sloop, held a short consultation together, after which the officers drew back into their places and left the Governor to speak.

"Dr Robson," he said, "Captain Ellison, in command of the sloop of war, has told me of his previous meeting with you at the mouth of one of the West African rivers, and the way in which your vessel was fitted out, and of the state of your papers. Everything, in fact, goes to prove the perfect truth of your story and the fact of your ignorance of the plan for the escape of the prisoner. I can offer you no apology for your being made prisoner and brought here, for I think that due consideration will prove to you that you were somewhat imprudent in your action and choice of friend. You and yours, sir, are perfectly at liberty to leave the island at once. As for you, Count Des Saix," he continued, "as the Governor of this island I have certain duties to perform, and after such an important and daring attempt as yours, I must tell you that in spite of peculiar circumstances which I will refer to shortly, this matter cannot end here. It is an affair of diplomacy in which others are concerned as well as England. For the present you and your people must consider yourselves prisoners pending the arrival of the dispatches that I must send to the British Government. Yours, sir, was a daring and extremely hazardous plot, designed in extravagance and I may say in ignorance of the impossibility of its execution. The prisoner was too closely guarded and watched, and, as you have seen, it was quite impossible for your vessel to approach this island without being seized. I gather that you have been a naval officer in the service of the late Government of France, and I presume that it was from a feeling of devotion to the Emperor Napoleon—I should say, our prisoner here—that you and your friends devoted yourselves to this task, which has proved so signal a failure. Sir, I can only admire your act and the devotion of the followers of the late Emperor."

"Sir, to us," cried the Count, "your way of speaking of our august master is little better than an insult. With us there is no late Emperor; he is still the ruler of the French Empire, our august master while he lives."

"Sir," said the Governor, slowly and gravely, "mine is the painful duty to announce to you that my words were well chosen and correct, that your designs were as hopeless as they were vain; the late Emperor Napoleon died two nights since."

The Count gave a violent start, gazing wildly in the Governor's eyes, as if asking whether his words were true. Then turning to his son he took off his cap and stood in silence with his head bowed down, before saying in a low broken voice that reached no farther than the ears of Uncle Paul and Rodd—

"Morny, my son, we were faithful to the end, even though we failed. Our august master is free at last. But our country lives, and in the future there is always for us *la France*."

There were several meetings between Uncle Paul, Rodd, and the prisoners—if prisoners they could be deemed, for their captivity was of the easiest kind—before the schooner set sail for England and home, and during one of these, when all seemed once more the best of friends, the doctor was heard to say—

"Yes, of course, I forgive him now, and you know, Des Saix, since that sort of a trial we had I have never said one word of reproach. I was not going to trample on a fallen man. But, you know, all that business, to use a coarse old English expression, sticks in my gizzard. It was not honourable, nor gentlemanly; I won't add noble. I don't think you ought to have done it to one who trusted you and helped you as I did. Now, look here; do you think it was a good example to set your son?"

"My friend," said the Count humbly—"May I still call you my friend?"

"As long as you live, sir!" cried the doctor warmly.

"Then I say to you, No; it was dishonourable, treacherous, and vile. But my sword was devoted to the service of my dead master, my life was his, and I was ready to give all to save him from his unhappy fate. Can I say more than this: I have sinned. Forgive."

As matters turned out it was many, many months, owing to an accident to the schooner and the delays in re-fitting at Las Palmas, and long stays made in the Mediterranean—the entrance to which could not be passed without a cruise within—before the *Maid of Salcombe* approached the English coast, and, oddly enough, once more Captain Chubb was driven to take refuge for a few hours at Havre-de-Grace, where one of the first things to be noticed was the familiar brig.

Inquiries followed at last, and Rodd and his uncle learned that the vessel had been lying there for some time while her captain, the Count, and his son were at Paris.

No: the officer in charge of the brig could give no information about their residence in Paris, but he had heard that they were not going to sail in the brig again, as they were about being appointed to a large ship in the King's Navy.

"Humph, Rodd!" said the doctor. "This sounds like good news."

"Yes, uncle, but we must try and see them again."

"Would you like to?"

"Of course!" cried Rodd warmly. "For a good long talk about old days."

"Perhaps," said the doctor, "they may hear of our return, and may try to see us."

"And if they do, uncle?"

"Well," said the doctor, smiling, "they know our address."